Back to Her Teens
A Lesbian Ageplay Spanking Romance

Back to Her Teens
A Lesbian Ageplay Spanking Romance

By Clarine Klein

http://clarineklein.com

Petite and oh so sassy college sophomore Rhen Mathews is being kicked out of her dorms to make room for new students, and is in desperate need of a place to live. And so, when Dana Johnson, her former boss and burgeoning dommy-mommy girlfriend, offers to let her move in with her, she accepts without a second thought.

The only condition?

When in public, she has to pretend to be her thirteen-year-old niece from out of town.

What follows is a forced regression/ageplay romance novel filled to the brim with super embarrassing moments for Rhen and lots of much-needed spanking and discipline from her loving, but very strict, Auntie Dana.

Chapter 1

A Case of Mistaken Identity

"Crap, crap, crap!"

College sophomore Rhen Mathews had been repeating that mantra to herself with ever-increasing panic ever since her smartphone's text message alert had jolted her awake some ten minutes earlier.

She was *so* late!

"Shit!"

Even though she was supposed to be starting her new job as an assistant at the Johnson Family Daycare that morning, her natural inclination toward being a night owl had kept her up until well past 4 AM the night before. Well, technically morning, but as far as she was concerned that was more based on when you fell asleep as opposed to when the sun decided to rise. Either way, she'd overslept *way* too much, snoring through the alarm she'd set right before burrowing under her covers, and now she was nearly an hour late!

Cutting loose with a rainbow of profanity and hoping desperately that she wasn't already fired before she'd even started her new job, she frantically hopped from foot to foot as she tried to kick her makeshift pajama pants off.

"God dammit, why do they have to make the ankles on these stupid things so fucking snug? I hate junior sizes!" she hissed, tumbling over the foot of her bed with a frustrated grunt as she struggled to wriggle free of the snug pair of leggings she'd been wearing since the day before.

She'd *planned* on dressing up in something nice and professional to make a good impression during her first day on the job, but with her being as late as she was already she opted instead to stick with what she knew. Stripping down to her simple white camisole and a snug pair of powder blue panties, she quickly pulled on a pair of black and white nylon short-shorts and a loose-fitting t-shirt with a faded video game logo on it that she picked at random from the pile of mostly clean clothes shoved underneath her desk.

Pausing in front of the mirror she shared with her room-mate, she winced and brushed a hand down her front in the vein hope that doing so would somehow make what she saw there look more professional.

It didn't help.

"Whatever. It's better than nothing, I guess."

Grabbing her backpack and shoveling her smartphone, wallet, keys, and just about anything else close to hand that looked like it might be important (Hey, maybe she *would* need her iPad while she was keeping an eye on a bunch of tweens, who could say?) she bolted out of her dorm room. She dashed down the hallway then, letting her door slam behind her even though she knew it drove her RA nuts, and wove her way between the few people hanging out and chatting with their friends, keeping up her litany of cursing as she pulled her long black hair into a loose ponytail that bobbed behind her as she sprinted toward the exit of the building.

"Double crap, triple crap, crap, crap, crap!"

Bursting outside and shielding her eyes from the bright sunshine of another crisp, cloudless, summer morning in Iowa, Rhen came to a sudden stop. The Johnson place was only about three miles away from campus, at least according to what she'd seen on her laptop the night before when she'd punched the address the Student Employment Center had given her into it. Again, she'd planned on leaving early enough to just walk there, but now that that wasn't an option anymore, she had a decision to make.

For a brief moment she considered digging her smartphone out of her backpack and calling for an Uber, but dismissed the idea just as quickly as it had come. The whole point to her taking up the stupid job in the first place was so that she could save money and build some capital, not blow it on frivolous taxi trips. Even if it cost her less than twenty dollars to get there, at the hourly rate she was being paid she'd basically be tossing two hours' worth of work down the drain before she'd even started.

So that plan was a no-go.

She then considered maybe taking the bus. It would be almost as fast as an Uber, and way cheaper, but she had no idea what, if any, busses even went to that part of town or when they might be leaving. She was already super late as it was. She couldn't afford to waste any more time waiting around for the right bus to arrive!

Which only left her with one real option.

The one that she'd been hoping to avoid.

Her bike.

"Dammit!"

Dashing over to the metal racks where she and her fellow students chained up their bicycles when they weren't using them, she squatted down onto her heels and quickly dialed in the combination for her lock and pulled the chain free from around her bike.

It was an old fashioned, white-framed monstrosity of a thing, with a wicker basket mounted to the front and little tassel streamers hanging from the ends of both handlebars. She'd picked it up for next to nothing at a garage sale over a year ago, and while it had definitely seen better days, it was at least sturdy and reliable.

The only problem was that it made her look and feel about ten years younger than she actually was.

Given her tiny frame (she liked to think of her size as "petite", but that was definitely stretching the truth, she knew), the childish bike did very little to help her project a more adult image in keeping with her actual age as a college sophomore. In fact, on more than one occasion she'd been stopped by the campus police wanting to know what she was doing riding around the college unattended when she should've been at home or in school.

Those were always just the most *pleasant* of conversations to have. Especially when she was forced to pull out her wallet to show them her ID to get them to back down and stop threatening to call her parents if she kept sassing them.

On the bright side though, at least the seat on her adorable bike was comfortable and low enough so that her feet could reach the pedals without any problems. Plus, it sure as heck beat walking or running to her job. And so, after checking her smartphone one more time to confirm the route she needed to take, she hopped onto its padded seat and started pedaling just as fast as she possibly could.

It would be fine…

Probably.

—

Fifteen minutes later, sweating and gasping for air (the life of a computer science major didn't usually attract the super athletic, and Rhen was certainly no exception), she skidded to a stop in front of a white brick, two-story house at the end of a non-descript cul-de-sac.

Breathing heavily, she double checked the house number painted on the side of the curb, comparing it with the one in her email from the Employment Center. It was the place alright. And while the outside looked just the same as all the other houses she'd whizzed past on her way over, she could clearly hear the sounds of children laughing and playing in the back yard, and even saw a few of them scampering around inside through the big bay windows that looked out onto the front lawn.

Rhen did her best to quash the nervous fluttering inside of her stomach as she swallowed hard. It was now or never, she supposed.

"Okay, here we go…"

Walking her bike up the driveway, she mulled her options over for a brief moment before deciding to just dump it on its side on the grass beside the big, red SUV parked in front of the garage. It was a safe enough neighborhood as far as she could tell. And besides, who in their right mind would want to steal her crappy bike?

Somehow she didn't picture any potential thieves being too keen to go riding around town on anything with shimmery tassels and a bell on it.

Looking at the door in front of her, she let out a long, slow breath, mustering her excuses and explanations. With any luck, she might yet still save her job.

Straightening up to her full five-foot-one-inch height, she squared her shoulders and then forced herself to climb up the stairs, cross the porch, and push open the front door; marching into the home with a sense of confidence and authority that she didn't actually feel. Hopefully Missus Johnson would buy her made up reasons for being late, and she wouldn't find herself turning around and marching right back out only a couple of minutes later.

"Uh, hello?" she called into the house, not receiving any response.

The Employment Center hadn't given her much in the way of information about her new job aside from the name of the business, an address and phone number, and the time she was supposed to be there by. Even so, picking Missus Johnson out of the crowd of milling preteens wasn't exactly difficult. She was a broad-shouldered woman in her mid-to-late forties, with bright red hair and wide hips who looked as if she were almost six feet tall. And at the moment she was looking more than a little frazzled as she pulled apart two bickering tweens and sent them each scampering off in a different direction with a hard slap to their seats.

SMACK! SMACK!

"And that had better be the last time I have to tell you two to knock it off!" she called after the retreating youngsters with a growl, before letting out an exasperated sigh and running a hand through her hair.

"It's going to be one of those days today, isn't it?" she asked aloud to nobody in particular as she shook her head.

Talk about crappy timing, the petite sophomore thought to herself with a wince. *Damn it.*

Rhen really wished that she'd been able to catch the older woman at a better time, but she was already pushing danger-ously close to being over an hour and a half late for her first day on the job as it was, and so she decided she'd better just introduce herself as fast as she could and then get out of her boss's way. If she was upset with her, she could just lie and say that the Employment Center told her to show up at noon.

Hey, that's not a bad idea!

Not only would she not be late then, she'd actually be *early*, which would most certainly impress her, wouldn't it?

Tiptoeing into the front room, she stopped a couple feet away from Missus Johnson and cleared her throat.

"Um, Missus Johnson?"

"Yes, what is it?" the older woman snapped, seemingly started out of her moment of peace. She cast a quick glance around the room, before looking down to find Rhen standing beside her, looking nervous.

"Oh hello, dear!" she said, her earlier irritation having been swapped out for maternal kindness as she smiled at her in apology for the outburst. She then gave her a quick once over, trying to match her face with a name and seeming to come up blank. "I don't think we've met yet. What's your name, cutie pie?"

Rhen felt her cheeks color at the other woman's tone. It had been a long time since any adult had talked to her like that. Well, aside from the campus police and maybe her grandma, that is. She supposed that it must be force of habit for her though, and tried not to hold it against her. After all, she could hardly run a daycare if she was constantly snapping and yelling at people.

Clearing her throat again, Rhen did her best to seem unconcerned and as if she hadn't just been frantically pedaling down the street as hard as she could as she met the other woman's warm gaze.

"I'm Rhen Mathews, ma'am," she said, offering her hand to her new boss and hoping that the churning in her stomach wasn't showing up on her face. "It's um... nice to meet you, um... ma'am."

Smooth, she thought to herself, mentally rolling her eyes.

Thankfully though, the other woman didn't seem to notice, or if she did, she didn't care.

"It's a pleasure to meet you, Rhen," replied Missus

Johnson, taking her hand and giving it a firm shake. "Did your parents just drop you off? Are they still around? I'd like to at least say hello to them before they leave, if that's possible."

"Um, no?" answered Rhen with a confused tilt of her head, regarding the other woman quizzically.

That was certainly an odd question to ask. Why would she even think that was an option? She was a sophomore in college for crying out loud! She was perfectly capable of getting places all on her own. And besides, her grandma lived more than twelve hours away.

"I biked here. Duh."

"Careful with that attitude, missy," warned the older woman, her expression darkening as she pinned her in place with a sharp glare. "I've been running ragged all morning thanks to my new assistant flaking out on me, damn college kids, and the last thing I need is lip from you. Now run off and go play with the others. Lunch will be ready in about an hour, alright?"

Rhen felt her stomach twist at the reprimand, and her cheeks color at being labeled as "flaky". She'd always considered herself to be a pretty responsible person, albeit one with a habit of running a tad behind schedule from time to time. Even so, she still held out hope that she could repair things between the two of them before she was well and truly fired.

Clearly the Employment Center hadn't given Missus Johnson much in the way of information either, and she would need to clarify some things for her.

"Um, I'm *really* sorry about that," she began to say, fighting hard to meet the other woman's gaze as her hands fidgeted nervously with the hem of her t-shirt. "But I'm here now, at least, and I'd like to start helping out if that's okay with you, um… ma'am."

"Oh never you mind, dear," dismissed Missus Johnson with a wave of her hand. "You just run off and play. It's fine."

"But... but..." protested Rhen, at a loss for words.

Why was she even bothering to show up in the first place if she wasn't going to actually *do* anything? Had she nearly pulled her hamstrings racing over here for nothing?

What the hell?

"Look," sighed the other woman when she saw the look on the younger girl's face, her patience starting to wear thin. "I appreciate the offer. Really, I do. But you're way too young to be of any help to me. Now, I've got a lot of things to do still, so run along or else I'm going to be helping *you* across my knee. You got that, kiddo?"

"Um, *excuse* me?"

That certainly managed to push a button for Rhen, and she found herself stomping her foot and snapping at her boss without even thinking.

"Oh my god, lady, will you open your god damn ears for one fucking second and listen to what I'm trying to tell you?"

Even as she was saying it, she knew it was a mistake, but she just couldn't help herself.

Given her diminutive size, being treated like a child was a major point of contention for Rhen, and it was a sure-fire way to send her temper through the roof in an instant. She absolutely *hated* being dismissed out of hand just because she looked younger than she really was. Being turned away half the time when she tried to get into bars, and having to show four different types of ID whenever she wanted to see an R-rated movie.

No matter how well she did her hair and makeup, how tight her jeans were, or how much she stuffed her bra, it didn't ever seem to make a difference, and it sucked!

Oh… crap.

She paused after her initial tirade was over, her breath having caught in her chest as she realized what she'd just said. Then she squeaked as she saw the look on her boss's face go from exasperated indulgence to grim and steely. She tried opening her mouth to apologize a moment later, but by then it was far, *far* too late.

She'd barely managed to get out a panicked "Wait, I'm sor-!" before Missus Johnson swooped down on her, grabbing her by the ear and dragging her off toward the couch on the other side of the room. All of the apologies Rhen wanted to make got stuck in her throat then, and came out instead as little yelps of surprise and pain as her boss plopped down in the middle of the leather couch and hauled her face-first across her knees.

Although it had been a long time since she'd found herself being draped across a maternal lap like this, Rhen was still all too aware of what was about to happen to her.

The last time she'd been in a similar position had been back during the summer of her junior year of high school, when she'd tried to sneak in four hours past her curfew. Her grandma had been up waiting for her when she'd tiptoed in, and after smelling the alcohol on her breath, had totally blown her stack. She'd immediately pushed her over the arm of the couch, yanked up her miniskirt, gotten even *more* upset when she saw the thong underneath it, and had then proceeded to go to town on her butt with the belt she'd already had waiting for her.

Needless to say, that had been one heck of a spanking. And although the actual pain from it had long since faded by now, it all came rushing back to her as Missus Johnson began slapping the seat of her shorts.

SMACK! SMACK! SMACK!

"Ow! Hey! Ow! Hold on!"

Her protests went unheeded however, as Missus Johnson continued to easily hold her in place across her lap. She tried to squirm and wriggle out of the line of fire, but her boss had a strong grip around her waist that kept her from going anywhere as the palm of her right hand exploded against each of her cheeks in a rapid-fire avalanche of pain.

"Young lady, I cannot believe you would speak to your elders like that. What on earth were you thinking?"

"Oh my god, I'm sorry, I'm sorry!" Rhen frantically tried to apologize as Missus Johnson shifted her aim further south to the unprotected backs of her thighs, making her *really* gasp and squirm then.

But no matter how hard she bucked or how much she squealed, her boss kept right on spanking her, having learned long ago to tune out the whining of the brats she put across her knee.

After what felt like forever to the petite sophomore, but was reality in no longer than two minutes at most, Missus Johnson's slapping came to a sudden stop. She gave Rhen's now toasty cheeks a satisfied rub, and then helped her back to her feet.

Standing up after her, she placed a firm arm around her shoulders and began guiding her toward an empty corner that faced the big bay windows behind the couch.

"If I wasn't so busy, I'd find a bar of soap to wash that potty mouth of yours out with, little girl," she growled, parking Rhen where she wanted her and grabbing her hands to put them on top of her head, interlacing her fingers and pushing her nose all the way into the corner. "Just be grateful that I still have things to do, and you stay here until I say you can come out. You got that?"

"Yes ma'am," squeaked the brightly blushing sophomore into her corner, not daring to move an inch while her boss still loomed behind her.

"Good."

Missus Johnson gave her smarting seat one more, firm pat, and then seemed to move out of the room with a frustrated huff. At least, Rhen assumed she'd gone. It was hard for sure since she had her face pushed so far into the corner, but she soon heard the sounds of pots and pans clanking together in a sink underneath running water, and was able to guess that the other woman had made her way into the kitchen and was starting work on getting lunch ready.

Well now, that certainly hadn't been how I was expecting the first conversation with my boss to go...

Rhen felt her face flush again as she tried to flex some of the heat from her bottom.

It didn't help.

Her boss certainly knew what she was doing when it came to handing out spanks, that was for sure. And by now it was also pretty clear that she thought she was someone else entirely, probably a new kid for her to look after or something. Given her general stature and attire, she couldn't exactly blame her. Even so, she knew she needed to clear things up between the two of them before they could get out of hand.

Okay, okay, she admitted to herself with a wry smirk as she pushed out of the corner and gave her tush a tentative rub, wincing. *Any more out of hand.*

Taking a few steps back, Rhen stood there contemplating the corner she'd been deposited into for a couple of minutes while she gathered her thoughts and tried to figure out what she was going to do next. She certainly didn't want to embarrass the other woman or make her feel awkward for what had just happened between the two of them. It had been an honest mistake, she was sure. And even though her bottom was smarting something fierce, she'd had worse. She just needed to march into the kitchen, look her right in the eye and set the record straight.

Besides, she'd just spanked her. She could hardly *still* be mad at her for being late now, could she?

Steeling herself and putting on her best "I'm a grown up, gosh darn it!" face, Rhen marched out of the front room and into the kitchen where she found Missus Johnson arranging slices of ham onto pieces of bread at the counter. She had her back to her and hadn't seemed to have noticed her yet, and so feeling her stomach fluttering with nervous butterflies, Rhen cleared her throat.

"Excuse me, Missus Johnson, I-"

"Oh my goodness," fumed the older woman, cutting her off as she whirled around to face her, glaring daggers with her hands planted squarely on her hips. "What did I *just* get through telling you, young lady?"

"Um, well I, uh… you see…" stuttered Rhen, all of her carefully rehearsed lines melting away under the heat of her boss's stare. "It's just that, um…"

Not bothering to humor her naughty charge and her hemming and hawing any further, Missus Johnson stormed over to where Rhen stood and grabbed her upper arm in a tight grip. With her face fixed into a mask of grim determination, she dragged her back into the living room and once again took up her seat in the middle of the couch, hauling the frantically protesting girl back across her knees with ease.

"It's time you learned that when Auntie Dana tells you to stay in the corner," she snapped, adjusting the younger girl so that her hips lay directly atop her right thigh. "You *stay* in the corner."

Rhen was just in the middle of trying to explain that she didn't *need* to stand in the corner and that none of this was even necessary when she felt Missus Johnson's fingers slip into the back waistbands of her shorts and panties. Going rigid, the heat in her face ratcheting up several degrees all at once, she let out a mortified squeak as the older woman casually yanked them both down to mid-thigh, exposing her still-pink buns to the cool air of the front room and the warmth of the sun shining in through the windows behind her.

"Oooh, someone's getting a spanking, someone's getting a spanking!" jeered an unseen juvenile voice from somewhere off to her right. "Hey everyone, one of the big kids is about to get spanked on her bare butt. Come and see!"

That certainly got Rhen squirming, though with Missus Johnson's left arm pinning her in place across her lap, all it did was make her seem even more like the little brat everyone else seemed to think she was.

"Jacob Reilly, unless *you* want to be the next one over my knee, I suggest you make yourself scarce," warned Rhen's boss, drumming her fingers impatiently against her naked right cheek. "Now."

"Yes ma'am!"

Rhen didn't dare turn her head to glare at him, having someone else see her like this was humiliating enough as it was without meeting their gaze and having it confirmed, but from the sounds of the rapid footfalls on the hardwood floor, it seemed like he'd taken the message to heart. That, or he was hiding behind some corner, out of sight and just waiting to peek in on what was happening once Missus Johnson started smacking away.

It's what she would have done, if she were him.

Swallowing hard, Rhen tried one last time to get her boss to hold off on spanking her and listen to what she had to say.

"Missus Johnson, please! I can explain..."

But once again her pleas fell on deaf ears.

For the second time that morning she felt a strong maternal palm slap down *hard* against her cheeks, first her left then her right, in lightning-fast succession. And without the scant protection of her shorts and panties, the spanks now echoed with a sharp report each time they impacted her tender tush, sending a ripple of pain through her hips and bouncing her buns as the lingering warmth from earlier was rapidly fanned into a flaming inferno.

SMACK! SMACK! SMACK! SMACK! SMACK!

Holy cow! Is this lady a professional spanker, or something?

Before she'd even realized she was doing it, Rhen had started to sniffle and whine as salty tears clouded her vision and began running down her cheeks.

"Owie! Oh my gosh. I'm sorry, I'm sorry, I'm sorry! Please-Owie! I'll be good!"

She spent a good deal longer than two minutes across Missus Johnson's lap this time around, and by the time the last spank had found its mark, her bottom and thighs were colored a vivid shade of cherry red and throbbed with a lava-hot fury that kept her squirming long after it was all over.

"Are we ready to behave now?" asked Missus Johnson gently, but firmly, letting her palm linger warningly against Rhen's right cheek.

"Y-Yes ma'am," hiccupped Rhen, struggling to get her sobbing under control as she wiped her forearm across her red-rimmed eyes.

Now *that* had certainly been a spanking that would have

made her grandma proud.

"Good girl."

Missus Johnson gave Rhen's seat one more firm pat, and then helped her up off of her lap.

The younger girl's hands immediately went to try and pull up the shorts and panties pooled around her ankles, but were intercepted before they got much further than her knees.

"Uh-uh," chided her boss, giving her hands a quick squeeze before moving them back up to her hips and letting go. "Those stay right where they are until you've finished your corner time, missy."

All of her earlier sass and indignation having been thoroughly spanked out of her by now, Rhen just sighed and sniffled again as she nodded.

"Yes, ma'am..."

She remained standing in front of Missus Johnson for several more humiliating moments, one hand awkwardly pawing at her throbbing caboose, while she used the other to wipe away tears and snot from her face. For the time being she forgot all about her dignity as she stood there naked from the waist down, occasionally sniffling and groaning.

Even though she was in fact a sophomore in college, at that particular moment she felt very much like the young teenager everyone so often seemed to treat her as.

And strangely enough, it didn't feel that bad this time.

—

Leaning back against her plush leather couch, Dana Johnson surveyed the contrite girl standing before her with smug satisfaction.

Even the sassiest ones changed their tune after their panties came down and they spent a few minutes over her knee, she'd found. And although this one had certainly been a harder nut to crack than most, she'd managed to get through to her eventually.

Honestly, the nerve of her speaking to her like that. It was just absurd.

Eventually, she let out a long breath, letting her earlier annoyance go with it, and then sat up a bit straighter and prepared to deliver her final lecture before she installed the sniffling girl into the corner.

She'd definitely be eating her lunch standing up, that was for sure.

She was just about to open her mouth and tell her to get moving, when she noticed the gleaming, slightly damp, black curls waving back and forth in front of her as their owner squirmed and shifted uncomfortably. She felt a trickle of something not quite right then, as a nagging sense of uncertainty and suspicion wormed its way into her thoughts.

Ever so slowly, giving herself time to let her brain catch up with what her eyes were reporting, she directed her gaze up from the thatch of pubic hair attached to the squirming pair of too well-rounded hips, to the small swell of an A-cup bosom, and then finally up to the young looking face still unable to quite meet her eye.

At which point things started to click into place, and it was her turn to blush.

"A-Ahem."

Swallowing hard, she flashed the younger girl, or rather the younger *woman*, a sheepish grin.

"Uh... what was it you said your name was again, dear?"

Chapter 2

You Do the Crime,
You Do the (Corner) Time

After she'd managed to explain who she really was, all the while still sniffling and cupping her scalded cheeks as she shifted awkwardly from foot to foot, Missus Johnson quickly leaned forward from her seat on the couch and pulled Rhen's panties and shorts back up for her, apologizing profusely for the mix up.

"Oh honey, I am *so* sorry! I just… I thought… I mean, you just look so…"

She made a broad sweeping gesture with her hand then, taking in Rhen's slight figure and the youthfully casual outfit she was wearing.

Standing as she was in a pair of flip-flops, nylon short-shorts, and a loose fitting t-shirt with her sleek black hair pulled back into a frazzled ponytail behind her, she looked every inch the young and sassy teenager. Especially as she bobbed in place, hands rubbing at the back of her shorts as she pouted.

"Yeah, I get it," she huffed, rolling her eyes.

Despite how humiliating it had been to be treated like a naughty thirteen-year-old, to say nothing of being spanked like one, Rhen was surprised to find that she wasn't actually all that upset with Missus Johnson. Dressed as she was amid the sea of preteens and tweens that she was looking after, it was easy for her to see how she could have been mistaken for just another one of her charges giving her way too much attitude. Part of her knew too that she should be outraged as she stood before the older woman, pawing at her sore bottom as she tried to massage away some of the heat and angry red coloring peeking out from just beneath the legs of her shorts, but she just... wasn't.

It had honestly been kind of fun in a strange way.

Rhen shivered again as she imagined how she must have looked flailing around across Missus Johnson's lap with her bare bottom bouncing and turning redder and redder under her relentlessly punishing palm. And even as she blushed at the memory of it all, replaying it over and over again in her mind's eye in exquisite detail, she felt a giddy little thrill surge through her as it dawned on her just how convincingly she'd been able to play the role of naughty tween without even trying.

Sure, it had been beyond humiliating to be treated that way. But on the other hand, it had also been *very* exhilarating. Knowing that she'd been able to fool the older woman so easily had her feeling like some sort of undercover secret agent who'd just gotten away with something big. Not to mention that the pleasantly-throbbing heat radiating out from her tush and gradually making its way in between her squirming thighs certainly helped make things feel a whole lot better in the aftermath.

Realizing that she'd been staring off into space with a lopsided grin for longer than was probably polite, Rhen shook her head to clear it and coughed. Missus Johnson was obviously expecting some sort of reply from her, but unfortunately for her, she hadn't really been paying attention for the last minute or so.

Deciding to take a shot in the dark, she adopted an easy, nonchalant air as she said.

"No really, I mean it. Um… don't sweat it, ma'am. It was you know…"

She made a vague swirling gesture with her free hand, the one that wasn't busy rubbing her bottom, as she tried to find the right words.

"Just an honest mistake, I'm sure. And plus, I mean…"

Again, she felt her cheeks flush and her stomach twist with an odd mixture of nervousness and excitement as she swallowed hard and added.

"I *was* kinda, sorta, super-duper late today and all."

Rhen flashed her boss a chagrinned smirk with her admission, feeling the butterflies in her stomach stirring up to new heights as she did so.

"So, you know… I suppose I kind of got what was coming to me and stuff."

"Hah, indeed you did," agreed Dana with a friendly laugh, all of her earlier worry having blown away in the face with Rhen's positive attitude and readily admitted confession of wrongdoing, being replaced once again by her good-natured, albeit stern and no nonsense, maternal confidence. "But now I suppose I really ought to figure out what I'm going to do with you, shouldn't I?"

She sighed, easing back into the comfortable leather couch behind her. Rubbing her chin thoughtfully, she ran a critical eye up and down the girl standing nervously before her.

"Hmmm…"

They both shared a look for a few heart-poundingly anxious moments, Dana's lightly challenging and Rhen's nervously hopeful. The woman's arched eyebrows made it very clear to her that her boss definitely had no regrets about spanking her now that she'd admitted she'd earned it, and that she should consider herself lucky that she'd gotten off so lightly. And as stomach-clenchingly mortifying as those thoughts might have been, it was the knowing smile quirking up at the corners of her mouth that made it even more clear that the dampness between her thighs hadn't gone unnoticed by her sharp eyes either.

And that *really* drove the embarrassment home for poor Rhen.

"So... am I not fired?" she wheedled, feeling hope well up inside of her chest as the moments dragged on without her being told to get out and never come back.

Surely the barn burner of a spanking she'd just received more than made up for her small (well, okay, *huge*) bit of tardiness, didn't it?

"Uh, ma'am!" she added hastily as she saw her boss's eyes flash with annoyance.

"Well, not yet, at least," conceded Missus Johnson with a stern look that let Rhen know that she was still on thin ice despite clearing the air just now. "I've still got to mull that one over for a bit more before I make my final decision. But for now..."

She heaved herself up off of the couch then, rising to her feet in a gracefully fluid motion that startled Rhen with just how swiftly she moved for a woman her age. Still frowning slightly, she gripped her firmly by the shoulders and spun her back around to face the opposite wall before propelling her toward the corner she'd been standing in earlier with a hard swat.

SMACK!

"You get that nose of yours right back where it was, missy."

"Ow, hey!" squawked Rhen, suppressing a yelp as she stumbled into the corner.

"College student or not," lectured Missus Johnson, her voice carrying an edge of unspoken warning as she stalked after the younger girl, stepping up behind her and once again threading her fingers together on top of her head for her. "Naughty little girls who get their bottoms spanked in *this* house do their corner time whether they like it or not."

"But- Eep!"

Rhen's protests were cut off suddenly by a mortified squeak of terror, feeling a pit open in the bottom of her stomach as her shorts and panties were whisked down to her ankles for the second time that morning with startling ease.

"Wait, hold on!"

SMACK! SMACK!

"Hush, child!" snapped Missus Johnson, punctuating her command with two heavy swats back to back against either of her bare cheeks, making her hips jerk forward and start to squirm with the reignited sting. "You did the crime, now you can do the time."

"But-!" whined Rhen again, trying to turn away from the corner with her hands still on top of her head so she could at least plead her case properly.

SMACK! SMACK! SMACK!

Three more rapid-fire spanks exploded across her bright red behind, and she frantically found herself whirling back around to face the wall, all but shoving her nose into the corner while she danced from foot to foot, hissing.

"Okay, okay, *fine*! I get it. I'll stand in the corner, geez."

"Hmmm... We'll just see about that," observed Missus Johnson darkly, keeping a firm grip on her shoulder and letting her right palm hover menacingly over the girl's cheeks for a few more moments just to make sure that she was really going to stand still before letting go and taking a step back.

"This time you'd better stay right where you are until I say you can come out. You got that, little girl?"

"Yes ma'am," sighed Rhen, feeling a fresh wave of humiliation wash over her as she heard the loud footfalls of over-excited tweens running around the room behind her, chasing each other.

She let out a low moan and opened her mouth to ask again if she *really* had to stand there with her ruby red cheeks on display for the whole world to see, especially with that stupid set of bay windows right behind her, but quickly thought better of it. The throbbing heat in her seat and Missus Johnson's looming presence only a foot or two away were more than enough to make her decide that it was probably better to just stay quiet and endure the embarrassment with some modicum of good grace.

"Good girl," chirped the older woman with evident self-satisfaction as she took in the delightful sight of the well-punished brat squirming in the corner for a few moments longer, drinking in the details of her adorable caboose as she pouted.

She then brushed her hands off with a sense of a job well done, and moved off back toward the kitchen and all the lunches she'd been preparing before she'd been so rudely interrupted.

"Just remember, Rhen, dear," she called over her shoulder as she walked away. "If we have to have this conversation again, you're going to find out just how unpleasant a spanking from Auntie Dana can really be, alright? I've got plenty of wooden spoons in the kitchen, you know, and they all hurt a *lot* more than my hand does. I can promise you that."

Rhen gulped and straightened up a little bit more at the warning, inadvertently thrusting her adorable, bare caboose even further out toward the room in the process.

"Yes ma'am!"

She continued to stay like that for what felt like forever, but according to the looks she routinely stole toward the old grandfather clock ticking away against the wall behind her, was only about twenty minutes.

Ugh. This sucks.

While Rhen had certainly had her fair share of spankings while growing up, her grandma had never been a big believer in corner time, and so it was only now that she was in the middle of it that she discovered that it was almost as bad as the spanking itself. It was *so* humiliating to be left standing around where anyone and everyone could see the evidence of what had just happened to her, and more than a few of the *actual* daycare kids running around and playing behind her stopped to point her out and snicker at her bare behind.

They'd ask her what she'd done to get in so much trouble with Auntie Dana. Tease her about how she was way too big to be getting spanked like a little kid. Or else maybe just let out a low whistle at how red her pale skin had turned. And as much as Rhen wanted nothing more than to whirl around on the little brats and tell them to piss off, she kept her smoldering face pressed firmly into the corner and her mouth shut tight.

It was bad enough already having everyone see one set of red cheeks on her. She wasn't in any particular rush to show off the others.

Plus she had a sneaking suspicion that Missus Johnson just might consider chasing off a bunch of gawking tweens as leaving the corner, and she'd already had enough spanking for one day, thanks.

—

Eventually her boss returned to collect her from the corner, and seeing that she'd been properly obeyed this time around, praised Rhen for her good behavior as she knelt down behind her and gently pulled her panties and shorts back into their proper place around her hips for her. She then took her hand in hers, all smiles and warm maternal affection once again, and led her out of the front room and into the kitchen.

"Come along, cutie pie, you must be starving."

Upon entering the kitchen, she took a moment to introduce her to the eight or so other boys and girls already gathered around the oversized wooden table waiting to eat, all of whom by Rhen's estimation were somewhere between the ages of ten and thirteen. Unfortunately for her though, her boss neglected to mention the fact that she was *supposed* to be her new assistant.

"Everyone, this is my new friend Rhen. Why don't you say hello to her?"

"Hi Rhen," the gathered kids all chorused back, many of them smirking at her.

"As I'm sure many of you noticed earlier, she was having a serious attitude problem, but we took care of that and she's ready to play nice with all of you now. Isn't that right, dear?"

Left with little other choice, Rhen had gone beet red in the face and gave a strangled nod.

"Um, yes ma'am..."

This introduction certainly had rankled the petite sophomore, whose first instinct had been to open her mouth and set the record straight, but the snickers she got from the others when she hissed upon sitting down too fast on the hard wooden chair beside Missus Johnson kept her quiet. Instead, she just pouted at her lunch.

She could always explain things later on when she wasn't

so busy wriggling around trying to find a comfortable position to sit in, after all.

—

After a surprisingly tasty lunch of ham and cheese sandwiches, wavy potato chips, and carrot sticks, Rhen was released along with everyone else to go play.

But while the others dashed off in seemingly every direction as soon as they'd been given permission to get up and go, she chose instead to linger behind and assist her boss with clearing off the table. Ostensibly to be helpful, but mostly so that she could reassert at least some shred of what remained of her professional dignity.

"So um…" she began, piling paper plates and napkins on top of one another and not quite meeting the other woman's eye as she spoke. "What would you like me to, um… you know, do… as like, your assistant and stuff?"

However, Missus Johnson just smiled and waved a dismissive hand at her.

"Oh don't worry about that, hon. You just go out and play with the others and have some fun. We'll talk things over like grownups after everyone's gone home for the day, alright?"

"Well, okay… if you're sure you don't need me…"

"Go on now, scoot!" laughed the older woman, turning her in the direction of the open back door and the kids running around outside playing tag.

She then propelled her along her way with a playful, but still commanding, swat to the seat of her shorts, and Rhen shot out the door like a rocket.

"Eep! Yes ma'am!"

Chapter 3

Bike Trouble

It was six o'clock in the evening by the time the last of Missus Johnson's charges finally went home, having been picked up by either parents on their way back from work or older siblings who'd been roped into babysitting them. Rhen, who was still far too embarrassed over being treated like a child herself earlier that afternoon to risk having someone's parents mistake her for one as well, spent her time hiding out in the back yard until the last of her playmates had been collected for dinner.

The house and its little square patch of a backyard was left surprisingly peaceful with nobody running around screaming and laughing anymore, but that quiet also brought with it a sense of foreboding dread now that there wasn't anyone left to distract her boss from paying attention to her.

If someone had taken the time to ask her what she was up to as she sat there staring at her flip-flops as they kicked idly back and forth above the dirt in front of her, Rhen probably would have told them that she was just getting in some last minute pumps on the swing set before she headed back home to her dorm. But that was a lie. Deep down, she knew that she was simply way too nervous to go inside and face her boss now that it was just the two of them.

So instead she continued to sit there lost in thought, chewing apprehensively on her lower lip and trying to formulate a plan for how to gracefully confirm that she wasn't fired without actually bringing the subject up or having to look the playfully stern older woman in the eye again.

What if I...? No, that would never work...

Several times that afternoon she'd been on the verge of marching back inside the house to try apologizing again, or to maybe find something to help out with that would show off how useful she could be as an employee, but each time she'd lost her nerve before she'd even managed to reach the back door. Her confident stride would gradually start to lose steam as she drew closer to the back porch, until finally she'd come to an awkward stop, rooted to the spot with indecision. Feeling like everyone was staring at her and laughing, she'd then cast her eyes around for any excuse to put things off for a bit longer, which invariably led to her back to throwing herself into whatever game the others happened to be playing at the time.

After all, she blended right in.

By the time everyone had gone home for the evening she was an exhausted and sore mess. Her shirt was covered in grass stains, she had a lightly skinned right knee from where she'd tripped during an intense game of freeze tag, and her black hair was a tangled nest with several strands sticking out at odd angles. Even so, she had to admit that she'd had a blast running, screaming, and laughing along with the rest of her new friends that day.

Even if she *was* a little over ten years older than most of them.

Well, she thought to herself with a shrug, plucking lazily at the silver lining of her situation with a wan smile. *That kind of, sort of, counts as being her assistant, right? I was just... keeping an active eye on everyone by playing with them. Yeah, totally...*

Seizing on that as her best defense, though not at all feeling confident about it, she was just about to stand up and march back inside when she heard her boss calling for her.

"Rhen, honey, come here! I want to talk to you for a minute," shouted the older woman, raising her voice loud enough so that any neighbors out and about would be able to hear as she waved an arm above her head.

"Coming, ma'am!"

Rhen let out a long sigh then, knowing that whether she liked it or not, it was time to face the music. With one last pump of her arms and legs to build up some momentum, she jumped off of the swing set and jogged over to the spot on the back porch where the woman who was hopefully still her employer was waiting for her.

"Did everyone get home okay?" she asked, doing her best to keep her voice light and breezy, and mostly succeeding. She hoped that asking a professional sounding question would make her look extra-responsible and ready to work, and decided to tack on one more for good measure. "Want me to do any cleaning up before I head out?"

"No, no, that's fine," answered Missus Johnson with a knowing twinkle in her eye as she surveyed her would-be assistant, a bemused smile tracing across her full lips as she took in the unkempt state of her. "Actually, I was wondering if you'd like to go out for some dinner with me tonight, my treat."

"Oh wow, thanks," said Rhen, taken aback by the kind gesture and feeling her confidence starting to rise a little more. This was certainly a good sign, wasn't it? You wouldn't invite the person you were planning to fire out for dinner, now would you? "I'd love to, ma'am!"

"I'm happy to hear that, cutie pie," smirked the older woman, amused by Rhen's youthful exuberance even as the temperature of her smile dipped by several degrees as she continued. "You haven't exactly been on your best behavior today, I know, but I still thought it would be nice to get out of the house for a little while so we could *chat*."

She let the word "chat" hang ominously in the air for several long moments, causing Rhen's stomach to clench and flutter as all of its possible implications rushed through her mind at once.

The slight and sweaty college sophomore couldn't help but notice too that she hadn't *actually* apologized yet for the spankings or bare bottom corner time she'd put her through earlier either, but in the face of free food that wasn't ramen noodles or crappy cafeteria meatloaf, she decided that she could let that one slide. Besides, as far as she was concerned, the less said about those things, the better. All she wanted to do now was put all of that humiliating business behind her and start over fresh with her boss, and a nice professional dinner sounded like just the thing to make that happen.

"Thank you, Missus Johnson, I would love to sit down and discuss things over dinner with you," said Rhen again, this time with as much propriety and dignity as she could muster.

The butterflies in her stomach were still stubbornly whirling around like crazy though, and she couldn't help but shiver as a tingle traced its way down over her tush, reminding her of the time she'd spent across this woman's lap only a few hours earlier and making her flush with sheepish excitement. Still though, she told herself that she wasn't trying to be on her "best behavior" or anything else as childish as that as she straightened up to her full height and schooled her features into a polite mask.

No, she was just being prudent and respectful to this fascinatingly intimidating older woman.

"That is very kind of you to offer, ma'am."

She tried to grin at her then, but found that she was already smiling.

Yeah… totally professional. Not smitten in the slightest, no siree.

"You're very welcome, dear," replied Missus Johnson, her mouth still set firmly in a knowing smirk as she eyed her up and down once again, apparently liking what she saw.

Keeping her back straight and her head held high, Rhen moved to step past her boss with as much good grace as she had available to her. But she was stopped in her tracks before she'd made it more than a few steps when a hand suddenly descended gently, but firmly, onto her shoulder, holding her in place.

"Not so fast there, kiddo," she purred from behind her, her words just as firm as the grip on her shoulder. "You wouldn't happen to know anything about that cute bike with the tassels that's been lying abandoned in the middle of my front lawn ever since this morning, now would you?"

Oh, um, yeah… that's mine," admitted Rhen with a squeak, not daring to look behind her as she felt those butterflies in her stomach kick into overdrive. "Sorry about that. I was just in such a rush when I got here that I totally forgot about it, my bad."

"Yes, that's what I thought."

Missus Johnson was clearly not thrilled to hear this, and before she'd even realized what was happening, Rhen felt the hand on her shoulder squeezing tight, tipping her forward to look at her knees. A strong arm then snaked its way around her waist and hauled her up off of the ground, leaving her suspended in midair with her arms and legs dangling uselessly well above the patio concrete as she was tucked in tight against her boss's wide left hip.

"Wha-?" she gasped as her flip-flops slipped free from her dirty feet and landed with a clatter somewhere behind her.

Rhen was just beginning to reorient herself to her new position when she felt Missus Johnson's strong fingers slipping into the back of her shorts again, causing her stomach to plummet after her shoes as a fresh wave of anxiety washed over her.

The fingers easily wrapped themselves around the stretchy nylon material as they gripped it, and half a heartbeat later her shorts were yanked down past her thighs, where gravity then took hold of them and tugged them the rest of the way off of her legs entirely. With their descent came the warm caress of the early evening summer sun along the tautly-stretched seat of her powder blue panties, making her shiver with a mixture of anxiety and anticipation as it suddenly became all too clear what was about to happen.

Oh no, not again!

She began to squirm like an eel as the reality of her situation slammed into her like a ton of bricks. She moaned and thrashed against the iron vice holding her in place in a futile attempt to escape her impending doom, knowing all the while that it was impossible. If it hadn't worked that morning, then there was no way it was going to work now.

SMACK! SMACK!

Two hard swats made abrupt contact with the centers of each of her cheeks, compressing them with the force of their impact before they sprang back into place for more. She squeaked with the shock of each blow, her eyes shooting open wide with panic as her arms and legs flailed reflexively from the sting.

"Oh my god, Missus Johnson, please! I'm sorry!"

"You're sorry, are you?" snapped the older woman, peppering Rhen's backside with sharp spanks all the while as she spoke. "That bike of yours has a kickstand doesn't it? You couldn't take the ten seconds required to park it properly around the side of the house with everyone else's?"

SMACK! SMACK! SMACK!

"Ow! Oh! I'm sorry, I was in a rush."

SMACK! SMACK! SMACK!

"Owie, ow! I wasn't thinking! Oooooh, ah, ah ah!"

SMACK! SMACK! SMACK!

"That's right, you *weren't* thinking!" she lectured, shifting her aim down to the delicate undercurves of the younger girl's gyrating caboose and pouring in even more ferocity to each swat so that she'd really be feeling this particular punishment all the while they were eating dinner. "Are you *trying* to tempt people into stealing that cute little bike of yours?"

"No, no, no I'm not!" Rhen frantically tried to reassure her, feeling her face flush almost as hot as her bottom was as she realized that her boss had definitely seen how age inappropriate her bicycle was.

Then again, given her current predicament and the furious inferno that was growing all the more painful with each and every relentless swat to the back of her panties, maybe it wasn't?

Dammit!

Why did she have to fit so perfectly under this woman's arm?

"And what about all the other boys and girls?" demanded Missus Johnson, delivering half a dozen truly scorching spanks to the backs of her thighs before moving back up to her sit spots. "How would you have felt if one of them had been running around out front and tripped over *your* bike and hurt themselves? Hmmm?"

"I'm sorry!" Rhen moaned, dragging the words out into a great hiccupping sob as she started to cry in earnest.

Her boss's lecture had easily cut to her core, and now big

fat tears were starting to trace zigzagging patterns down her cheeks as she considered what might have happened to her new friends because of her carelessness; forgetting for the moment that she'd been told repeatedly that they weren't allowed to play out front.

"Sorry isn't good enough, young lady. You need to do better!"

"I will, I will!"

SMACK! SMACK! SMACK!

As the pain in her seat boiled over into something truly unbearable and her guilt over disappointing her boss washed over her, again, Rhen let her body sag, accepting her punishment like the good girl that she wanted so desperately to be just then.

"There, there," sighed Missus Johnson about a minute later, delivering one final swat to the center of Rhen's tight little rear end, before setting her back onto her feet with casual ease.

She drew the crying girl in for a long hug then, gently stroking the back of her frazzled hair until she finally calmed down enough to be let go.

It was clear to her that she was one of those girls who cried easily from a prolonged spanking, but just as quickly was able to bounce back and get herself under control once it was all over. Her bottom would be sore and swollen for a long while to come, but as she'd seen already once before that day, that wouldn't be enough to keep her bubbly personality in check for long.

After a couple more minutes of cuddling, Missus Johnson untangled herself from her assistant and stepped back, keeping one hand firmly gripped on her shoulder while the other wagged an admonishing forefinger at her still sniffling face.

"This had better be the last time we have to talk about this," she warned, keeping her voice stern, but with enough warmth to let her know that all was forgiven. "Because if I see that bike of yours out on my lawn like that ever again, I promise you that you're going to be one *very* sorry little girl. You understand?"

"Yes ma'am," sniffled Rhen, shivering in spite of herself and wishing very much that she could grab her shorts and pull them back on to restore at least some semblance of her identity as a twenty-year-old college sophomore.

She already felt like a very sorry little girl as it was just then, and she definitely didn't want to even imagine how things could possibly get any worse.

Well, at least I still have my panties on.

That was better than nothing, wasn't it?

"It won't happen again, I promise."

"Good."

Missus Johnson flashed her a motherly smile and ruffled her hair then, before turning on her heel and moving back inside the house as if nothing had just happened. Then, pulling open the screen door in front of her, she paused to call over her shoulder.

"Come along now, cutie pie. Put your shorts on and let's get going. I don't know about you, but I'm *starving.*"

Chapter 4

Dinner and Decisions

After a quick trip to the bathroom to wash her hands, scrub the dirt and tear tracks from her face, and attempt to wrangle her hair into something at least somewhat approaching presentable, Rhen and Missus Johnson piled into her red SUV and set out for dinner. Some twenty minutes later they pulled into a parking spot out front of Papa Italiano's, a modestly priced, family-friendly Italian restaurant. It wasn't exactly the fanciest place to go out to eat, but the food was tasty and just then Rhen felt hungry enough to eat a horse.

She'd certainly worked up one heck of an appetite from playing tag and hide-and-seek all that afternoon.

The restaurant was loud and crowded as they pushed their way inside, filled to the brim with the cacophony of clinking silverware on plates and music being blasted from unseen speakers overhead, while people talked and laughed over all the noise. Moving through the din, she couldn't help but blush and squirm a little bit as she thought about the image that she and her boss must have made as they sat down side-by-side on the little padded bench next to the reservation stand.

Surely the two of them must have looked like the spitting image of a mother and her young daughter out for a quiet dinner together as they waited to be seated. Especially with the way Missus Johnson kept clucking disapprovingly at her for fidgeting as she sat wedged in close beside her on their narrow perch.

Even with a well-padded seat to help, sitting was still very much an unpleasant experience for Rhen as the heat in her bottom continued to simmer and throb beneath her.

Thankfully though, whether by some miracle of happenstance or the woman manning the reservation stand taking pity on her and her clearly sore bottom, they managed to get a table after only a relatively short wait of about ten minutes. But as she showed them to their booth and they sat down, they must have indeed looked very much like a mother-daughter pair to the woman. Because as they'd settled into their respective sides, their waitress had laid out a kids menu and a packet of crayons in front of Rhen with a friendly smile rather than the laminated adults menu she offered to Missus Johnson along with the wine and dessert lists a moment later.

"Um, excuse me," the younger girl piped up, the twinge of pain in her rear end as she shifted uncomfortably in her seat acting as a keen reminder to keep her tone civil and polite. "Can I get a regular menu instead, please?"

"Oh, I'm sorry, sweetie. I just assumed you'd be more comfortable with the kids menu," apologized the young woman acting as their waitress, not sounding the least bit remorseful at all as far as Rhen was concerned.

The girl looked like she was just barely out of high school, but even so, the chest and hips straining against the black and white pinstripes of her uniform more than put Rhen's own shallow curves to shame. It was no wonder she'd pegged her as a tween who'd be ordering from the kids menu. She certainly looked the part just then, especially when compared to her and her boss.

"If you don't mind waiting for a while, I can go get you a regular one instead," she offered with an insincere smile that bore an unmistakable edge of condescension to it. "I'd do it now, but I've got four other tables to take orders for first. Do you think you can you be a good girl and wait patiently for me while I take care of that?"

"What?" demanded Rhen, feeling the tips of her ears starting to heat up with righteous indignation as she glared at the still sweetly-smiling girl standing beside her.

Be patient for her? *Sweetie?*

Oh, she was so going to put this bitch in her place!

"Listen here, you-"

"Don't worry about it, dear, she can just use mine," cut in Missus Johnson smoothly, preempting her before she could really let fly with some choice words and flashing the younger woman an apologetic look as she waved her hand dismissively. "She's just being cranky because she got a spanking before we came to dinner tonight. I'm sure you understand how kids can be sometimes."

That certainly stopped Rhen's tirade in its tracks, the words dying on her lips before she'd even had a chance to spit them out at the stupid waitress. She was still seething at being treated like a child, but the look her boss flashed her from across the table was a clear warning that there would be another trip across her knee right there and then if she didn't behave herself, and she took it to heart.

"I'm sorry!" squeaked Rhen, looking away from the two smirking women and staring down at the kids menu in front of her with newfound interest.

"That's okay, sweetie pie, I forgive you," chirped their waitress, practically the living embodiment of smugness now as she turned to focus her full attention on Missus Johnson.

Seeing that she'd managed to squash the impending temper tantrum before it had a chance to take root, Missus Johnson cleared her throat and went on, driving one final nail into the coffin of Rhen's humiliation.

"Besides, I'd rather have something to keep this one

occupied with while we wait on our meals. She has a tendency to get kind of antsy when she's bored. Isn't that right, Rhen, honey?"

"Ugh. Yes, ma'am…" grumbled the petite sophomore, scowling at the two of them and hardly believing her ears.

She was definitely still tempted to say something sharp and biting, but the frosty twinkle in her boss's eyes and the unspoken warning not to test her, kept her mouth shut tight as she looked down at the piece of paper in front of her again and blushed.

That seemed to amuse their snotty waitress all the more, and she laughed right along with Missus Johnson as she pulled out a pad of paper and a pen and took their drink orders. Rhen asked for a Diet Coke, doing her best to ignore the clucking from her boss about how the caffeine would keep her up all night, *again*, before she too ordered one for herself. Their waitress jotted the easy order down, told them that she'd be back in a few minutes, and then turned around and flounced away.

Part of Rhen burned with the desire to give the smirking woman sitting across from her a piece of her mind, but the tingling warmth in her nether cheeks kept her from doing much more than scowling petulantly as she leaned across the table to snatch up the adults menu. Missus Johnson didn't protest as she dragged it over to her side of the booth and flipped it open. However, after spending only a few minutes squinting through all of the entrée choices, Rhen found herself frowning and fighting off another blush as she set the menu aside and picked up the piece of paper in front of her that had the kids entrée options printed on the back of it.

"Not, a, *word*," she growled to her boss good-naturedly.

"Not a word," agreed Missus Johnson with as low laugh, retrieving her menu and folding it open.

True to her word, their waitress returned around five or so minutes later with their drinks. She set the tall glasses of soda down on top of small square napkins in front of each of them, offering Rhen the choice of a regular straw or one of the Papa Italiano's branded crazy straws, before pulling out her little pad and pen once more to take their food order. Rhen felt her insides boiling at the amused smirk on the other girl's face as she took her order, which just so happened to be the macaroni and cheese with chopped up slices of hot dog from the kids menu. She wisely decided to keep her temper in check however, and instead quietly ground her teeth as Missus Johnson took her time asking about the house specials for the night, before finally settling on the grilled salmon and roasted peppers with a lemon glaze.

"Careful there, cutie pie," she cautioned after their waitress had sashayed away again, keeping a pleasant smile fixed on her face that took on a decidedly teasing edge to it as she leaned in a bit closer over the table. "If you keep on pouting like that, you might not get dessert."

In spite of the fireworks her boss's words and expression set off inside of her stomach, Rhen couldn't resist the urge to stick her tongue out at the older woman.

"Meanie!"

She just laughed at her however, and then they both smirked, each acknowledging how silly the whole situation was as they settled back to wait for their meals to arrive.

—

Much to her own annoyance, Rhen quickly found herself getting more and more bored as time seemed to crawl by at a snail's pace for them as they waited. She'd been so flustered from her earlier spanking in the backyard at the daycare that she hadn't even thought to grab her phone from her backpack on their way out the door, and now was left with seemingly nothing to entertain herself with as her stomach growled.

Well, except for one thing.

Huffing and pouting as she stared out of the corner of her eye over the twists and turns of her crazy straw at the piece of paper she'd shoved as far away from her as she could, she blew some annoyed bubbles into her drink and then caved. She snatched up the plastic-sealed packet of crayons from beside her along with the kids menu as fast as she could, just like she was ripping off a Band-Aid, and flipped it over to the side with the maze and word search printed on it.

If I'm going to be treated like a little kid in this stupid restaurant, then I might as well enjoy myself, at least.

She'd just finished circling the second to last word on the surprisingly challenging word search (it was "risotto") when their food finally arrived.

And it smelled delicious.

Well, at least hers did.

Rhen couldn't help but wrinkle her nose at the scents of sizzling salmon and peppers wafting up at her from her boss's plate across the table. Even so, they began to dig in with gusto, both of them famished from a long day's work.

After a few minutes of near-silent chewing, save for the occasional question of how each other's meals tasted, Missus Johnson sighed through her nose and set her utensils down on either side of her plate.

"Rhen, honey, I'm really sorry to say this, but I don't think I can keep you on as my assistant."

Even though she'd had a feeling that this was how things were going to turn out, the news still hit Rhen like a punch to the gut. Swallowing hard, she set her own spoon down beside her plate, finding much to her embarrassment that she could already feel the beginnings of tears prickling at the corners of her eyes as she did. She'd certainly had enough first-hand experience with the sensation today to know what it felt like by now.

"*Please*, Missus Johnson," she begged, actually bringing her hands together in front of her in a supplicating gesture. "I really need this job. Please, please, *please* can't you give me another chance? I know I screwed up really badly today, but I promise I won't ever be that late again. I'll be the best assistant you've ever had, just give me another shot!"

Taken aback by the sincerity and desperation in the younger girl's pleading, Missus Johnson found herself automatically reaching out across the table to comfort the poor thing.

"Honey, honey," she soothed, wrapping her hands over Rhen's smaller ones and giving them a reassuring squeeze. "It's just a silly summer job. Really, it's not a big deal. You're a wonderful girl and I'm sure you'll find another one eventually."

She heaved out another long sigh and shook her head sadly.

"But even though I really like you, dear, there's just no way that I can let you be my assistant."

"But why?" whined Rhen, not even caring how childish and petulant she sounded just then as she forced herself to meet her boss's dark eyes. "I know I messed up, but *come on*. It wasn't *that* big of a deal, was it? And besides, didn't I do a really good job keeping an eye on everyone this afternoon? All the kids seemed to really like me! Shouldn't that at least count for *something*?"

Missus Johnson felt the corners of her mouth twitching up into a half-smirk at the display before her. She should have known that what this silly girl needed was another dose of

Auntie Dana's tough love to get through to her.

"Well, if you really want to know," she said, pursing her lips into a disapproving frown as she squeezed Rhen's hands again before letting them go. "The truth is, you're a child, Rhen."

Seeing the look of hurt outrage on the younger girl's face, she quickly clarified.

"Oh, don't get me wrong. You're clearly a very smart girl from what I've seen on your transcripts, your school sent them over with your application, and you've got a wonderfully bright and friendly personality that, quite frankly, I think is just adorable, but when it comes to being an actual mature adult, you still have a *lot* of growing up to do."

Rhen felt her back stiffen at the sharp accusations, only the apologetic look in the older woman's eyes dulling their sting enough to not make them painful and cruel. She opened her mouth to argue that she was in fact plenty mature enough for the stupid job she was being fired from, but Missus Johnson held up a hand to keep her quiet as she plowed forward with her dressing down.

"I see you're about to argue with me, so let me lay it out for you, hon," she said, keeping her voice stern, but not cruel, as she began to tick off points on her fingers. "For starters, I personally consider being well over an hour late on your first day of work to be a *very* big deal, young lady. Especially when it was just because you'd went to bed way too late the night before and slept through your alarm. Before we cleared up our little case of mistaken identity, I was *this* close to calling your university and giving them hell for sending me someone so flaky."

She held up her thumb and forefinger in front of her, barely half an inch apart.

"That kind of crap would *never* fly in the real world, and

you're damn lucky that a little spanking and some time in the corner was all you got out of it. A bad referral like the one I was planning to give you would have definitely not made finding a new job nearly so easy, I can tell you that for a fact, missy."

"I'm sorry, ma'am…" mumbled Rhen, unable to meet the other woman's gaze anymore as she stared down at her half-finished macaroni and tried to ignore the roiling going on inside of her stomach as the first hot tear trickled down her right cheek.

"You should be, and I'm glad to hear you say it," sighed Missus Johnson, waving off her apology. "But I forgive you, and it's in the past now. More to the point, even if you *had* been on time today, you're unfortunately way too young, and pardon me for being blunt but it's the truth, immature to be riding herd on a bunch of grade schoolers."

"What? But I'm nearly twenty-one!" protested Rhen, her indignation overcoming her embarrassment enough to force her to look back up at the older woman sitting across from her, still frowning.

"I know you are, but parents get antsy about who's watching their kids, and unfortunately you just don't fit the bill for what they're expecting in a care taker."

She sighed again, and this time flashed Rhen an apologetic look of her own as she shrugged. The gesture seemed to convey the message that she didn't like it either, but there wasn't anything she could do about it.

"But even if that weren't the case, there's no way that any of those kids would ever take you seriously as an authority figure. Not when at least half of them look like they're a year ahead of you in school. To say nothing of the fact that most, if not all of them, had a front row seat for your trip across my knee this morning and your time reflecting on your bad behavior in the corner. A bright red bottom and a sobbing face, a person to listen to do not make, I'm afraid."

She paused again, this time to enjoy the sight of Rhen's adorably cherry-red face as she took a long sip from her drink, savoring its flavor and the cute little dimple that formed between the younger girl's eyebrows whenever she scowled. She really was *such* a cutie pie. It was a shame that she wouldn't be seeing her again after tonight. She would have enjoyed getting the chance to mother her some more.

To say nothing of getting her hands on that cute little caboose of hers again.

"I'll at least admit that you're right about how well you did with the kids this afternoon, they definitely liked you. But unfortunately it's all too clear to me now that you fit in far better as one of my charges than you ever did as my assistant. I'm sorry to say it, hon, but that's the long and the short of it."

"But... but..." spluttered Rhen, more tears gathering at the corners of her eyes as she stared desperately at the woman sitting across from her who'd just so thoroughly fired her. "You don't understand. I really, really, *really* need this job!"

"Hey, hey, it's just a part-time gig, kiddo," soothed Missus Johnson, moving on instinct to slide over into Rhen's side of the booth and wrapping an affectionate arm around her trembling shoulders. "There's no need to make such a big fuss about it. I'm sure you'll find another one sooner or later. You're a clever girl. You just weren't a good fit for me is all."

"But... but you don't understand," moaned Rhen miserably, feeling all of the pent up anxiety and pressure from the last few weeks finally catching up to her all at once as hot tears started pouring down her cheeks in earnest.

She turned in her seat and clung to the older woman, not caring how childish it made her look or feel just then as she buried her face into her ample bosom and sobbed.

Missus Johnson squeezed her gently and rubbed her back, rocking her softly as she waited for her to calm down. Clearly there was much more to this silly sophomore's story than met the eye, and she was going to get to the bottom of it before they had dessert.

"Why don't you tell me what's really going on?" she suggested a few minutes later when Rhen's crying had finally subsided to just the occasional sniffle.

Still leaning against the older woman's side for support, Rhen heaved out a long and tired breath before she began to explain her situation to her in a mumbling, embarrassed, little voice.

To say money was tight for her was the understatement of the century.

She'd received a scholarship to attend her university that covered her tuition and books, but not much else. With her grandma's limited finances and no parents in the picture to speak of, she was the very definition of a lean and thrifty college student. Thankfully though, she'd been able to avoid one major expense up until now, rent. She'd been allowed to live in the dorms rent-free ever since she'd started school, but now that she was about to be a junior, she'd been told that she'd accumulated too many credits and had to move out to make room for newer students.

She'd known that this was something she'd have to take care of at some point ever since the start of fall semester the year before, but she'd kept putting it off and hadn't done anything about it ever since she'd gotten the email informing her she had to move out by the start of August the following year. Her plan had been to take care of it somehow during winter or spring break, but she'd been distracted by tagging along with some of her friends to go get wild and loose, and hadn't figured anything out yet.

Her grandma had told her that she could help her out a little bit with the first month's rent and a security deposit on an apartment, but she wasn't exactly well off to begin with and what little she said she could provide wasn't nearly enough to cover getting a proper lease anywhere. Not to mention the fact that she had no idea how to even go about *finding* an apartment to live in in the first place.

Up until now, she'd either just lived with her grandma, or had been told where she would be staying by the university. How did you even start looking for an apartment that didn't cost an arm and a leg? She'd tried searching for places close to campus on the internet, but all of the listings she'd found had been for luxury student housing that was *way* outside of her non-existent budget.

So Rhen had taken to fretting and worrying whenever she laid down to go to sleep at night, while during the day telling herself that everything was fine and that she still had plenty of time to take care of things later. Whenever she'd felt that little twinge of worry about the future in the pit of her stomach, she'd pushed it down by repeating to herself that she was just way too busy with classes and exams to stress out about anything else.

That had worked fine for a while, but now summer semester was almost over, and to her absolute horror it had dawned on her that she was about to be homeless in only a few short weeks if she didn't think of something, and fast!

Last Monday morning, she'd run in a panic to the Student Employment Center and picked the earliest available job offering they had on hand so she could at least start saving *some* money. But now that she was fired, that plan had fallen apart, and she was terrified that she'd ran out of time and options, and wasn't going to have anywhere to stay next semester.

One of the girls working at the Employment Center had suggested she look into maybe getting a student loan, but unfortunately that wasn't something she had any chance of securing in the short amount of time she had left before the semester was over. She'd have to drop out of school and return home to live with her grandma, so close to finishing her degree, but now with no hope of actually ever graduating; at least, not any time soon.

"Oh honey…" cooed Dana Johnson, patting the back of Rhen's hair and rocking her gently in her arms. "There, there, it's going to be alright, I promise."

She could feel her heart breaking for the poor thing, even if she'd largely brought her situation down onto herself with her procrastination. Despite that though, she hardly felt like she could just turn this little waif of a college student out on her own without forever feeling horrible about herself.

From what she'd seen and heard from the time she'd spent with Rhen that day, she was a very clever and well-meaning girl, but she was also in desperate need of someone to rein her in with a *very* firm hand. And as that thought bubbled up in her mind, a plan began to form. One that would solve Rhen's little housing troubles, give her the structure she so clearly needed, and would allow Dana to have more than a little fun with the cutie pie nestled in against her chest for a long time to come.

"I like you a lot, kiddo," she said, tipping Rhen's head back to look at her with a delicate hand under her chin and flashing her a reassuring grin. "You've got plenty of heart and spunk, even if you *are* a total sass-mouth."

Rhen smiled in spite of the tears still marring her red-rimmed eyes, looking just as cute as a button to Dana.

"So how about this? How would you like to stay with *me* next semester, and every other semester too for that matter if you'd like?"

She raised an eyebrow and hoped very much that the other girl would say yes.

"I would just *love* to have you around as my 'niece' if you're up for it."

"What, really?" asked Rhen, sitting up a little bit straighter and feeling the first real glimmers of hope sparkling within her in what felt like forever. "But… what about the daycare and all that other stuff?"

She felt herself blushing, but she knew that she had to keep going as she plowed on.

"You know, the spankings and all the other kids who think I'm one of them?"

"You mean the spankings you one-hundred percent earned with your bratty behavior today?" clarified Dana, her voice taking on a decidedly stern tone as she fixed Rhen with a dis-approving look. "And the friends you had so much fun play-ing with all afternoon?"

"Um, yes?" squeaked the younger girl, looking away as her blush deepened even more, only making her cuter. "So, uh… where would those fit in to all this?"

Dana smirked.

From the embarrassed look on Rhen's face as she chewed at her lower lip, it was pretty clear to see that she wasn't nearly as upset about the possibility of another trip across her knee as she was trying to make out. That was good. It was nice to see that she too, at least on some level, saw the appeal and need for her to be taken in hand.

"Here's the way it's gonna be, cutie pie," Dana explained, keeping her voice stern, but still kind, as she tipped Rhen's chin back again so that she had to look her in the eye. "I'm more than happy to have you living with me. I've got a spare guest room nobody ever uses that would be just perfect for you, and I make more than enough money between my daycare and my side business as a design consultant to cover anything that you might need. But if you *do* decide that this is what you want, then there's going to be rules, and you best believe that there'll be consequences too."

She paused long enough to make sure that Rhen was fully paying attention now before she went on.

"As far as I'm concerned, you're *far* closer to thirteen than you are to twenty when it comes to your behavior, and if you decide to come live with me, then that's exactly how I'm going to treat you. I mean it, kiddo. From that point onward, you're not going to be a twenty-year-old college kid who gets to make all her own decisions anymore. You're going to be thirteen, and I *will* be keeping you in line just like I have been all day today. I'm not going to charge you any rent, and I'll be happy to do whatever you need to make sure you do well in school, but the moment you say yes, you're going to officially become my bratty little niece."

She let that all sink in for a few moments, running her free hand down Rhen's back and giving her well-rounded caboose a hard squeeze through her shorts.

"And as you found out today, Auntie Dana runs a *very* tight ship, doesn't she?"

Rhen gasped and squirmed in the other woman's clutches, trying not to moan as she winced from the fresh pain her fingers digging into her tender flesh elicited.

"But... but... Um, won't that be weird? I'm in college for crying out loud!" she whined, realizing only after the words had tumbled out of her that she wasn't actually denying that she could or should be spanked and treated like a naughty teen, but instead just complaining about how embarrassing it would be.

"And what about your husband?" she added quickly, hoping to distract the broadly beaming woman from thinking too hard about turning her over her knee again anytime soon. "Don't you need to discuss this all with him first?"

Dana couldn't help but snort and roll her eyes at that.

"Rhen, honey, you already pass for thirteen without even trying to. In fact, I bet with the right outfits, and a couple other adjustments, I could get you looking closer to twelve, easily."

She released the younger girl's chin, but deliberately chose to keep her other hand right where it was on her backside as she gave a dismissive wave of her free hand toward the discarded kids menu and the half-finished plate of macaroni and cheese, winking at her.

"Besides, you're just too damn adorable *not* to spoil and spank. And as far as being concerned about what others might think, well... I know it may not be the popular norm for a lot of kids these days, but nobody is going to bat an eye at a bratty teen getting her just desserts over her auntie's knee when she's in trouble."

"Humph. I guess..." conceded Rhen begrudgingly, not quite willing to admit that the other woman had a point or to acknowledge that today had easily been one of the most simultaneously exhilarating and relaxing days of her entire life.

She knew that she should be upset about being treated this way, or at the very least offended that she was being talked down to like this, but... the prospect of being this vivaciously charming older woman's young "niece" (and all that would entail) was just too tempting.

"And as to your other question," continued Dana, interrupting her thoughts with a tinkling laugh. "There is no Mister Johnson. Well, at least not anymore, there isn't. We got married right about the time I was your age, and then divorced eight months later. Johnson is actually my maiden name, and as to the title, well…"

She shrugged and flashed Rhen an impish smirk.

"I decided to hold onto that one when I started the day-care. You know, for marketing reasons. Parents really do prefer a more homemaker, married type of woman to look after their kids, you know."

Rhen couldn't help but chuckle at that revelation, the laugh carrying away with it the last of her anxieties and fears from the previous weeks. She swallowed hard, realizing that she'd already made her decision. Now all she had to do was say it out loud.

"If you'll have me, ma'am, I think I'd really like to live with you."

Missus Johnson, now for all intents and purposes Rhen's Aunt Dana, gave her right cheek an affectionate squeeze and they both smiled.

"Oh honey, I would *love* that."

Chapter 5

Details and Dessert

Once the last of Rhen's tears had been dried with an unused napkin and their dessert order had been placed, Dana pulled out her smartphone and offered it to her new "niece".

"Why don't you give your granny a call and tell her the good news?" she suggested in a way that Rhen suspected she wasn't supposed to ignore. "I'm sure she's still worried sick about you finding somewhere to live. Plus I'd also like to have a quick chat with her as soon as possible. You know, introduce myself and make sure we're both on the same page on a few things and all that."

"Oh, good idea," agreed Rhen, accepting the device from her former-boss-turned-aunt and punching her grandma's phone number into it from memory.

The call went through after only a handful of rings, and her face lit up as she heard the warm voice of the woman who'd raised her ever since she was a small child pick up on the other end.

"Hi Grandma, it's me… No, I'm using someone else's phone… Because I forgot mine… No, no, it's fine. I just left it in my backpack at her house is all. It's safe, I promise… Yeah, today was my first day… It was alright, I guess. Kinda fun, actually. But uh… Yeah, no the job kinda sorta fell through in the end… No, no, it wasn't anything like that. It's just that I kinda, um… Well, I kinda messed up a bit and got fired. But it's all good now, I promise!"

Rhen blushed as she blurted out her last couple of

sentences as fast as she could, hoping that they'd be over-looked while her newly-acquired aunt sat across from her watching the display she was putting on in open amusement, her eyes crinkling at the corners as she smirked. Crossing her fingers underneath the table, she silently prayed that her grandma wouldn't go ballistic or ask her too many questions just then. She could practically *feel* the sharp accusations and impending lecture brewing on the other end of the line like an oncoming summer storm, and she very much wanted to avoid getting a double dose of scolding from the two authority figures in her life in one day if it was at all possible.

"No really, it's fine, I swear!" she squeaked. "Actually, it's even better than fine! I'm out to dinner with the lady I was working for, her name's Dana by the way and she's super nice, and she offered to let me move in with her next semester after I told her about the whole dorm thing."

She paused for a moment then while her grandma took it all in, sounding rather dubious.

"Yes, *really*," she huffed. "We talked the whole thing out, and she said she'd let me live with her rent-free if I wanted to. I just had to agree to uh… to be on my best behavior is all."

Eager to sweep past that last bit before her grandma could puzzle out its meaning, Rhen quickly added.

"She's *super* nice, Grandma. I think you'd like her a lot."

I know I sure do.

Rhen felt her cheeks flush at the sudden personal revelation, and swallowed hard as her grandma picked up on her evasive tone, but by some small miracle she ended up letting her off the hook with only a stern warning to try and do better after she eventually managed to drag the whole story of her disastrous first day of work out of her. Eager to keep her return to childish discipline a secret, she'd been *very* careful to avoid making any mention of Missus Johnson's preferred method of discipline at all costs.

"I guess you could say she's super strict, but that's okay. I honestly don't think I mind it all that much with her," she admitted with another rush of heat up her face, wondering why it was that she couldn't seem to stop herself from gushing on and on about the woman sitting across from her, only to realize then that she'd totally developed a crush on her. "It's like, you know... tough love or something. It's nice."

Oh well... There's no sense in trying to deny it now.

"*Yes,* I'm serious!" she snapped in exasperation a moment later when her grandma pressed her on that point. "Look, can we talk about something else instead, *please?*"

The petite sophomore couldn't help but heave out a sigh of relief when they finally moved on to discussing the arrangement she'd reached with her former boss, content to let her grandma steer the conversation for a little while so her motor mouth couldn't embarrass her further. But that relief was quickly replaced by a nervous twinge in her chest when her grandma asked her to pass the phone off to Dana so that they could talk.

"Um, yeah... Sure, no problem. Here she is," she said, trying to sound nonchalant as she held out the phone to her aunt. "She wants to talk to you."

"Hello there, this is Dana Johnson," greeted the older woman smoothly as she accepted her phone back and brought it to her ear with a knowing look that made the butterflies in Rhen's stomach flutter even harder. "How're you doing this evening?"

Rhen sat there awkwardly fidgeting with one corner of her kids menu and staring shyly at the tabletop, wishing very much that their molten chocolate lava cake would arrive already and cut the phone call short as her new "aunt" and her grandma fell into a surprisingly long and easygoing conversation. She knew from personal experience that her grandma held very similar beliefs to Dana when it came to child rearing and discipline, though by some miracle of luck (and being really good at not getting caught) she'd managed to avoid experiencing anything quite like what she'd gotten that afternoon since her junior year of high school. Nevertheless, apparently her grandma and Dana had sensed that they were kindred spirits, because before she knew it, the two of them were chatting away like old friends who hadn't seen each other in years.

By now the all too familiar sensation of dread and anticipation was gnawing away at Rhen's insides, and she found herself straining hard to try and overhear what her grandma was saying on the other end of the line. Unfortunately it was far too loud in the restaurant to pick up anything comprehensible, but judging by all the fervent nodding and the things Dana was saying, she had a pretty good idea what they might be talking about with regard to her and their new living arrangement.

Phrases like "needs discipline", "put on a tight leash", and "proper schedule" kept coming up and Rhen didn't like the sound of any of it, especially since it seemed pretty obvious that her grandma was agreeing right along with whatever it was her new aunt was telling her. Something about wardrobes (or maybe it was closets?) kept coming up too, but try as she might, she wasn't able to make heads or tails of that remark. Not that it mattered much, she decided.

Given the older woman's penchant for swift and immediate action whenever she got out of line, Rhen was sure she'd find out what she meant sooner rather than later.

After a minute or two more of letting her mind fill in the gaps from the little bits and pieces she was able to pick up, and not at all liking what they were shaping up to look like, she turned her attention back to her rumpled kids menu and tried not to listen any longer. She told herself that it was because eavesdropping on a private conversation was rude, but the truth was simply that she didn't want to find out for sure whether or not her grandma really thought she was still young enough to spank at the ripe old age of twenty.

Practically twenty-one, she thought with a sullen pout. *Humph!*

Dana wasn't a tyrant though, she reminded herself. She'd be fine so long as she acted like the mature adult she knew she was. Even though her new aunt had made it very clear that she would be assuming the role of a thirteen-year-old while living with her, that was more for show and fun, wasn't it? Today had just been an unlucky fluke. She wouldn't be getting spanked *that* often... right?

Mercifully the phone call eventually ended with Dana promising that she'd be in touch again soon, and a few moments later their dessert finally arrived.

More than ready to put the entire embarrassing incident and all of its stomach-twisting possibilities behind her, Rhen snatched up her fork, and she and her aunt dug in.

—

The drive home that night was a quiet one for the both of them. Rhen, who was stuffed to the brim with pasta and cake, could feel herself drifting off to sleep with each passing streetlight as Dana drove her back to her dorm.

They'd had a brief conversation once they'd piled back into the car about whether or not they should swing by Dana's house to grab her bike first before she dropped her off, but fatigue and her aunt's insistence that it would be fine where it was for the night quickly convinced her that it wasn't worth the effort.

The big seats of the SUV were just so *comfy.*

She could just walk to class tomorrow.

Besides, who cared? If she left her bike at her aunt's house, then that would just be one less thing she'd have to worry about moving later.

Or something.

I'll figure it out in the morning...

—

By the time they pulled up in front of her dorm, Rhen was fast asleep.

For a brief moment Dana considered carrying the gently snoring girl inside and tucking her into bed herself, but reluctantly decided against it after it occurred to her that she had no idea where Rhen's room actually was inside the building.

"Oh well, there'll be time enough for all that later, I suppose," she sighed to no one in particular with only a twinge of disappointment, contenting herself with snapping a quick photo of her snoozing niece as she drooled adorably onto her seatbelt.

Reaching over, she softly shook her by the shoulder to rouse her.

"Wake up, cutie pie. We're here."

A blurry-eyed Rhen stretched in her seat and yawned then.

"Oops, I must've fallen asleep..."

"Just for a minute," conceded Dana with a twinkle in her dark eyes as she surreptitiously checked the picture she'd just taken on her phone.

Oh yes, that one was definitely a keeper.

"Do you want me to walk you inside?"

"Nah, that's fine," replied Rhen with a half-hearted wave as she stepped out of the car onto a pair of wobbly legs. Letting out another long yawn, she turned back toward the older woman and flashed her a tired smile. "Thanks for everything, Aunt Dana. Today was a lot of fun."

"You're very welcome, dear. Now go get some sleep. I'll call you tomorrow, alright?"

"Deal."

—

The next day, after she'd finished up with watching her usual gaggle of eight or so kids for the day, Dana drove back to Rhen's school with her bike mounted to the back of her car. After dropping it off in front of her dorm and sticking around to make sure that she locked it up properly, the two of them decided to go grab some dinner.

This time they opted for simple fast food from one of the nicer "restaurants" on campus since neither of them was really in the mood for anything more extravagant just then. Rhen was honestly just grateful to find herself spending two nights in a row now not having to try and stomach lousy cafeteria food. Being a bratty thirteen-year-old certainly had its perks, even if her aunt tut-tutted at her disapprovingly when she admitted to her that she'd actually already had most of a bag of potato chips only just half an hour earlier.

"Honestly, Rhen, you're going to give yourself a tummy ache if you keep snacking like that before dinner."

"Um, sorry, Aunt Dana."

"Oh never mind, it's fine, cutie pie. Now why don't you tell the nice lady what you'd like to eat?"

Rhen actually recognized their cashier as one of the girls who lived in lived in one of the floors above her in the dorms, but thankfully she didn't seem to recognize her. At least, she sure hoped she didn't. Either way, she took their orders with a bland, professional smile, and although it irked her to no end to accept it, she even let Rhen pick out whatever toy prize she wanted to go along with her meal.

"Thank you, dear," crooned Dana, accepting her credit card back along with a receipt once the cashier had finished running it.

"Yeah, thanks…" mumbled Rhen, refusing to meet her eye as she shuffled awkwardly in place.

Hey, at least it's free, she told herself with an internal shrug. *I can live with a little embarrassment if it means not having to spend any money on something yummy.*

The two of them ate outside at a picnic table underneath the sprawling limbs of a tall oak tree that provided enough relief from the lingering summer heat to be enjoyable as the sun finally started to dip down below the horizon for the day. Over their modest meal, a cobb salad for Dana and chicken nuggets for Rhen, they hammered out a few more of the details of their new living arrangement.

It was quickly decided, mostly by Dana (although Rhen had to admit that she did have a point), that it was silly for her to wait until the start of the next semester to move into her house. She pointed out that her guest room was far, *far* nicer than Rhen's cramped little dorm room was. And once she was settled in there, she'd have a lot more room to spread out and wouldn't have to cram herself into a tiny corner whenever she wanted to study or use her computer.

It was hard to argue with that, agreed Rhen. Plus she was also getting pretty sick and tired of constantly having to wear headphones at night so she wouldn't wake up her roommate. Having a room all to herself was going to be pretty sweet.

"Besides," added Dana with a playful grin that she hid

behind her napkin as she patted her lips. "The sooner you settle into your new home, the sooner you can start getting used to acting your age, little girl."

Rhen felt an excited shiver run straight down her spine and in between her pressed-together thighs at those words, especially when her aunt winked at her and went on to remind her (and anybody else who might've been listening at the time) about their agreement that she was to assume the role of her *thirteen*-year-old niece, not her twenty-year-old niece when she moved in. And while the words definitely brought a hot flush of mortified heat to Rhen's cheeks, there was no denying that the prospect *did* intrigue her, and she found herself nodding her head obediently.

"Yes ma'am, you're totally right. So um… when can I move in?"

"Hmmm… Now let me see," mused Dana languidly as she leaned on an elbow and surveyed her new niece with an open display of amusement. She was just so *cute* when she got all bashful and squirmy. "My schedule is pretty much locked down until around six every Monday through Friday, but anytime other than that works for me. How about you? What's your class schedule look like right now?"

After a bit of back and forth coordinating their schedules, they both decided that it would be best if Rhen moved in that Friday evening after the daycare closed. The petite sophomore had told her that she needed some time to take care of a few things on campus and to talk to her RA before she left, which wasn't *exactly* the truth but she found herself telling the fib anyway, and Dana had agreed that that would be fine.

"Friday it is, then," she declared with a broad smile once the matter had been settled. "That'll give us all weekend to get you properly put together as my new niece. And don't you worry about a thing, hon. You just pack up your stuff, and we'll get you settled in, no problem. I've already told all the boys and girls at the daycare that your granny was going to have you stay with me while you're going to school, and they're all so excited to have you around again. Oh, this is going to be so much *fun*!"

Rhen wasn't quite sure if she liked the way the words "put together" sounded in her ears, nor the eager gleam her aunt had in her eyes as she said them, but she quickly decided that it would probably be better if she didn't ask her to elaborate. Somehow she had a sneaking suspicion that the answer wasn't something she wanted the random strangers walking all around them overhearing away. Even so, she was excited to have an actual plan in place now.

"Hell yeah, I'm stoked!"

"Language, dear," chided Dana with a smirk.

"Oops, sorry."

Rhen felt as if she was on the cusp of a brand new adventure as Dana walked her back to her dorm and sent her jogging back inside with an affectionate pat on her rump.

And before she knew it, the rest of the week had flown by in a flash.

Chapter 6

Dorm Room Discipline

Dana's dire prediction that drinking too much soda with her dinner would keep her up all night proved to be an accurate one for Rhen later that Thursday. Especially after the three other cans of Diet Coke she chugged over the course of the next few hours after that. With the big move less than twenty-four hours away now, she was way too excited to even *think* about going to bed at a reasonable hour.

Not that she would have anyway.

She certainly hadn't crawled under her covers until the wee hours of the morning any other day that week. Well, with the exception of Monday night, that is. Despite how embarrassing it might have been, Rhen had to admit that a sore bottom and a full tummy were an excellent way to knock her out well before her usual "bedtime". She just hoped that her aunt wouldn't ever figure that one out. Especially not after the sizzling lecture she'd given her over dinner the night before when she'd found out just what time she'd gotten to bed that morning.

Whatever, she told herself, feeling a giddy little thrill surge through her lower abdomen at the rebellious thought. *It's not like she'll know whether or not I stay up late tonight anyway. Even if I sleep in, by the time she gets here, I'll have been up for at least a few hours and she'll never be able to tell the difference. Check and mate, bossy lady. No spankings for me this time, heh.*

As the hours ticked by one by one, slowly transforming

from night, to late night, to early morning, Rhen kept telling herself that she was just too excited to go to sleep yet. She chose to ignore the role that all of the caffeine coursing through her system might have been playing in her inability to get tired, and instead tried to unwind by playing games and chatting with her friends online until some time just after 5 AM.

Eventually fatigue won out over her urge to keep on grinding for rare loot, and stifling a yawn so she wouldn't wake her roommate, she shut down her computer and flopped into bed. Once she'd nestled herself under her covers just the way she liked it, cocooning herself in two layers of blankets up to her chin and around her forehead, she set a handful of alarms on her phone spaced out at five minute intervals.

She was determined not to oversleep (too much) tomorrow, and quietly thanked her lucky stars that she didn't have any classes scheduled for Fridays.

Settling back against her pillow, exhausted but still feeling a frisson of electric anticipation (and maybe just a *little* bit of apprehension) about what things were going to be like starting tomorrow, she felt her stomach lurch in a not all-together unpleasant way as her lips quirked up into a secret smile. Then, double-checking the display on her phone one more time and stifling a snicker, she quickly corrected herself.

She was excited about what her life was going to be like starting later *today*.

—

Rhen slept fitfully that night (or morning, depending on your perspective on the situation), and was eventually pulled back to full consciousness by her roommate slamming the door behind her as she left for her classes a few hours later. Rolling over, she tried to get comfortable again and maybe

squeeze in a couple more hours of snoozing, but the lingering knowledge that she was going to be moving out in just a
few more hours kept her from being able to settle back down
enough to drift off again.

"Humph!"

Flopping back against her pillow with an annoyed huff, she
glared up at the ceiling and let her mind wander as she gradually came to grips with the fact that she just wasn't going to
be catching any more Z's for a while.

"Whatever."

Not that it really mattered, she supposed. It wasn't like she
had anywhere to be just then anyway.

Rhen had only signed up for three classes that semester.
All of them painfully easy, entry level programming and web
design courses, that while not actually required for her major,
were at least close enough to it that she felt she could justify
taking them instead of more of the super boring general education classes that she'd been putting off.

Ostensibly she'd picked the lighter course load so that
she'd have plenty of time to find a job and work during the
summer. Or at least, that had been her *plan* when she'd been
flipping through the course catalog back in April at any rate.
But procrastination and the ever-increasing worry that she
wasn't going to have enough money to move out at the start
of the fall semester had kept her from accomplishing nearly as
much as she'd been hoping to. Instead, she'd wound up whiling away most of her free time either messing around on her
computer, pretending to do her homework usually, or else just
wandering campus listening to podcasts on her smartphone.

Every now and then she'd stop by the student activities
center, figuring that she might at least find something promising on one of the job fliers people sometimes posted on the
corkboard in there. Unfortunately though, none of the gigs on

offer ever sounded like things that she'd be good at, or were anywhere near interesting enough to actually bother with contacting the person who'd posted them for more information. Occasionally she'd snap a picture of one that looked like it might be up her alley, but would then immediately forget to follow up on it as soon as she'd left the building. More often than not, she'd just wrinkle her nose at all of the pathetic job offers on display, grab a handful of free snacks from the card tables by the doors, and then high-tail it back to her dorm as she tried to ignore the gnawing feeling in the pit of her stomach that kept on getting worse and worse with each passing week.

Thank god that was all over now.

But like, seriously. Who wanted to stand around for three hours straight without moving a muscle just so that a bunch of doofus art students could paint dumb, stupid pictures of you? And in the nude no less!

No thank you.

Up until very recently, Rhen had managed to avoid having anybody see her even partially undressed if she could at all help it. It wasn't that she was particularly ashamed of her body per se, but being as petite and virtually lacking in curves as she was, she always felt rather intimidated whenever one of the more well-developed girls in her dorm saw her less than fully clothed. It was hard to tell for certain, but it always seemed like they were sneering at her whenever they watched her strip down to her camisole and panties before walking to the showers.

One of them had even asked her once if she was someone's visiting little sister!

After that humiliating incident and the torrential downpour of profanity it had elicited from her, Rhen had gotten her process for changing in and out of her clothes down to an exact science. She'd wait until her roommate was either fast asleep or out of their room entirely before she'd even think about stripping down, and after the second time someone had asked her if she'd graduated from high school a few years early, she'd taken to showering during the times when she knew that nobody else was going to be in the big communal stalls.

As much as she loved to let her mind wander as she luxuriated under the flow of hot water, scrubbing herself clean and mulling over whatever programming project she happened to be working on at the time, her anxiety over being seen ensured that she always kept her ears sharp and her mind alert. At even the slightest hint that someone might be about to walk in on her, she'd find herself frantically dashing for her towel and fleeing back to her room with it pressed tight against the minimal swell of her breasts. Doing her best to ignore the view of her butt she was giving everyone as she scurried past them and not caring at all how much water she dripped onto the carpet as she dove for cover behind her slamming door while her RA stuck her head out into the hall to yell at her to slow down.

If she could avoid being seen, then she could avoid being mistaken for someone younger, and that was well worth any amount of annoyed scolding from her RA in her opinion.

Although, I guess it's a bit of a moot point now, Rhen thought to herself with a wry grimace.

Somehow she had a sneaking suspicion that those days of avoiding people seeing her undressed were long gone for her. At least if her time with Dana so far was anything to go by. Apparently, not having everyone see your bare ass as it was painted a bright shade of cherry red was a privilege only afforded to good girls. Who knew?

Thankfully though, she was at least good at pulling off her adopted age of thirteen.

As far as she was concerned, it was *far* more tolerable to have people thinking that she was a spoiled teenage brat being taken to task by her old-fashioned auntie, rather than having them know that she was actually a college sophomore who still needed to be punished like a little girl.

"Oh well..." she sighed, shaking herself out of her blush-inducing contemplation as she threw back her covers and sat up. "I guess I'm just going to have to behave myself then."

Checking the display on her phone, she saw that she'd managed to drag herself out of bed only just a little bit past noon. Not too bad for one of her days off, really. Then, after taking a quick shower, and definitely not regretting no longer having to bathe in public, she found herself pacing back and forth in her room as she put together a mental checklist of all the things she still needed to do before Dana came to pick her up that evening.

"Hmmm... Let's see," she murmured aloud, rubbing her chin thoughtfully as she cast a critical eye around the cramped dorm room she'd been sharing with her friend Abby all semester.

She definitely still needed to pack, but that wouldn't take too long. All she really had to do was shove her clothes into her backpack and the duffle bag she'd moved in with as a freshman, and then unplug her computer and wrap up the cables. So that could wait until later, especially since she still wanted to use her laptop that afternoon.

"Honestly, I should probably focus on cleaning up a bit in here first," she mused as she prodded at a pile of dirty laundry with her big toe, grimacing.

She had a feeling that her aunt Dana might just take a dim view to the pyramid of empty soda cans she and her room-mate had been working on for the last month. To say nothing of all the random bits of snack wrappers, crumpled pieces of paper, and dirty clothes that obscured a large portion of their cheap and stained carpet floors.

"Yeah, definitely better take care of that first," she concluded. "Unless I want her going ballistic when she gets here."

Rhen shivered at the mental image that that thought produced, trying hard to hold back a smile as a sensation of nervous anticipation and excitement pulsed between her legs.

With a lopsided grin plastered across her face, she began piling up some of the junk from the floor onto her bed with the intention of sorting it out into what were things she'd need to hold on to for later, and what was just useless trash that she could throw away. To her chagrin, a lot it turned out to be clothes that she'd been meaning to wash for a while now, and she found herself wishing very much that she had more time to run them down to the little coin-op laundry machines at the end of the hall.

Oh well…

She shrugged to herself then, sighing inwardly.

I guess I'll just do it at Dana's tomorrow and save my quarters for snacks.

Heck, maybe her aunt would even do her laundry for her if she asked her nicely? Surely there had to be *some* perks besides a sore bottom and a heaping helping of humiliation to being her niece, right?

"Well, I suppose there's all that free room and board stuff," she snorted, tossing another t-shirt that she'd thought she'd lost forever onto her "to pack" pile. "Not to mention all of the love and attention. That's not such a bad deal… Hehe."

After about fifteen more minutes of hyper-focused cleaning Rhen had managed to put a somewhat noticeable dent into the disaster area that was her and Abby's dorm room. She'd just finished knocking over the Great Soda Pyramid of Giza and had tossed the last of the sticky cans into a trash bag, when a rumble in her stomach had her thinking that maybe it would really be better if she grabbed some lunch first before she kept going. Obviously, she'd be much more efficient if she was working on a full stomach, and her aunt *had* been commenting just the night before about how worried she was that she wasn't eating enough.

Or was it eating *well* enough? Maybe it was both?

Deciding that it was better to be safe than sorry, Rhen told herself that the cleaning could wait for a bit longer as she slipped on pair of faded socks and a battered pair of sneakers. Then, tossing her trash bag into a corner by the door, she skipped off to the campus cafeteria for a late breakfast/regularly-timed lunch.

—

After picking at some crusty lasagna and then setting it aside in favor of two thick slices of chocolate cake, Rhen was feeling much better. With her energy now fully restored, she was just about ready to get back to work. She'd returned to her dorm and was starting to sift through the junk pile on her bed again, when she suddenly remembered that she had an assignment for her web design class that she still needed to work on.

It wasn't due until Monday, true, but it really would be bad if she kept putting it off until the last minute, wouldn't it?

Aunt Dana did say that studying was supposed to come before anything else, she reasoned while chewing on her thumbnail, conveniently ignoring the context in which that little admonition had been given. *I really should do at least some work on it before I forget. There'll still be plenty of time for cleaning up later, I'm sure.*

And so, after borrowing one of Abby's sodas from her mini fridge, she settled in behind her computer and got to work. However before she could really get into the swing of things, she'd only just pulled up the PDF for the assignment from her class's website, she found herself getting distracted again.

Flicking over to another tab, she saw that three of the channels she was subscribed to on YouTube had uploaded new videos since the night before. Staring at their thumbnails, she briefly debated whether or not to watch them later, but after mulling the issue over she decided that it would probably be best if she just watched them now. After all, she didn't want them distracting her while she tried to focus on her homework, did she?

Rhen felt a guilty twinge of worry flutter inside her stomach at the thought, knowing that watching all three of them back-to-back would eat up the better part of an hour at least, but she did her best to ignore that feeling as she clicked on the first one and cracked open her soda. She'd watch it for a few minutes and then let it play in the background while she got started on her assignment. It would be fine.

Probably.

—

After watching all three videos and scrolling through their comment sections to see if everyone else thought that they were just as awesome as she did, Rhen decided that she really needed something to help her clear her head so that she could focus on her work. And so, she soon found herself playing one or two (or ten) quick rounds of her favorite arena shooter, promising herself that she'd get straight to her homework just as soon as she and her team won one more match.

Unfortunately though, she was on a total hot streak and before long she'd completely lost track of time. The next thing she knew, her stomach was grumbling again, demanding dinner, and she was just toying with the idea of making a quick trip to the dorm vending machines for some cookies when her phone buzzed with a text message from Dana.

[Hey, cutie pie. I'm on my way. See you soon!]

Something which brought her crashing right back to reality as she caught sight of what time it was.

"Crap, crap, crap!"

Now in a panic, Rhen bailed out of her game and pulled up her homework PDF, starting to outline database tables just as fast as she could manage. It was way too late to start cleaning now, she knew, but she could at least try and look busy when her aunt showed up in a few minutes.

It's better than nothing, right?

—

"Knock, knock," came a familiar maternal voice from behind her door some ten minutes later, pushing it open without waiting for a response. "Rhen, honey, are you in here?"

"Oh!"

Rhen jumped in her seat as her door suddenly swung open, having been caught up in watching a short highlight reel from one of her favorite esports teams as she'd been scrolling through her Twitter feed.

"Um, uh, hey Aunt Dana. How's it going?"

As she spoke, she surreptitiously moved her mouse cursor to pause her video and switch back over to the PDF with her homework assignment on it, but there was no mistaking the guilty look on her face and the way she kept shifting in her chair.

"Hello, young lady…" answered Dana slowly, dragging out the greeting as she surveyed the messy room and her nervously smiling niece.

She pursed her lips into a disapproving frown then. Somehow she'd had a feeling that things were going to turn out this way. She definitely had her work cut out for her when it came to helping Rhen overcome her procrastination issues, that was for sure.

"Are you ready to go?"

"Almost," replied the younger girl quickly, shooting to her feet as if she were the very picture of punctual obedience. "I just need to uh... finish packing."

"Finish?" asked Dana, arching an eyebrow skeptically as she took a few steps into the room and turned in a slow circle to take it all in. "It looks to me like you haven't even *started* yet."

"Well, uh, I mean…"

Rhen gave a nervous chuckle, rubbing at the side of her neck as she tried (and failed) to find a positive spin to put on things.

"Yeah, I guess you could say that. I kinda got caught up working on, um… on homework and stuff."

"Didn't you tell me that you were ready to go when I texted you earlier this afternoon?" pressed her aunt, keeping her voice steady and calm, but now with that same low, dangerous purr she used whenever she was starting to lose her patience.

Her change in tone definitely hadn't gone unnoticed by Rhen, who swallowed hard. She'd certainly gotten to know that particular cadence pretty well during that first, and final, day on the job as her assistant.

"I mean, *technically*, yes I did, but that's because I kind of *am* packed… sort of. Mostly. I just have to, you know…"

She gestured weakly at the mound of clothes and other miscellaneous bits of trash she'd piled up on top of her bed before lunch.

"Pack."

"Uh-huh. And what about the state of this place, hmmm?" cut in her aunt, not even bothering to acknowledge her lame excuses as her nostrils flared. "I *know* you're not going to tell me you plan on leaving this place looking like a pig sty for your roommate to pick up all on her own, are you?"

"Of course not!" snapped Rhen, feeling her cheeks flush with heat at all of the embarrassing questions and hard looks she was getting. Not to mention the fact that the door to her room was still wide open and anyone else with theirs open, or who just so happened to be standing out in the hall just then, could easily overhear what was going on. "I was *planning* on cleaning up after lunch, you see... but then I needed to do some homework, and time just sort of... slipped away from me."

She shrugged, hoping that appealing to her need to study hard would help defuse the situation.

It didn't.

"So was that homework you were doing when I walked in here just now?" demanded Dana, planting her hands on her hips and not budging an inch from her spot in front of her niece's open door. If she thought that she could get away with not having all of her little friends overhear her getting into trouble, then she could think again. "Because it sure looked to me like you were just playing around on your computer, little girl."

Rhen's blush deepened to a dark pink then, and she knew she'd lost.

"Well?" pressed her aunt, tapping her foot impatiently.

"Um... No ma'am, it wasn't," she mumbled at her shoes, fighting to work some moisture back into her suddenly dry mouth. "I'm sorry."

"Mmhmm. That's what I thought."

With the matter now settled, at least as far as she was concerned, Dana turned toward Rhen's bed and cleared away a spot in the middle of it to sit on. Once she'd settled onto the edge of her niece's mattress, she patted her lap expectantly and gave her a hard look.

"Take off those jeans and get over here, Rhen."

"Oh come on!" whined the younger girl, her hands automatically flying back to clutch her rear end and its snug denim covering.

Oh my god, she can't be serious.

She threw a pleading look toward her open door and the two or three people she could see watching the drama unfold, her stomach lurching with an unsettling mixture of embarrassment and excitement as she locked eyes with them.

"Can't we do this later, *please*?"

Dana just shook her head though, smirking at the way her niece couldn't even say what she knew was about to happen to her out loud.

No matter, she could do it for her.

"No, we are *not* going to do this later!" she snapped, slapping her right palm against her thigh and biting back a wince. "You've more than earned this *spanking*, and now you're going to get it and that's final!"

"Yes ma'am!" squeaked Rhen, jumping in spite of herself at the noise of her aunt's hard palm against her soft capris. "But um... can't I at least shut the door first?"

She jerked her head ever so slightly toward the open hallway then, her face still tomato red, hoping that her aunt would pick up on what she was trying to say and cut her at least a little bit of slack.

She didn't.

"I'm afraid not, cutie pie," replied Dana, not sounding the least bit sorry as she flashed her an amused smirk and twisted the proverbial knife. "I don't know why you're complaining so much all of a sudden. It's not like this is the first time someone else has seen you get your little tushy spanked, now is it?"

"Humph," pouted Rhen, crossing her arms in front of her and glaring at a bit of trash beside her desk while she tried to ignore the titters of laughter drifting in from the hall. "I guess not..."

"That's right, it's not," agreed Dana with a roll of her eyes. "So quit your whining and get those jeans off. *Now*. If I have to come over there and do it myself, you are not going to like what happens next, I can promise you that, missy."

Now that certainly got Rhen's heart pumping and her hands moving! Clearly her aunt wasn't going to budge on her decision to spank her. That much was clear from the fiery look in her eyes. And so she decided that the best thing she could do just then was to get this over with as soon as possible before anybody else happened to notice what was going on.

In a flash she had her jeans unbuttoned and unzipped, and half a heartbeat later they were tangled up around her ankles.

"Okay, okay, I'm coming!"

Shuffling over to her aunt at a painfully slow pace thanks to the pants wrapped around her calves acting like a pair of makeshift manacles, she tried not to pay attention to all of the snide comments drifting in from the hallway.

"Hah! Little Rhenny's about to get her bratty buns busted!"

"I *knew* she was younger than she kept telling us she was."

"Oooh, that lady looks *scary*. I sure wouldn't want to be

her right about now."

"I know right? But doesn't her little heinie look just adorable in those panties?"

"Oh my god, you're right, it does!"

"I wouldn't mind putting her over my knee if I had the chance, hehe."

Rhen's face grew even hotter if that were possible as she carefully picked her way across her cluttered floor and over to her aunt's right side. At least her back would be to the door in a minute, and once she was over her lap she wouldn't have to actually see who was taunting her.

"Let's just get this over with," she grumbled.

Apparently though, this just wasn't her night.

"Uh-uh, not so fast," interrupted Dana, holding up a hand and stopping her in place before she'd made it more than a couple of steps across her messy room. "I said I wanted those jeans *off*, Rhen."

That got a fresh chorus of snickering from the peanut gallery outside, and Rhen opened her mouth to protest, but quickly thought better of it. She was already in enough trouble as it was. There was no sense in making it any worse now. And so, trying to ignore the spikes of anxious humiliation twisting around inside her stomach, she kicked her feet back and forth until she was finally able to send her inside-out jeans flopping hard against the wardrobe behind her.

"There! Happy?" she demanded with a huff.

If she was going to be treated like a little brat, then she figured she might as well indulge herself and brat it up.

Her aunt was more than ready for her though.

"Panties too," she ordered coolly, pointing down at the floor with a disapproving frown. "And unless you want a taste of my brush before bedtime, I'd ditch the attitude while you're

at it, little girl."

"Yeah, Rhen," crooned someone from the open doorframe as she and her friends dissolved into a fit of giggles. "Be a good girl for your mommy!"

"Auntie," corrected Dana with a mischievous wink, sending the others into even more hysterics.

"I'm *waiting*," she added a moment later when it became all too clear that Rhen was frozen with indecision. "Come on now, cutie pie. We've still got things to do tonight, you know."

Oh god dammit. Me and my big fucking mouth.

Moaning to herself in utter humiliation as she rolled her eyes up toward the dusty drop-ceiling tiles above her head, Rhen clamped down on every urge she had to complain about how totally unfair and unnecessary this all was.

That's just what she wants me to do too, I bet, she thought to herself with an inward smirk, picking up on the other woman's game.

She knew full well that her aunt was a big believer in embarrassment being an integral part of her punishment process. She'd told her just as much only two days earlier over dinner, after all. And she knew too that she couldn't have asked for a more perfect scenario to drive her lesson home with than the one they both found themselves in right then. So instead of complaining further and giving the giggling girls in the hallway more ammunition to tease her with, Rhen just took hold of the waistband of her pastel pink panties with a harrumph.

"Fine. Have it your way, meanie pants," she grumbled.

Pouting as hard as she possibly could at nobody in particular, she pushed them down off of her hips, letting them fall to the floor around her ankles with a stomp of her foot.

"Happy?"

Clarine Klein

"Very. Now come here."

Stepping out of her panties, feeling her heart thundering like a jackhammer in her chest, Rhen scampered over to her aunt's side then with her hands clamped over the thick patch of pubic hair between her thighs just as fast as her dignity would allow, abandoning her underwear (along with whatever remained of her old reputation among her peers as a mature college student) in the middle of the floor as she went.

"There we go, that's more like it," cooed Dana, nodding in self-satisfaction as she took her firmly by the upper arm and hauled her across her waiting lap. "Upsa-daisy, honeybuns."

"Oh my god, *honeybuns!*" squealed someone from the hallway. "*Yes.* I love it."

Dammit. Why didn't I just clean up when I had the chance?

The beds in Rhen's dorms were elevated several inches higher than normal to allow room for storing suitcases and other bulky items under them so that they wouldn't get in the way. As a result, she found herself dangling across her aunt's wide lap with her hands and feet nowhere near the floor as she was settled into position face down and bottom up across her knees.

"Hang on tight now, cutie pie," breathed Dana, leaning over to murmur into her ear quietly enough so that only she could hear as she gave her bare left cheek a reassuring squeeze. "You're in for a bumpy ride."

"Yes ma'am…" sighed Rhen, feeling her stomach do several flip-flops in a row as she let her body relax across Dana's knees. "If it makes you feel any better, I'm really sorry."

"It does, actually. And I want you to know that I've already forgiven you," she replied with a couple light pats as she straightened up, admiring the goosebumps her touch raised on

84

the younger girl's pale skin. "But I'm afraid that's not going to get you out of what you've got coming, though."

"I know..."

"Good girl."

SMACK! SMACK!

Rhen's aunt didn't give her much time to dwell on how she must have looked like a bratty child just then as she lay stretched out across her lap. Nor did she allow her to fully take in the fact that her totally bare bottom was angled right toward the open door behind her, providing the best possible view for the gathered gaggle of girls spying on her just outside

No sooner had she tightened her grip around her waist, than she began to pepper her rear end with hard and fast spanks that made her squeal and squirm.

SMACK! SMACK! SMACK!

"Ah! Oh! Ouch!"

"You should be ashamed of yourself, Rhen Mathews," she began to lecture as she settled into a punishing rhythm, punctuating certain words with a particularly hard swat or two. "I cannot *believe* the state of this room. It's *filthy!* And of course there's the fact that you haven't even *started* packing yet either. I know you didn't have any classes today, so what on earth were you doing all this time, hmmm?"

At that moment, Rhen wanted nothing more than to grit her teeth and take her spanking as quietly as possible, but clearly that wasn't going to happen. Her aunt was dead set on extracting answers from her it seemed, and she knew instinctively that she wasn't going to slow down until she got them.

Unfortunately it was rather hard to concentrate with her cheeks constantly bouncing and stinging, growing all the more uncomfortable with each passing second. The relentless and way too loud *SMACK! SMACK! SMACK!* of her aunt's palm against her naked flesh was driving away pretty much any thoughts other than the ones about how much her bottom hurt from her mind just then, which made trying to come up with a believable fib pretty much impossible.

"I'm- Ow! I'm sorry, Aunt- Ack! Dana," she whined, scissoring her ankles back and forth behind her in a futile attempt to shake off some of the sting from the steady downpour of spanks. "I just got distracted on my computer is all! Owie, owie, owie!"

"Uh-huh," grunted the other woman, clearly not impressed in the slightest and making her displeasure known with an extra-hard volley of smacks to the backs of her flailing thighs. "And what time did you get to bed last night, hmmm?"

"Ah! L-Late!" gasped Rhen, squeezing her eyes shut tight as she clutched her sheets in a white-knuckled death grip. Holy crap those thigh swats *hurt*! "Sometime after- Oh! After five, I think."

"After *five*?" bellowed Dana, not surprised, but definitely not happy to hear it either. She redoubled her grip around Rhen's waist then and poured even more strength into the spanks she was dulling out against her thighs, painting them an angry shade of red all the way down to just above the backs of her knees.

"I'm sorry, I'm sorry, I'm sorry!"

Rhen squealed out the apology in a high-pitched wail, no longer caring for the moment who might overhear her as she fought to endure the agonizing tattoo being beat out against the backs of her legs.

"I should hope so, young lady," huffed Dana, landing two real zingers back-to-back before shifting her aim up to focus on the undercurves of her niece's chubby bottom. "Until we can get this whole staying up 'til all hours of the morning thing under control, your bedtime is nine-thirty on school nights, is that clear?"

SMACK! SMACK! SMACK!

"Okay, okay, okay!" Rhen frantically gasped, willing to accept going to bed at just about any time so long as it meant an end to her spanking.

"Good."

Dana continued to pepper Rhen's desperately squirming seat with hard smacks for several more minutes as her cries grew more and more shrill and plaintive. She made sure to keep her pace brisk and relentless the whole way through, but varied how hard she actually swatted enough to keep her from getting too comfortable or caught up in a single pattern. And by the time it was all over Rhen's thighs and her swollen caboose were each sporting a matching shade of fire engine red, and she'd been reduced to a sobbing mess.

"Shhh… There, there," soothed Dana, giving the girl's scalded buns a soft caress before rolling her over onto her side and gathering her up into her arms to sit on her lap. "It's all over now, sweetie."

Even though part of Rhen wanted nothing more than to put this whole humiliating ordeal behind her and get dressed, the rest of her was far more in need of a warm cuddle just then. And so she clung to her aunt's soft bosom as she sniffled and sobbed.

After a minute or two of solid crying, letting all of her pent up stress flow out with her tears, she managed to get herself back under control enough to speak coherently. Swiping at her red-rimmed eyes with the back of her left forearm, she looked up at her aunt hopefully as she silently asked if she was forgiven.

Dana just smiled back down at her, all traces of her earlier disappointment and anger long gone, replaced by nothing but maternal affection and maybe just a little bit of smug satisfaction.

"You ready to start cleaning up?" she asked, tapping a playful forefinger against the tip of her still-sniffly nose.

Not trusting herself to speak without hiccupping out a half-sob quite yet, Rhen just nodded and then hissed as she was set back onto her feet, hands flying back to massage her scorched buns.

Yep. I'm definitely going to be feeling this one for a while... Yeesh!

Her aunt followed after her not a moment later, and still smiling, put a strong hand onto her shoulder and squeezed it gently.

"Then let's get to it."

Nodding obediently, Rhen gave one final, heaving sniff, and then stooped down to pick up her discarded pink panties, before being stopped by a light slap to her right cheek.

POP!

"Uh-uh," chided Dana, gently plucking the cool material from her hands before she could turn them right-side-out again. "You can have these back *after* you've finished packing and cleaning, young lady. Not before."

"But..." whined Rhen, dancing in place with pent-up frustration as the snickering from outside her door started up again. She could feel a fresh wave of brattiness welling up inside of her despite the throbbing in her still very much naked backside, and it took a supreme effort of will for her not to continue arguing with her aunt.

One spanking was more than enough for one night, she decided.

"No buts, cutie pie," warmed Dana, quirking a challenging smirk at her pouting niece. She certainly did bounce back quickly from a spanking, that was for sure. "Unless you want *your* bare butt back over my knee."

"No thanks," huffed Rhen, trying to sound more contrite than she actually was, and not quite managing to suppress a grin of her own as she sighed and began to gather up trash and clothes from off the floor.

"Heh, that's what I thought."

—

Rhen was amazed at how much faster her chores seemed to get done when she had a second pair of hands helping and a hot and sore bottom to keep her focused. She just hoped that this wouldn't become a regular thing for her since the boost in performance definitely wasn't worth the price in her opinion. With her aunt's help though, they managed to clear away almost all of the clutter from both hers and Abby's sides of the dorm room in what felt like record time.

There was no way to know for sure who or how many people might have seen or heard her getting spanked, but she had to assume that it had been a lot of them. And all the while they were cleaning and packing, she could hear her fellow dorm buddies snickering as they lingered by her open door, most of them talking loudly enough to one another for her to overhear snippets of their condescending conversations.

"Wow, her butt sure is *red*."

"Yeah, no kidding."

"She totally deserved it though. I mean come on, five am is way too late for a girl her age to be staying up."

"Tell me about it. And did you see how messy her room was?"

"Heck, if I had known she was so young, I probably would have spanked her myself that time she was blasting her music so loud you could hear it from the lobby."

"Oh my god, for sure! Remember how much she swore at you when you told her to turn it down? I think *someone* is pretty lucky she didn't get her mouth washed out, hehe."

Rhen's ears burned with the shame of it all, each teasing remark sending a fresh twinge of embarrassment roiling around inside her stomach before it wriggled its way down to between her squirming thighs, knowing that any hope she might have had of being thought of as an adult by the people who lived in her dorm was long gone. Whether she liked it or not, she'd been reduced to the role of a bratty teen in their eyes, and there wasn't a thing she could do about it.

Not that she could really blame them.

She'd certainly acted like it more than enough in the past to sell the idea several times over, and her aunt's *very* public discipline session just now had removed pretty much any doubt that might have still been lingering.

She knew too that she was going to be the prime topic of conversation for the rumor mill for a long time to come. Though hopefully some juicy new scandal would rear its ugly head in a couple of days, and they'd move on.

Hah, yeah right.

—

As if the overheard snatches of conversation weren't bad enough all on their own, the worst bit of humiliation for Rhen came when her RA suddenly popped into her room some time later while she was on her hands and knees fishing things out from underneath her bed.

"Hi there, Missus uh…"

"Dana Johnson, dear," her aunt introduced herself, taking the RA's hand in hers and giving it a firm shake before answering the other question that she knew was on the pretty coed's lips with a conspiratorial wink. "I'm Rhen's... *auntie.*"

"Ahhh, I see," came the far too knowing reply from the other girl. "Well, it's nice to meet you, ma'am. I'm Courtney, her RA."

Rhen swallowed hard as an all new flush that had nothing to do with her current exposure crept up her neck, plastering a lopsided grin across her lips.

She could practically *feel* Courtney's eyes staring down with open delight at her ruby red caboose as it bobbed from side to side in front of her. Moreover, judging by the gentle caress of the air conditioning along some of her most intimate parts, she had a sneaking suspicion that she was leaving very little to the imagination just then with her on her knees and her butt up in the air while her torso was wedged underneath her bedframe. But as much as she hated being in such a compromising position though, it was far easier to hide and pretend that she wasn't on display as she did her best to reach a skirt that had somehow gotten itself wedged all the way back against the wall than it was to have to meet the other girl's eye.

"It's a pleasure to meet you too, dear," replied her aunt, never once sounding anything other than smooth and confident as she and the RA watched her struggle and squirm beneath her bed. "I hope we weren't too loud earlier. Unfortunately my little Rhen here's room was a total mess, you see, and I felt it was better to take care of things sooner rather than later."

"Oh not at all," laughed Courtney, waving a hand dismissively. "I've got two little sisters back home, so I totally know how that goes. Actually, I just wanted to come by and thank you. You have *no* idea how many times I've wanted to put this one, and a few others around here as a matter of fact, over my knee."

"Yes, I can imagine so," snorted Dana. "Well you can rest assured that she'll be taking regular trips across my knee in the future. We've got a *lot* of bad habits to work on, that's for sure. Which reminds me, I don't know if she's told you or not yet, but Rhen is going to be moving in with me tonight, so you probably won't be seeing her again for a while."

"Ahhh, that's a bummer!"

"I know, I'm sorry, but I just can't help but want her all to myself though," snickered Dana. "But don't worry, she'll still be around campus, so I'm sure you'll run into each other again eventually."

"Boy, I sure do hope so. She's a real firecracker, even if she *is* a bit of a brat."

"Isn't she though?" sighed Dana wistfully. "Well, if she ever gives you any trouble in the future, I want you to know that you have my full permission to warm her tush as much as you like."

"Ooooh, I'll definitely be sure to keep that in mind, ma'am. Thanks!"

"Of course, dear."

Much to Rhen's horror and burning humiliation, the two of them continued to chat on like old buddies for several more minutes. During that time she'd eventually managed to grab her skirt, and had then pretended to look for other lost pieces of clothing, but after a while she knew that she'd have to face the two smugly smirking women standing behind her. And so, blushing and trying not to think about how she must look, or what they'd just been talking about for that matter, she wriggled back on her hands and knees until her head cleared the gap between her bed and the floor.

"Phew!"

Heaving out a relieved sigh, she used the edge of her mattress to lever herself back up to her feet, and then brushed off several crumbs and bits of lint clinging to the front of her shirt and her knees.

"Bye, Rhenny, I'm going to miss you," cooed Courtney, swooping in behind her and wrapping her up in a tight hug before she could stop her. "You behave yourself now, you hear?"

"Oh! I-I'll do my best, Courtney," the younger girl squeaked, stiffening and flushing tomato red as her RA surreptitiously groped her sore bottom and chuckled darkly into her ear.

"We'll see about that, bratty buns."

Rhen shivered.

Huh… Now I'm kinda bummed I'm moving… Weird.

After spending what was probably far longer than was really necessary to say goodbye, Courtney finally left them alone. And although her visit had been beyond humiliating, and Rhen wasn't quite sure how literally she'd taken the permission her aunt had given her to spank her in the future if she misbehaved, she at least had the decency to close the door after her as she sashayed out of the room.

Even better, her aunt had been true to her word, and after every piece of scrap paper and cookie wrapper had been thrown away, and the last of her clothes had been stuffed into her backpack and duffle bag, Rhen was allowed to put her jeans and panties back on.

As she was pulling those up however, wincing and hissing at the feel of the elastic waistband of her panties rasping against the backs of her sizzling thighs, she was not at all surprised to find that there was at least one more bit of acute embarrassment still left in store for her that evening as the door to her room flew open once again, and her roommate came flying in talking a mile a minute.

"Oh my god, Rhen! I just heard from Chelsea Stevenson that some girl from our floor got spanked by her mom a little bit ago. Can you believe that? *Spanked!* Like a little kid! The door was open too and she did it with her bare ass out and everything. Apparently you could totally see her pus-"

Taking in the sight of the older woman standing beside her half-bent-over and unfortunately still very bare bottomed friend, Abby came skidding to a stop with the door open behind her.

"Oh! Um, uh... h-hello..."

"Hello, dear, it's nice to meet you. I'm Rhen's Auntie Dana."

Chapter 7

Settling In

"I know it's still kind of early, but why don't you go ahead and get changed into your jammies for me?" suggested Dana in that same casual tone of voice she often used whenever she was actually giving an order, drawing in close behind her niece and giving her a friendly pat on the seat of her jeans after they'd finished the grand tour of her new home. "I don't want you staying up all night tonight."

"Oh, um, yeah... sure," mumbled Rhen, absent-mindedly rubbing at the spot where Dana had just popped her as she dumped her two bags off at her new desk.

Though the world outside of her second-story window was bathed in the dim glow of soft summer twilight, the overhead lights mounted to the base of her ceiling fan were more than up to the challenge of illuminating her modestly-sized bedroom with a warm and friendly glow. The room itself wasn't all that much bigger than the one she'd had back on campus, but with only a single desk and a dresser to take up most of its space, along with a queen-size bed dominating the far wall, it truly felt like a palace to the broadly grinning sophomore.

Oh yeah, this is way better than living in the dorms, she mused as she walked in a slow circle around her brand new bedroom, only half-listening to whatever her aunt was saying as she ran her hands across the smooth surfaces of the furniture, marveling at how soft the carpet felt between her toes. *I could definitely get used to this... even with all the spankings.*

"Rhen... Rhen! Are you even listening to me, young lady?"

"Oh!" she squeaked, coming to a sudden stop as her aunt's pointed question popped the contemplative bubble she'd been caught up in for the last minute or so. "Um, sorry about that. What were you saying?"

Dana fixed her with another hard glare then, and Rhen thought for sure she was about to find out firsthand just how it felt to be put over her knee while she was sitting on the edge of her new bed, or perhaps maybe how sturdy her desk chair was as she bent across the back of it. But instead her aunt just blew out an exasperated huff and flashed her a tolerant smirk.

"I *said* that I want you to get ready for bed," she repeated, letting some steel creep into her voice as her smirk twisted into something a bit more dangerous. "Better be careful there, cutie pie. You don't want to spend your first night here sleeping on your tummy, do you?"

"It's kind of a little too late to start worrying about that now, wouldn't you say?" snickered Rhen, giving her bottom an overdramatic rub.

"Oh is that so?" countered Dana, not missing a beat, a wicked twinkle in her eyes as she took hold of the younger girl's upper arm and started dragging her toward her bed. "Because it sounds to me like someone needs to have her attitude adjusted, *again*."

"Yes ma'am! Er, I mean, no ma'am!" spluttered Rhen excited panic seizing hold of her lower abdomen as she broke free from her aunt's loose grip and scurried over to her desk and the backpack full of clothes she'd left there. "I mean... Right, okay! Get changed. Got it. I can do that!"

"Are you sure?" asked Dana with mock-concern, staring the younger girl down as she began to wriggle out of her jeans and pursing her lips to hold back a snort of laughter threatening to escape from her. "I really don't mind, you know, cutie pie."

"I'm sure!" squeaked the younger girl, hauling her t-shirt off and tossing it in the general direction of where her jeans had flown when she'd kicked them away.

"Well, if you say so..." replied the auburn haired older woman with a seemingly unconvinced shrug. "In that case, I'll go fix us some dinner, then."

Turning on her heel, she began to make her way out of the room, calling over her shoulder as she went.

"Oh, and by the way, don't worry about unpacking anything tonight. We'll take care of all that tomorrow morning. You just come down and help me out after you've finished changing, alright?"

"Sure thing," nodded Rhen, flashing her retreating back a thumbs up and sighing in relief as the butterflies in her stomach started to settle down now that it was clear that she wasn't about to take another trip over the intimidating older woman's knee.

Or was she?

She felt her stomach tighten up with panic again as she watched Dana stop in the doorway suddenly, but relaxed just as quickly as she turned back to regard her with a warm, maternal smile.

"I'm really glad you're here, Rhen. Welcome home."

Touched by the simple gesture, Rhen beamed, unable to do much more than that just then as her heart swelled with joy in her chest. Swallowing hard, she crossed her new room in three quick strides and threw her arms around the equally-beaming older woman, burying her face into her chest.

"Thanks, Aunt Dana! I'm so excited to be here!"

—

Fifteen minutes later, Rhen finally got around to slipping

into something comfortable to sleep in, pulling on the first things she found shoved in near the top of her backpack that looked like they'd more or less fit the bill. She would have done it sooner, but after Dana had left her alone, she'd gotten caught up in exploring every nook and cranny of her new bedroom and the little bathroom that was all hers just down the hall from it. And while her initial explorations might have eaten up a decent chunk of her time, what really held her up had been the ten or so minutes she'd spent ogling her bottom and thighs in the full-length mirror beside her closet door.

Rhen hadn't had a chance to properly survey the results of a trip across her aunt's lap yet since the first two times it had happened she'd been whisked away into a corner immediately after she'd been put back on her feet, and she hadn't dared try checking herself out in her mirror back in the dorms that evening since she still had an audience watching her every move as she cleaned her room. As a result, she was very curious to see what state her rear end had been left in. It had certainly *felt* like her bottom was on fire at the time when she'd been getting spanked, that was for sure. But now that the heat had faded away to only a mild soreness, how bad could it really be?

"Holy crap!"

The sight that greeted her as she'd slipped her panties down to her knees had been enough to take her breath away.

Her tush was just so... so, *red*!

Rhen was no stranger when it came to admiring her own well-spanked butt in the mirror. She'd certainly been punished enough times growing up with her grandma to be familiar with the sight, but clearly her Aunt Dana was in a league all of her own when it came to dishing out discipline.

Not that that's much of a surprise, she snickered to herself as she kneaded her tender flesh, reveling in the ache her questing fingers produced and gnawing at her lower lip to suppress a moan. *She's clearly gotten more than enough practice running her daycare.*

She could feel her knees wobbling beneath her as she found a particularly sensitive spot and gave it a hard squeeze, imagining that it was the older woman's strong hands gripping her.

"Oh god!"

My poor ass.

So far Dana had already spanked her three times in less than a week. And although Rhen fully acknowledged that she'd earned each and every swat, it was still a rather inauspicious way to start things off between the two of them as far as she was concerned. Then again, she supposed that she was still trying to look at the situation through the eyes of Rhen, the twenty-year-old college sophomore who was majoring in computer science. Three spankings in the span of just a handful of days was probably pretty normal for Rhen, the bratty thirteen-year-old who'd just moved in with her strict auntie.

Now *that* thought made her swallow hard as a smile began creeping toward the corners of her lips.

She'd definitely need to make more of an effort to behave herself from then on if she ever wanted to sit down comfortably for more than two days in a row.

Or not.

She shrugged.

If spankings were going to be a regular part of her life from then on anyway, then she might as well have fun earning them, right?

She certainly thought so.

—

Drawn ever onward by the alluring scents of garlic bread

and simmering meat sauce, Rhen quickly padded her way on bare feet across the cold hardwood floor of the hall outside her bedroom and down the stairs.

Scurrying into the kitchen, she found her aunt standing in front of the stove there, shaking out a box of spaghetti noodles into a bubbling pot of boiling water.

"There you are! I thought you might have gotten lost up there," she teased by way of greeting as Rhen stepped up to the stove beside her, practically drooling.

However a frown quickly replaced her sly grin, dragging the corners of her mouth down with it as she caught sight of what the younger girl was wearing.

"Um, excuse me, little girl," she growled, voice growing low and dangerous as she turned her head to look her up and down more closely. "I thought I told you to get ready for bed?"

"I uh… I thought I did?" answered a confused Rhen, feeling a twinge of worry in her stomach at the disapproving look her aunt flashed her.

She cast a quick glance down to confirm that she hadn't accidentally forgotten to change her clothes in her haste to run downstairs for food.

She hadn't.

"What's wrong?"

"I told you to put on your *pajamas*, dear," explained the older woman patiently, rolling her eyes heavenward as she stirred the pot of spaghetti beside her without even looking. "Not some ratty old gym clothes."

"Oh, oops. Yeah, I don't have any of those," laughed Rhen as the tension eased from her shoulders.

She gestured offhandedly at the oversized t-shirt and loose pair of basketball shorts she was currently wearing as makeshift sleepwear and shrugged her narrow shoulders. Her outfit honestly wasn't all that different from the one she'd worn that day the two of them had first met, although her current ensemble was far baggier.

"I usually just wear something like this to bed, or whatever I happen to have on at the time, you know?"

"Oh no, this will never do," clucked her aunt, plucking at one of the sleeves of her bulky t-shirt and wrinkling her nose. "I guess we'll just have to add jammies to the list of things to get you while we're out tomorrow."

"Tomorrow?" asked Rhen with a sly grin, cocking her head to the side curiously. "What's going on tomorrow?"

"Ah darn it! That was supposed to be a surprise," huffed Dana, lightly slapping her forehead in annoyance. "Well, I guess there's no real harm in telling you now that the cat's out of the bag."

Turning the heat on her burner down to low, she turned to face her with an ear to ear grin, clapping excitedly.

"You and I are going to the mall tomorrow so I can buy you a brand new wardrobe!"

"Wait, we are?" asked Rhen, not quite believing what she was hearing.

"That's right," confirmed Dana in a self-satisfied sing-song. "I was kind of on the fence about whether or not we should, but after getting an up close and personal look at what you have wear, or more to the point, what you *don't* have, while I was helping you pack, I thought that it would be best if we just started over totally fresh with all new, and actually age appropriate, clothes for you. Now doesn't that sound like fun, cutie pie?"

"Oh wow, that's really nice of you, Aunt Dana," gushed the younger girl, honestly taken aback by the kind gesture. "But um… are you sure? I mean, that's a *lot* of money to be spending on me, and my clothes are pretty okay for the most part… kinda. You really don't have to do that, you know."

"Of course I'm sure, dear, and I'm more than happy to do it," replied Dana with an airy wave as she moved over to pull open the door to the oven a few inches.

After peering inside to check on the garlic bread for a moment, she nodded to herself and pulled the door the rest of the way down. Then, slipping on a pair of thick mittens, she waggled one of them at the black haired girl in her raggedy gym clothes in an admonishing gesture.

"You're my niece now, and I won't have you running around like some sort of scrappy ragamuffin. So quit trying to talk me out of it unless you want another spanking, missy."

"Hah! Well, if you insist," snorted Rhen, feeling her chest flutter at the wink her aunt gave her in spite of the fact that she knew that she was just joking about spanking her again.

Probably.

"Is there anything I can do to help pay you back at least?" she pressed, thighs squirming together in spite of herself as she watched her slide a cookie sheet with half a dozen pieces of garlic bread out of the oven and set it onto a cooling rack on the island behind her.

The question was mostly rooted in a genuine urge to want to be helpful, but part of her also hoped to use it as a means to help preserve some small sliver of her adult identity. Somehow she felt that if she at least *worked* for her new clothes, then it would be a mostly equal exchange between two adults, rather than a doting aunt spoiling her favorite niece.

"Oh, think nothing of it, sweetie. I'm your aunt, and it's my job to make sure you have everything you need to be happy and healthy," dismissed Dana, giving her a tender look as she quickly plucked pieces of hot garlic bread from off of the cookie sheet and stacked them onto a paper plate beside her. "But now that you mention it, I *will* be giving you a list of chores that you'll need to take care of while you're living here. I know that school keeps you pretty busy, but part of the reason why you're here in the first place is so that I can instill some actual discipline into you, and no niece of mine is going to spend all her free time just lying around doing nothing. Is that understood?"

"Um, yes ma'am!" squeaked Rhen, blushing as she shuffled in place, awkwardly fidgeting with the hem of her oversized t-shirt.

"Awww, I love how polite you get whenever you're feeling shy," Dana cooed, reaching out to gently run her fingers through the loose tresses of the shorter girl's midnight black hair. "Now be a good girl for me and take those shorts off."

"What, why?" squawked Rhen, her hands flying back to clutch her still tender tush as panic gripped her heart. Had she really somehow just stumbled into another spanking so soon after her last one? "I've been good!"

"Oh honey, you're not in in trouble," laughed the older woman, her face breaking into a wide grin at the sudden and vehement reaction she'd managed to get from her niece. She reached out and put a reassuring hand on one of her shoulders, locking eyes with her and letting her see that she wasn't upset or angry in the slightest. "However, in *this* house, little girls wear their jammies to bed. But since you don't have any of those, I'm willing to make an exception and let you sleep in your shirt and panties for tonight. But those shorts *are* coming off. *Now*."

Dana gave the shoulder in her hand a light squeeze then, lending her words an extra edge of authority that quelled any potential whining as they sent a surge of nervous exhilaration pulsing between Rhen's still-squirming thighs.

"And you can go ahead and throw those ratty things away while you're at it too. They're full of holes, and I can see them fraying in at least two spots from here. We'll be getting you a couple new pairs tomorrow though, so don't you worry your cute little caboose one bit, alright?"

"Yes ma'am," sighed Rhen with a mixture of relief and acute embarrassment as she slipped her hands beneath the tattered hem of her oversized t-shirt and let her faded shorts fall to her feet in a heap.

Well, at least my shirt sort of covers my butt, she thought to herself with a grimace as she gathered up her discarded shorts from the floor and moved to throw them away in the trash can beside the back door. She gave the front of her t-shirt's hem an experimental tug as she went, trying to coax another inch or two of coverage out of it, but all she succeeded in doing was inadvertently making the back of it ride up to more fully expose the seat of her pastel pink panties. *I just wish there was something I could do about the thighs...*

"That's *much* better, dear. Thank you," cooed Dana, once again stirring around the noodles in her pot. "Now why don't you go ahead and set the table while I finish up here?"

"Uh, yeah, sure... no problem," answered a red-faced Rhen dutifully, moving over to one of the cabinets above the sink and rising up onto her tiptoes to get at the plates inside.

"Good girl."

Despite how mortifying it was to be forced to spend the rest of her evening pantsless, Rhen had to admit that the cool caress of the air conditioning blowing through the kitchen was a welcome relief indeed on her sore bottom as she bustled about the room gathering up dishes and silverware to set the table with. Even better, once she was actually seated, her bare legs and thighs were all but invisible thanks to the broad oak table covering them.

It was just too bad that the chair she was sitting on was so hard and uncomfortable.

"You know, Aunt Dana, you really ought to think about buying some of those little cushions you can tie to the backs of your table chairs to make them more comfortable."

"Awww, is someone having a hard time sitting down for dinner?"

"Um, no!" squeaked Rhen, quickly averting her gaze from her aunt's smug grin. "It was just uh, you know… just a suggestion. Never mind!"

"Uh-huh," she answered slowly, her eyebrows quirked upward in a knowing look. "I'll tell you what, honey. If you're still sore tomorrow, you can sit on your pillow for breakfast. How's that sound?"

Rhen didn't say anything, but the flush of hot pink in her cheeks as she busied herself with twirling her fork around some spaghetti was answer enough for her aunt.

—

After another delicious meal wherein she found herself eating far more than she'd been expecting to, apparently non-cafeteria food tasted way better than she'd remembered, Rhen could feel exhaustion creeping in all around her. She'd managed to polish off over half the pieces of garlic bread all by herself in between two heaping helpings of spaghetti and meat balls, and now all she wanted to do was curl up somewhere and fall asleep while her body digested it all.

It was such a shame that no matter how much she seemed to eat, her figure still remained so lithe and tiny.

"I think it's about time that someone climbed aboard the Beddy-Bye Express. How about you?" cooed Dana as she

Clarine Klein

gathered up their plates and moved to deposit them beside the sink where she could take care of them later.

"But it's not even nine yet," whined Rhen as she stretched in her chair and stifled a yawn. "I thought you said my bed time wasn't supposed to be until nine-thirty."

"It's actually ten-thirty on weekends," the older woman corrected her with a patient laugh as she moved behind Rhen and eased her chair back from the table for her. "But I think it would be best if we started getting you used to actually going to bed before the sun rises as soon as possible."

Helping her niece back to her feet, she gave the tip of her nose a playful tap and then grinned from ear to ear as her brows dipped down into an adorable little scowl.

"Come along now, cutie pie. I'll tuck you in."

For a brief moment Rhen considered trying to come up with some excuse to stay awake longer. Maybe she could squeeze another hour or two out of her aunt by claiming that she needed to work on homework? But the tingling warmth still radiating from her backside coupled with the weights pressing down on her eyelids were more than enough to get her to abandon that train of thought almost immediately. Instead she just yawned again and let herself be led back upstairs by the hand and into her bedroom, where her aunt tucked her in under the covers, and kissed her forehead goodnight.

"Sweet dreams, hon."

Rhen tried to respond, to say goodnight and thank the marvelous red haired woman for all of the kindness she'd shown her over the last week, but all that managed to escape her lips was an incoherent mumble as her eyes drifted closed and she slipped off into dreamland.

"I'll see you in the morning."

Chapter 8

The Transformation Begins

The next morning Rhen awoke to the mouth-watering scents of bacon and eggs wafting up to greet her from somewhere down below in the kitchen. Heedless of the fact that she was still in just a rumpled t-shirt and the same pair of panties she'd been wearing since the day before, she let her groggy limbs carry her on autopilot down the stairs and into the kitchen where she found her aunt waiting for her in front of the stove once again. She was already fully dressed and looked as if she'd been up for at least a couple of hours now as she glanced over her shoulder to level a warm smile in her direction.

"Well good morning, sleepyhead," she greeted her as she scooped out some scrambled eggs onto two different plates next to one another on the counter beside her.

One of the plates was definitely piled higher than the other, and that was the one she set before Rhen as she pulled out a chair from the kitchen table and flopped down onto it. Thankfully though her bottom was totally back to normal by now and the press of the cold, hard wood against her sleepy seat was only a minor annoyance as she shifted around on it, trying to get comfortable.

"Morning," she yawned, reaching over for the bottle of ketchup her aunt already had waiting for her in the center of the table and proceeding to all but drown her eggs in it.

"Did you sleep well?"

"Uh-huh," she grunted groggily as she picked up her fork

and speared a hunk of scrambled egg onto the end of it. Her eyes remained half-lidded as she brought it up to her lips, but a happy grin spread across them as she began chewing.

"Mmmm, yummy…"

"Hah, I'm happy to hear you think so," laughed Dana, her eyes twinkling with fond amusement as she sat down across from her with a cup of coffee in one hand, and a tall glass of orange juice in the other. "Here, make sure you drink all of your juice now, hon."

"Yeah, yeah," sighed Rhen around another yawn, accepting the glass and taking a sip from it before setting it down beside her plate with a dull thunk.

The two of them ate their breakfast in near total silence after that, with only the occasional clinking of their silverware against their plates for company.

Rhen was still definitely not a morning person. Despite having woken up feeling far more well-rested than she had in a long, long time, at that particular moment she was much more interested in filling her grumbling stomach with her aunt's delicious food than she was in talking. Which suited Dana just fine, who was content to sit by watching her niece stuff her face like she'd been starving for days as a pleased half-grin tilted up one corner of her mouth.

She was just so *cute.*

Once the table had been cleared and Rhen had finished rinsing and drying their dishes before loading them into the dishwasher, something that seemed rather redundant in her opinion but which she wasn't going to start arguing about without a pair of pants on first, Dana wrapped a strong arm around her slim shoulders and steered her out of the kitchen and back up toward her bedroom.

"Come on, cutie pie. Let's go get you ready to greet the

day, shall we?"

Upon seeing the state of Rhen's unmade bed however, Dana wasted little time in yanking up the back of her over-sized t-shirt and landing three hard swats to the seat of her panties in quick succession.

SMACK! SMACK! SMACK!

"The first thing you do when you get up is you… *Make! Your! Bed!* Is that understood, young lady?" she demanded, punctuating her lecture with three more sharp spanks.

SMACK! SMACK! SMACK!

"Oh! Ah! Oof! Yes ma'am. I'm sorry, ma'am!"

"Good," huffed the older woman a moment later, evidently satisfied as she released her grip on Rhen's t-shirt and sent her scampering over to her bed with one final smack. "Now you take care of that while Auntie Dana finds you something nice to wear on our trip to the mall today."

With one hand still rubbing at her lightly stinging bottom, Rhen made quick work of tugging her covers back into place and tucking the edges under her pillows. The whole process took less than two minutes to finish, and all the while she was doing it she found herself blushing at the oversight. She really should have known better. After all, her grandma had been a stickler for her making her bed as well when she'd been grow-ing up.

Though she never usually spanked her for forgetting to do it.

Most of the time, anyway.

Clearly her Aunt Dana took this kind of thing far more seriously than she'd been expecting. She'd need to be more careful from then on if she didn't want to risk another sore bottom before the day had even begun.

Then again, half a dozen swats were hardly even worth

thinking about in the grand scheme of things. After all, she was *supposed* to be a bratty teenager, right?

Oh well, whatever.

Now wide awake, Rhen perched herself on the edge of her bed and idly kicked her feet back and forth above the plush carpet as she watched her aunt dump all of the clothes from her backpack and duffle bag out on top of her dresser. Frowning at what she saw in the pile, she clucked her tongue in quiet disapproval and then left the room, returning a minute later with an empty cardboard box.

"I'm sorry to say, hon, but most of this is going to have to go," she declared with a disappointed shake of her head as she began picking through the pile of clothing in front of her, tossing most of what she grabbed into the box at her feet without so much as a second glance as she continued to frown and tut-tut under her breath. "Unbelievable, just unbelievable…"

"Wait, why? What do you mean?" whined a suddenly very petulant Rhen, bouncing up and down in annoyance on her bed and craning her neck to try and see what was bugging her aunt so much about her clothes. "There's nothing wrong with my stuff!"

"What I mean, *Rhen*," Dana replied in that low, dangerous purr of hers she used whenever a full-on spanking was brewing. Scowling, she rounded on the younger girl and held up a miniscule red thong between her hands that was barely more than a few bits of string connected by a tiny scrap of cloth in the middle. "Is that just about everything here is totally inappropriate for a girl your age!"

Rhen squeaked at that, and she felt her face go about as red as the thong in her aunt's hands.

"Oh come on," she groaned, suddenly sounding far less sure of herself as she crossed her arms in front of her with an indignant huff. "That's not like, *that* bad. It actually looks pretty cute on me, you know…"

"Completely inappropriate, or else it's falling apart at the seams," the older woman repeated, steamrolling over the petite sophomores feeble protests. Letting out an indignant huff of her own, she dropped the offending bit of underwear into the box beside her, before turning back around and tossing in several more pieces of clothing after it for good measure. "And I don't care how cute they might have looked on you, young lady. No niece of mine is going to be strutting around in undies that are *clearly* intended for a girl twice her age. No ma'am. Not on my watch."

"Ahhh, you're no fun!"

"Keep it up, little girl, and you're going to find out just how not fun I can be," warned Dana, not bothering to look back as she tossed another pair of panties into the box at her feet.

"Eep!" squeaked Rhen in response, cheeks clenching beneath her on reflex. "Yes ma'am! I'm sorry!"

"Mmhmm, we'll see about that."

With her back still turned to her, Rhen was unable to see the huge smirk plastered across Dana's lips as she continued to sift through her clothing, adding almost all of it to the rejected pile at her feet as she went.

She knew that it was useless to keep arguing about her aunt's decision, not unless she wanted a trip across her lap for her trouble. Plus she had to admit that a lot of her clothes actually had seen better days and were in dire need of being replaced anyway. So instead of whining more, Rhen kept her mouth shut in a silent pout as she bid a fond farewell to all of her miniskirts, most of her panties, the two or three padded bras she owned, and the majority of her jeans. Along with just about anything else that her aunt deemed too old and tattered to hang onto, or that she decided was simply too mature for her niece's adopted age.

Which, as it turned out, was just about everything.

By the time it was all over, Rhen was left with a depressingly small pile of socks, two pairs of panties (including the ones she was currently wearing), four camisoles, the nylon short-shorts she'd worn on that fateful Monday a few days earlier, and the jeans she'd had on the night before. On the bright side though, her aunt had at least left her with several of her old tops. Unfortunately, all of those were graphic tees, which she knew would look right at home on a young teenager.

Mostly because that had been the age she'd been when her grandma had bought them for her in the first place.

Oh well... At least I'm getting new clothes out of all of this, she thought to herself with a put-upon huff, pouting for all she was worth as she watched the last of her adult wardrobe being packed away before her very eyes.

"Awww, cheer up, cutie pie," Dana cooed once she'd finished folding over the edges of the cardboard box and had set it on the floor beside her door. "We'll drop all this off at a charity shop on our way out later. I'm sure your old clothes will find a nice new home with someone there."

"If you say so..."

Rhen resisted the urge to point out the fact that they'd already *had* a very nice home crumpled up and stuffed into the drawers of her dresser and lost underneath her bed. She knew that a remark like that would most likely just earn her some more swats for being sassy, and so instead she just kept quiet and watched as her aunt sauntered over to her nightstand and picked up her wallet.

"Now let's just see what's hiding out in here, shall we?"

Without a moment's hesitation, she opened the little clasp

on the younger girl's wallet and began plucking things out from it.

Rhen watched in mounting horror as her driver's license, her debit cards, and just about anything else that she might've been able to use to prove she was actually an adult disappeared into her aunt's front pocket.

"Wait, hold on! What're you doing?" she whined, springing up from her spot on the edge of her bed and rushing over to her aunt's side. "Come on, I need those!"

"Oh hush now, you silly goose," chided Dana as she raised her left hand up above her head to put the wallet out of her niece's reach. "Your granny and I talked about this last night and we both agree that while you're staying here, I should keep an eye on your finances so you don't overdraft any of your accounts like you have in the past. And since you don't have a car, and you *definitely* won't be going to any bars in the near future, you won't be needing your driver's license either."

"But... but!" floundered Rhen, unable to formulate anything more articulate as her mind desperately started scrambling to figure out just how much her grandma might know about her little arrangement with her new "auntie".

"And besides," added Dana smoothly, grinning from ear to ear again as she lowered her arm and waggled the now mostly-empty wallet at her. "People might start asking some embarrassing questions if they notice a thirteen-year-old girl running around with a driver's license and a bunch of debit cards. Do you *really* want to try explaining to them why a supposedly mature college student such as yourself is spending so much time across her auntie's knee getting her bare bottom spanked like a little girl?"

The taunting question immediately threw Rhen through a loop, and her cheeks flushed stop sign red as she pictured just such a scenario.

"Um, no, not really..."

"Good. I'm happy to hear that," chirped her aunt, snapping the wallet shut and setting it back on the nightstand beside her lamp, bringing the matter to a close. "And don't you worry, cutie pie. I'll be sure to keep all of this safe for you until you're ready to have it back."

She patted her front pocket affectionately and winked.

"Besides, all *you* really need in your day to day life is your student ID, your phone, and your allowance. Speaking of which, that reminds me..."

From her other pocket, Dana produced a crisp twenty dollar bill. She stretched it out and gave it a quick snap between her hands, holding it up at eye level in front of her niece, before setting it beside her wallet on the nightstand.

"Try not to spend it all in one place, alright?"

"Humph... whatever."

As bad as losing most of her clothes and the contents of her wallet had been, what followed next was a million times worse in Rhen's opinion.

Taking her by the hand, her aunt led her out of her bedroom and into the little bathroom down the hall that she had all to herself. As they entered, she grabbed a fluffy green towel from the rack beside the tub and laid it out on top of the equally-fluffy bath mat in the middle of the floor.

"Go ahead and lay down there on your back for me, please, honey," she said, gesturing at the towel she'd just laid out with a negligent wave of her hand.

Not bothering to wait and see if her niece did as she was told, she turned her attention to one of the drawers beneath the sink and began fishing out supplies for whatever it was she had in mind from it.

"Um...?" stalled Rhen, chewing on her lower lip and shuffling her weight from foot to foot as she watched her aunt set out a pair of chrome-plated body hair trimmers, a couple of hand towels, and a pink bottle of some sort of cream onto the counter in front of her. She couldn't see the label on the bottle from the angle she was standing at, but even so, she still had a sinking feeling in the pit of her stomach about what was in store for her. "What's all that stuff for?"

Rather than answer immediately, Dana just flashed her a reassuring smile through her reflection in the mirror before turning to look her up and down with her hands on her hips.

"I know this is probably going to be a little embarrassing for you, sweetie," she began to explain after another half-minute or so of watching her niece squirm. She couldn't help but smirk a little at her obvious understatement, knowing full well just how much the girl before her was going to be blushing in just a few moments. "But it's something that I've been thinking about for a while now."

Still smiling, she advanced on Rhen until she was looming over her and placed her hands gently, but firmly, onto her shoulders. She then turned her in place until her back was directly to the towel she'd laid out for her, and with a bit of insistent pressure against her shoulders, pushed her down so that she was squatting on her heels before toppling onto her back across the waiting towel behind her.

"I know a lot of girls start developing early these days, but, well..."

She paused to smirk impishly down at the petite sophomore before she began to work the hem of her t-shirt up past her hips until it lay in a rumpled heap just above her bellybutton.

"Given your general appearance, and quite frankly, your *very* immature attitude, I think it would be best if we adjusted the appearance of your privates to be more in line with your overall level of behavior."

"But... Wait! You don't mean...?" spluttered Rhen, unable to put together a complete sentence as she watched in horror as her panties were wriggled off of her hips and down to her ankles, before being pulled free of her legs entirely. "Oh come on!"

She couldn't bring herself to admit out loud that her pubic hair was one of the only things she could really point to as a sign that she was in fact a mature adult woman. Even though she might not have had the chest to match any of the girls in her dorm, she'd at least had *that* much to mark her as one of their own.

As she continued to mouth and gape, trying to muster at least some semblance of a resistance, her aunt just looked at her in that condescending "I'm in charge, and this is happening whether you like it or not" way of hers that Rhen had grown so accustomed to in the last week. She watched with mounting dread and excitement as she carefully folded up her panties into a neat rectangle and then set them onto the countertop beside the sink, before casually scooping up her hair trimmers and kneeling down in front of her again.

"Okeydokey, go ahead and spread your legs for me, cutie pie," she instructed, gently prying Rhen's knees apart to help coax her into the position she wanted. Once her thighs had been parted wide enough to expose the thick tufts of black curls hidden between them, she gave her another reassuring smile. "Now you just hold still and we'll be done before you know it. Alright?"

"Ugh, fine, whatever..." grumbled the younger girl with another harrumph. "This freaking *sucks*."

That definitely got a chuckle from her aunt as she scooted in closer and eyed her target.

"Careful now," she warned in a low purr. "There's plenty of soap in that cabinet too, you know."

"Eep!"

Unable to bring herself to watch, Rhen let her head lull back against the towel beneath her and hid her scarlet face behind her hands as she listened to her aunt flick on her trimmers. She gasped a moment later then as the cold, vibrating metal came into contact with her warm, sensitive skin, and tried not to squirm too much as the razor began making quick work of her damp patch of pubic hair.

Dana took her time to carefully run her trimmers back and forth and up and down across every square inch of her exposed groin, making sure to perform several passes over each and every spot to ensure that she'd gotten everything there. And although Rhen couldn't see her as she worked, she could definitely hear her humming to herself all the while and could tell that she found the whole ordeal to be just the most entertaining thing ever based on the way she kept chuckling darkly whenever the vibrating head of the trimmers brushed up against any particularly sensitive areas of her skin.

Which happened to be pretty much everywhere, as it turned out.

Whenever she touched upon a spot that made the younger girl hiss in a sharp breath of air through her nose, she'd pause and hold her hand in place. Watching with naked amusement as Rhen panted and squirmed from the vibrations of the razor head as it tickled and teased her, driving her crazy as she moaned into her cupped palms, pushing her ever closer to the edge of release.

Oh god! I think… I think I see now why people l-like those magic wand things so much… H-How much allowance did she give me again?

After she'd managed to clear away most of the dark curls

between her legs, Rhen's aunt leaned in close and blew a long burst of cool air across her glistening lips, ostensibly to help dislodge any clinging bits of hair she might have missed when she'd brushed the rest of it off a moment earlier, and then smirked.

The bratty sophomore squealed with surprise at the sudden burst of sensation across her hyper-sensitized labia, and lifted her head up high enough to glare at the other woman playfully.

"There we go, things are starting to look *much* better now," cooed Dana, locking eyes with the younger girl as she deliberately kept her lips tantalizingly close to her molten sex.

"H-Hey, watch it!" Rhen gasped around a pout, the tickle of the older woman's breath on her swollen folds nearly pushing her over the edge right there and then as she flopped back against the towel behind her and groaned. "Meanie."

"Oops, pardon me," snickered Dana, sounding not the least bit apologetic as she straightened up and smirked down at her in self-satisfaction.

"Wh-Whatever..." grumbled Rhen, clawing desperately in her mind to get herself back under some semblance of control.

The trimmers had left her with only a thin covering of stubble across her folds now that felt coarse and itchy as she snaked a hand down to run her fingers experimentally along her tingling vulva.

"Uh-uh, no touching until we're finished, cutie pie," tut-tutted her aunt, batting away her hand and giving her a light swat between the thighs that made her squeal and arch her back.

"Aieee!"

"Just be patient for a little while longer, alright?"

Flopping back against the towel again, Rhen gave a

breathless and silent nod as she chewed at her lower lip, not daring to take her eyes off the spot on the ceiling she was trying to bore a hole into with her mind.

A moment later she squealed again as she felt her aunt begin to slather on a thick coating of an acrid-smelling cream across what was left of her once proud pubic hair. Clamping down on the urge to squirm and struggle as she worked the ice-cold cream over all of the spots the trimmers had touched, Rhen crossed her arms over her chest and grumbled quietly to herself in an attempt to restore some small modicum of her dignity.

All that seemed to do though was just encourage Dana, who began cooing about how adorable she looked just then.

"I'm so proud of you for being such a good girl for me," she crooned as she rose to her feet and took her time rinsing her hands off in the sink before moving to loom above her between her splayed thighs, grinning from ear to ear as she surveyed her handiwork. "I didn't even have to threaten to get out the pull-ups. Way to go, honey."

She flashed Rhen a thumbs up, and that combined with the stomach-churning mention of pull-ups possibly being in the equation ratcheted up the temperature in the younger girl's face by several hundred degrees. Surely she didn't have anything like that in her size! She was just teasing her, right?

Right?

Oh god, I sure hope so, she thought to herself with a worried grimace, reflexively reaching up to chew on her right thumbnail. *This is already bad enough as it is!*

Ten excruciatingly embarrassing minutes later, her aunt finally stooped back down between her knees and began to wipe away the harsh smelling cream with a damp towel. Its passing took all of her remaining hair with it, leaving her skin silky smooth to the touch after it was gone. And honestly, despite her utter humiliation, Rhen had to admit that she rather liked the look and feel of her now totally bare front. Though at the moment she wasn't in any kind of mood to say so out loud.

Especially not with the way Dana kept grinning knowingly down at her.

"There we go, nice and *smooth*," she declared with smug satisfaction as she pat, pat, patted between her legs with a fresh towel to dry her off. "That cream is so wonderful. I use it all the time for my arms and legs. You should stay just like this for at least a month or two, so I'd get used to it if I were you."

Not quite sure what to say to that, Rhen just nodded weakly. And thankfully that seemed to be enough for the broadly beaming older woman, who went on.

"Maybe if you behave yourself until then we can discuss letting things grow out again when it's time to for a touch up, but for now…"

She set her towel aside and traced a teasing fingertip up and down along the length of Rhen's totally smooth mound, running it over her folds before idly twirling it around her engorged clit.

"I think this look suits you just perfectly. Wouldn't you say?"

"Ah! Y-Yes ma'am," squeaked Rhen as her toes curled and uncurled behind Dana, hovering so tantalizingly, frustratingly close to the edge of bliss but still being denied release.

"Good," her aunt chirped, dusting off her hands as she casually sprang back to her feet, before reaching out to help her stand as well. "Now let's get you dressed so we can go shopping!"

Turning Rhen by the shoulders again and pointing her

toward the door, she sent her sprinting off in the direction of her bedroom with a sharp swat to her bare bottom.

"Go on, shoo!"

Scurrying away, the bare bottomed college sophomore turned bratty teen could tell that it was going to be a long, *long* day.

Chapter 9

Shopping for a Brand New Look

The mall seemed to be even busier than it usually was for noon on a Saturday to Rhen as she and Dana passed by row upon row of parked cars. All of them neatly crammed in side-by-side like sardines between the painted lines, making use of every available square inch of space they could manage to squeeze from the massive parking lot.

I guess it's because the start of school is just around the corner…

She grimaced at the thought and tried not to imagine herself being lumped in with the rest of the back to school shoppers all out that weekend looking for deals before the semester began.

Of course today would *be the day that we decide to go do this. Ugh. How freaking appropriate.*

For a while though it looked like they might need to turn around and come back later as they searched seemingly in vain for somewhere to park, and oddly enough Rhen found herself feeling more than a little disappointed at the prospect in spite of how embarrassing going out "school shopping" with her new auntie was. But once again fate and luck seemed to be on their side, and after nearly ten minutes of circling around the crowded lot with nothing to show for it, a spot miraculously opened up near one of the smaller side entrances and Dana swooped in before anyone else could snatch it up.

"Hallelujah!"

Preening at the small victory, clearly taking it as a good omen for things to come, the older woman killed the engine on her large, red SUV and pushed open her door. She then circled around to the passenger side and helped Rhen down, before taking up her hand and pulling her excitedly after her toward the sprawling three-story shopping center and its busily bustling corridors.

"Come along, cutie pie. Time's a wastin'."

As if the packed parking lot outside weren't proof enough already of how busy things were that day, the milling torrent of shoppers making their way in and out of stores and moving in seemingly every direction that greeted them upon entering the blessedly air conditioned building more than confirmed it.

"Oh my, it sure is busy today," observed Dana with a bemused little chuckle as she navigated them through the press of people and off toward their first stop on her list of stores to visit. "Stick close to me now, Rhen. I don't want you getting lost, alright?"

"Uh-huh," grunted the petite sophomore with a faint blush as she begrudgingly stepped in beside her aunt to avoid being trampled by a passing knot of high schoolers, silently thanking her lucky stars that she hadn't insisted on continuing to hold her hand like she was a small child once they'd gotten inside.

She was already feeling way too young as it was without that added embarrassment on top of everything else that she was still trying to get a grip on.

There were way more people thronging the walkways of the mall than Rhen had been expecting there to be, and the sight of them all sent an electric thrill of secret excitement down her spine and between her legs as she passed them by. Even though she was currently dressed in what she still considered to be at least a mostly mature pair of jeans and a t-shirt, the feel of the front of her panties rubbing against her now totally smooth groin wasn't lost on her at all. And she had to fight hard not to let her cheeks burst into flames as her snug jeans shifted against her bare front with each step, underscoring just how immature she knew she must look beneath her clothes.

How many of the dozens of random strangers walking past her and her aunt already saw her as just another young teen out shopping on a Saturday?

It was hard to say for sure one way or the other, but she had a sinking suspicion in the pit of her stomach that the number was only going to get higher as the day wore on.

It's fine, it's fine, it's totally fine, she tried to reassure herself. *I'm sure that if I just act like the mature adult I actually am, nobody will really notice anything odd or treat me any differently...*

Swallowing a curse, she breathed out a long sigh through her nose, trying to silence the cloud of butterflies inside her stomach.

Probably.

As they continued to pick their way through the chaotic corridors, Rhen's wandering thoughts were soon ensnared by one of the stores they passed. Slowing down and drifting away from her aunt, she found herself drawn like a moth to a flame toward the front entrance of the busy video game store off to her right. It was packed practically from wall-to-wall with kids around her age, all examining the toys and games on display as some of them debated which systems were better, while still others begged their parents to buy them something.

Wait a minute...

Flushing scarlet, Rhen shook her head in an attempt to clear it as she quickly corrected herself.

It was packed with kids all around the same age as her

adopted identity, not her actual one. Wincing, she felt her stomach do a few flip flops at the notion that she'd just inadvertently thought of herself as a bratty thirteen-year-old instead of a mature twenty-year-old college sophomore without even realizing it.

Yeesh. I guess I'm just better at this whole pretending to be younger than I actually am thing than I realized, she tried to joke to herself as she forced a wobbly smile onto her lips.

As troubling as those worries might have been to her just a few days earlier, they quickly rolled off her back now as she came to a stop in front of a grouping of cardboard cutout displays near the front of the store that showed off some of the hot new games that had just come out.

"Oh wow, that looks awesome," she breathed excitedly, ogling a voluptuous, blonde-haired mage woman who was in the midst of fending off a horde of scaly monstrosities with fireballs.

"I thought I told you not to wander off?" came a low murmur against the side of her ear a moment later.

"Ah!"

To Rhen it seemed as if her aunt had just materialized directly behind her from out of nowhere, and the shock of it all caused her to let out a high-pitched squeak of surprise, jerking as her hands suddenly came down to rest affectionately atop her shoulders.

"Oh… um, oops. Sorry about that," she apologized with a little shrug, trying not to give away just how much the older woman had startled her despite having just yelped like she'd seen a ghost. "I just, uh… kinda got distracted is all…"

"Yes, that does seem to happen quite a bit with you, young lady," observed Dana with a wry smirk as she tugged her in a bit closer so that her back was nestled up against the warmth of her torso. She gave her shoulders a little squeeze that seemed to say "And you're going to be paying for it with your bottom if it *keeps* happening" as she continued. "So, did you see something you liked in there?"

"Um... maybe," admitted Rhen, trying to ignore the sensation of butterflies in her stomach as she eyed a few of the new releases hungrily.

"A lot of those *do* look pretty fun," cooed Dana as she slid her hands down from the younger girl's shoulders to rub her upper arms.

She actually had no clue if any of the video games on display were any fun or not, she hadn't touched one in decades, but she was willing to trust Rhen's expertise on the matter.

"Tell you what, cutie pie. If you're a good girl for me while we're out shopping today, I'll buy you a game when we're finished. How's that sound?"

"Whoa, really?" gasped Rhen, her excitement temporarily overshadowing any urge that she might have had to not sound like a giddy tween. Suddenly this trip to the mall had gotten a whole lot more exciting! "You mean it?"

"I sure do," confirmed Dana with another laugh, holding onto her niece's upper arms as she bounced up and down with a burst of pent-up energy. "But first thing's first. We're going to get you some new clothes, then we'll have lunch, and then after that I want to stop by a few other places to pick up some odds and ends that you're going to need while you're living with me. You definitely need at least a couple new pairs of shoes, and I want to pop by that organic hair care place too while we're at it. Oh, and then there's..."

Rhen was only half-listening now as the older woman continued to rattle off their shopping itinerary to her. She was far too busy trying to decide which game she wanted most to really care about what stores they'd be going to later. Besides,

Dana was in charge of all that stuff anyway. All she needed to do was follow along and remember to say "yes ma'am" and "no ma'am" whenever she asked her a question.

Her ears did perk up though a minute or two later as she gave her arms a light squeeze, as if she could tell that she wasn't paying attention to her anymore.

"So after we take care of all that, *then* we can come look at games. Deal?"

"Deal," agreed Rhen, leaning her head back against the older woman's comfortable chest and smiling up at her from ear to ear. "Thanks a lot, Aunt Dana."

"Awww, anytime, hon," she cooed, ruffling the younger girl's unbound hair. "I love seeing you smile."

Taking her niece's hand in hers, Dana led her away from the game store and back the way they'd been going toward other end of the mall. There, she ushered them into the massive, multi-story department store that dominated the entirety of the west end of the building.

Upon entering the store, they were immediately set upon by a perky sales clerk. She appeared to be only a few years older than Rhen was, but that was about where their similarities ended. Dressed in a flattering, but still very professional, dark skirt and white blouse with a matching blazer, she had a modest bust and wide hips, and a neon smile that she directed at the two of them as she swooped in before they'd made it more than a few steps past the doors.

"Hello, and welcome to Cashman's! My name is Julia, how may I be of service to you today, ma'am?"

Rhen's first instinct was to open her mouth and tell the overeager young woman that they were fine and didn't need anything from her, but her aunt beat her to the punch before she could say anything.

"Well hello to you too, Julia. I'm Dana, and this little cutie pie is my niece, Rhen," she said, her voice and demeanor the very picture of a confident middle-aged woman gearing up to spend a lot of money in the very near future.

Beaming fondly at her adopted niece, she guided her forward half a step with a firm hand along her lower back so that she was now the center of attention.

"Say hello, Rhen, dear."

Rhen could feel her face flushing hotter and hotter with each and every embarrassing word of her aunt's little introduction. She'd been hoping that if she stood with her shoulders back and her head held high, her too-small jeans and baby blue t-shirt wouldn't subtract too much from the age others perceived her as. But just like that, she knew that any hope she might have had of being seen as a fellow adult in this woman's eyes had slipped away before she'd even had a chance to snatch it up.

Pouting at the positively effervescent clerk standing in front of her now, she crossed her arms over her chest with a huff and chirped sarcastically.

"Hello, Rhen, dear."

SMACK!

"Ack! Hey!"

Rhen bunny-hopped forward another step as both of her hands flew back to rub furiously at the seat of her jeans where a hard smack had just landed.

"Manners, young lady," warned her aunt darkly, before turning her attention back to the now smirking clerk. "Sorry about that. *Someone* here has been pouty all morning, I'm afraid."

"Oh don't worry about it, ma'am," waved away the younger woman with a tinkling laugh. "It's always nice to see a parent who actually believes in firm discipline. You wouldn't *believe* some of the little hellions that we get running around in here unattended, like it's their own personal playground or something. It drives me crazy sometimes."

"I can imagine so," laughed Dana right along with the other woman.

Rhen could feel her face burning even hotter with each passing moment now as the two of them continued to make small talk about child-rearing and the importance of a well-spanked bottom from time to time for the next couple of minutes. More and more she found herself wishing that the stupid clerk would latch onto someone else to help instead. Eventually though, the younger woman mercifully brought the conversation back around to sales and Rhen was able to let out a small sigh of relief.

"So what brings you two into Cashman's today?"

Rhen didn't even bother trying to answer the question as she stood off to the side. Instead she just stared intently at the scuffed up toes of her well-worn sneakers so that she wouldn't have to meet either of the other women's gazes just then.

"Well now that you mention it," said her aunt with a low chuckle as she held up a finger and grinned. "We're actually here for a bit of everything. You see, my niece is going to be staying with me for the next year or two, and due to some unforeseen circumstances, pretty much all of her clothes, except for the one's she's wearing now obviously, have disappeared."

"Oh no," gasped their sales clerk, or rather, Julia, as her aunt had started calling her now that they were so bud-dy-buddy with each other. "Did the airline lose your luggage while you were on your way to your auntie's house, hon?"

"Um, yeah... Something like that," mumbled Rhen around a fresh blush, unable to bring herself to look at the sickly sweet expression of concern that the other woman was giving her for more than a few seconds.

"Well that's just *awful*," she tut-tutted to nobody in particular, before switching back on her bubbly saleswoman persona an instant later as she turned her full attention to Dana once again. "But on the bright side though, you two have definitely come to the right place. From shirts to shoes, panties to socks, and just about everything in between, Cashman's has got you covered. Literally!"

Julia snorted at her own joke, and Rhen couldn't resist the little twitch it brought to the corners of her mouth either. Much to her own annoyance.

"I was hoping you might say that," crooned Dana with a grin of her own as she stepped over to her niece's side and put an arm around her shoulders. "Did you hear that, kiddo? By the time we're finished here, you're going to have a brand new wardrobe. Isn't that exciting?"

"Hooray for me," cheered Rhen in a deadpan voice, unable to stop herself from pouting at being called "kiddo" so casually in public.

She felt a small shiver run down her spine as her aunt's hand tightened for a brief moment in a silent warning.

"You know, we also have an excellent selection of wooden spoons in housewares," added Julia with a wink. "Or if you'd prefer, our men's department also has a wide variety of genuine leather belts, as well."

Rhen's stomach clenched at the suggestions and she felt her knees wobble just a bit, but a moment later her tension eased as her aunt let out a low chuckle.

"Thanks for the tip, hon, but I'm sure we won't be needing anything like that today."

She let her hand slip down from around her niece's

shoulders so that it could cup her right cheek as she added.

"Will we, Rhen?"

"No ma'am," squeaked the younger girl as Dana pinched her cheek. Thankfully though, this time she managed not to hop forward. "I'll be good!"

That managed to get a set of matching smirks from both her aunt and Julia that left the tips of her ears sizzling.

"So Julia, would you mind showing us around?" Dana finally asked after a few more terribly embarrassing moments of silence. "I have a feeling that it's going to be a pretty big task to get this little lady set up with everything she's going to need, and I'd appreciate having an extra pair of hands to help lighten the load."

"Oh absolutely," the clerk agreed readily, her wide smile seeming to gain another tooth or two as she ran a cool professional eye over Rhen. "Hmmm… I think juniors would probably be the best place to start looking for things in her size. Most of the items from our teen sections would probably look way too big on her smaller frame, I'm afraid. Plus we're having a buy two get one free sale on all of our outerwear in juniors, so that'll help save you some money. Oh! Oh! And we just got in the most *adorable* little skirts that would go perfectly with your niece's eyes. Come on, I'll show you!"

Not waiting long enough to give either of them a chance to say no, the clerk took Rhen by the hand and began leading her and her aunt off in the direction of the juniors section and a huge display of pleated skirts in a wide range of colors and patterns.

Rhen had a feeling that it was going to continue be a long, *long* day.

—

For the next two and a half hours, or possibly more (it sure felt like an eternity to poor Rhen), the three of them shopped like there was no tomorrow.

After picking through the skirts that Julia had been so eager to show off to them, and coming away with half a dozen options to try on, they continued to work their way deeper and deeper into the juniors section of the massive department store. Her aunt and the sales clerk were two women on a mission it seemed, and the pile of things for Rhen to try on grew far faster than she could have imagined.

Holy crap, I don't think I've ever even owned this many clothes in my entire life…

Her only consolation was that while the hideously adorable pile of potential clothing options grew, she was at least given a chance to voice her opinion about the things that her aunt and the eager clerk were picking out for her. The only problem was though that the choices she was offered usually consisted of things like picking between a pale green top with short frilly sleeves, or a bright pink one with the word "Princess" written across the chest in rhinestones and glitter.

More often than not Rhen found herself caught up in chewing on her thumbnail while she tried to decide which would be the least embarrassing item to be seen wearing out in public, only to have her aunt just shrug and decide she could have both instead.

"You need options, dear, and they're both just so cute. We might as well have you try them both on and see how they look. If they fit right, we'll just get them both and be done with it. I don't mind."

Of course Julia was no help at all in that regard either, as she busied herself with bustling away their selections to the changing rooms in back for later, and pulling out new and enticing items for them to inspect from seemingly nowhere at nearly every turn. Clearly the woman was a master of her craft when it came to talking people into buying new clothes, and with the huge commission she was sure to walk away with by the time they were finished, Rhen knew there was no chance in hell she could talk her into slowing down.

So instead she just followed after the two of them and tried not to pout too much. Especially after the first time her aunt had gotten fed up with her attitude and casually asked her if she wanted a spanking before they kept going. That had definitely been enough to get her to perk up and at least *try* to participate in picking out her new clothes from then on.

She just wished they weren't all so… juvenile.

Rhen's aunt and the ever vivacious Julia quickly fell into a steady rhythm of picking out four or five things each that they thought might look good on her, before marching her off to the back of the store and into the changing rooms there. Since they had so many things to try on, and were shopping with a member of staff who could ensure that nothing disappeared while they were under her supervision, they didn't bother with picking a room for Rhen to change in. Instead they just had her strip down to her camisole and panties in front of the three-sided floor-to-ceiling mirrors at the end of the row of cubicles so that they could have enough room for their selections and the three of them to stand comfortably.

Well, two of them at least. Rhen hardly felt all that comfortable standing on the little raised platform in front of the mirrors, stripped down to just her undies in front of the two no-nonsense women as they critically inspected every inch of her body and the way it filled out the clothes they'd picked out for her to try on.

The first time this happened, Julia had clucked her tongue in disapproval, looking aghast as she said, "Oh honey, those panties have *definitely* seen better days."

"No kidding," her aunt agreed, frowning at them as well. "I can't believe you decided to go out wearing those today, young lady."

"But- I didn't-" Rhen started to argue, only managing to catch herself just before blurting out the humiliating truth behind why she was currently dressed the way she was.

Ugh. I should have known that something like this might happen.

Her hands fluttered anxiously at her sides as the two women standing before her eyed the faded and threadbare panties her aunt had left her with after confiscating the rest of her clothes that morning with matching scowls. Blushing as her fingertips brushed against the hole near the waistband on her left side where they'd torn some time ago. She resisted the urge to try and cover herself up, knowing that they'd just tell her to stop fidgeting and move her hands anyway if she did so. And as bad as things were just then, she didn't at all feel like having the other people using the changing rooms all around her hear the pair of them admonishing her to behave herself.

Again.

Plus the huge mirrors looming behind her made maintaining just about any sliver of modesty all but impossible anyway, so it was kind of a moot point, she supposed.

After eying her thoughtfully for what felt like a very, very long time, the two older women seemed to reach some sort of unspoken decision, and a moment later they disappeared back out into the store as her aunt called over her shoulder.

"You just stay right there for a minute, cutie pie. We'll be right back."

With little other choice than to do as she was told, Rhen folded her arms across the front of her white camisole and let out a mighty harrumph.

"Damn it."

Now she was well and truly stuck.

All of the changing rooms required a member of staff to unlock them before a customer could enter them, so she had no chance of hiding out in one of those unless she wanted to try squeezing through the six inch gap between the floor and the bottom of the door. Worse still, she knew that putting her clothes back on would just annoy her chaperones and might even earn her a swat or two for her trouble. So instead she contented herself with heaving out a long, put-upon, sigh, remaining atop the raised dais in front of the mirrors with a petulant scowl on her face as she tried not to think too hard about the fact that she was basically standing in the middle of a department store in just her underwear where anybody might see her.

As it turned out though, quite a few people *did* in fact see her waiting around in just her camisole and worn panties, but rather than be scandalized as she'd been expecting, the mothers escorting their daughters and the few young adults out shopping on their own paid her little more than a fleeting glance before going on about their business. After all, why shouldn't they? She was just another young teen waiting around while her aunt went to fetch something for her to try on, wasn't she?

"I'm not sure whether I should be happy or offended," Rhen huffed to herself as she cocked one hip out to the side with a sassy grimace. "Ugh. This freaking *sucks*."

Her aunt and Julia were gone for nearly ten minutes, or at least somewhere around that long. It was hard to tell for sure since Rhen had left her phone in one of the front pockets of her jeans, and she didn't want either of them stumbling across her digging around for it whenever they finally got back, lest doing so might give them more fodder to tease her with. So she resisted the urge to retrieve her phone, and instead tried counting out the seconds in her head to pass the time as she grew steadily more and more bored with each passing minute.

When the two older women at last returned, they each bore half a dozen pairs of panties, mostly in varying shades of pastels and degrees of childishness, along with a couple of plastic wrapped three-packs of tightly rolled panties as well. And while the loose pairs of underwear they carried seemed mostly bearable to Rhen, the ones she spotted in the three-packs were a totally different matter altogether. Those all had what appeared to be cute animals, or else little flowers or fruits printed all over them, and were undeniably childish.

Oh well... At least they'll match my new hair style, she thought to herself with a wince as the fingers of her right hand slid subconsciously across the smooth front of her tattered panties. *How... wonderful.*

Her shopping escorts quickly set the bulk of their new selections off to one side, apparently not interested in giving Rhen a say in whether or not she went home with any of them. And from there, Dana thumbed through the individual pairs she'd brought with her, before selecting one and holding it up in front of her for a quick inspection. They were mint green with pink trim around the legs and waistband, and had a little bow on the front.

They were sickeningly cute, and Rhen knew immediately that they would look absolutely perfect on her as her aunt nodded in satisfaction.

"Here you go, Rhen, honey," she said as she tossed the brand new undergarments over to the mortified sophomore, who managed to almost catch them as she flailed her hands out in front of her. "Change into those, and let's see how they look on you."

Rhen opened her mouth to argue as the soft cotton

material flopped against the tops of her white ankle-socks, but the sharp look her aunt gave her as she started to speak caused her words to stumble and fall short before she had a chance to let them out. And so, heart pounding a mile a minute and blushing a brilliant shade of stop sign red, she quickly slipped her old panties down and off as fast as she could, before all but flying into her new ones.

"Oh yes, very cute," declared Julia with a self-satisfied, professional nod as she eyed Rhen's hips and smiled. "Pastels *definitely* compliment your pale complexion."

"Um, th-thanks," the younger girl squeaked as she craned her head back over her shoulder to try and see how she looked in her new panties for herself, before turning in a slow circle to admire them from the front as well.

As much as she hated to admit it, Julia had definitely been right about the color looking nice on her. Taking in her reflection in the mirror, Rhen felt a terrifying little thrill of panic mixed with a strange sense of excitement surge through her. If she hadn't known any better, she would have sworn that a brightly blushing younger version of herself from nearly a decade ago was staring back at her just then.

"Alright, I'll admit it. You were definitely right about those," conceded her aunt to the sales clerk with a good-natured grin as the two of them eyed the chubby twin orbs filling out the seat of Rhen's brand new panties. "I'm glad you talked me into going with some fun lighter colors instead of sticking with those plain old whites and navy blues. Those panties are absolutely Rhen's style, for sure."

Not bothering to wait and hear what *she* actually had to say on the matter, her aunt stooped down again and picked out two skirts and a couple of different tops from their other piles of clothes they'd collected.

"Alright, cutie pie, now let's see how these look on you

next."

—

By the time they were finally, finally, *finally* finished shopping for clothes, shoes, and just about anything else her aunt and Julia could think of that she might need, Rhen was one exhausted young lady.

But she was also very happy.

Although a lot of the things that her aunt had picked out for her had way more pleats or ruffles than she would have preferred, she at least took solace in the fact that it was all (for the most part) mature looking enough that she wouldn't be immediately mistaken for a ten year old. Maybe a twelve year old on some days, but thankfully the majority of her new wardrobe was decidedly in line with her new identity as her aunt's bratty, young, *teenage* niece. Moreover, Julia had certainly known what she was doing as she'd suggested things for her to try on, and Rhen had to admit that she and her aunt had picked out some very cute and flattering things for her to wear.

This was especially good news, considering the fact that she was now decked out in one of her brand new outfits as she stood patiently beside her aunt and waited for Julia to finish ringing up the last of their purchases. Her old jeans, panties, and t-shirt were gone, shoved down into the bottom of one of their bags, and in their place she now wore a lavender pleated skirt and a long-sleeve pink top. The outfit went incredibly well with her long dark hair as it flowed behind her in a ponytail, and their enterprising sales clerk had even taken the time to point out that the darker colors of her skirt and hair helped to highlight the minty green hue of her panties as well.

Not that Rhen had any plans of letting *anyone* see that for themselves anytime soon.

On her feet too, she now wore a fresh pair of comfortable, soft pink high-tops, still curling and uncurling her toes inside of them as she got used to the feel of them. Her aunt had bought her three other pairs of shoes as well, and Rhen couldn't wait to find excuses to wear them around campus later.

Despite how odd it felt to see herself dressed down so effectively in the reflections she caught of herself from the various mirrors hung up throughout the store, it all somehow felt right to Rhen as well. For years now she'd been trying to find clothes that made her look more like an adult, to make her feel more like who she wanted her friends and peers to see her as, but the things she'd worn had never felt comfortable. Never felt like they truly belonged on *her*. And yet, as she swished the pleats of her new skirt around her hips as she bobbed in time with the rhythm of the pop music playing from somewhere overhead, she knew that she'd finally found a look that truly worked for her.

It's just too bad that it shaves years off of how old I look, she snorted to herself, before smirking. *Oh well… Some people spend fortunes trying to make themselves look younger. I suppose I should just be grateful that my body is so accommodating in that regard.*

Truth be told, it was all a little overwhelming to think about the fact that she now had so many new clothes to choose from when she got dressed in the morning. And when she saw the final total for their little excursion through the juniors section of Cashman's, her stomach immediately plummeted to her ankles.

Holy shit, that's a lot of money!

She cast a shocked look from the register and its little display, to her aunt, and then back again, as a pit opened up in her stomach and worry gnawed at her. Were they going to have to return some of the things they'd picked out? She *knew* she shouldn't have said yes to all those stupid dresses and tops. She just knew it!

But rather than baulk at the figure, her aunt just produced her debit card from her purse and fed its chip into the little machine beside the register without a moment's hesitation.

"Wow, we got some pretty great deals today huh, Rhen?" she observed with an extremely satisfied look on her face as she reached for the plastic pen tethered to the card reader and quickly scrawled out her signature with a flourish. "I was expecting this to all be a *lot* more expensive."

"Our junior's section always has really great deals," chirped Julia as she closed out the sale and stuffed Dana's absurdly long receipt into one of their many, many bags. "Thanks for spending the day with us at Cashman's. I had a wonderful time, and I hope you both did too."

"Oh, most definitely," agreed the broadly grinning older woman with a nod. "And thank *you* again for all of your help, Julia. You were a lifesaver out there. I don't even want to imagine how much longer it would have taken us if Rhen and I had had to do this all by ourselves."

"Of course, ma'am, it was my pleasure," beamed the all but glowing sales clerk from behind her register before turning her high-wattage smile on Rhen one last time. "Bye-bye, Rhenny, dear. Come back and see me again sometime, alright?"

"Um, yeah, sure," mumbled a blushing Rhen as she snatched up as many bags as she thought she could carry in an attempt to put an end to her humiliation in this particular store as fast as possible. "Bye."

Taking hold of their remaining bags, Dana quickly fell into step beside her retreating niece, and the two of them made their way out of the department store and off to their next adventure in the mall.

Rhen just hoped that it wouldn't be nearly as embarrassing as this last one had been.

Chapter 10

A Brush with Danger

After making a quick pit stop in the parking lot to unload their recent purchases into the trunk of Dana's SUV, the two of them hustled their way back inside the mall and made a beeline for the food court.

With their stomachs rumbling, they shared a brief discussion about where they wanted to eat and soon settled on Chinese from a big name chain, due in no small part to the fact that its line was one of the shorter ones. A few minutes later, laden down with trays piled high with steaming plates of tasty food and tall cups of soda, the two of them wove their way through the milling press of their fellow shoppers in search of a place to sit.

They eventually managed to find a small table that a couple out on what appeared to be a first date had just vacated, and they quickly claimed it for themselves before anyone else could.

"Oh my god, finally!" exclaimed an exasperated Rhen as she plopped down across from her aunt at their wobbly table. "I'm *starving*."

"You and me both," agreed Dana with a low laugh, amusement sparking behind her dark blue eyes as she slid out her chopsticks from their paper sleeve, while the younger girl opted instead to use a plastic fork. "Now eat up before it gets cold."

That was an order Rhen didn't have to be given twice as she began to all but inhale her chow mein and orange chicken, only pausing occasionally to dribble soy sauce onto her noodles. Her aunt kept pace with her remarkably well. Their whirlwind shopping trip inside of Cashman's had drained most of her energy as well, and she found herself chowing down with just as much gusto as her niece. Although as *she* ate, she did so with far more grace and without the need to be reminded to chew her food thoroughly before trying to swallow it.

"Oh god, that was so freaking *good*," moaned Rhen with immense satisfaction some fifteen minutes later, slurping up the last of her chow mein and letting out a quiet burp.

"Manners, Rhen," chided Dana without much energy as she too slurped up the last of her noodles.

It had indeed been a surprisingly good meal, especially for mall food.

Ignoring the way her aunt's mouth had tightened with disapproval at her antics, Rhen flopped back against her seat back and let her body go limp, sliding a few inches beneath the table as she sighed.

"Thanks for lunch, Aunt Dana. I'm stuffed."

"You're more than welcome, dear," the red-haired woman replied around a pair of pursed lips that were struggling to hold back a smile, dabbing at the corner of her mouth with a napkin as she glared mildly at her not-niece.

She held her stare in place for another moment or two longer, hoping that the bratty girl sitting across from her would take the hint and straighten up. But seeing that her dirty looks were going completely ignored, she decided to let things slide for the moment as the corners of her mouth tugged upward once again with barely-restrained excitement.

"So, are you ready for round two? We've still got a lot of

shopping to do, you know."

"I sure am!" agreed Rhen, visions of her promised video game dancing around in her head as she straightened up in her chair and smirked. "But only if you promise that there won't be any more frilly skirts or glitter tops involved."

Or stupid sales clerks getting a good look at my panties and telling me how cute I am, she added silently with a little shudder. *Once was more than enough for me, thank you very much.*

"We'll see, cutie pie," her aunt chuckled wryly, as if reading her thoughts as they both pushed back from their table and gathered up their trays. "We'll see."

With their stomachs now full and no longer feeling like they were trying to eat themselves from the inside out, they dumped their trash out into one of the many cans scattered throughout the chaotically-packed food court, and set off to do even more shopping.

Now that the major hurdle of outfitting Rhen with an entirely new wardrobe had been taken care of, they were free to adopt a more casual pace as they meandered from floor to floor and store to store, browsing at their leisure. And although some of the places they visited were boring beyond belief for her, Rhen still managed to keep a lid on her urge to complain and misbehave.

For the most part, anyway.

No amount of sass or disobedience, no matter how small, seemed to escape her aunt's sharp gaze as they browsed and window shopped. And any time it seemed like she was about to step out of line, Dana's hand would casually drift down to give her tush a meaningful little pat and squeeze through the pleats of her dark skirt. Regardless of who happened to be standing around them at the time.

"Uh-oh, does someone need a spanking?" she'd ask smoothly.

Those words, along with her warning touch and challenging half-smirk were more than enough to send an anxious shiver slithering up Rhen's spine from the spot where she'd been gripped. One that when it reached her face, set her cheeks ablaze and made her stomach roil with swarms of anxious butterflies.

"No ma'am, I'm sorry!"

Letting out a small squeak and apologizing quickly, she'd then make a heroic attempt to reel in her brewing annoyance before it could get her into any *actual* trouble as she scurried out of arm's reach and tried to steer the older woman's attention over to just about anything else that happened to be close to hand at the time.

"Oh, now would you look at that? Uh... candles! I wonder what those smell like. Let's go find out... Heh, heh..."

The only silver lining Rhen could see to these humiliating and heart-pounding little exchanges was that at least the various sales clerks and their fellow shoppers who happened to witness them didn't seem to find them all that notable. They'd just smirk to themselves, or maybe snicker and point, but that was about the extent of it. To them, she wasn't a college sophomore being asked in public if she needed a spanking. Instead she was just another young teenager out for a day of shopping with her doting, but stern, aunt. And that was all.

Oh well, I guess it could always be worse, she tried to reassure herself with a mental shrug. *At least they're just seeing a little pat on the behind, and not anything more... strenuous.*

Rhen shivered.

Hopefully things would stay that way.

Somehow though, she doubted they would.

Why was it so hard to stay on her best behavior?

—

An hour and a half or so later, Rhen's Auntie Dana had bought her several more things that she would need for school or else that she thought might spruce up her bedroom back home, including a brand new winter coat. It was puffy and bright pink, of course, but it was also very warm and she knew that it would keep her nice and dry when it started snowing in a few months.

"Look here, Rhen, honey, it even comes with a pair of matching mittens. Isn't that wonderful?"

"Um… uh… yeah, I guess so," the younger girl had answered, unsure of how to respond to that question in a way that didn't make her sound like a child, or else come off as being overly sassy. "Oh hey, they work with smartphone screens. Nice!"

Dana also bought her a new backpack as well, one that was mercifully free of any glittering bedazzlement or Disney princesses. Although the stylized cat ears at its top and the little black and pink paw-print pull tabs for the zippers did little to make her look any more mature with it on. Especially when she caught a glimpse of herself in a mirror and saw how it looked slung over her shoulders while she was wearing her new outfit.

Oof. Now I really do look like I graduated from high school a few years early… Or else I'm just about to start it, she thought to herself with a grimace, rolling her eyes at the pouting teenager she saw reflected back at her in the mirror. *I guess I should just be grateful that nobody from my old dorms is here to see me like this, at least.*

Rhen deliberately chose to ignore the embarrassing reality

that *everyone* on campus would soon be getting the chance to see her dressed like an adorable thirteen-year-old when she went to class next Tuesday. That was something she could worry about later. For the moment she was just determined to enjoy the shopping trip out with her aunt.

—

With the bulk of their shopping now behind them, there was only one more stop Dana had in mind for herself and Rhen before they headed home for the day. (Well, aside from visiting that game store she'd been mooning over all afternoon, that is.)

After making another quick trip to the parking lot to drop off their latest crop of purchases alongside the rest of the stout bags taking up a large amount of the space in her trunk, Rhen's aunt took her niece's hand in hers and steered her back inside one final time. Thankfully the crowds had thinned out a fair amount by then, and she was able to easily guide them through the corridors and into a little boutique nestled in a quiet corner of the mall.

Prismatic was a store that specialized in high-end hair care supplies and accessories. And it was a place that Dana had been meaning to visit ever since Rhen had agreed to come live with her last Monday. She'd actually planned on visiting the little specialty shop the day after they'd made their living arrangement, but upon mulling things over further, she'd decided that it would be a lot more fun to wait until she had her new cutie pie coed by her side; especially after she'd had a chance to have a nice long chat with her granny that following Tuesday.

Given the younger girl's temperament and the general level of behavior she'd seen from her so far, Dana had a sneaking suspicion that it would end up being a far more entertaining and effective little outing for the both of them if she brought her along with her. Plus it would provide some valuable insight into just how willing the raven-haired girl was to fully embrace her new role as a bratty teen while she slowly relearned how to be a mature young woman.

With the emphasis being on *slowly*.

As they stepped into the quiet shop and breathed in the soothing scents of tea tree oil and lavender, Dana's eyes lit upon exactly what she'd known she'd find in there.

Oh yes, this was going to be fun.

—

"Hello ladies, welcome to Prismatic. Can I help you find anything?" spoke up a sleepy sounding sales clerk, stifling a yawn as she roused from where she'd been dozing behind her cash register upon catching sight of the two of them.

Rhen guessed that she couldn't have been much older than she was, as she watched her step out from behind the front counter and join them beside the glass display case her aunt had stopped before. Though of course, at the moment she looked about a decade younger than the pretty clerk did. Turning away from her and her welcoming smile with a pout after noting with irritation that her full attention seemed to have shifted entirely to her aunt and not her, Rhen studied the wares on display in front of them.

The metal and glass display case came up to just above her bellybutton, and was lit from within by a long strip of bright white LEDs that cast a cool glow over the neat rows upon rows of hairbrushes inside of it.

"Why yes, I do believe you can," answered her aunt smoothly as she turned from studying the display to address the young woman beside her with a friendly smile. "I'm looking for a very special hairbrush for my lovely little niece, Rhen."

She wrapped an arm around Rhen's trim shoulders and gave them an affectionate squeeze to indicate just who it was that she meant in case there had ever been any doubt.

"Oh, well I can definitely help you there, ma'am."

The clerk nodded eagerly as she moved behind the display case and slid it open from the back, the prospect of a fat commission reinvigorating her tired movements.

"These brushes here are our top of the line models," she explained, indicating the top row of dark and highly-polished wooden hairbrushes gleaming in the glow of the lights just a few inches above them. "They're all made from Cameroon Ebony that's been sourced by one of our *three* fair-trade certified distributors, and are hand-crafted by a team of Prismatic Style Specialists working out of our headquarters in Vermont."

She frowned appreciatively at the brushes before them as she lovingly traced her fingertips across the glass.

"They're a bit pricey, yes, but well worth the money in the long run, if you ask me. Especially since each of them comes with a lifetime warranty and a free bristle reconditioning once a year."

Not giving either of them a chance to say they weren't interested, she eyed Rhen's inky black hair thoughtfully for a second and then pointed to a group of three brushes near the end of the display case.

"For your niece, I'd recommend any of our paddle brushes here. They're perfect for straight hair like hers, and will keep it shiny and clear out any tangles that might pop up."

Rhen's face colored at the phrase "paddle brush" and she felt a twinge of apprehension coil itself around her stomach then. Surely her aunt didn't mean…

"Hah! You know it's funny that you should mention *paddle* brushes, dear," Dana laughed, an amused smirk quirking up one side of her mouth.

Oh come on, do we really have to do this, Aunt Dana? whined the aghast sophomore internally, rolling her eyes but keeping her mouth shut.

"Because aside from keeping my little Rhenny's hair looking its best, I'm also looking for a brush that I can use a little further down south whenever the need arises as well."

As if to make it even more humiliatingly obvious just what it was that she meant, her aunt reached over and gave her bottom a couple of firm pats and then winked at the preening younger woman.

Rhen desperately hoped that the clerk would baulk at her aunt's implication, or at the very least have the good grace to blush, but instead she just flashed her a knowing smile before looking back up and locking eyes with Dana.

"Oh yes ma'am, I totally understand. If that's the case, then I would recommend you pick one of these three," she indicated three of the shiny black hairbrushes with wide backs of various shapes and sizes as she continued. "Which are all more than up to the task of roasting a pair of bratty buns."

As she said it, a faint hint of color traced across her freckled cheeks, and Rhen was left wondering just which side of the discipline equation the pretty young saleswoman had been on to become so familiar with which brushes were the best for giving a spanking.

"I see," observed her aunt, drawing out the words as she pursed her lips and stepped in a bit closer to the display case, leaning over to more closely examine the brushes that the clerk had pointed out to her. "Oh my, they all look so lovely, it's hard to decide which one to pick."

She turned her head and arched a teasing eyebrow toward Rhen.

"What do *you* think, cutie pie? It's your hair and tush that we're shopping for, you know. Do any of these stand out to you in particular?"

Rhen's stomach gave another apprehensive twinge as she stepped up closer beside her aunt and glared down at the hairbrushes on display.

"I don't care, they all look the same to me," she grumbled.

That seemed to touch a nerve with the sales clerk, who apparently had more than a little bit of professional pride tied up in the products she was charged with selling. Even if the downtime between sales as she waited for customers to wander in bored her to tears.

"Well, that's not too surprising to hear," she cooed in a sickly sweet voice as she began extracting the three brushes in question from their glass case, laying them out carefully on the countertop before her. "I wouldn't expect a *little girl* like you to immediately be able to spot the subtle, nuanced differences between three high-end hair care accessories."

It took a supreme effort of will for Dana not to burst out laughing at the glare her niece leveled at the saleswoman behind the counter.

The clerk let Rhen stew in her indignation for another moment or two as an idea began to form in the back of her head, drinking in the sight of the pouting little brat in front of her with an unabashed smirk. She planned out her next words oh so carefully, rehearsing them a couple of times in her mind, and then once again turned her full attention back to her aunt. Her smugness gone in an instant as she locked eyes with the older woman, replaced once more by her all too sweet professional smile as she continued.

"If you'd like, ma'am," she offered helpfully, gesturing once again at the brushes she'd laid out on the counter as she flashed her most dazzling smile. "I'd be more than happy to let you give these three a small test drive. After all, with the price tag they each come with, you might as well be sure that you're getting the very best brush for handling *all* of your niece's needs. Both top... and *bottom*."

She winked.

And in that moment Rhen could have reached across the counter and strangled the grinning girl her as her stomach dropped and all of the color in her face drained after it toward her feet.

Oh, you bitch.

"Now that sounds like an *excellent* idea," crooned Dana at the same time as her niece's thoughts turned venomous. "But are you really sure you don't mind?"

"Not at all ma'am," answered their sales clerk with a broad grin as she waved away her concerns. "Please, by all means, help yourself."

"Well, in that case, I do believe I will. Thank you very much, young lady."

With the matter now settled, she turned her attention to the three brushes laid out in front of her, and eyed them thoughtfully for a moment before picking up the one on the left. She hefted it experimentally, getting a feel for its weight and the shape of its handle in her palm, before she looked over to her niece.

"Why don't you go ahead and bend over the counter right here, honeybuns?" she ordered, indicating a clear spot just to the right of the array of brushes with the one she currently had gripped in her hand. "This shouldn't take more than a few minutes, I'm sure."

"What?" demanded an aghast Rhen, clamping down as hard as she could on the urge to grab her bottom protectively as she eased back from the counter in front of her. "Aunt Dana, *please*, you can't be serious!"

"Oh honey, don't be such a baby," chided her aunt with a cluck of her tongue, as she transferred the brush to her left hand and advanced on her.

With a gentle, but firm, push along her lower back, she guided her forward a few steps and then over the front of the display case so that her elbows and forearms were resting against its glass top.

"I'm just going to give you a few whacks with each of these to see which one I like the most. You're not *actually* getting a spanking, you silly goose."

"But…"

Rhen groaned with embarrassment as her aunt said the "s" word out loud for anyone and everyone to hear, not really caring about the distinction between "just a few whacks" versus an "actual spanking" just then. That groan quickly morphed into a squeal of surprise and panic though, as she felt the back of her pleated skirt being raised up and out of the way.

"Wait, Aunt Dana, please!" she moaned, squirming her hips from side to side in a futile protest as the seat of her mint green panties was revealed to the store at large.

Thank god the stupid place was all but empty just then, save for the three of them of course. She just wished that her back wasn't angled directly toward the open entrance to the mall.

"Oh hush," snorted Dana, not impressed by her theatrics in the slightest as she gave the middle of her cheeks a sharp pat. "Nobody cares about seeing some bratty little girl's undies… Or her bare bottom for that matter."

"No wai-!"

Where her bottom happened to be pointed to at that particular moment quickly became the least of Rhen's worries as she suddenly felt the older woman's slim fingers slip into the pink-trimmed waistband of her panties and then tug them down to just below the crease of her sit-spots. She gasped at the sensation of the cold mall air caressing along her naked tush, as all of the blood that had drained from her face a moment earlier rushed back into it with a vengeance.

"Oh come *on*! It doesn't have to be on the bare, does it?"

Her aunt just ignored her protests entirely however, not bothering to say anything more as she swapped her selected brush back to her right hand.

A moment later Rhen felt the back of that first hairbrush explode in quick succession against her unprotected rear end.

CRACK-CRACK! CRACK-CRACK!

Quick as a striking snake, Dana doled out four sharp swats, two to the centers of each wobbly cheek. And while they were definitely not as hard as they could have been, they were still more than enough to make her niece squeal and gasp with shock and pain in a way that brought a self-satisfied smirk to her lips.

"Hmmm… That's not bad," she said with raised eyebrows, hefting the wide-backed brush appreciatively as she eyed the two sets of slightly overlapping pink rectangles it had left in its wake. "What do you think, Rhen?"

"I think that damn thing stings like a mofo," the petite sophomore bit out around a wince, shifting her weight from one foot to the other as she struggled to master the sting in her behind.

CRACK!

"Ah!"

"Watch your language, young lady," warned her aunt darkly, before bringing the brush down on the other cheek to emphasize her point.

CRACK!

"That's not the kind of thing I want to hear coming out of your mouth, especially not when you're in this position. Is that understood?"

"Okay, okay, I'm sorry!" hissed Rhen, bouncing adorably on the balls of her feet. "It just slipped out."

"Well it had better not happen again, or else you're going to be chewing on a bar of soap for dessert tonight."

Dana circled the back of the brush along the expanse of Rhen's exposed cheeks to drive her message home.

"Is that clear?"

"Yes ma'am," the younger girl quickly reassured her. "It won't happen again, I promise!"

"We'll see…"

A little snicker from their sales clerk brought an end to the tense exchange, and Dana cleared her throat.

"Ahem. Well, that was choice number one," she said smoothly, setting the brush aside and picking up the next one. This one had a rounded back that was shaped into a wide oval. "And here comes number two. Are you ready, cutie pie?"

She tap, tap, tapped the new brush against the faint pink splotches she'd left behind on Rhen's left cheek as she waited patiently for a response.

Oh god… Here we go again.

Swallowing her embarrassment, she nodded.

"Yes ma'am."

CRACK-CRACK! CRACK-CRACK!

Sticking to the exact same pace that she'd used with the

first brush, Dana delivered four more no-nonsense smacks to the centers of her cheeks. And once again she squealed and squirmed like she'd just been set upon by a group of angry bees, though this time her feet shot up off the floor and flailed for a moment in the air with the stinging impact as it exploded across her seat.

"Ack! Owie, owie, owie!"

Planting her feet back beneath her once again, she hissed out a sharp breath through clenched teeth as she tried to ride out the pain. And much to her own annoyance, she realized that the snotty clerk had been correct.

Although at first it seemed like both brushes had struck with about the same amount of unyielding force as they'd crashed against her naked rump, upon further reflection it was pretty clear to Rhen that the second one had felt slightly different. Its rounded edges and more compact size had seemed to focus its point of impact into a smaller, tighter area. Which made it hurt far more than the last one had in her opinion.

"Oooh, I *like* this one," declared her aunt excitedly as she looked down at the brush in her hand with a newfound respect. "How about you, Rhen?"

"Ugh, it *sucks*," she begrudgingly admitted with a miffed pout, not daring to say anything more colorful as she clenched and unclenched her sizzling cheeks behind her.

"Yes, that one does tend to get a pretty good reaction out of naughty girls," mused the smiling clerk from her vantage point behind the counter. "You definitely can't go wrong with that one, ma'am."

"Indeed," observed the older woman with a matching smile as she drank in Rhen's adorable squirming for another moment longer.

"Well then, let's just see how this last one fares, shall we?"

Shrugging, Dana scooped up the final of the three brushes that had been laid out for her, a broad rectangular monstrosity that felt surprisingly heavy in her hands.

"Ready?" she asked one last time, holding the back of the brush poised and ready to strike just above Rhen's naked cheeks.

"I guess so," grumbled the girl with a roll of her eyes. "Ah!"

CRACK-CRACK! CRACK-CRACK!

Just as before, the back of the brush in her aunt's hand exploded across her unprotected seat, and just as before, she found herself hissing in air through flared nostrils as she stomped her feet and waggled her seared bottom.

That last one had stung a *lot*, but coming so soon after the oval one, Rhen was able to tell that its wider profile had helped to take away some of the bite from its initial impact. And chewing on her lip as she compared the sensations from all three, she had to admit that it had been the easiest to bear of them all.

It had still stung like crazy, but it was clearly the lesser of three evils.

Keeping her fingers crossed and hidden beneath her torso where she lay bent over the display case, she silently prayed that her aunt wouldn't pick up on that as well.

"Hmmm…" murmured Dana as she rubbed her chin thoughtfully and eyed the back of the brush in her hand before setting it aside with the others. "This one is nice too, but… I think we'll take the second one, the oval one."

Well, shit.

"An excellent choice, ma'am," complimented the sales clerk as she returned the two rejected brushes back to their spots inside the display case, before fishing out an oversized piece of parchment paper from beneath the glass case and smoothing it out on top of the counter. "I'll just wrap that up for you."

While the smug saleswoman busied herself with going about wrapping up their selected hairbrush in the thick material, even going so far as to tie a little bow around it with a shiny red ribbon, Rhen's aunt casually restored her niece's panties back to their proper place over her pink tush and then smoothed down her skirt in back.

"There we go. All done, cutie pie. Now that wasn't so bad, was it?"

"I guess not..." the younger girl managed to grumble, face still smoldering but unable to quite ignore the damp spot she felt between her still squirming thighs.

Pushing herself up from the display case, Rhen resisted the urge to reach back and rub at the furious sting still sizzling in her cheeks from those dozen or so test swats her aunt had given her. Instead she did her best not to pout too hard as the three of them all moved over to the cash register to pay.

"Thank you so much for your business, ma'am," chirped the clerk in a cheerful voice as she slid their ribbon-wrapped package across the counter.

"You are most certainly welcome," replied Dana with a smile of her own as she deposited their purchase into her purse. "And thank *you* for all of your help, young lady."

She paused long enough to wink at her as she added.

"And your expertise."

With an amused twinkle in her eye, she wrapped an arm around Rhen's shoulders once again and gave them a light squeeze.

"Isn't there something you would like to say as well, Rhen, honey?"

"Um, thank you," mumbled the younger girl, face

positively crimson.

"Anytime... *Rhenny*," crooned the smug clerk from behind her register. "You behave yourself now, you hear?"

Rhen resisted the urge to unleash the bevy of curse words that sprang to the tip of her tongue at that condescending dismissal, and instead just nodded as politely as she could manage. And as her aunt turned her away and guided her out of that stupid, pretentious, totally overpriced store, she let out a quiet sigh of relief.

That had certainly been more than a little humiliating. Although she knew too that it could have been much, *much* worse. Even so, as she ground her teeth and mumbled darkly to herself about overeager sales staff, she couldn't help but feel a nervous and giddy flutter in her chest as she wondered just when it was that her new hairbrush would be properly put to use for the first time.

Oddly enough, she couldn't decide if she wanted it to be sooner or later.

I guess we'll just have to wait and see...

—

Mercifully, it seemed that buying her a hairbrush for both her hair and her bottom had been the last thing that her aunt had had on their shopping itinerary, and Rhen's mood immediately started to pick up as they neared the game store they'd been passing off and on all afternoon since having lunch.

As the store and its life-sized cardboard cutouts of grizzled space marines and whimsical dragons came into view, her focus zeroed in on it immediately and any lingering sting in her tail was all but forgotten. She gravitated toward the open doors that were beckoning her ever onward as the strong plastic scents of new games wafted over to her on a phantom breeze.

"Whoa now, hold on there, cutie pie," ordered Dana as she dropped a firm hand onto her shoulder that stopped her in her tracks before she could cross the threshold into the store. "Not so fast."

Feeling butterflies starting to stir up inside the pit of her stomach again, Rhen turned to regard her with what she hoped was an innocent look of confusion.

"Um... yes, Aunt Dana, um, ma'am?"

It didn't work.

"I believe our deal was that I would buy you a game only if you were on your best behavior while we were out shopping today," she said with a frown, releasing her shoulder and planting her hands firmly on her hips. "Are you *really* going to stand there and tell me that you've been a good girl for me all day, Rhen?"

"Um, well..."

Rhen's face heated up as she directed her gaze down toward the tops of her new sneakers. Digging the toe of her right foot into the carpet in front of her, she wasn't sure just what to say right then that might help turn things around for her. Part of her wanted to protest that she *had* been on her best behavior, or at the very least as good as could reasonably be expected from her given the circumstances, but she knew that doing so would only invite more trouble for her.

That, and it wasn't remotely true.

Being a brat was just too easy for her. And too fun.

As if on cue, the heat from those test swats started to pulse quietly beneath her skirt again, and she suddenly found herself not in the mood to tempt fate so soon after having had her panties pulled down for her.

"No ma'am, I guess I haven't," she admitted, heaving out a

dejected sigh.

She cast a wistful glance back behind her at all the games that had been calling for her since their arrival late that morning and huffed with annoyance at herself.

Oh well, maybe next time…

"I'm sorry, Aunt Dana."

Then, just as she was sure that the twisting in her stomach was going to drive her to start sniffling as she teared up, her aunt spoke.

"I forgive you, dear, and thank you for the apology."

Dana reached out and tipped her head up, making her lock eyes with her as she smiled fondly.

"I know today hasn't exactly been easy for you. Lord knows I hated shopping and trying on clothes all day back when I was your age as well."

She paused to give Rhen a wink as if to say that she meant that she'd been like that back when she'd been her niece's *adopted* age, rather than her actual one.

"And so in light of that, I think you've earned yourself a little treat. I'll still buy you a game if you want one."

Rhen's jaw fell open, or would have if Dana's hand hadn't still been tipping her head back, and this time the fluttering inside her stomach had nothing to do with nerves.

"Oh Aunt Dana, thank you, thank you, thank you!" she squealed as she all but tackled the older woman and squeezed her around the waist just as hard as she could.

"Oof! Oh! A-Anytime, kiddo," her aunt managed to get out around a wheeze, grinning in amusement and maternal affection as she released her death grip on her and turned to scurry off into the game store.

"Good god, that girl is far cuter than she has any right to be," she laughed to herself as she slowly followed after her a

moment later
Today had been a very good day.

Chapter 11

Bedtime Surprise

Upon returning home, Rhen and her newfound aunt spent the next half hour getting her properly settled in to her new bedroom.

Rhen arranged her alarm clock and stuffed animals with the greatest of care on top of her nightstand. She got her laptop and all of its accessories set up just the way she liked them at her desk, and then found homes on her walls for all of the posters that her aunt had bought for her of her favorite bands, shows, and video games. She knew that it was perhaps a bit childish to cover the majority of her walls in glossy two by three foot pictures of the things that she loved, but she really didn't care.

She thought they added a nice personal touch to the room that helped make it her own.

While the younger girl busied herself with decorating, Dana took care of sorting out her new clothes. Most of them she just hung up inside her closet, while still others she arranged within the various drawers of her dresser, taking extra care to ensure that every skirt and pair of panties was in its proper place by the time she was finished. Once her clothes had been dealt with, and she'd collected the final bits of price tags and other pieces of trash that had started to accumulate as they'd stripped away the wrappers and packaging off of the things they'd purchased, she fished Rhen's high-end hairbrush out from her purse and grinned.

"Just one more thing, and then I think we'll be finished."

With a flourish, she pulled free the ribbon bow that had been tied around the thick parchment paper that it was wrapped in, and then set it alongside the small stuffed bear and penguin that her niece had arranged alongside her alarm clock on her nightstand.

"There we go, perfect," she declared, taking a step back and surveying the little table with her hands on her hips. "We'll just leave Missus Hairbrush right here for whenever we need her. Sound good to you, cutie pie?"

Rhen frowned at the highly-polished ebony brush, not liking at all the idea of it being within easy reach of where she was sure to be taking many trips across her aunt's knee in the future, but resisted the urge to say anything about it other than an extra-polite, "Yes ma'am."

At least it's not a freaking paddle or something else super obvious like that, she tried to tell herself as she turned away from her nightstand and resumed fiddling with the angle of her mouse pad on her desk. *Nobody should be able to tell what it's actually there for just by seeing it laying there, so I guess it's not a big deal.*

By the time the two of them were finished organizing and decorating, arranging and unpacking, Rhen's bedroom at last felt like it truly belonged to her. Gone was the quiet little guest room she'd woken up in that morning, and in its place now stood her very own private sanctuary that she had all to herself.

Her very own bedroom inside of her auntie's house.

"This place sure shaped up pretty nicely, wouldn't you say?" asked the older woman as she stepped up behind her and wrapped her in a gentle hug.

"It sure did," agreed Rhen, smiling dreamily as she leaned back against her comforting warmth and breathed in the scent of her perfume. "Thanks a bunch, Aunt Dana. Today has been just… just, awesome."

As she said those words, meaning every single one of them with all of her heart, Rhen's mind couldn't help but flash back to all of the humiliating ordeals that she'd suffered through since breakfast that morning. The short spanking she'd received for not making her bed, having her old clothes and driver's license confiscated, her pubic hair being shaved away, Julia and her condescending smiles as she and her aunt picked out childish clothes for her to wear, and of course that awful hairbrush testing at Prismatic. But even as all of those things washed over her, flushing her delicate features with heat and making her heart flutter, she found that she really didn't mind.

Sure they'd been humiliating, and of course she didn't want another spanking if she could avoid it, but none of that really mattered now. Yes, deep down she knew that she was still Rhen, the twenty-year-old college sophomore majoring in computer science, and come next Tuesday she'd be back on campus attending lectures and preparing for the finals she'd be taking in just a couple of weeks. But the truth of the matter was that that version of her had been stripped away and folded up for storage like an old set of clothes over the course of that morning and afternoon. She'd probably come out to play in those moments later on when she and the older woman got more intimate. There was no denying the sizzling, natural chemistry between the two of them, that was for sure. But for now, and into the foreseeable future as she integrated herself more and more into daily life with her Auntie Dana, she was content to just be little Rhenny Mathews, the bratty and sassy thirteen-year-old who was more often than not in need of an attitude adjustment.

It was fun.

She was happy.

She was home.

Now I just have to stay on my best behavior.

Rhen smirked as that thought crossed her mind and she found herself honestly wondering just how long she'd be able to keep that up for before the sternly playful and heart-poundingly intimidating older woman managed to find something to take her to task over.

Somehow I doubt that I'll be going unpunished for all that long around here...

"Well, I think I'll leave you to it then," said Dana a moment later, breaking her from her reflective musings as she gave her torso a quick squeeze, leaning in to kiss her on the cheek before letting go. "I'm sure you've got lots of things you want to do on your own now that we've got you all settled in."

She ruffled Rhen's hair affectionately from behind, and then began to make her way toward her open bedroom door.

"Dinner's in about an hour and a half. Does pizza sound good to you?"

"Oh heck yeah it does," agreed Rhen with a wide grin. "Pile it high with pepperoni and sausage for me please!"

"You got it," laughed the older woman as she stepped out into the hall and disappeared toward the stairs. "I'll call you when it's here."

"Thanks!"

After her aunt had gone, Rhen padded her way over to her bedroom door and quietly eased it the rest of the way shut. She wasn't sure if she was actually supposed to keep it open all the time or not, but since Dana hadn't said one way or the other, she decided that she'd take the risk and ask for forgiveness later if she ended up getting into trouble for it.

"Now then," she declared, skipping over to her desk and settling in behind her laptop. "I do believe I have some dailies

I need to take care of."

As she was logging in to the server that she played on for her online RPG, her stomach gave an unpleasant twinge as she suddenly remembered that she still had that web design assignment that she needed to take care of before Monday night. In the whirlwind of events since her aunt's arrival in the dorms the day before, she'd all but forgotten about it.

"Half an hour," she promised herself, her hand automatically reaching for a can of soda that wasn't actually there and cracking a smile. She'd have to grab one from the fridge later. "I'll play for half an hour, and then I'll work on it. It'll be fine."

—

Nearly two hours later, Rhen jumped in surprise as she heard the doorbell ring from downstairs, swearing viciously.

Sort of.

She didn't want to actually risk her aunt overhearing her and have her decide to make good on her earlier threat to wash her mouth out, after all.

"Shi- I mean, crap!"

She'd completely forgotten about doing her homework after she'd finished with her daily quests and started installing the new game that Dana had bought for her.

"Whatever, it's fine," she said to nobody in particular as she pushed back from her desk and stretched her arms above her head, stomach growling. "I'll just take care of it after dinner."

"Rhen, pizza's here!" she heard her aunt calling for her from the foot of the stairs a moment later. "Get your butt down here, cutie pie, I'm starving!"

Springing up from her solid, wooden desk chair, Rhen shot out of her bedroom like a rocket, thundering down the stairs on sock-covered feet.

"Coming!"

—

As a happy bonus (aside from being greasy and delicious), their meal that evening required no cleanup from Rhen when it was finished. Since they'd just used paper plates to eat off of, she was able to scurry back up to her bedroom without any delay once her aunt had decided that she'd eaten enough.

"Thanks for the food," she called over her shoulder as she scampered out of the kitchen and toward the stairs again, taking them two at a time, eager to get back to her new game and the group chats that she'd left waiting for her up there.

"You're welcome," Dana called after her with a laugh, raising her voice loud enough so that the younger girl would be able to hear her from the hallway upstairs.

—

Just as the large grandfather clock in her front room chimed nine o'clock that evening, Dana padded her way upstairs and popped her head into her niece's bedroom.

"Rhen, honey, you can have twenty more minutes of screen time on your laptop, and then I want you in the shower and getting ready for bed. It's been a long day, and you need to get a good night's sleep, alright?"

"Okay, Aunt Dana," chirped Rhen, turning her attention away from her laptop just long enough to nod at her before zeroing in once again on the game she was playing.

"I'll be by to tuck you in later," replied the older woman with a bemused look on her face as she spent a few more moments watching her niece blast some sort of magical spell at the monsters she was fighting in what she could only assume was her new computer game.

Chuckling to herself, she wondered briefly for a moment just how likely it was that she'd actually find the girl in her jammies and ready to go to sleep when she returned later.

Somehow, she had a feeling that it probably wasn't a particularly safe bet.

Which was just fine with her.

Deciding that she'd find out one way or the other soon enough, Dana eased her niece's door shut behind her, as she said one more time, "Half an hour, cutie pie. I mean it."

"Yeah, yeah…" mumbled Rhen, only half paying attention now. "I heard you."

"Oh yes, I'm sure you did," Dana muttered to herself under her breath as she rolled her eyes. "You little sass muffin."

—

Once her aunt had gone, and the battle encounter that she'd been locked into had finally ended, Rhen cast a quick glance behind her at the white-enameled alarm clock that the older woman had bought for her that afternoon. Noting the time, she did a bit of speedy mental math, and then grinned. If she was quick in the shower, she could probably squeeze in another half an hour or more on her laptop without Dana ever being any the wiser! She just had to be ready for her to tuck her in when the time came was all.

She could do that.

She'd be fine.

—

At five minutes to ten, possibly cutting things just a *little* bit closer to the wire than she should have since she'd played for nearly an hour instead of twenty minutes like her aunt had said, Rhen put her laptop to sleep and casually made her way out of her bedroom and down the hall toward her bathroom.

It would be fine.

She could still totally make her bedtime rendezvous with Dana without a problem.

She'd just have to be quick in the shower, that was all.

Humming to herself all the while as she went, she pulled her hair free of the loose ponytail that she'd tied it back in earlier and beamed.

She was very much looking forward to a nice, hot, and above all else, private and uninterrupted, shower.

"Oof. Geez…"

The sight that greeted Rhen in the mirror as she slipped her panties down a moment later as she got undressed in her bathroom caught her completely off guard. Between catching up on YouTube videos, chatting with her friends online, and the triple-rare loot that the last boss in her game had dropped, she'd honestly forgotten all about the fact that her aunt had "adjusted" her pubic hair to better match her general level of behavior. She'd gotten so used to the feel of it by then, or rather the lack of a feeling she supposed, that the sight of her totally bare sex had momentarily startled her.

She stared transfixed at her own reflection for several long moments as her panties hung all but forgotten around her knees, running the fingertips of her right hand oh so gently over the smooth folds of her labia and marveling at how silky smooth it all felt. Much to her own surprise, she found that she was able to push past her initial spike of embarrassment far faster than she'd been anticipating. And rather than be mortified at the loss of her hair and the clear and stark reminder of her new regressed-age status on such open display before her, she just blushed slightly and flashed herself a secret little smirk.

"You know, it really doesn't look all that bad," she told herself as she shrugged off the rest of her clothes and stepped into the shower. "I just hope to god that nobody else besides me Aunt Dana ever gets a chance to see for themselves…"

—

A little over half an hour later, a pink-skinned and well-scrubbed Rhen emerged from her bathroom amid a billowing cloud of steam. Clad in just a towel wrapped around her chest, she hummed happily to herself once again as she made her way at an easy pace across the hall and back into her bedroom.

"Did you enjoy your shower, dear?" greeted her aunt with a small grin from her perch on the edge of her bed as Rhen stepped onto the plush carpet from the hallway.

"Ack! Geez, Aunt Dana!" she choked, hands flying up to cling to the front of the towel around her chest as she jerked to a sudden stop in the doorway. "You scared the shi- I mean, *crap*, out of me."

"Sorry to spook you, sweetie," purred the older woman, a flicker of amusement tinged with warning in her dark eyes. "I'm just here for your bedtime spanking, is all."

Rhen stumbled as she took another step into her bedroom. Tightening her grip around the top of her towel, she found herself swallowing hard.

"My uh… my what?"

She'd heard her of course, but at that moment her brain was having a hard time coming to terms with reality.

"Your bedtime spanking," her aunt repeated smoothly, the amusement in her eyes giving way to a direct and unyielding stare that made Rhen's thighs squirm. "Did you honestly think that you could sass me like you did all afternoon and *not* get into trouble, young lady?"

Hooking a thumb to her right to point at the alarm clock on Rhen's night stand, she frowned as she continued.

"And I thought I told you I wanted you to be ready for bed nearly twenty minutes ago? It's almost ten-thirty now, and you're not even in your jammies yet. That's two strikes, Rhen, and I don't think we're going to wait around for a third before we nip this in the bud."

"But I wasn't- I mean to say- That's not fair!" spluttered the red-faced younger girl, excuses springing to her lips and then falling flat as her aunt just stared her down, waiting.

With her heart thudding hard against her chest as if it were trying to escape, she heaved out a long sigh. She knew that there was no way around what was about to happen, and she had to admit that her aunt did have a *bit* of a point, maybe, she supposed. Not that she liked it in the slightest.

"I guess you're right, Aunt Dana... I'm sorry."

It was all she could really say just then, and she knew it was her best chance to possibly mitigate what she knew she had coming.

Dana nodded approvingly at her admission of guilt, and her frown cocked partway up into a satisfied smirk.

"That's right, little girl," she crooned as she crooked a lazy finger to beckon her over to her. "If you want to act like a brat while you're out with Auntie Dana, then you'll pay for it with your cute little caboose. Now drop that towel and get over here."

"Oh god..."

Rhen let out a low, mortified groan as she took a couple of tentative steps forward on a pair of wobbly legs toward her waiting aunt. She held onto her towel for dear life for as long as she dared to, before finally letting it drop to the floor as her face all but burst into flames. Swallowing hard, she scampered the rest of the way over to her right side, closing the distance in a fraction of the time it had taken her to get around to losing her towel.

Only then did she notice the round oval head of her brand new hairbrush nestled against the side of her aunt's hip on top of the bed.

"Oh come on!" she whined, curling her hands into little fists at her sides as she stomped a foot. "I wasn't *that* bad today! Do you *really* have to use the hairbrush?"

"Now is definitely not the time to be getting an attitude with me, cutie pie," Dana warned in a low purr, arching an eyebrow as she regarded her coolly. "And you'd better get that squeaky clean tush of yours across my lap right now before I decide to give you something to *really* whine about. You hear me?"

"Eep! Yes ma'am!" squeaked the nervous sophomore, all but diving across the other woman's waiting thighs, even as part of her rolled her eyes at the fact that she'd just used such a cliché threat on her.

I guess that really doesn't matter all that much if it still works... she snickered to herself, trying not to think too hard about how vulnerable her bare bottom was just then.

"There we go, much better," cooed Dana as she settled into place, drawing her out of her musings as she patted her bottom affectionately and then squeezed, digging in her nails.

Hard.

"Ah!"

Rather than start spanking her right away however, Dana took her time adjusting her position further until she had her just the way she wanted her. She wrapped an arm around her thighs, pulling them up and onto the bed so that her torso and legs were both supported by the mattress as she lay sprawled across her ample lap. Then, once that was done, she took two great handfuls of bottom cheek in each of her hands, and squeezing, pulled her forward until her rounded caboose was angled directly across the middle of her thighs.

"Perfect."

She gave Rhen's cheeks a couple more light pats, and noted with wry amusement that her soft and scrubbed seat no longer bore even the faintest hint of the earlier swats from her hairbrush that she'd been so pouty about. Resolving to fix that, she felt the other corner of her mouth quirk up to replace her satisfied smirk with a full on grin.

Wrapping her fingers around the handle of her niece's hairbrush, she gave her jiggly buns a few light taps as she got a feel for her aim.

"Now you just hang tight and we'll be done before you know it. Okay, honeybuns?"

Rhen just huffed and flopped the side of her face down against her folded arms in front of her, not willing to risk saying anything that might get her into any more trouble right then.

Even so, her aunt took that as a sign of acknowledgment and raised her hairbrush up high over her shoulder, before beginning to bring it crashing back down in a swift and forceful repeating arc.

CRACK! CRACK! CRACK!

Not rushing in the slightest, Dana kept her pace steady and even as she spent the next several minutes bouncing the back of Rhen's hairbrush off of her bare bottom with moderately hard swats, watching with grim satisfaction as the petite sophomore's cheeks grew steadily pinker and pinker as the minutes ticked by at a snail's pace. With each reverberating crack of the hairbrush, the round splotches left behind by its oval-shaped head gradually began to blend together until they formed an all-encompassing burning, stinging sensation from the tops of her cheeks down to just below her sit-spots. One that had her crossing and uncrossing her ankles and clinging to her bedspread as she gasped and yelped, wriggled and squirmed.

Dana didn't bother with lecturing this time around, and instead basked in the increasingly-frantic litany of promises to be good and apologies that started tumbling out of the younger girl's mouth as her squirming grew steadily more panicked and pained.

It was music to her ears.

By the time she was finished, both of Rhen's rounded cheeks were painted a lovely shade of dark pink and were warm to the touch as she lay there clenching and unclenching them in time with her panting breaths. And although her heart was still pounding hard and her stomach fluttering with the thrill and embarrassment of being spanked totally naked across the older woman's lap, she knew too that she'd gotten off far, *far* lighter than she'd been expecting to.

That spanking had definitely stung, that was for sure. And the little gasps and yelps it had wrung out of her as the brush had drummed out its relentless and unyielding rhythm against her gyrating cheeks had most certainly been genuine. But now that it was all over, rather than be left with a furious inferno that would be smoldering for at least an hour or two more after she'd finished sobbing, Rhen's tush merely tingled with a not-all-together unpleasant glow.

The message to behave herself in the future had still been loud and clear however, and had her making a silent vow to avoid provoking a proper performance from that damn hairbrush of hers for as long as she possibly could. She could still remember how bad her aunt could *really* make that strong oval back on it sting, and she knew too that the next time she decided to pull it out for a spanking, she wouldn't be let off with just a few minutes of mild swatting.

She'd be a sobbing mess standing with her nose pressed firmly into a corner.

Heaving out a tired sigh, Rhen felt an odd mixture of anticipation and dread roil around inside her stomach at that particular mental picture as her aunt helped her back up onto her feet and hugged her tight.

"Am I going to have any more sass from you, young lady?" she asked with a challenging twinkle in her eyes as she untangled herself from around her and held her out at arm's length, both hands planted firmly on her shoulders.

"No ma'am!" Rhen hastened to assure her, heedless of the lewd display she was making of herself as she danced in place in her grip while using both of her hands to gingerly massage away some of the lingering sting from her only slightly-swollen seat.

"I'm glad to hear that," purred Dana with a low chuckle, her face breaking out into a warm smile that did little to disguise the hungry look in her eyes. "Now let's get you into those cute new jammies of yours and then all tucked in. What do you say?"

Rhen cast a sidelong glance at her alarm clock and saw with some small amount of amusement that she was actually up past her bedtime. The thought of it sent a little twinge of rebellious satisfaction through her stomach, despite the fact that she was currently standing there in nothing but her birthday suit with a sore, pink bottom.

"Sounds good to me."

Rising up from her perch on the bed and returning her hairbrush back to its spot on the night stand, Dana then took her by the hand and guided her over to her dresser.

"Come on then, cutie pie."

Pulling open Rhen's top drawer, she retrieved from it the brand new pair of pajamas that she'd bought for her earlier that afternoon. They were an absurdly cutesy long-sleeved pants and shirt combo made from a wonderfully soft sky blue material. Puffy white clouds were printed all over them, and they had stretchy elastic cuffs around the ankles, wrists, and waistband. And worst of all, it had a big, smiling rainbow emblazoned across the chest.

Rhen absolutely *hated* how adorable they made her look.

To say nothing of the fact that in them she most definitely passed as a cute tween, rather than a young teen beginning to edge her way out of more childish clothes (and punishments). But she knew better than to argue as her aunt held out the pants in front of her for her to step into, and instead just put one foot and then the other into them and tried not to grimace as they were pulled up to cover her still bare and very pink bottom.

Apparently naughty girls didn't get to go to bed with panties on.

Humph, whatever.

She then raised her arms up high over her head and tried not to think too much about how hard her nipples were just then as she waited patiently for Dana to shake out her matching top and pull it down over her torso for her.

"Awww, don't you just look *precious*!"

"Heh, thanks," snickered Rhen as her blushing head emerged from the neck-hole of her pajama top a moment later, unable to stop herself from doing a little twirl to show off her new outfit from all angles. "Ta-da!"

"Very nice," nodded Dana, clapping appreciatively and grinning from ear to ear. "Now stop spinning around before I decide to pull those jammy bottoms down before I tuck you in."

Feeling loopy from sleepiness and a post-spanking high, Rhen grinned goofily at the older woman.

"Trying to get into my pants are you, Miss Bossy Boots?"

"It's a tempting offer, cutie pie," purred Dana in response, closing the distance between the two of them and capturing her lips in a hungry kiss. "But *someone* is up past her bedtime, and unless you want to eat your breakfast standing up, I'd stop stalling for time."

Slipping her hands beneath Rhen's pajama bottoms, she captured her warm cheeks in a strong grip and then dug her nails in.

Hard.

"Eep! Yes ma'am!"

"Good girl."

Releasing her iron grip and chuckling darkly, Dana slipped her hands free of Rhen's pajama bottoms and then led her by the hand back over to her waiting bed.

Still flushed a delicate shade of neon red, the younger girl watched with a mixture of fond amusement and just a bit of sheepish chagrin as she pulled back her covers for her to climb under, and then tucked her in just as she'd done the night before.

"Sleep tight, honey," Dana said after she'd leaned in and kissed her forehead goodnight. "I'll see you in the morning."

"Goodnight, Aunt Dana," Rhen yawned as she stretched out and then curled her blankets around her just the way she liked them, adding almost as an afterthought as her eyes drifted shut. "Love you."

Sleepy as she was, she missed the hard swallow and the misty eyes that her words elicited from the older woman, who after taking a moment to compose herself, murmured back extra fondly.

"Love you too, cutie pie."

And god help her, she meant it. She'd fallen for the petite sophomore something fierce, and was overjoyed beyond words to hear that she felt the same.

As the lights overhead flicked off, and her door was shut behind Dana as she slipped out of the room, Rhen thought for sure that she would be wide awake for at least a couple more hours. If nothing else, she was going to bed far earlier than she was used to, and she was convinced that all of the thoughts and emotions swirling around inside of her head from the day's events would have her tossing and turning for a long while to come, to say nothing of the aching need pulsating between her thighs. But, as her left hand snaked its way down beneath the covers to caress the warmth radiating out from underneath the thin material of her pajama bottoms, she decided that all of that could wait until tomorrow.

Today had been a long, *long* day.

Chapter 12

Sitting Sore in a Whole New Way

By the time Monday morning finally came and went, that entirely all too familiar sense of looming dread and panic had started to settle in along the bottom of Rhen's stomach once again. She'd had every intention of finishing off her web design homework the day before, but somehow she'd wound up going to bed having still just barely touched it. Now it was noon at the start of a brand new school week, and her assignment was due by nine o'clock that evening.

Shit. Why the hell does this keep happening to me?

Rhen knew that she needed to start buckling down as she sat at the kitchen table with her aunt and the rest of the day-care kids eating lunch. And as she occupied herself with pushing around the carrot sticks on her plate, trying to scrape up the few remaining dollops of tangy ranch dressing, she made a promise to herself that she'd get to work right away after she and the others had been dismissed to go play.

Then again...

As she sat there mulling the problem over, chewing thoughtfully on the end of a ranch-covered carrot stick, she started to think that maybe she might have been overreacting just a *little* bit. Now that she had a full stomach to think things through on, she was pretty sure that she still had more than enough time to take care of her assignment. After all, it was just dumb old web design, right? She'd been fiddling with server-side development as a hobby for years now. She could handle it. There was no way she wouldn't be able to easily throw together an elegant little algorithm for whatever the assignment decided to throw her way.

She had plenty of time for at least one or two games of tag first.

I'll just run around for a little bit outside to clear my head and work off some of the food I just ate, she told herself, feeling her old sense of fly-by-night confidence starting to slide back into place as she did her best to suppress the gnawing worry in the pit of her stomach. *That way I'll be at peak performance when I actually sit down to work later on. In fact, now that I think about it, it would be silly not to take a quick exercise break!*

With her decision made, Rhen bussed her dishes over to the sink with the rest of her friends (she'd begrudgingly accepted that she rather liked them, and they seemed to think she was cool and interesting despite having seen her bright red bare bottom on display last week) and joined them as they spilled out into her aunt's backyard to run, scream, and generally make a ruckus while the sun still shined high overhead.

It would be fine.

—

Or... maybe not.

By the time the last of her fellow daycare kids had been picked up by either their parents or older siblings, and it was just about time to eat dinner judging by the smells wafting up from downstairs, Rhen knew that she was in trouble. Deep trouble. Her homework was due in less than an hour now, and it had become readily apparent that she'd made a grave miscalculation about how long it was going to take her to complete it.

As she scrolled her way through the PDF outlining the

details for her assignment and finally got a proper look at the full list of things that she still needed to do for it, she could feel her heart rate skyrocketing as her stomach twisted and roiled.

"Crap, crap, crap… *shit*!"

Oh yes, she was royally screwed.

"Rhen," Dana called from the foot of the stairs on the floor below, drawing out her name as she made her voice loud enough to be heard all the way up in her bedroom with the door only slightly ajar. "It's time for dinner. Put down the games and come on, cutie pie."

"Shit, shit, shitty shit, shit on a shit sandwich!"

If she hadn't been so busy freaking out, Rhen probably would have been very grateful to know that her aunt hadn't heard the torrent of curse words pouring out of her mouth at that particular moment.

"Did you hear me, young lady?"

"Uh… yeah!" she managed to yell back a moment later, only half paying attention as she frantically ran her eyes over the grading rubric for her homework. "Hold on just a sec. I'll be down in a minute."

"Now means, *now*, kiddo," was her aunt's only response, and Rhen knew that she was rapidly crossing into dangerous territory with her delays.

"*Alright*. I said I'll be there in just a second!"

"Don't make me come up there, little girl…"

Rhen winced, cheeks clenching reflexively beneath her at the warning tone in the older woman's voice.

If there was one thing that her newfound aunt couldn't stand, it was being deliberately disobeyed when she gave someone a direct order. And not doing as she was told as soon as soon as she was told to do it most definitely counted as deliberate disobedience in her book.

She'd learned that lesson the hard way more than enough times by now.

"Okay, okay, I'm coming! Geez."

At least everyone else has already gone home by now…

Hoping that things weren't nearly as bad as they seemed to be just then, Rhen did her best to ignore the thin ice that she was waltzing across with her aunt as she continued to remain seated at her desk, panicking. In a last ditch effort to mitigate an impending academic disaster, she pulled up her course syllabus and double-checked it for any signs of a way out of the hole that she'd managed to dig for herself. But rather than ease her worries, it instead just made them much, much worse.

Of fucking course the majority of her final grade *would* be based on how well she did on her homework assignments. Which she begrudgingly had to admit at least made some small amount of sense given that they made up the lion's share of her workload in that class. Unfortunately though, that also meant that there would be no catching a break by having this one not count for anything major.

"Shit!"

Rhen stomped her feet and let out a frustrated moan as she glared at her laptop, her mind churning through possibilities and contingency plans.

She definitely didn't want to fail the class that she'd so casually written off as being an easy A for her. That would be beyond humiliating, and probably more than a little painful once her new auntie found out about it.

Heh. Never mind what Dana would think, she mused to herself with a little shiver, smirking in spite of the roiling panic gripping her insides. *Grandma would totally hit the roof if that happened.* Hell, *she'd probably drive down here so the two of them could take turns whipping my ass raw.*

Shaking her head to clear it before that particular scenario could fully manifest itself in her mind's eye, Rhen redoubled her focus, staring hard at her computer screen.

"Come on, there's got to be something I'm missing here…"

Scrolling back up to the grading rubric in her syllabus, she started doing some quick mental math, trying to figure out just what the bare minimum was that she'd need to do to avoid outright failing her assignment and severely damaging her grade in her web design class in the process. And as she did so, a plan began to form in the back of her mind. Not a great one, but it was at least still *something*.

"Hmmm… I might just be able to pull this off if I hurry," she murmured to herself, nibbling on the end of her thumbnail and feeling a small ember of hope starting to kindle within her chest. "It's not going to be pretty, but it'll at least be good enough to pass… probably."

With her decision made, Rhen pushed her chair back from her desk and sprang to her feet, the slim chance of not failing (another) homework assignment because she'd forgotten about it or put it off until the very last minute lending her a burst of speed as she dashed out of her bedroom. Sprinting as fast as she could to avoid having her aunt come looking for her, she took the stairs down two at a time, and managed by some small miracle to avoid slipping on the hardwood floor in her socks as she hurried.

"Whoa now, careful there, hon," admonished a worried-sounding Dana with a hand over her heart as she came barreling into the kitchen.

Just as quickly as she'd entered, Rhen had come to an abrupt halt as she bonked hard into the side of the island in front of where the older woman had been standing, waiting for her.

"I know you're hungry and all, but slow down, would you? I've already had to patch up one overeager beaver today, let's not make it two, alright?"

Rhen couldn't help but smirk a little bit at the light scolding her aunt was giving her. It was definitely nice to know that she cared, and part of her did have to admit that she had a point. Just that afternoon she'd seen one of the hotter-headed younger boys split his lip open after he'd ran face first into the edge of the island she'd just collided with. And after Dana had patched him up, he'd wound up getting a spanking and spending half an hour in the corner with his shorts and briefs around his ankles for playing tag inside the house.

It had been rather gratifying to watch him standing there with his nose pushed into the corner as he fought against the urge to rub his flaming bare bottom. But at the same time it had also been more than a little embarrassing to see that her bossy boots auntie really didn't treat her all that differently from any of the other "kids" she looked after. Although Rhen was willing to bet that her tush saw a lot more of the woman's displeasure than any of the others' did.

To say nothing of where her fingers had been wandering last night while they'd been cuddling on the couch in front of the TV before bedtime.

"Can't talk now, Aunt Dana, really busy," Rhen panted as she straightened up with a wince from where the edge of the countertop had just jabbed in against her ribs. The blow hadn't really hurt all that much though, and she'd already forgotten about it by the time she dusted herself off. "I'll take my food to go, please."

"You most certainly will not," huffed the red-haired older woman, planting her hands on her hips and glaring at her in disbelief. "In this house we eat our dinner at the table, young lady. I'm not running a hotel, and I won't have you getting your crumbs all over the carpet in your room.”

“But Aunt Dana, I’m *busy*,” whined Rhen, actually stomping a foot before she could stop herself.

Seeing the way that just caused her aunt’s right eyebrow to arch up dangerously however, she quickly decided to try a different tactic instead. Hoping that appealing to her strict belief that school should come before anything else, she added in the same petulant tone as before.

“I’ve got homework to do still, and it’s due in an *hour*! Can’t you just make an exception this one time, please? Or maybe we could just eat later?”

Rather than being her ace in the hole however, all Rhen’s admission seemed to do was darken the glare on the other woman’s face into a full on scowl.

“And why weren’t you working on this assignment after we finished lunch today, or sometime yesterday during the afternoon?” she demanded coolly. “I *know* you’ve had more than enough time this weekend to do your homework, little girl.”

“Well…”

Rhen looked away from her aunt’s stern countenance as she suddenly found herself going on the defensive. Tracing a fingertip along the granite surface of the island beside her, she did her best to think of a way to soften the truth even as she spoke it aloud.

“I did, *technically*, start it a few days ago, but I kinda… sorta… forgot to finish it.”

Her last few words came out all at once in a jumble as her face heated up. The admission hadn’t sounded any better coming out fast than it had in her head, and she could tell by the way Dana was frowning at her that she hadn’t liked what she’d heard one bit either.

"Um, sorry?"

"Uh-huh," her aunt grunted skeptically, clearly unimpressed with her meandering admission of wrongdoing and her halfhearted apology.

Crossing her arms over her ample chest, she eyed her with that same look she always used whenever she was attempting to sniff out the rest of a half-truth one of her kids was attempting to sell her.

"And this wouldn't happen to be that same 'bit of homework' you said you were 'working on' when I came to get you on Friday, now would it?"

Uh-oh... I don't think I like where this is headed...

Rhen grimaced and tried to think of some excuse or explanation that might help cast things in a better light for her. For a brief moment she considered just outright telling her aunt that it wasn't the same assignment, but she knew that that would most likely only make things much worse for her. Even if she did believe her, she'd still be upset about her letting things lapse until the very last minute, again, anyway. But if she happened to figure out that she was lying, and Rhen was almost certain that she would (she had a terrible poker face and she knew it), then there would be hell to pay.

Unfortunately, honesty really was the best policy in this situation. And so, heaving out a sigh and quietly hoping that things wouldn't be too bad for her, she nodded.

"Um, yes ma'am, it is."

Dana closed her eyes and let out a long, slow sigh of her own at hearing this, though hers was laced with far more exasperation and strained patience than Rhen's had been. When she at last opened her eyes again, they were hard and unyielding. Her back was straight and her lips were pursed into a tight line. She had once more fully slipped into disciplinarian mode.

"Bend over the counter, Rhen. Now."

"But Aunt Dana," the younger girl immediately began to protest, balling her hands into indignant little fists at her sides as her whining ratcheted up an octave or two.

"One…"

Her aunt held up a finger, her face set into a mask of grim determination as she stared her down, silently daring her to see what would happen if she kept defying her.

"I still need to do my homework!"

"Two…"

"Can't this wait until later?"

"Two and a half…"

Not at all wanting to find out what would happen if and when the stern older woman at last reached "three", Rhen turned and all but dove across the island beside her.

"Okay, okay, geez! I'm sorry, alright?"

"Humph, we'll just see about that," sniffed Dana in annoyance, rolling her eyes as she turned her back on her. "Now you just wait right there while I find something appropriate to deal with your attitude, missy."

Rhen watched with a mounting sense of dread as the now smirking older woman sashayed her way confidently over to the stove, and in one fluid motion plucked up a very sturdy looking, long-handled wooden spoon from the ceramic crock she kept beside it.

Oh crap. That's definitely not going to feel nice.

"The procrastination ends *now*. Do you hear me, Rhen?" demanded Dana as she rounded on her once again and stalked over to her side, all traces of her earlier self-satisfied levity gone from her hard eyes.

"Yes ma'am!" squeaked Rhen, her cheeks clenching and unclenching nervously beneath her skirt as she caught sight of the storm brewing behind the older woman's stormy gaze.

She'd known full well just what kind of danger she'd been putting her caboose into by not doing her homework all weekend, and she felt a shiver run down her spine now as she tried not to imagine how that scary looking spoon was going to feel against her bare bottom in only a few moments. At the same time, she also felt her face heating up as the realization that she wouldn't have been in this mess in the first place if she'd just done her homework like she was supposed hit her like a ton of bricks. And while that was certainly more than a little humiliating to come to terms with, in a much bigger way it was also oddly comforting.

She'd been naughty, and now she was going to be punished for it.

Well what do you know? I guess these spankings are actually teaching me something, after all, she thought to herself with a bemused smirk as she shifted around in a vain attempt to find a more comfortable position across the cold granite countertop beneath her. *I just wish I didn't have to experience the whole thing now that I've clearly learned my lesson. Dammit.*

"It's high time that you learned how to manage your time better, little girl," her aunt barked, snapping her out of her musings as she smacked the wooden spoon down beside her on the counter with a hard clatter that made her jump. "Because if you don't, you're going to end up with a lot more unpleasant things to deal with than just a sore bottom, believe you me."

There was no arguing there, Rhen knew, and so she just nodded.

"Yes ma'am, you're right. I'm sorry."

"I'm really glad to hear you say that, dear, but you know that being sorry doesn't mean that you get to escape your punishment, don't you?"

"Yes, ma'am," sighed Rhen again as she tried to ignore the butterflies inside her stomach that having to answer that last question aloud had stirred to life.

As she continued to lecture, Dana ran a hand along the curve of her niece's bent waist, searching for the hidden clasp that held her pink skirt in place around her hips. Half a heartbeat later she found it, and her practiced fingers made quick work of the button and zipper there.

With a whisper of fabric on skin, Rhen gritted her teeth against the far too familiar embarrassment that welled up within her as she felt her skirt slide free of her hips and slip down her legs to pool limply around her ankles. She squirmed in place as the wafting air from the kitchen caressed along the backs of her exposed thighs, and flexed her cheeks beneath the taut material of her panties, savoring the feel of them before they too were taken away from her. There was no way her aunt *wouldn't* be pulling them down in just a moment, she knew, and despite how little protection the ruffles on the back of them would have actually afforded her, she was still going to miss them. If for no other reason than that they at least preserved some small sliver of her dignity.

At least everyone else has already gone home for the day...

"By all rights I *should* be sending you off to cut me a handful of switches so I can *really* show you what happens to naughty little girls who don't do their homework," Dana continued to scold as she took hold of the waistband of her panties on either side of her hips, and then whisked them down to join her skirt around her ankles. "But since we're on a bit of a time crunch here, we'll just have to make do with the wooden spoon, I suppose."

Rhen moaned and chewed on her lower lip as molten heat rushed up her neck to the tips of her ears. She fought hard against the urge to try asking if her aunt could just let her go as she shifted her weight from one foot to the other and back again, the movements making her naked cheeks bounce and wobble with each step, as if they were just begging the scowling older woman to punish them thoroughly.

Traitors!

"Please, Aunt Dana, I'll be good!"

Although Rhen didn't actually have any firsthand experience with what being switched actually felt like, her grandma had threatened her enough times with one while growing up to know that it was something that she most certainly wanted to avoid at all costs. And she definitely counted narrowly escaping finding out what one was like, from multiple switches no less, because they were pressed for time as a good thing. Even if the situation she found herself in just then was still all sorts of humiliating for her.

This isn't that bad, she tried telling herself while at the same time doing her best to not think about the fact that she could feel cool air tickling her between her partially parted cheeks and thighs. Just how much of herself was she showing off to Dana right then? *Well at least that damn "haircut" of hers is being put to good use. I might as well actually look the part of the bratty young teen if I'm going to get spanked for not doing my homework like one.*

"After we're done here, I want you to get your laptop from your room and bring it down here to the kitchen. You can finish your homework at the table, and then you and I are going to have a nice long talk about how you're going to be doing things differently from now on when it comes to managing your time. Is that understood, young lady?"

Rhen shivered as she felt the hard, smooth back of the

wooden spoon being tap, tap, tapped against her bare right cheek, patiently waiting for her to reply. She let out a resigned sigh, accepting that this was just how things were going to go whether she liked it or not, and then reached out to grip the edges of the countertop on either side of her as she grimaced.

"Yes ma'am."

The words had barely left her lips, when the wooden spoon started falling against her upturned tush. And *fast*.

THWAP! THWAP! THWAP! THWAP! THWAP!

In the interest of not taking up too much time from her niece's homework and its rapidly approaching deadline, Dana kept her pace brisk and relentless.

Usually she liked to pace herself when delivering a spanking. She'd make sure to spread the individual swats out evenly across both bouncing bare bottom cheeks and thighs to ensure that they all got full and equal coverage. And as she did that, she'd also make little adjustments here and there to her speed and strength based on the reactions she was getting from the brat she happened to be punishing at the time.

But not this time.

Instead she focused on dishing out as many spanks with her wooden spoon to Rhen's frantically gyrating bare bottom just as fast as she possibly could within the next two minutes. Going for a quantity over quality approach, knowing that in the end the results would be close enough to not matter all that much, she kept her aim zeroed in exclusively on the delicate undercurves of the squealing girl's chubby cheeks. She was intent on whipping up a highly-concentrated, fiery inferno directly over where she knew she'd be resting most of her weight when she sat down to do her homework after they were finished. Taking solace in the fact that while this wasn't nearly so severe spanking a spanking as the girl actually deserved, what she had in mind for her next would make sure that the silly little thing remembered this particular lesson for a very long time to come.

She would learn to do her homework on time, or else they'd be having this discussion again out in the back yard with some switches from her crepe myrtle.

THWAP! THWAP! THWAP! THWAP! THWAP!

Exactly two minutes, and around nearly one hundred and fifty rapid-fire swats, later, Dana came to a sudden stop.

Setting her spoon down on the countertop next to her gasping and groaning niece, who hadn't even started properly sniffing yet (the little minx!), she gripped her by the scruff of her shirt and hauled her back up to her feet.

"Laptop, now," she ordered, pointing toward the stairs before sending her scrambling out of the kitchen with a hard swat to her sizzling right sit-spot.

"Okay, okay, okay!" squealed Rhen.

With all thoughts of modesty and dignity cast aside for the moment, she hopped forward and then started making a beeline for her bedroom.

Unfortunately for her though, the panties still tangled up around her ankles slowed her progress considerably, and she lost precious time dancing around and stumbling as she tried to kick her way free of them. Eventually however she managed to fling them off of her left foot and in the general direction of where her skirt had fallen, and then bolted her way up the stairs, hands clamped to her stinging backside as she ran.

Time was ticking away, and she knew that she couldn't afford to waste any of it. Not if she wanted to save her grade, or her poor boiling bottom.

"Oh that sweet and sassy cutie pie of mine," sighed Dana wistfully once she was all alone again, her hands planted on her hips as she stared off toward where Rhen had just disappeared. "One of these days she'll figure out how to channel some of that energy of hers into something productive."

She smirked.

"Though hopefully not *too* soon."

———

After spending about as much time as she dared to ogling her swollen backside in the full-length mirror beside her closet door, Rhen snatched up her laptop and wireless mouse from her desk and hightailed it back toward the kitchen just as her aunt was starting to call for her again.

"Time's a-wastin', Rhen. Get your butt back in here right now, young lady!"

"I'm coming, I'm coming!"

Not wanting to risk dropping her precious laptop on the stairs, especially since there was no way that she could afford to replace it anytime soon, Rhen took them one at a time and at a far more reasonable pace than she had coming up them just a couple minutes earlier. Thankfully though, her aunt had heard her and didn't come looking for her as she carefully padded her way down the stairs at a frantic speed-walk. She was already in enough trouble as it was, and she sure as heck didn't need any more just then.

But as she stepped back into the kitchen, using her closed laptop as a temporary means to hide her naked front from view, she found herself stopping short.

"Uh… what's that for, Aunt Dana?" she asked tentatively, approaching the chair that the tightly-smiling older woman already had pulled out and waiting for her at their broad, wooden table.

It wasn't the chair itself that had given her pause as her stomach roiled with a fresh wave of butterflies, but rather

what she found laid out across its seat. For some reason, Dana
had placed a welcome mat right where she was supposed to
sit.

Uh-oh…

Rhen had never seen the mat before, but judging by the
way it was lying along the seat, only bending a little at the
edges, she could only assume that it was brand new. And if the
smug grin that was on open display on her aunt's face right
then was any indication, she'd been waiting for just the right
moment to spring it on her for a while now.

Taking a couple of hesitant steps forward toward the ominously innocuous looking mat, she saw that it was made from
some sort of rough brown fiber with stiff rubber bristles for
scraping off mud and dirt from shoes poking up all across the
entirety of its surface. Whatever her aunt had in mind for her
with it being there, it did *not* look pleasant at all.

Which Rhen suspected was probably the point.

"It's called a punishment mat, dear," Dana explained far
too casually for her liking as she sauntered over to her side
and slipped her laptop from her grasp.

She set it down gently on the table in front of the chair
she'd prepared for her, before plucking the mouse from her
grip as well and setting it beside it.

"Like I said earlier, I *should* have taken you out back and
worn out some switches on that dilly dallying little derriere of
yours after the way you've been letting your homework slide,"
she continued in that coolly casual disciplinarian way of hers.
"As far as I'm concerned, you fully deserve to not be able to
sit down for the rest of the night, but right now that would
just be counterproductive. So instead we're going to use an
alternative approach to make sitting down for you *almost*
impossible for the next little while until I think that the lesson
has, shall we say… sunk in."

And here I was thinking I'd gotten off relatively easy all things considered, thought Rhen with a grimace, barely managing to suppress a snort at the notion of how naïve she'd been.

Not giving the younger girl a chance to argue, Dana gripped her firmly by the shoulders and spun her around so that her back was facing the waiting chair. Then with a squeeze, she pushed her gently, yet undeniably firmly, down until she was sitting with the full weight of her freshly spanked bare bottom and thighs resting against the coarse and pointed surface of the mat beneath her.

Rhen immediately saw just why her aunt had called it a punishment mat then.

After less than ten seconds sitting on the stupid thing, her bottom felt like it was being rubbed raw by its prickly and scratchy woven fibers, while at the same time the stiff rubber bristles standing at attention in a tight grid pattern across its surface dug in mercilessly against her tender thighs and sit-spots. It was definitely *not* a pleasant experience to say the least, and at that moment she found the evil, evil mat anything but welcoming.

"Ah! Oh! Oof," she hissed, fighting hard against every instinct she had to spring back up and clutch her aching caboose. "Aunt Dana, come on! This is way too mean. I'm sorry I kept putting off my homework, but there's no way I can focus with this thing digging into me, please."

She was half a breath away from offering to let her spank her again later if she'd just let her up off of that awful mat now, but the throbbing heat that was being reignited and fanned into a whole new level of unpleasantness below her kept her from making that mistake.

"That's why it's called a *punishment* mat, cutie pie," countered Dana breezily, leaning in to tap the tip of the blushing girl's nose playfully with a finger before straightening up and surveying her handiwork with smug satisfaction.

She smiled at the little hisses and moans that bubbled up from Rhen as she tried desperately to shift her weight around to find some small semblance of relief from the non-stop discomfort that she was now in, all the while knowing full well that it was a futile endeavor that would only make things worse for her in the long run. All she'd accomplish by trying to shift her weight around would be to dig another area of her punished hindquarters in even harder against the cruel expanse beneath her. There was no escaping this punishment, and definitely no minimizing it either.

Which was exactly why she'd chosen it.

Still grinning, she stepped around behind her whining niece, and with a firm grip on either side of her chair's laddered back, slid her forward until her squirming thighs were hidden beneath the table in front of her and she was directly facing her laptop.

"Now get to work," she ordered sternly.

Rhen immediately nodded her head, if for no other reason than to avoid making her current situation any worse by showing even the faintest hint of defiance, as she leaned forward to flip open the lid of her computer. She winced and pouted as the movements dug the tips of the bristles in harder against her sit-spots, as if to taunt her and the areas where she'd gotten so many swats just a few minutes earlier.

"Yes ma'am, I'm starting now," she hastened to assure her.

"Good."

All the while she was scrambling to obey, Dana continued to hover just behind her shoulder, watching her movements with a critical eye and taking note of every wince and grimace. She was beyond pleased with the results she was getting so far from her repurposed welcome mat, and was silently congratulating herself on the stroke of creative genius that had given her the idea to make use of it in the first place. And based on the dramatic shift in attitude it was producing in her niece, who as far as she was concerned had *barely* gotten a spanking at all, she would definitely be making use of it again in the future.

It was no public corner time, but it certainly had its merits.

"Oh, and Rhen," she decided to add with a low purr against the squirming girl's ear after she'd snatched up the wooden spoon from where she'd left it on the island, setting it down beside her laptop with a hard clack. "If I catch you doing *anything* other than working on your homework, young lady, you're going to find yourself standing for breakfast, lunch, and dinner for the rest of the week. Is that understood?"

"Yes ma'am!" squeaked Rhen again, meaning it with every ounce of her being as her fingers flew across her keyboard, punching in her password at top speed as her laptop awoke from its hibernation.

"Good, then I'll leave you to it," cooed Dana, giving her shoulder one more quick squeeze as she kissed her cheek.

Straightening up, she made a show of checking the small watch she wore around her left wrist.

"You've got about fifty minutes before that assignment is due, and if I were you, I'd make the most of them."

Rhen didn't bother to answer her this time as she moved off. She was far, far too busy doing exactly as she'd been told to waste any time on idle promises to be good.

—

The better part of the next hour flew by in a blur of wildly unpleasant discomfort and hyper-focus for Rhen as she did her best to ignore the sensation of the punishment mat beneath her cheeks as she wriggled her aching bare bottom again and again atop its cruel surface.

As she lost herself in database layouts and backend APIs, the stiff bristles of the mat continued to work themselves in against her tender flesh. Urged ever deeper thanks to her naturally short legs, which made it impossible for her *not* to rest her full weight against the rasping fibers and protruding points beneath her. With her diminutive height, the balls of her feet barely grazed the tile floor underneath the kitchen table in front of her where she sat, and as a result she was unable to use them to try and possibly leverage some of her weight up and off of the horrible mat.

She was stuck both literally and figuratively, and it *sucked*.

And so Rhen was left hissing and fidgeting constantly as she worked, attempting off and on to try to find a more comfortable position to sit in as she toiled away at her homework. Unfortunately though nothing she did ever seemed to provide any real relief for her exposed skin, and she was forced to endure the sensation of her bottom and thighs being scrubbed raw non-stop, the heat of it almost akin to a never ending barrage of light spanks. It was never enough to really push her past the point of being unable to endure it, but it was always just far enough out of her comfort zone to make ignoring it or tuning it out for more than half a minute at a time impossible.

In short, it was awful.

But at the same time, Rhen's focus seemed to experience a miraculous improvement as well. Spurred on (literally) by the punishment mat beneath her naked caboose and the ever-present threat of wooden spoon looming just off to the side, she quickly fell into a hypnotic work rhythm. Blocking out the world around her, save for the feel of the stiff bristles and coarse fibers relentlessly shifting beneath her squirming thighs, her fingers danced across her keyboard as her mind swirled with ideas and algorithmic solutions.

And much to her own surprise, she actually finished her assignment in its entirety with time to spare, submitting it a whole five minutes before the deadline passed.

"And… done!"

Clicking the submit button and seeing that it went through successfully, she sighed with relief and leaned back in her chair, exhausted. After spending a few moments basking in the afterglow of a job well done, she wiped a forearm across her sweaty brow and tried not to wince too much as her movements pulled free some of the bristles near the tops of her thighs, only to dig in still others around her cheeks even harder.

"Phew."

That had been way too close for comfort, but in the end it had been some of her finest work… somehow.

"I think you mean 'finished', dear," teased Dana as she swooped in beside her with a plate of steaming food fresh from the microwave.

Closing the lid on her niece's laptop for her and pushing it and its mouse aside, she set the plate in front of Rhen, along with a fork and knife, and then pulled out a chair beside her to sit down in.

"Now eat up, and while you do that, you and I are going to have a nice long chat about the importance of not procrastinating."

"Oh goody…" deadpanned Rhen with an impudent smirk as she picked up her utensils and dove into her meal.

All of the running around earlier that afternoon along with the intense thinking she'd just been doing had worked up quite the appetite for her, and she did her best to ignore the glare her aunt gave her for that last bit of sass as she speared a piece of broccoli on the end of her fork and started chewing.

"Go on, I'm listening," she said around a mouthful of vegetables a moment later.

She waved her fork dismissively at the older woman as she chewed, before swallowing hard and shifting uncomfortably as it became clear that her patience was starting to wear thin.

"Uh, ma'am."

"Careful, cutie pie," purred Dana, resting the side of her face against her cupped palm as she smirked and watched the younger girl spear another mouthful of broccoli. "We've got all the time in the world for another spanking now, you know."

"Eep!"

Snickering quietly at the worried squeak that last remark of hers elicited, she went on.

"Now then, let's talk about your homework schedule, shall we?"

—

"Thanks for dinner, Aunt Dana, and I'm sorry again about letting my homework go to the last minute like that," apologized Rhen after she'd finished eating and Dana's lecturing had finally wound down to a close.

She had to admit that the older woman had definitely had more than a few good points to make about how irresponsible it had been of her to let her work pile up unfinished like she had. And when she'd pointed out how her near-catastrophic housing crisis had been largely caused by her dragging her feet on finding a job and not taking it seriously once she had one, Rhen's face had glowed about as red as her bottom beneath her. But even so, she'd somehow managed to power through it all without sniffling too much, and while her aunt had been frank and honest in her assessments of how poorly she'd been behaving, she'd never been unkind about any of it, and when it was all over she'd wrapped her arms around her in a big hug and told her that she was still proud of her.

That had meant a lot to Rhen. Far more than she thought it would.

She just wished that she hadn't kept her perched atop her punishment mat throughout it all.

Well, I guess it certainly helped to drive her points home, she thought to herself with a wry smirk.

Aloud though she said, "I'll just go ahead and take care of these..."

Gathering up their dishes with one hand and pushing her chair back from the table with the other, she kept her face polite and helpful despite the flash of pain it produced in her as she slid far enough back to expose her bare legs and everything in between to the kitchen at large once again. Then, with a grimace, she mentally prepared herself for the herculean task of standing up. Ostensibly so that she could bus their plates to the sink like she was supposed to do whenever dinner was over, but in reality she was prepared to seize upon any excuse she could find to escape that god awful punishment mat for even a moment.

The lecture was over now, so it would probably be fine, she assumed.

Or, at least she hoped.

Apparently though, it wasn't.

"Uh-uh," said Dana with a firm shake of her head, snatching the plates away from her niece before she had a chance to rise, and flashing her a knowing smirk. "Nice try, cutie pie, but you're going to keep that caboose of yours parked right where it is until I say otherwise. You hear me?"

"Ugh, fine," conceded Rhen with a good-natured, though rather petulant, pout as she crossed her arms in front of the minimal swell of her breasts. "But you can't blame me for trying."

"No," agreed the older woman with a laugh as she whisked their plates off to the sink and gave them a quick rinse before placing them inside the dishwasher. "But I can most certainly spank you if you try doing anything like that again, little girl."

Rhen couldn't resist sticking her tongue out at that playful threat, doing her best to ignore the surge of butterflies and the throbbing ache between her legs that those words and her impetuous actions stirred up inside of her.

"Meanie."

"You know," snorted Dana, beaming in open amusement at her bratty antics as she dried her hands off with a dish towel. "You're *very* lucky that you're cute, missy."

That made Rhen blush anew, and coaxed another gratified snort from the older woman as she returned to her seat beside her at the table.

"Alright, hon. Let's take a look at that schedule, shall we?"

During the course of their meal and Dana's scolding, the topic of Rhen's fall semester school schedule had come up. Pursuing a hunch that had been itching at the back of her mind her ever since she'd pulled down the bratty girl's panties over an hour ago, she'd pressed her about it, and Rhen had ended up confessing that she'd been putting off taking several of the required general education core classes that she needed to graduate. This of course had not done her any favors with her aunt, and for a brief moment it seemed as if she might be taking another trip across her knee right there and then, but instead she'd just let out a long sigh through her nose and told her that they would be going over her schedule after dinner.

"You know, I'm not just here to dish out discipline and fondle your adorable backside," she'd said with a mildly annoyed shake of her head. "I'm also going to help you graduate on time and make sure that you learn how to behave like an *actual* adult."

Rhen had bristled slightly at the implication that she wasn't mature enough to handle her own life, but then a twinge of discomfort had made itself known right along her naked left sit-spot and she'd swallowed whatever it was that she'd been about to say. The unfortunate truth was that, yes, she was definitely still a child in a lot of ways, and as much as she hated to admit it, she did in fact need a firm hand to help keep her on track. That had been made abundantly clear to her that evening, if nothing else.

That didn't mean that she had to like it though!

And now that the time had come to revise her schedule, she could definitely feel her heart starting to thud against her chest, hard. She'd just about run out of classes that she could reasonably justify to herself to take instead of her boring general education ones. And as her university's schedule manager loaded up in her web browser, she had the distinct impression that she was about to get another earful from her aunt.

She was right.

"Rhen, honey, are you serious?" demanded the older woman a few moments later as she pinched the bridge of her nose in exasperation. "You're taking Intro to Bowling *and* the Historical Roots of Competitive Dodge Ball next semester? Aren't you supposed to be a computer science major?"

"I mean..."

Rhen shrugged noncommittally and tried not to wince too

much as the movement shifted her weight beneath her against the punishment mat, producing yet another sharp stinging sensation as if it too was expressing its outrage at the ridiculous schedule she'd concocted for herself.

"Um, yeah… I guess so."

"No."

Dana shook her head as she poured all of her disapproval into that single word. She then scrubbed a hand through her long red hair as she rolled her eyes skyward.

"No, no, *no*. This is totally unacceptable, little girl."

Rhen swallowed hard at the other woman's tone, and felt a nervous twinge in her stomach. Being called "little girl" like that tended to end in a very specific way for her, she'd found.

Shaking out her hair, Dana glared at the monitor display before her, running her eyes over her niece's schedule one more time as she cross-referenced it with the very helpful graduation roadmap the website provided for students to see what they still needed to do before they finished school.

"It looks to me like you haven't taken almost *any* of your general ed classes. You're still missing credits for basic math, general science, *and* English. Is that really what I'm seeing here?"

"Maybe…" Rhen only half-confessed, not quite able to bring herself to fully admit just how much she'd been avoiding those classes.

As she stared down at the swirling wood grain of the table in front of her however, a faint trace of color warming her cheeks as she dragged a fingertip along its surface, she knew that her aunt already had the cold hard truth staring her right in the face.

"Well, um… Probably, yeah."

There, I said it. Geez, that was way harder than it should have been. I freaking hate having to own up to stuff like this directly.

"Well this is just totally unacceptable, and we're going to do something about it right now, young lady," declared Dana with a huff, seizing the mouse beside her with a bit more force than was strictly necessary as she dragged the on-screen pointer over to the big green edit button and clicked it. "No niece of mine is going to while away her time in college avoiding taking the classes she needs to tak just because she doesn't like them. No ma'am, uh-uh. Sometimes we have to do things we don't like, and taking boring classes is just one of those things."

Unable to deny that the older woman had hit the nail pretty much square on the head, Rhen just nodded and let out a quiet hiss through her gritted teeth as she scooted her chair in a bit closer so that she could get a better look at her laptop's screen. And together the two of them spent the next half hour carefully pruning and rearranging her schedule for the upcoming fall semester until it at last met with Dana's strict approval.

In the end it wasn't exactly the course load that Rhen would have picked if she'd had her way, obviously. But she had to admit that her aunt had done a pretty good job of filling things out in a way that would definitely keep her busy, but wouldn't crush her under the weight of too many assignments. Assuming of course, that she actually did them on time; which she very much intended to.

One time on the punishment mat was more than enough to drive that particular lesson home.

It was definitely going to be a much busier semester than she was accustomed to, that was for sure, but at least she'd be that much closer to graduating once it was all over. Plus she still had Mondays off along with most of Friday, and as a happy little bonus, she even got to keep her Intro to Bowling class.

All in all, Rhen found that it was a schedule that she could live with. And truth be told, it was long overdue.

Chapter 13

Sandcastles and Spanked Bottoms

Rhen soon fell into a steady routine as the weeks flew by and the summer semester wound down to a close. Every morning her aunt would wake her up around eight. Either in person by throwing back the curtains on her window to let in the early rays of morning sunshine as birds chirped away happily in the distance. Or else by calling for her from the foot of the stairs after she'd slapped the snooze button on her alarm clock one too many times, coaxing her out of bed with the mouth-watering scents of a hot breakfast wafting up from somewhere in the kitchen down below.

They would then share a quiet breakfast together while she gradually shook off the last vestiges of drowsiness still clinging to her like cobwebs. Fully coming awake as she filled her stomach with whatever her aunt had whipped up for her that morning and drinking down a tall glass or two of orange juice. Truth be told, she would have much preferred a soda or maybe even some coffee instead of the pulpy juice, but whenever she asked for either of those things Dana would just cluck her tongue disapprovingly and shake her head, putting a stop to the discussion before it even had a chance to get started.

"You're way too young to be relying on caffeine to get you going in the morning, dear," she'd admonish with a warm smile around the rim of her own steaming mug of premium dark roast. "A healthy breakfast and some juice is exactly what a girl your age needs to grow up nice and strong. Now quit giving me that dirty look and finish your eggs before you wind up eating them standing up."

After their breakfast dishes had been cleared away they would then typically split up and go about their separate ways for the rest of the day. And on those days that Rhen didn't have off from school, this usually involved her riding her bike over to campus since Dana had her hands full with the daycare and couldn't give her a ride. Which was honestly just fine with her since the university was only a few miles away from their house and the ride there gave her plenty of time to clear her head and attempt to adopt a more mature air about herself so that she hopefully wouldn't stick out quite as much in her young teen attire.

Unfortunately though, that never seemed to quite work out, and more often than not she found herself having to deal with the amused snickers or dismissive eye-rolls of her fellow students as she sat among them in lectures or else waited in line to ask her professors a question after class was over. It was definitely annoying and more than a little embarrassing to be sure, but she supposed that it could always have been worse.

At least most people just assumed that she was a freshman in high school getting an early start on her college credits, as opposed to being smack dab in the middle of seventh grade, or else something even worse. It wasn't much, but it was better than nothing. And after that mother of a spanking she'd received in her dorm room with so many of her friends watching on from the open doorway on the night that she'd moved out, Rhen was only too happy to take whatever little victories she could get.

She just wished that her former dorm buddies would stop saying hello to her with a casual slap on the butt, or else asking her if she'd been behaving herself lately.

The jerks.

Those little swat-greetings weren't unbearable though, and she'd quickly gotten used to them, but that didn't stop her from finding excuses to stay home whenever she could. Which meant that on the days that she didn't have to be on campus, she wound up spending a lot of her free time hanging out with the other kids that Dana looked after for her daycare.

Mostly by choice.

If she'd had her way, she would have spent the majority of those days hiding out inside her bedroom playing around on her computer and only emerging at noon to eat lunch with the others so that she could at least pretend that she wasn't actually supposed to be one of them. But her bossy boots auntie would have none of it, and insisted that she at least spend a couple of hours, up until lunch time at the very least, playing with all of the kids who'd been dropped off by their parents after breakfast that morning.

"Nobody likes a grumpy goose who spends all day sulking in her room just because she thinks she's too old to have fun with children a bit younger than she is," she would scold, wagging an admonishing forefinger at her that carried a very real, silent promise that a spanking would be forthcoming if she didn't do as she was told. "Besides, it'll do you a world of good to socialize more and get some of that pent-up energy out of your system before you hit the books. Now you get that cute little caboose of yours moving before I move it for you!"

Although the warning was a serious one, the words were always accompanied by a sly grin and a little wink that dulled the edge of them enough to make them easy to swallow, and Rhen would scurry off to join in on whatever game was already in progress on the floor below without needing a swat or two to send her on her way. And more frequently than she would have liked to admit, she found herself being swept up into some silly shenanigan or another with the other kids her aunt looked after, and would wind up spending all of her afternoon playing with them instead of hanging out by herself in her bedroom like she'd planned.

In fact, it happened enough times that after a week or two she was willing to admit that Dana *might* have had a point about her needing to socialize more.

Not that she'd ever tell her that without one heck of a spanking to loosen her lips first, of course.

After everyone else had gone home for the day, the two of them would then meet up again to eat dinner either at home, or else at a nearby restaurant so that Dana could have a chance to get out of the house for a little while. They'd talk about their respective days as they ate, enjoying each other's company and just unwinding as they tried to decide what they wanted to do that evening, before Dana would ask about whether or not Rhen had any homework that she still needed to take care of.

As much as the both of them enjoyed spending their time together at night as a burgeoning couple, she refused to budge an inch on making sure that her adorable little "niece" lived up to her full academic potential. And if she decided that she'd rather play all afternoon instead of working on her home-work, then she had nobody to blame but herself when her panties came down for a brisk spanking after dinner.

After all, rules were rules, weren't they?

And if there was one thing that Dana Johnson loved doing with the raven-haired sophomore that she was now involved with, it was enforcing the rules.

Later on at night, about an hour before it was time for her to go to bed, Rhen would usually slip away to indulge herself in a long and luxurious shower, basking in the delicious heat of the steaming water without having to worry about anybody barging in on her. Well, most of the time. Dana liked to wait until she'd been soaking for a while before poking her head in to give her an earful if she'd noticed that she hadn't finished doing some chore or another. Though thankfully so far she hadn't made good on any of her threats to haul her out and show her what a spanking on a wet bottom felt like.

Not yet anyway.

After showering, Rhen would then brush her teeth and change into her sky blue pajamas, and Dana would tuck her in under her covers with a kiss goodnight. And if she'd behaved herself well that day, then she'd fall asleep comfortably resting on her back.

More often than not however, she wound up drifting off to dreamland lying on her side with her bottom cheeks bearing at least a faint trace of redness to them from some spanking or another that she'd managed to collect during the day. As it turned out, she apparently had a natural talent for finding new and creative ways to nettle her aunt. Ways that always seemed to end with her being draped bare bottom up across her lap so that she could return the favor tenfold.

But on the bright side, at least Missus Hairbrush had yet to make a return visit since that bedtime spanking nearly three weeks ago. (Although she had a gut feeling that her luck was swiftly running out in that regard as well.)

All in all though, Rhen found that she really didn't mind getting spanked all that much.

Well, after the fact at any rate.

In a strange, stomach-churning way, she'd discovered that courting danger and the risk of a going to bed with a sore bottom was actually a lot of fun. And while she most certainly made an effort to behave herself and adhere to the rules and schedule that Dana had provided for her (something that she was actually quite grateful for now that she was starting to see some of the benefits from them), she didn't let herself get too upset whenever her panties inevitably found their way south for a spanking.

After all, it was just a part of life for her now, and something that a growing part of her understood that she needed.

Something that she *craved*.

She just had to be extra careful not to slip up too much until after everyone else had gone home for the day, or else she'd wind up with a giggling gaggle of preteens and tweens teasing her all afternoon.

—

On one particularly sunny and warm afternoon, just after Rhen had finished off the last of her finals for the semester, her aunt decided that it would be a fun idea to shepherd everyone off to the local neighborhood park for an impromptu field trip. While her back yard was certainly big enough for running around and swinging, it definitely couldn't hold a candle to the mammoth playscapes, winding jogging paths, and various other sport courts and fields that the park a few blocks away from her house had to offer.

"We've got to take advantage of the nice weather before it starts to turn. Fall is just around the corner, and before you know it it'll be way too chilly to run around and play without bundling up. So come on, kiddos, it's off to the park we go!"

Rhen had at first tried to say that she wasn't interested in going when Dana had made the announcement over lunch that afternoon, but her feeble excuses had been brushed aside by the older woman without a second thought.

"You know that 'I don't feel like it' isn't a valid excuse in this house, young lady," she'd said with a casually dismissive wave of her hand that made it obvious that the matter wasn't up for discussion. "And based on your behavior these last few weeks, I'm not sure you're actually responsible enough to be left on your own at home quite yet anyway. So you're coming with us, and that's that."

Rather than protest further and risk finishing her lunch with her shorts and panties bunched up around her ankles, Rhen had wisely chosen to keep her mouth shut and just nodded as she busied herself with taking an extra-large bite of her turkey sandwich.

The prospect of being lumped in with a bunch of tweens out in public, as opposed to the privacy of her and Dana's home where she at least had the high fences in their back yard to shield her privacy, had butterflies roiling around inside of her stomach. Thankfully though, the older woman's refusal at least didn't seem all that out of the ordinary to any of her gathered friends who were also hard at work scarfing down the rest of their lunches as fast as they could so that they could go play sooner. After all, she *was* just thirteen as far as any of them knew. Of course her aunt would want to keep an eye on her instead of leaving her home alone all day.

And so after a quick round of cleaning up in the kitchen once every plate had been cleared of food, they all threw on their shoes and socks and began making the short trek down to the park, Rhen in tow right beside Dana at the head of them all.

—

Much to her own mixed relief and annoyance, Rhen found that she had no problems blending right in with everyone else running around and having a blast at the park that afternoon. Not a single person, adult or otherwise, pointed her out as being out of place among the other playing kids, and she quickly found herself being drawn into a pick-up game of red rover that left her winded and sweaty by the time she finally decided that she'd had enough of it.

As much as she would have liked to believe that her easy anonymity was a result of her flawless acting abilities and not just her natural inclination toward behaving like someone nearly half her age, she knew that a large part of why she went unnoticed by all of the adults around her was due to the outfit that she happened to be wearing. Dressed as she was in a pastel pink t-shirt with a smug emoji emblazoned across its front and a pair of snug denim shorts that ended just above her knees, to say nothing of the white ankle socks peeking out from the tops of her tennis shoes, she knew that she fit the picture of an overexcited teen running around the busy park at top speed all too well.

And to her own great surprise, she found that she really didn't mind.

She was having way too much fun playing with her friends to worry about whether or not a bunch of random strangers mistook her for just another kid out with her aunt, instead of a whip-smart college sophomore enjoying her day off from classes.

She was dressed the part, so she might as well enjoy herself and act like it, right?

—

An hour or two later however, Rhen came to regret that blasé attitude of hers just a little bit. Because as she soon discovered, blending in as well as she did with the other kids around her also meant that nobody batted an eyelash when she wound up being disciplined like one as well.

After she'd gotten her fill of running around the open grass fields and seeing who could jump the furthest from the swing sets, she'd decided to unwind by spending some time alone amid the volleyball courts. But it wasn't the sport itself that she'd had in mind. No, instead she'd spent the last half-hour playing around in the sand of an unoccupied court, doing her best to arrange it into something at least sort of resembling a sandcastle.

It was a lot harder going than she'd originally thought it would be since she didn't have a bucket or trowel to work with. As a result, she'd been forced to move around the loose, summer-warmed granules using just her cupped hands, and at first she'd had very little luck in getting them to cooperate. But after a bit of trial and error, she'd managed to dig up some wetter and more malleable building materials from about half a foot below the sun-kissed surface of the court, and with that her little fortress had started to shape up quite nicely.

Albeit somewhat primitively.

It's more of a mud hut than it is a fancy castle, but I still like it, she mused to herself as she hummed happily, carefully patting the sloping walls of her creation with her palms to help firm them up against possible attacks from enemy forces.

She'd already had one side collapse on her earlier, and she didn't want a repeat of that tragedy if she could at all avoid it.

"Heads up!"

Rhen heard the warning just as a white and black soccer ball came careening into the back wall of the fortress that she'd just finished repairing, obliterating it along with most of the central tower and the armory as it embedded itself into the sand before her.

"What the hell?" she spluttered, spitting out dirt and debris as she beheld the ruins of the once beautiful seat of power for the Sand Kingdom.

"Sorry about that," panted a boy of around twelve as he

jogged up to where she sat kneeling amid her destroyed sand-castle, her face flushing hot scarlet with anger. "Hey, throw the ball back, would ya?"

"You want your *ball* back?" she snarled, livid as she shot to her feet to tower no more than an inch or two above the shocked boy as she continued to berate him. "Just *look* at what your stupid ball did to my sandcastle!"

She pointed at the crumbled mound of semi-moist sand that was all that remained of her masterpiece as she glowered.

"Hey, back off! It was just an accident!" snapped the boy as he got over his initial shock at being yelled at by some random girl and started to go on the offensive himself. "It wasn't even that good to begin with, so why are you making such a big deal about it? Just build another one, geez."

His friends, a few of them kids from her aunt's daycare among them, had gravitated toward the two of them now, drawn in largely by Rhen's yelling and wild arm-flailing at her ruined work. They stood by and watched eagerly to see what would happen next, knowing that a fight was surely brewing.

Having an audience to her momentary freak-out pushed Rhen past the point of caring about her actions for the time being as the other boy's words made her see red. And without thinking, she took a quick couple of steps forward and pushed him as hard as she could. Caught off guard by the sudden move, he lost his balance almost immediately and flopped down hard onto his rear end on the volleyball court, its loose sand cushioning the blow significantly.

"How about *you* go fuck yourself, you little shit!"

Her words drew out a chorus of horrified gasps from the knot of on-looking children. She had definitely not been quiet as she'd shouted them, and that combined with pushing the boy had been more than enough to shock them all into a momentary stunned silence.

But before a proper fight could break out between Rhen and the boy she didn't even know however, Dana had swooped in to interpose herself between the two of them, separating them with a tight grip on her still-fuming niece's shoulder that kept her from taking another step.

"Rhen Elizabeth Mathews, just what on earth has gotten into you, young lady?" she demanded, shaking her slightly as she brought the girl's full name to bear against her. "I cannot *believe* what I just saw! Have you lost your dang mind, little girl?"

Her aunt's sharp words and the use of her middle name were enough to drain the anger right out of Rhen, making her knees wobble as the cold twisting horror of what she'd just done poured like an avalanche into the pit of her stomach to replace it.

"Oh my god, I am *so* sorry!" she blurted out all at once, panic-stricken and waving her hands in front of her as if she could somehow use them to take back the last couple of minutes. That wasn't going to work though, she knew, and so instead she forced herself to relax as much as she could and swallowed hard against the rising tide of anxiety roiling around inside of her. "Um, are you okay?"

"Uh… yeah," the boy answered awkwardly as he scooted away from her a bit and climbed back to his feet.

As he stood there dusting off the back of his shorts, it was pretty obvious that only his pride had been hurt in their little scuffle, thankfully. Now he was clearly doing his best to look disinterested so that his friends wouldn't have more ammunition to tease him with later. Being pushed over by a girl was bad enough as it was already.

"Don't worry about it, um… it was nothing."

Oh thank god, thought Rhen to herself with a little choked out sigh. She had no idea how she would have been able to handle it if she'd actually hurt the little twerp.

Her relief was short-lived however as Dana's hand shifted itself down from her shoulder to her upper arm in a silent warning that things were far from over.

"What's your name, sweetheart?" the older woman asked the grimacing boy, her gentle tone in direct opposition to the vice-like grip she had around the spot just above Rhen's elbow.

"Kyle Delaney, ma'am," he answered, his voice cracking slightly as he did so.

Honestly, it would have been cute if Rhen hadn't been so busy trying to deal with the aerial armada of butterflies swarming around inside her stomach just then.

"Well, Kyle, I'm very happy to hear that you're not hurt," continued her aunt, keeping her tone civil and polite even as Rhen heard the grim resolve bubbling just beneath its surface. "And since you were the wronged party here, I think that it's only fair that you have a front row seat to the spanking that my bratty little niece is about to get. Wouldn't you say?"

With those words, she gave Rhen's arm a slight tug, forcing her to take half a step forward as her face flushed with heat once again.

"Aunt Dana, no, please," she started to whine, one hand flying back to cover the seat of her sand-encrusted shorts as she bobbed her weight from foot to foot. "It was just an accident! He said he was fine, can't we leave it at that and move on?"

Rhen's pleas fell on deaf ears however, going completely ignored by Dana as she continued to smile warmly at the boy in front of her.

He looked about as shocked as she felt right then, though without any of the thigh-squirming panic that was churning around inside of her.

Thank god I look as young as I do. So long as nobody here ever finds out how old I really am, I should be fine... Oh god, what am I saying?!

"So, young man, does that sound okay to you?"

The question had the boy's, Kyle's, face lighting up as his initial trepidation gave way to no small amount of vengeful glee. Apparently he wasn't as willing to let things go as he'd originally seemed to be as he nodded his head emphatically. The prospect of watching a cute older girl get hauled across her aunt's knee for a spanking like a small child more than making up for any loss in reputation with his friends as far as he was concerned.

"Oh heck yeah, that sounds *awesome*!"

Dana just chuckled at his enthusiasm and flashed him a tight smile that sobered him up a bit.

"Uh, ma'am," he added quickly with a chagrinned look that didn't quite reach his eyes.

"Yes, I doubt that Little Miss Rhen here will be forgetting this lesson anytime soon either," observed the older woman dryly, returning the boy's smirk with a wink of her own. "Now then, come along you two. There's still plenty of sunshine left, so let's get this taken care of and then you both can get back to enjoying it, alright?"

Mortified, Rhen kept her eyes locked firmly on the toes of her tennis shoes as she was frog-marched by the elbow away from the volleyball courts and over to the stone and wood pavilion that Dana and a few of the other parents had been sitting at, making idle small talk while their kids ran around and played.

"Sorry in advance for the noise, folks, but someone here needs a spanking, I'm afraid."

Any hopes that she might have had to postpone this particular punishment for until after she and her aunt had gotten home were dashed as the gathered adults around the various tables under the shade of the pavilion only broke away from whatever it was they'd been doing long enough to give a dismissive wave or flash an approving look toward them as they strode through their midst.

"No problem."

"Go for it."

"Be my guest."

"Yeah, tan her butt good," piped up one particularly haughty sounding mom. "I saw how she pushed that poor boy down. You make sure that girl learns a thing or two about playing nice, you hear?"

"That's the plan," answered Dana with a low laugh as they stepped past the woman, Rhen flashing her a dirty look that only seemed to deepen her smug satisfaction.

Although she'd only extended the offer to watch her spank her niece to Kyle, that hadn't stopped the rest of the kids that he'd been playing soccer with, or who'd just so happened to be standing around at the time when the confrontation had taken place, from following after them as well. And so instead of just one witness to her humiliation, Rhen looked back to discover that she now had close to a dozen kids eagerly trailing after her and her aunt.

Eep!

"But Aunt Dana, it was that stupid ball of his that ruined my sandcastle in the first place!" she started to whine again, throwing a dirty look over her shoulder toward the widely grinning Kyle who was keeping an easy pace with them just a few feet behind.

Panic over her impending, and unfortunately very public,

spanking had overridden her initial embarrassment and acceptance that she'd been the one at fault as she continued to press
for leniency.

"I swear it won't ever happen again, and that I'm really,
really, *really* sorry! Can't I have just one more chance, pretty
please?"

"That is no excuse at all, and you know it!" snapped her
aunt, tightening her grip on her upper arm and not slowing
her long-legged stride in the slightest as they neared an unoccupied bench at the far end of the pavilion. "And we *both*
know that you know better than to act that way, Rhen. Flying
off the handle like that over something so trivial is completely
unacceptable, young lady. To say nothing of that *filthy* language I heard coming from your mouth, either."

Indignant despite the hot blush staining her cheeks a bright
shade of red, Rhen opened her mouth to argue that she hadn't
really said anything all *that* terrible, but immediately thought
better of it. Clamping her jaw shut again and gritting her teeth
instead, she fixed Dana with an impudent scowl and let her
lead her on toward her doom.

"Oh yes, little girl," confirmed the older woman in a low
purr, completely unfazed by her glower. "You and I will most
certainly be addressing that potty mouth of yours later on
when we get home, believe you me."

Well, shit.

Rhen continued to pout silently, if for no other reason
than to have something to do while her heart thudded like a
jackhammer against the inside of her chest and her stomach
writhed with that all too familiar mixture of anticipation and
anxiety. Much to her own dismay, she found that she was
unable to muster up any kind of viable excuse or counter-
argument to anything that her aunt had just said to her and
instead just let out an irritated little huff, resigning herself to

her fate as they at last came to a stop in front of a low stone bench near the far edge of the pavilion.

With her usual confident grace, Dana let go of her arm and turned to sit herself down in the middle of the backless, armless bench. She then fixed her with a cool, assessing look as she ran an eye over her from head to toe, frowning. Deliberately ignoring the small crowd of children they'd managed to gather during their short march to the bench she now sat perched upon, she clucked her tongue in disapproval and then leaned forward to spend several long and embarrassing moments attempting to brush away the crusted-on sand and dirt that was still clinging to Rhen's once clean clothes.

She shook out her still mostly-lovely pastel pink t-shirt a few times and then slapped the back of her shorts hard enough to make her wince, before doing much the same with the fronts and sides of her thighs as well. And while she managed to knock away a fair bit of the crumbly sand from the girl's grimy garments, there was little she could do about the darker stains still plastered across her knees and the seat of her shorts.

"Goodness gracious, what a mess. These are definitely going to have to go straight into the laundry as soon as we get home," she tut-tutted to herself at the state of Rhen's filthy outfit, plucking at the hem of her t-shirt with her thumb and forefinger as she pursed her lips into a grimace. "And *you*, my dear, are going straight into a bath after dinner."

Rhen merely bit her lower lip at her aunt's mild scolding and nodded, the tips of her ears growing all the hotter as Kyle and his stupid jerk friends snickered from somewhere just behind her.

Oh shut up, you dweebs…

Shifting her voice from stern disapproval to steely determination, Dana's full lips twitched upward into the barest hint of a challenging smirk as she locked eyes with the blushing girl standing in front of her.

"Let's get you ready then, shall we?"

"Ready?" squeaked Rhen, already knowing what the other woman meant, but hoping that stalling would somehow get her to change her mind about what was about to happen all the same. "Um, is that um... really... uh, you know... necessary?"

"Oh yes, I think it is," cooed Dana with a knowing look that made her squirm adorably as she leaned forward to take hold of the waistband of her denim shorts on either side of her hips. "Now you just hold still for a bit while Auntie Dana gets you ready for your spanking. Okeydokey, cutie pie?"

Oh god, here we go... lamented Rhen internally, even as a mortified groan of despair squeezed itself out from between her pouting lips.

The elastic waistband of her shorts gave only the faintest hint of resistance as her aunt's tugging fingers pulled at it, stretching away from her slim hips more than enough so that the soft denim material could easily be tugged down to hang bunched up around her knees in one smooth motion.

"My goodness, that girl at Cashman's was certainly onto something when she suggested we buy you shorts with an easy-pull waistband," she observed with open amusement as Rhen's hands fluttered helplessly at her sides, curling and uncurling themselves into little fists as a fresh wave of humiliation washed over her. "These are *so* much easier to get down than those ratty old jeans of yours were."

Yeah, who would've ever been able to guess that?

The fact that she was wearing a relatively non-childish pair of panties that afternoon, ones that were snow white with hot pink trim running along their waistband and leg holes, was of very little comfort to Rhen as she felt well over a dozen pairs of eyes moving to trace along the chubby curves of her bottom inside of them.

"Guess I should've worn a belt then," she murmured darkly, attempting to distract herself with a bit of snarky sass and choosing to ignore the fact that her shorts didn't actually have any belt loops. "And I hope that stupid clerk choked on her commission."

Dana's response to this was to whisk her panties down to join her shorts around her knees without any warning.

"What was that, dear?" she asked with an arched brow, the edges of her mouth tightening into a disapproving line at the grumbled words. "Don't tell me we need to schedule a visit from Missus Hairbrush before bed tonight for that attitude of yours, do we?"

"No ma'am!" squeaked Rhen as one hand flew down to cover her hairless front, while the other hovered awkwardly behind her in an attempt to shield her as yet still pale backside from view.

Her knees bowed slightly under the weight of another potential spanking, let alone a session with that awful ebony hairbrush laying ready and waiting on the nightstand beside her bed for whenever it was needed next, and she quickly added, "I'll be good, I'm sorry."

That definitely got a round of chuckles from Kyle and his friends, along with several of the parents who'd turned now to watch the show.

"That's better," replied her aunt sharply, before pointing at the tops of her thighs with a manicured fingernail. "Now you get that tush of yours over my knee right now, young lady. Chop, chop!"

"Right, okay, I'm coming!"

Definitely not in the mood to argue anymore at that point, Rhen shuffled her way over to Dana's right side just as quickly as she could, the shorts and panties bunched up around her knees slowing her progress considerably. Once there, she looked down at the expanse of wide lap waiting for her and swallowed hard, before allowing herself to be tipped forward to lay across her strong legs with a little grunt.

"Oof."

Well, at least my front is out of sight now, she tried to tell herself, clamping her thighs together nice and tight in an attempt to avoid showing off anything more than she absolutely had to while she squirmed into as comfortable a position as she could manage along the stone bench beneath her. *Not that it really makes much of a difference, I suppose...*

Gritting her teeth, she felt a hot flush creep up her neck to the roots of her long, black hair as the warm summer breeze still managed to trace a tickling fingertip along the naturally-parted crevice between her cheeks. Making her wriggle slightly as her semi-exposed rosebud clenched and unclenched in anticipation of her impending punishment.

This freaking sucks.

"Young lady, do you have anything to say for yourself before we begin?" asked Dana sternly, her right hand palming her left cheek as she spoke. "Anything, perhaps, that you might want to say to young Mister Kyle here?"

Grinding her teeth and clamping down on every instinct she had to remain quiet and avoid embarrassing herself further, Rhen turned her head to the side where she found the boy and his friends staring at her stretched out across her aunt's lap with rapt attention, mouths practically hanging open with shock and delight.

"Sorry for pushing you," she mumbled half-heartedly at him, not quite meeting his eye.

SMACK-SMACK!

"What was that? Speak up now, dear."

"Ack!" grunted Rhen, jerking forward and squirming her hips more from surprise than any actual pain caused by the two sharp swats that had just landed directly against the centers of each of her cheeks.

Forcing herself to take a deep breath, she sighed through her nostrils and turned her head once again to the side to say nice and clearly for all to hear.

"I'm sorry for pushing you, Kyle."

"And...?"

She felt her stomach tighten once more as Dana's hand squeezed her right cheek warningly, and then she squeaked.

"And for swearing at you!" she added hurriedly, the words coming out in a jumbled mess as her legs straightened out behind her as if she'd just been shocked by lightning.

"There we go," cooed Dana, patting her jiggly rump affectionately before giving it a little rub. "And you, Kyle? Is there maybe something that *you* would like to say to Rhen as well?"

Seemingly startled to be addressed so directly by the intimidating older woman with the young teenage girl stretched bare bottom up across her knee, Kyle jumped and nodded as fast as he could, swallowing hard before answering.

"Um, I'm sorry that our ball ruined your sandcastle."

"See, now was that so hard?" asked Rhen's aunt in that patronizing way that adults sometimes used whenever they were explaining something to very young children, arching an eyebrow as she drummed her fingertips over the handprint she'd left on her niece's right cheek.

"No ma'am," the two youngsters both answered at the same time.

"I thought not."

232

With her impromptu lesson in conflict resolution now over, Dana gave Rhen's bouncy buns a few more test pats as she prepared herself to settle into her usual spanking rhythm.

Still mortified, even more so now as she realized just how much of a child she'd been acting like, Rhen nevertheless quickly stuck out her tongue at the smugly-smirking boy standing beside her while her aunt's attention was focused on her lower cheeks.

"You're still a jerk," she mouthed at him before flashing him a sheepish grin.

To which he had the nerve to actually wink at her before darting his own tongue out for a brief moment.

Oh, you little brat!

"Now then, let's get this over with, shall we?"

"Humph. Yes ma'am…"

With those last few words, Rhen folded her arms under her chin with a pout while her aunt began to swat the upturned, naked bottom perched across her lap hard and fast.

SMACK! SMACK! SMACK!

Though much of her initial anger had cooled off by then, that didn't stop Dana from bringing her palm down at full force over and over again for several long and extremely painful minutes. She had every intention of reducing the bratty sophomore to tears with this spanking, and resolved not to ease up on her in the slightest until she'd at least reached that goal and then some.

As it turned out though, she didn't have to wait for long before Rhen started sobbing.

Between the roiling fury in her frantically gyrating cheeks and thighs from the non-stop smacks raining down on them, and the massive amount of humiliation that her aunt had been so careful to mix in throughout it all, she began to cry less than five minutes into her spanking.

"Oh my god- Ack! I'm sorry- Oh! I'm sorry I pushed him!"

"That's right, little girl, you *should* be sorry," scolded Dana, feeding off of the younger girl's frantic energy and doing her best to provide her with a memorable punishment. "I cannot believe you thought that that was okay. We use our *words* to solve our problems. Do you understand me?"

"Owie, owie, owie! Yes ma'am- Ah! I do!"

SMACK! SMACK! SMACK!

After continuing for an additional five minutes to *really* make sure that the lesson had fully been driven home, Dana finally slowed down and then eventually stopped, panting slightly as she rested her stinging palm along the undercurve of her niece's bright red and burning backside.

She allowed Rhen to continue to lie across her lap for several long moments after that, as she gasped and sniffled, working hard to regain her composure and master her sobbing. When she had at last quieted down enough so that only the occasional sniffle or hiccup escaped from her wobbling lips, she helped her back to her feet, intentionally leaving her shorts and panties right where they were, tangled up around her ankles. Dana then rose up to follow after her, placing her hands firmly on her shoulders as she turned her around to face Kyle and his friends.

By now their wide grins had shrunken back into merely satisfied up-tilts at the corners of their mouths, tempered in no small part by the tears they'd just seen the sniffling girl in front of them shed. And as she was turned to face them, all of their faces went about as red as Rhen's bottom and thighs were as they caught sight of the unobstructed view between her legs that was suddenly put on display before them.

Not that she really noticed any of that at first.

Rhen was far too busy shifting from foot to foot, trying to massage away some of the throbbing ache from her ruby red caboose to really care about something so trivial as modesty or dignity at that particular moment.

"Okay you two, shake hands and let's put this whole unpleasant incident behind us, alright?"

Despite the order and the bit of steel that still remained in the older woman's voice, neither Rhen nor Kyle took a step toward one another, both of them too absorbed in the moment to make the first move.

Rolling her eyes at the pair of them, Dana then gave her niece a sharp swat on the behind that had her bunny-hopping forward a step or two with a hiss.

"Now."

That certainly got them moving.

"Uh, sorry about you know…"

Despite being the one who had been pushed down in the first place, Kyle still made the apology as he took Rhen's proffered hand with his and gave it a couple of awkward shakes before letting go and taking a step back into the perceived safety of his knot of friends.

"Me too," sniffled Rhen, her face lighting up in a watery smile even as her left hand did its best to surreptitiously pull down the front of her t-shirt in an attempt to cover herself up.

"There we go, no hard feelings," declared Dana with a broad grin as she squatted down behind her niece and tickled the backs of her knees before she began to disentangle her clothes from one another.

After a few deft movements, she had her white and pink panties pulled free from where they'd gotten caught in her shorts and then had them traveling back up her legs, arranging them around her now swollen cheeks once again. She then paused for a moment to admire the pink glow that managed to shine through the tautly stretched material, before reaching for her shorts next. They too followed up her legs, and Rhen hissed as the comparatively rough-feeling denim rasped over her tender thighs and bottom before it too was once more secured in place around her waist.

"Now then, why don't all of you go play some more?" she suggested gently as she rose back to her feet and dusted off her hands. "There's still about half an hour left before we need to head home, you know."

"Sure," agreed Kyle with a shrug as he and his friends turned to leave, Rhen giving one last great big sniffle as she made to follow after them.

"Oh, and Rhen," Dana added in a low purr, halting her in her tracks with a firm hand on her shoulder. "Don't think I've forgotten about that potty mouth of yours, little girl. You and I will definitely be addressing *that* as soon as we get home, understand?"

She did, and only all too well.

"But Aunt Dana, come *on*!" protested Rhen, a pit yawning open in the bottom of her stomach as she whirled to face the older woman, hands balling into fists at her sides as she stomped a foot in petulant disbelief. "You *just* spanked me. That is so not fair!"

But her aunt just met her glower with a cool disapproving arch of her brows that had the younger girl backing down almost immediately.

"I mean... Um, please, Aunt Dana, wasn't that spanking enough to cover both the fighting and the swearing?"

It wasn't, and they both knew it, even as Dana shook her head with a frown.

"After the things I heard coming out of your mouth, cutie

pie, you'd better believe that there's a bar of soap with your name on it waiting for you at home. And unless you'd like me to throw in *another* spanking before we get to that, I'd suggest you stop arguing and go enjoy the time you have left at the park."

Not waiting to hear out any more of Rhen's excuses or whining, she spun her back around gently by the shoulder and sent her scurrying off toward the playscapes with a hard slap to the dirty seat of her denim shorts.

SMACK!

"Go on now, shoo!"

Leading the charge past Kyle and his friends, all of whom had slowed down to eavesdrop on the two of them, Rhen sped away as fast as her feet could carry her. Her ponytail bobbing after her as she ignored the winces of pain that each sprinting stride produced in her sore and swollen bottom.

"Yes ma'am, I'm going!"

Snorting to herself in wry amusement, Dana watched the adorable younger girl's retreating form as it disappeared somewhere among the swing sets before she moved off to rejoin the other adults she'd been chatting with before this little interruption. She wiped a forearm across her sweaty brow and sighed as she leaned back against the edge of one of the picnic tables under the pavilion, gratefully accepting a bottle of water from the mom who'd cheered her on as she'd dragged Rhen over to the bench earlier.

"Geez, now *that* was a workout."

Chapter 14

A Taste of Discipline

Despite the looming dread starting to gnaw at the base of her stomach, Rhen still made a valiant attempt to try and look on the bright side of things as she and Dana led the gaggle of kids from her daycare back home through the neighborhood after they'd had their fill of playing in the park that afternoon.

Instead of dwelling on the punishment that she knew she still had coming, she did her best to try and focus on the fact that it was only a few short blocks from the park to her auntie's house, which meant that she only had to put up with the uncomfortable sensation of having her snug denim shorts rubbing against her still-tender bottom with every step for a little while longer. Once they were back home she could slip away to her bedroom and change into a loose skirt and ditch her panties so that her buns could have a chance to cool off for a bit before dinner. Not to mention that once everyone else had left for the evening, she'd be able to hide out in her bedroom and forget all about the embarrassing stuff that had happened to her at the park that afternoon as she played some video games and chatted with her friends online.

Really, honestly, things were starting to look up for her.

Kind of...

Unfortunately though, the trip back home being a short one also meant that they made it back that much sooner, which in turn meant that an end had come to her brief reprieve from further punishment. At last the time had come to deal with her "potty mouth" as Dana had taken to calling it as she'd tut-tutted to herself disapprovingly all the way back to their house. And that cast a rather dark shadow over the meager bright side that Rhen had been trying to warm herself in.

Well, shit.

Even with the impending mouth soaping that she knew she had coming, she couldn't help but smirk a little at the rebellious thought. Although she *did* make doubly sure to keep her lips firmly pressed together while she thought it, just in case.

Once they were all inside, everyone else except for Rhen and her aunt immediately dashed off to go play some more before their parents or older siblings arrived to pick them up in an hour or so; though in reality both she and Dana knew that they were actually just retreating to out of the way hiding spots from which they'd be able to watch all of the upcoming excitement without running the risk of being scolded for it. Which left just the two of them standing "alone" in the entryway hall, with Rhen waiting anxiously for whatever was about to happen next as she kicked off her dirty tennis shoes and toed them over to join the rest of the recently discarded sneakers and high-tops piled up beside the welcome mat.

She wasn't left waiting for long.

Planting her hands on her hips, the stern, red-headed older woman fixed her with her best no-nonsense glare.

"Young lady, those clothes are absolutely *filthy*, and I want you out of them this instant," she said in a tone that made it very clear that she wasn't making a request. Extending out a hand, palm up, she went on to add. "I need to get them into the washing machine before they stain, so hurry up. You can keep your panties and camisole on if you'd like, but I want you down to your undies. *Now.*"

Although Rhen had been expecting something like this to happen just as soon as she'd walked in through the front door, the order still had her stomach tightening and her heart leaping in her chest.

Everyone has already seen me in my panties once today, so it's not that big of a deal, right? she tried to reassure herself, even though she wasn't quite able to buy her own line of logic.

"Fine…." she said with a roll of her eyes, stretching the word out into a petulant groan as she reluctantly moved to do as she'd been told.

Balancing on first one foot and then the other, and managing to only hop around a little bit, she slipped off her dirty socks from her feet one at a time and handed them over to her patiently waiting aunt. Then with a grimace, she gripped the hem of her t-shirt as a fresh wave of butterflies started to stir up inside her stomach, and pulled it up and off of her slim torso as well.

Shaking it out a couple of times, Rhen winced as she saw just how dirty she'd somehow managed to get it, and part of her had to wonder just how it was that she'd been able to get some of the grass stains she saw on there where she had. But she knew too that such thoughts were just her attempts at stalling for time and knew even better that that would get her nowhere. And so with another groan, she forced herself to set those musings aside as she passed the still mostly pastel pink garment over too.

Ugh. You'd think I'd be used to this by now with how often Aunt Dana likes to spank me, but of freaking course it's still just the absolute worst, she silently grumbled to herself. *I mean, I guess I should at least be grateful that she's not stripping me out of my clothes herself. I'm pretty sure I'd wind up showing off a lot more than just my panties if that were the case, but still…*

Heaving out an embarrassed sigh at what she knew had to come next and blushing despite having tried to convince herself that it wasn't that big of a deal, Rhen moved her hands to grip the waistband of her shorts on either side of her hips. Doing her best to ignore the stifled giggles she heard coming from just around the corner, she hooked her thumbs into the elastic and then pushed them down her thighs as quickly as she could while still avoiding accidentally catching her panties in the process.

Dana had said that she only wanted her down to her *undies*, after all, and she fully intended to not expose anything more than she absolutely had to if she could at all help it.

Rhen let gravity take care of sliding her shorts the rest of the way down her legs for her as they plopped to the floor, pooling around her ankles for the second time in less than an hour that day. Now left standing in just her white and hot pink panties and their matching camisole, the reality that she was just a naughty teenager being treated like a child hit her like a ton of bricks. And in an effort to channel some of that mortified energy that was currently flushing her cheeks a delightful shade of crimson, she found herself folding her arms defiantly across her chest and kicking her feet until her shorts at last came free, turning them inside-out in the process as they flew off to land in a tangled heap in front of her smugly smiling aunt.

"Happy?" she demanded with a huff, only just barely managing to stop herself from stomping a bare foot with the question.

"I sure am," answered Dana smoothly, her voice sugary sweet as she squatted down to scoop up the shorts at her feet.

Seemingly without a care in the world, she laid them out across her forearm along with her niece's t-shirt, and then leaned in to playfully tap the end of Rhen's nose with her forefinger, just a couple of inches below where her eyebrows had knitted themselves together into an absolutely adorable little frown.

"Cutie pie."

Unfazed by the dirty look that this produced, she flashed the pouting girl in front of her an indulgent smirk as she straightened up to her full height once again.

"Now, I want you go ahead and park that nose of yours in the corner while I take care of these, alright?"

She hefted Rhen's still warm, discarded clothes in her arms and flashed her a look that made it all too clear that she was on very thin ice and that giving her any more attitude just then would not be a smart idea.

"Yes ma'am," squeaked the younger girl, taking the hint and dashing off to do as she'd been told before her aunt could change her mind about wanting to wash her panties as well.

But the older woman just chuckled to herself as she watched her scurry out of sight, before she too turned and started to move off at an easy pace toward the laundry room.

"Goodness gracious, that girl is *very* lucky she's so cute."

—

Once Dana had finished going over the worst spots on her naughty niece's dirty clothes with a stain remover pen and had set the laundry machine for a very thorough wash cycle, choosing not to rush so as to give Rhen plenty of time to stew in her own worries over what was coming next, she casually made her way back through the house and into her cozy front room. There she was pleased to find the younger girl still pouting but exactly where she'd been expecting her to be.

With her arms folded in front of her as she glared at her usual spot facing the corner in front of the big bay windows that looked out onto their front lawn.

"Well I'm glad to see that you managed to *mostly* do as

you were told," she tut-tutted, stepping up behind her and giving the taut seat of her panties a few hearty swats.

SMACK! SMACK! SMACK!

"But little girls who're sent to stand in the corner are supposed to do so with their hands on their head and their noses actually *in* the corner. Aren't they, young lady?"

"Ack! Okay, okay, I'm sorry!"

Rhen yelped and danced in place as her aunt's unexpected smacks reignited the flames in her nether cheeks from earlier, but much as she wanted to do so now she found that she was unable to move her hands up to where they were supposed to have been already due to the grip she had on her left elbow.

"Yeah, Rhen, don't be a brat," teased a blonde-haired girl suddenly, leaning out from around a corner to snicker at her before ducking back when Dana flashed her a disapproving frown.

Rather than reprimand the taunting twelve year old though, she just rolled her eyes and heaved out a false-ly-long-suffering sigh as a faint smile traced itself across her lips. She knew full well just how much the younger girl still squirming around in her grip hated having others see her get punished like the child that she truly acted like so much of the time.

Which was just fine with her, since Dana intended for this to be the one and only time that she had to have this particular discussion with the college sophomore turned thirteen-year-old she was looking after.

"Alright then, come along, cutie pie," she ordered breezily, guiding her niece away from the corner and steering her toward the kitchen by her elbow. "Let's get this over and done with so that you can get back to your corner time."

Stepping into the kitchen, she marched them both right

up to the front of the sink, where she at last let go of Rhen. Dana then squatted down onto her heels and pulled open the cabinet beneath the counter, rummaging around in it for a moment or two before at last emerging with a bar of soap wrapped in thick white paper and pushing herself back to her feet.

"Ahhh, Ivory," she cooed, running her fingers lovingly across the waxy paper before she began peeling it away, piling it up into a neat little stack on the countertop beside her as she went. "So cheap, and yet so very, *very* effective for fibbers and potty mouths."

Yeah, I just fucking bet it is…

Rhen continued to grumble some decidedly unladylike things under her breath as she glared daggers at the bar of soap in her aunt's graceful hands, feeling the butterflies inside her stomach starting to return in force. Thankfully though, her words were lost amid the sounds of tearing paper and the flow of water as Dana reached out and twisted the tap on the sink in front of her, and so she avoided getting herself into any further trouble.

Pointedly ignoring the younger girl and her pouting, Dana rolled up her sleeves and brought the freshly unwrapped bar of soap beneath the warm, running water, taking her time to work up a nice frothy lather on its slick white surface. Though it was actually rather rare for her to have to make good on her threats to wash out a dirty mouth, she'd done so enough times by now that the preparation movements were second nature to her.

They were rather simple, actually.

She just had to get the soap nice and bubbly so that there was no escaping its horribly bitter taste once it was inside its intended target's mouth. The real trick was making sure that the naughty boy or girl who it was about to be used on watched her do it, and to give them ample opportunity to squirm and regret their actions. So once again she did not rush as she worked the bar in her hands into a lather, humming quietly to herself as she cast sidelong glances toward her blanching niece from time to time to gauge how she was feeling.

Oh yes, she was definitely one regretful little girl at that particular moment.

Which was perfect.

Faster than Rhen would have liked her to, Dana had gotten the bar of soap in her hands sufficiently bubbly enough to be put to use, and she turned to face her with a determined look in her eyes after she'd finished shutting off the flow of water from the sink.

"Now I know that this isn't going to be pleasant, but I hope that I won't be having any undue dramatics or whining from you, Rhen, dear," she scolded lightly, wagging a sudsy forefinger at her as she frowned ever so slightly. "There will be no trying to hold your mouth shut so that I have to pinch your nose to get you to open it. Is that understood, young lady?"

Mortified that she would even be asked something like that, surely she was more mature than to stoop to something *that* childish, Rhen's face flushed with color once again and she nodded at the challenge.

"I... I won't, Aunt Dana," she said, sounding much less confident than she'd been hoping to as the reality of what was about to happen made her stomach drop to her feet. "Um, if it makes you feel any better, I'm really, *really* sorry about swearing earlier."

"Well... It's not going to get you out of your punishment, *but*, I do appreciate the apology, cutie pie."

Dana's mouth quirked up into a gentle smile with those words, and she reached out to tap the end of the younger girl's nose with the tip of her forefinger, leaving a dollop of bubbles on the end of it in the process.

"Now be a good girl for me and say 'ahhhh'."

Balling her hands into worried fists at her sides, Rhen danced in place for a moment or two as she shifted her weight from one foot to the other, trying (and failing) to mentally prepare herself for what she knew was not going to be an easy time. But after she'd gotten the last little bit of exasperated moaning out of her system, she did indeed tilt her head back and opened her mouth nice and wide for the soap.

"Ahhhh…"

It was then that Dana surprised her by snaking her free hand out and around to grip the back of her head, threading her fingers through her long, dark hair and squeezing tight.

"To keep you from getting too far," she explained with a sympathetic smile as she brought the wet and dripping bar of soap up to Rhen's lips and began easing it into her still open mouth. "You'll just have to take my word for it when I say that it's for your own good, I'm afraid."

Humph, if you say so…

The bitter taste that flooded Rhen's mouth was just a little bit worse than she'd been expecting it would be and she immediately tried to spit the foul thing out as her aunt started to scrub it up and down over the top of her tongue. But the grip on the back of her head kept her from moving far enough to get away, and she was forced to stand there and endure it as the bar of soap was slowly and inexorably worked in and out of her gaping mouth.

And it was just, *awful*.

"Doesn't taste so good, does it?" crooned Dana with a

knowing look.

She took her sweet time pushing the slippery bar of soap into every nook and cranny of the petite sophomore's formerly foul mouth. Working up a foamy lather against the insides of her cheeks and even rasping it along the edges of her molars so that little pieces were left embedded between the gaps there, ensuring that she'd be remembering this lesson for a long, *long* time to come.

"Uh-uh," came Rhen's grunted reply, her words coming out in a barely intelligible burble as she shook her head as much as the smugly preening older woman's grip on her hair would allow.

Tears pooled at the corners of her eyes and soon began to slide down her cheeks to intermix with the river of drool and bubbles already dribbling down her chin to soak the front of her camisole and panties; thankfully obscuring the damp spot between her legs, but doing very little to hide the twin, diamond-hard points of her nipples pointing out in front of her. Despite the pure unadulterated unpleasantness that was being wrought upon the inside of her mouth though, part of her couldn't help but snort a little as it occurred to her that Dana could have just left her in her dirty clothes to begin with instead of making her strip for this.

She was certain that she would have had them sparkling clean by the time they were through.

"Good," chirped her aunt after a couple more vigorous pumps of the soap in and out of her mouth, yanking Rhen out of her attempts to distract herself.

Her eyes were dancing with grim amusement and self-satisfaction now as she continued to twist and turn the somewhat-mushy bar against her teeth.

"I want you to remember this awful, yucky taste every time you so much as even *think* about saying a bad word, little girl.

And I want you to remember too that if I *ever* hear anything like what I heard coming out of your mouth today, we'll be right back here to do this all over again, and next time I won't be nearly so nice. Do you hear me?"

Rhen just made a grunting, whining, gurgle of a noise as she continued to gently cry around the bar of soap wedging open her aching jaw. Thankfully though, Dana chose to interpret that as a "yes".

"Good."

—

"Alright, sweetie, I think we're just about done here," Dana cooed a couple of agonizing minutes later, giving the back of Rhen's head a reassuring little squeeze as she at last pulled the bar of soap out of her mouth completely.

Still holding it in her hand in case it was needed again, she let go of the hair she'd been gripping and took a step away to retrieve a clean glass from the cabinet beside them, before returning to hold it out to the miserable looking girl.

"You may rinse as much as you'd like to for the next minute," she said in a firm, but not unkind, voice before hefting the bar of soap in her other hand and waving it warningly as she added with a bit more steel. "But then you're going straight back into the corner until dinner time, okay?"

At that moment Rhen was prepared to stand in the corner until the end of the world if it meant getting some relief from the horrible taste inside her mouth. Accepting the glass from her aunt with a frantic nod, she gave a great, heaving sniffle and then turned toward the sink, spitting out a fat globule of bubbly saliva into it.

"I'll take that as a 'yes'," the older woman said with a light laugh, ruffling the back of her hair and tossing the spent bar of soap into the sink before reaching past her to turn on the water for her. "Alright then, cutie pie, get rinsing. You've got sixty seconds, starting... now!"

SMACK!

Rhen squeaked as Dana landed a hefty swat directly in the middle of her slightly soggy bottom to kick off the start of her countdown, but decided to save her pouting for until after she'd finished clearing out as much soap from her mouth as she could.

She made the next sixty seconds count as she filled her glass, took a swig from it, swished the water around inside her mouth, and then spat it out, before repeating the entire process all over again. It did very little to help get rid of the little bits and pieces of soap still wedged in among the gaps in the tops and sides of her molars, but little by little, mouthful by mouthful, the disgustingly bitter taste of Ivory soap began to disappear from her mouth. Not completely, but enough so that it was at least no longer overwhelming.

By the time her aunt declared that time was up, actually nearly two minutes later though Rhen had no idea, she plucked the half-full glass from her fingertips and gave her another swat in the middle of her jiggly caboose.

SMACK!

"That's enough rinsing for now," she said as she poured the remaining water out before setting the glass aside to clean the soapy residue off of later. "You can do some more after your corner time, alright?"

It was a rhetorical question, Rhen knew, but not wanting to tempt fate, she still reluctantly nodded her head anyway and allowed herself to be escorted back out into their front room without complaint. There, she was once more parked in the corner she'd grown so familiar with over the last few weeks.

"Remember to keep your hands on top of your head this time," Dana admonished, moving her wrists up for her so that she could interlace her fingers on top of her inky black tresses. "I don't want to have to give you another spanking today, you know."

"Oh yeah, I'm sure," deadpanned the petite sophomore with an unseen roll of her eyes.

Dana ignored her though, smirking to herself as she gently pushed on the back of her head, forcing her face forward so that she had no other choice than to arch her back and part her legs slightly, thrusting her bottom out toward the room as her nose was guided all the way into the spot where the two walls met.

"Hmmm, and I think we'll have these down as well while we're at it."

Suiting actions to words, she stooped down behind Rhen and whisked her panties down to her ankles in one smooth motion. Although this time, she didn't bother with letting them stay there.

"Ah!"

Well, I guess I probably should have seen that one coming...

"Step out, please," she ordered, lightly slapping the backs of the younger girl's thighs to help encourage her to move as she waited patiently for her to do as she'd been told.

A moment later she scooped up her discarded panties from off of the floor and pocketed them as she straightened up to admire her handiwork and the adorable sight of her bedraggled niece.

Rhen stood there facing the corner in nothing but a wet, white camisole that clung to her arched back like a second skin as her still fairly dark pink and very naked bare bottom poked out toward the half-drawn curtains of the bay windows looking out onto their front lawn.

"Perfect."

Dana cast a quick glance toward the great, old grandfather clock that dominated the wall beside her, and smiled. Dinner time was in just over two hours from now.

"I'd get comfy if I were you, cutie pie," she said with a low chuckle, reaching out to adjust the way the hem of her niece's camisole fell across her rounded hips before giving her tush a couple more affectionate pats. "You're going to be there a while, I'm afraid."

Chapter 15

Sunday School Surprise

One surprise that Rhen had not seen coming when she'd agreed to move in with Dana was her insistence that she attend church with her every Sunday. Thankfully though she hadn't been all that pushy about it, and had also made it very clear that first morning when she'd awoken her with the rising sun and told her that it was time to get ready for services, that she didn't expect her to come with her if she had any moral objections to it.

Well, any moral objections that weren't rooted in a belief that she should be allowed spend her Sunday mornings sleeping in until noon.

Dana had went on to explain as she waited patiently for Rhen to roll over from where she was curled up and cuddling her stuffed teddy bear and penguin that she attended a small community church that preached a nicely modernized version of Christianity. One that eschewed all of the fire and brimstone in favor of a more progressive stance on social issues, and that didn't try pushing an agenda of returning to an idealized version of America that had never actually existed. She did however make it a point to mention that while they didn't adhere to any archaic views on things like same-sex marriage, they were still firm believers that parents should raise their children to be well-behaved and respectful to their elders.

Apparently it didn't matter to them *who* your parent or parents were, so long as you obeyed them like a good boy or girl should.

That managed to coax an amused, although still quite sleepy, snort from Rhen as she finally started to stir beneath her sheets. Judging by her aunt's own views on the subjects of child rearing and discipline, she was willing to bet that her fellow churchgoers weren't afraid of baring a bottom or two from time to time themselves.

"So spare the rod and spoil the child, eh?" she teased around a yawn as she at last sat up and stretched her arms over her head.

"I think most parents prefer to use a paddle or belt," countered Dana with an amused twinkle in her eyes, not missing a beat. "But yes, that would be an accurate summary of the church's stance on discipline in the home. So I'd be on my best behavior if I were you, cutie pie."

Rhen felt an icy finger trace down along her spine at those words, and she shivered just a little bit as the sobering implications of what they might mean for her settled in along the bottom of her stomach like a heavy stone.

"Um… r-right, of course. Best behavior, got it."

Noticing the air of trepidation radiating out from the younger girl, Dana flashed her a reassuring smile.

"Look, hon, I'm not expecting you to convert or buy into anything that you don't personally agree with, alright?" she went on to clarify, bracing one hand on her hip as she gestured airily with her other.

She most certainly didn't want to scare the poor girl off or make her feel like she didn't belong if she could at all help it.

"But I think you'd really enjoy going to church with me if you gave it a chance. Father Jacob's sermons are usually pretty fun, and there're a lot of kids around your age to play with. Like I said though, I'm not going to force you to come with me if you have an *actual* reason for not wanting to go that isn't just 'it's boring' or 'I'm tired'. I know religion can be a touchy subject with a lot of people, but I really do think that having you get a nice strong dose of community values every Sunday will help do you a world of good when you're older."

Rhen scowled grumpily at the thinly veiled reference to her adopted age, but the look coupled with the tangled bird's nest that was her hair just then only seemed to make her aunt smile wider, and she decided not to press the issue further.

It was far too early to get spanked, in her opinion.

"Okay, okay," she sighed, kicking off her blankets with another yawn as she wriggled around to angle her feet over the edge of her bed. "I get it, I'll go. You've convinced me, and I'll be happy... Well, not *exactly* happy, but you know..."

She gestured vaguely and then shrugged.

"Happy-ish to go to church with you. But um... can we have some breakfast first?"

Right at that moment, her stomach decided to make itself known as it rumbled loudly, and Dana's smile burst into a full-on grin.

"Sure thing, cutie pie," she chirped, back to her far-too-bubbly in the morning self as she helped her niece out of bed and ruffled her hair affectionately.

Still smiling, she then took Rhen by the shoulders and turned her back around to face her abandoned mattress.

"But why don't you go ahead and make your bed first before you forget? I wouldn't want to have you spending your first day of services sitting on a sore tushy, after all."

She then leaned in closer behind her petite cutie patoo-tie sophomore, bringing her lips right next to her ear as she added teasingly.

"Those pews can be *awfully* uncomfortable on a fresh-ly-spanked bottom, you know. And I don't think you'd enjoy finding out what typically happens to naughty little girls who can't stop squirming when they should be sitting still and listening."

With those ominous parting words, along with a quick kiss to the cheek and a couple of firm pats to the puffy white clouds adorning the seat of the younger girl's pajama bottoms, Dana stepped away and began making her way toward the open bedroom door.

"I'll go ahead and get breakfast started," she called out over her shoulder as she went, waving a casual hand toward her pouting niece. "We're in a bit of a hurry though, so it'll have to be quick. Does oatmeal sound good to you?"

"Yeah, that's fine," answered Rhen, not bothering to look after her auntie's retreating form as she busied herself with straightening out her sheets and pillow.

Her mind was already swimming with exciting and terrifying visions of what might be awaiting her if she stepped out of line while she was at church that morning.

Oh my god! What if I'm the only teenager there who still gets spanked like a little kid?

She felt her cheeks clench beneath her pajama bottoms at the thought, and she resolved to be on her very best behavior that morning.

—

As it turned out, Rhen was not the only girl (or boy) in her early teens who still made the occasional (or in her case, fairly regular) trip across a parent or guardian's knee for correction whenever she misbehaved.

Knowing what signs to look for, she'd been able to easily spot at least one or two of her fellow young parishioners shifting uncomfortably on the lightly padded pews every week since she started attending church with her aunt. And in short order, playing "Spot the Sore Seat" had quickly become one of her favorite pastimes during the sometimes rather long-winded sermons, especially after Dana had decided to make it a rule that she had to leave her smartphone at home after it had gone off during the closing prayer one morning.

Rhen had definitely wound up not sitting so comfortably herself during lunch that afternoon.

It was surprisingly reassuring, and yet still rather humiliating, to have it so thoroughly confirmed for her once again that her auntie's views on discipline weren't really all that far outside of the norm as she'd at first thought they were. And as if her time being outfitted with a brand new wardrobe and shopping for a hairbrush at the mall hadn't made it clear enough to her already, being introduced to everyone as Dana Johnson's niece from out of town certainly helped to highlight for her just how much of a bratty little kid she was seen as in the eyes of most adults.

And on more than a few occasions, even her own, if she was being honest.

Whenever the other adults in the congregation looked at her, they didn't see a nearly twenty-one-year-old college student dressed down to look like a teenager. Instead they just saw what her Aunt Dana had seen from that very first moment they'd met, an impetuous little girl who was prone to ignoring her chores and had a tendency to get too big for her britches. In short, a mostly well-meaning girl who needed a very firm hand to keep her in line. And while spanking as a means of discipline might have declined in popularity some-what in recent years, the practice was still very much alive and well in the tight-knit little community of churchgoers.

And she fit right in.

In fact, spankings were such a common enough occurrence

that one time Rhen had even overheard a girl several years older than her own adopted age being told very loudly by her irate father that she and him were going to be having a "very long talk" when they got home later that afternoon. He'd said the words so casually, and in front of all of her friends passing her by on their way out the door, that at first Rhen had thought that she might have misheard him. But the way the other girl's face had crumpled into a mortified mask of despair as she started frantically begging her father to reconsider had made it all too clear that she hadn't.

Rhen definitely had a pretty good idea of just what kind of talk the girl's father had in mind for her when they got home. Based on the way he kept tapping his beefy forefinger against the side of his silver belt buckle, it had been pretty obvious. And feeling for her fellow teen, she'd flashed the pouting girl a sympathetic smile. One that had been rebuffed almost immediately with an annoyed scowl, as if her attempts to commiserate with the doomed young lady had only served to underscore the childishness of her impending punishment all the more.

That had rankled Rhen, who'd reacted on instinct by sticking out her tongue and blowing a raspberry at the jerk of an older girl, much to the amusement of her aunt who'd been standing right beside her at the time. Amusement which had at least allowed her to keep her panties on when she inevitably went over her knee later that afternoon for a brisk spanking of her own for teasing the other girl and being disrespectful in the chapel.

As far as Rhen was concerned though, it had been totally worth it. And she'd forgotten all about the warmth in her rear end practically as soon as she'd been let up off of Dana's lap to go play again. Taking far greater pleasure in the knowledge that her bottom was almost certainly *much* better off than that stuck-up older girl's had been just then.

—

The knowledge that she wasn't the only one getting her bottom warmed from time to time did a lot to help Rhen relax and let herself enjoy the weekly services without feeling like the odd one out among the other "teens". After a few weeks she'd even managed to settle into the role of class clown among the half-dozen other kids in her Sunday school class. Unfortunately for her though, this would inevitably lead to her learning one very valuable lesson that she hadn't thought to consider.

Not only did she fit in perfectly well as just another semi-regularly spanked young teen among the other youths of the congregation, but that as such, there were plenty more people other than her aunt who didn't see anything wrong with tanning her hide for her if she was being a brat.

Now *that* had certainly been an eye-opening experience for her.

Rhen was most definitely a disruptive influence in her Sunday school class. But in her mind, she just couldn't help it.

Off and on while growing up, she and her grandma had attended a fairly similar church to the one Dana dragged her to every week. And even then, she'd found the hour long classes that she and all of the other kids had been forced to endure while their parents got to mix and mingle after the main sermon was over to be interminably dull.

So she'd taken it upon herself to try spicing them up with her naturally charming personality and sparkling wit.

It was just too bad that her teacher didn't see things the same way.

While the priest who usually delivered the sermon every

Sunday morning was youthful and energetic, often tying the subject he was pontificating on back to modern day references and cultural touchstones, Rhen's Sunday school teacher was anything but. Where Father Jacob was fun and vibrant, Sister Miller was a total stick in the mud, and she had a *very* small amount of patience for any kind of, as she liked to put it, "horseplay" in her classroom. And as if she weren't bad enough all on her own, her pretty young assistant (and daughter), Sister Anna, wasn't that much better either in Rhen's estimation.

The girl was all of eighteen and had just started her first semester of college only two weeks earlier, though thankfully by some small miracle their paths had yet to cross on campus. She was willowy and condescending, thought she knew everything there was to know about life now that she'd graduated from high school, and was pious to the point of being snotty beyond belief. And although her mother ran her class with an iron fist, that didn't stop Anna from taking every opportunity she could find to exercise her meager authority over the students that made up their little Sunday school group as well, reveling in any and every chance she got to lord it over the thirteen and fourteen-year-olds that she thought she was so much wiser and more sophisticated than.

Not that that usually amounted to much more than shushing someone, usually Rhen, whenever it was clear that they were starting to get on her mother's nerves.

Even so, it still dug mercilessly at Rhen's pride to have a girl who was in reality only two years younger than she was being able to order her around with impunity. She'd taken to silently hoping that the ever-prissy Sister Anna would eventually slip up in some way during class that would be enough to provoke her mother into promising to turn her over her knee once they were home. But so far though, she hadn't had any luck in that area. Instead all she'd gotten was an unpleasant twisting feeling in the pit of her stomach that seemed to say that if her adopted age was only a couple of years younger, she probably would have already taken a trip or two across Anna's lap for all the glaring and times she'd stuck her tongue out at her while her mother wasn't looking.

Which just might have been worth it as far as Rhen was concerned.

To say that Sister Miller's lessons were boring would have been a massive understatement in Rhen's opinion. They typically consisted of studying a single story from the Bible every week, everyone in the small class taking turns reading a verse or two each aloud, followed by an awkward group discussion where she'd do her best to try and coax out some meaningful answers from her students that weren't just rote responses given out of habit.

Truth be told, part of Rhen felt kind of bad for the woman. Trying to steer a bunch of young teenagers into an actual discussion of their thoughts and feelings on a subject was no easy task on even the best of days. And she also knew that if she were really as mature as she liked to believe she was (and liked to whine about to Dana whenever she was in the process of yanking down her panties for a spanking) she would have helped get things moving and tried to get her fellow students to participate more, but her teacher was just so… *boring*.

For the first week or two that Rhen had started attending church with her aunt, she'd managed to behave herself well enough during her Sunday school lessons to avoid drawing the ire of Sister Miller any more than any of her fellow students usually did. The prospect of being the new girl in the congregation and trying to integrate herself into an already established group of friends who'd been in the same classes together for almost a decade now had been a daunting one. So instead, she'd decided to just keep quiet and gradually insert herself into the edges of their conversations until at last she felt comfortable enough to start actually taking part in, and often leading them, in cracking wise and goofing around.

Unsurprisingly for her, she'd found that it was remarkably fun to be the center of attention in their little group. And with her eight years of extra experience being a brat under her belt, she was able to keep them all in stitches with her running commentary of dumb jokes and biblical puns with ease.

That always seemed to get a rise out of Sister Miller too, who would stumble over whatever it was that she was reading aloud to the class when it became clear that nobody was listening to her anymore. She'd then go tomato red and start blustering on and on at them about the importance of understanding the teachings of the stories they were reading, and how she expected them to pay attention and not just make a racket. And all the while she was doing that, her daughter would move to stand beside her with her arms crossed, nodding her head fervently and occasionally repeating something her mother had just said as if it were her own idea.

Honestly, the two of them made quite the amusing pair, and if it wasn't for the fact that Sister Miller was so imposing when she was angry, Rhen might have egged them on even further. But instead, she just kept her mouth shut with the rest of her class as they waited for her to run out of steam whenever they upset her to the point of stopping a lesson.

The older woman's lecturing was usually enough to cow them all, including Rhen, to the point of being quiet for the next twenty minutes or so (usually enough time to wrap up their lesson) while she plodded on with whatever point it was that she'd been trying to make earlier. But sometimes a stern lecture wasn't enough to keep her students in line for long, and in those moments she'd wind up asking the room at large, far too sweetly in Rhen's opinion, if any of them wanted her to go get their parents.

The threat of getting a parent involved was always the point at which the snickering came to a sudden and complete halt. Nobody wanted to risk ruining the rest of their weekend by getting into trouble at home. Plus there was of course the added tension that said trouble might involve having their pants pulled down or their dresses flipped up in back for some swift and decisive correction. Rhen wasn't sure just how often her fellow students found themselves taking trips across their parents' knees, but she had a feeling that being called in because their kid couldn't keep their mouth shut during Sunday school would be enough to get most of them to decide that a spanking was in order.

And so when Sister Miller started to get *really* angry, everyone knew that it was time to shut up and look sorry.

Rhen had managed to adhere to this philosophy as well, and so far it had worked wonders for her. That is, until one fateful Sunday morning a couple of months after she'd moved in with Dana when she'd gotten just a little too cocky for her own good

She'd just finished off a major writing assignment the night before and didn't have any other homework due right away, and the prospect of being able to laze around all that afternoon and her day off the following Monday had emboldened her to the point of being careless. And so on a whim she'd decided to see just how far she could push her grumpy old Sunday school teacher before she finally snapped completely.

That day they'd been studying a story from the Old Testament about God speaking to a man through a talking donkey, and for obvious reasons, Rhen had found the whole thing to be very amusing. All throughout their lesson she'd been mouthing off, derailing the discussion her teacher was trying to lead at seemingly every opportunity.

If anybody had stopped to ask her why she was being such a brat, she probably would have argued that it really wasn't her fault. Obviously it was impossible for her *not* to take delight in finding excuses to work the words "ass" and "talking ass" into the conversation whenever she could, especially given the way it made everyone laugh at how bold and daring she was, so why should she get into trouble for it? Besides, it was Sister Miller who had picked out the story for them to study in the first place, not her. She should have known what kind of reaction she was going to get from them once they started reading it.

Well, mostly just from her, but still… that was beside the point as far as Rhen was concerned.

"Young lady, you will stop all the potty talk this instant, or else I'm going to go get your aunt and see what *she* has to say about it!" fumed a livid Sister Miller, steam all but billowing out of her ears as she glared daggers at the newest addition to her little flock of somewhat-eager young minds.

"Potty talk? What potty talk is that, Sister?" wheedled a smug Rhen, doing her best to sound wholly innocent as she held up her bible to point at the verses she'd ostensibly been quoting from. "It's not a swear word if it's in the Bible, right?"

She flashed the older woman a saccharine sweet smile as she thought of another audacious little jab.

"Oh! Is this the story where the phrase 'talking out of your ass' comes from?"

Just as she'd been hoping, all of her fellow students burst into another fit of irreverent giggling at that, thinking that her jokes were the absolute peak of hilarity just then. Which of course only made Sister Miller all the more annoyed with her.

Wow, her face is almost as red as Aunt Dana's hair!

"Rhen Mathews, if I hear one more word coming out of that mouth of yours before closing prayer is finished, and I mean just *one*, I'm going to show you just how I handle naughty little girls in my classroom. And believe you me, young lady, you are *not* going to like it one bit. Is that understood?"

Although Rhen didn't know for sure just what her teacher might do to her if she kept it up, she was willing to take the older woman at her word that it wouldn't be pleasant.

Apparently her fellow students were all well aware of what she meant however, because her sharp reprimand sent a ripple of nervous excitement through them all. Eliciting a chorus of grim "Ooos" from the lot of them as they shifted in their seats to grin in snide amusement at her, wordlessly taunting her as she now found herself toeing the edge of disaster, their teasing expressions egging her on to call Sister Miller's bluff.

Sensing that she wouldn't find any support among them now that the declaration had been made by their teacher, Rhen decided to follow her instincts and clamp her mouth shut, nodding in silent confirmation that she did in fact understand and would be quiet.

"Good," sniffed Sister Miller, clearly doing her best to regain her grip on her composure as she exhaled sharply through her nose and turned back to the blackboard to finish writing out the bible references that they would be going over next. "Now, as I was saying…"

But as she scratched out chapter and verse after chapter and verse for them to take turns reading aloud, Rhen found that she just couldn't contain herself. No sooner had her grumpy goose of a teacher gotten back to their lesson than a golden idea for a joke had bubbled up to the surface of her mind.

Oh come on! Why didn't I think of this earlier?

Pouting, she sat there for nearly a minute straight with her arms folded tightly across her chest, her mouth pursed into a tight line with the effort of staying silent, and her knee bouncing in front of her with pent-up energy as Sister Miller scratched out several more scripture references in her cramped handwriting across the board in dusty, yellow chalk.

Come on... Just keep it together, Rhen. There's not that much time left in class, you can tell it after prayers are done.

In the end though, Rhen's need to get her joke out of her system won out over her worries about what might happen to her if she did so.

"Oh man, I had no idea that Shrek was based off of a Bible story," she stage-whispered to the boy and girl sitting beside her that she'd had the most success with cracking up so far that lesson.

She grinned slyly at the confused looks they both gave her, ignoring the butterflies starting to stir around inside her stomach as she continued loud enough for everyone else to hear.

"You know, because of the talking donkey?"

Her smirk broadened as their faces lit up with understanding, and she pitched her voice down into her best Eddy Murphy impression as she added.

"I bet that donkey was all like... We can stay up late, swappin' Bible stories, and in the morning... I'm making *falafels!*"

The room immediately burst into laughter again, although that may have just been from the sheer stupidity of the joke she'd just told, rather than because it was actually all that funny. Either way, Rhen cackled right along with her fellow students, far too proud of her lame little joke to care about the storm that was surely brewing where Sister Miller stood as she wiped away a tear from the corner of her eye. In that moment she was far too busy reveling in being the center of attention again to care about what might happen next.

And boy was she ever.

It seemed as if pretty much everyone had thought that her joke was funny, even the always so prim and proper Anna had cracked a slight smile. Well, everyone except Sister Miller that is, who slammed her oversized large-print Bible shut as she thundered.

"That is *it*!"

All of the laughter was choked off immediately as everyone in the room, save for the furious teacher, jumped at the loud *THWUMP* of the leather-bound book smacking down heavily onto the little table beside her.

"Anna, honey, would you please go get Rhen's aunt for me and let her know that I'd like to have a word with her?"

Though her nostrils still flared, Sister Miller's initial fiery temper had cooled into that same ice-cold calm that Rhen had seen Dana adopt every time she was about to dish out some serious discipline.

It did not bode well for her confidence.

"Now."

Uh-oh…

"Sure thing, Mom," chirped Anna, positively giddy with the importance of the small task she'd just been given.

Popping up from the hard plastic seat that she'd angled off to one side away from the others, she sashayed her way out of the classroom and made a beeline toward where the rest of the adults were off enjoying a post-sermon cup of coffee and some donuts while their kids were forced to endure a double dose of church.

The room was dead silent for the entire time that she was gone, and Rhen was left to fidget in her seat as her face flushed with heat and her heart fluttered nervously in her chest.

Crap, crap, crap! Why couldn't I just keep my freaking mouth shut?

Far sooner than she would have preferred, Anna returned with Dana in tow only a step or two behind her.

"Hey there, Janice," she said by way of greeting to the other woman, way too casually for Rhen's liking, as she strode into the small classroom and put her hands on her hips.

She cast a quick sidelong glance toward her niece, noting the way she was blushing and squirming in her chair, but otherwise kept her attention fully focused on the still quietly fuming teacher in front of her.

"Anna said you needed to see me right away. Something about asses and falafels?"

Rather than darken the other woman's mood, Dana's teasing half-grin and irreverently arched eyebrow seemed to come as a welcome relief to Sister Miller, who snorted in amusement.

"Oh sure, it's fine when *she* does it," grumbled Rhen quietly enough so that only the boy and girl sitting beside her could hear her.

Thankfully though they remained silent as they watched the two older women continue to talk.

"Yes, something like that," confirmed Sister Miller with a dismissive wave toward Rhen. "You see, the problem is that this one here just can't seem to help herself and keeps interrupting my class with all of her smart-mouth comments. And while I usually don't mind a bit of horseplay here and there, she's been a constant distraction all lesson."

"Oh she has, has she?" asked Dana in that dangerously low purr of hers she used whenever Rhen was a hair's breadth away from a spanking, turning to regard her niece with an unimpressed look. "Young lady, is this true?"

"Well…"

Rhen fiddled with the bunched-up folds of her pale yellow church dress as she did her best to think of some way to spin things that wouldn't end up getting her into even more trouble. Try as she might though she couldn't come up with anything, and she wound up just sighing as she dipped her chin down to look at her knees with a barely-concealed pout.

"Yes ma'am, it is."

"I see," was all the response she got from her aunt before she turned her attention back toward the Sunday school teacher she was apparently so buddy-buddy with. "I am *so* sorry she's been behaving like this, Janice. Rhen *knows* that she's supposed to be quiet and pay attention when she's in class, and church is no exception. Isn't that right, little girl?"

Heat staining her face a bright shade of strawberry red, Rhen blew out a long breath, her cheeks puffing out with indignation. But as she looked up toward her aunt to argue that she hadn't been being *that* bad, the words stalled in her throat and she swallowed them.

Now was definitely not the time to argue, especially not with all of her friends watching on in open amusement.

"Yes Aunt Dana, I'm sorry."

"Humph, yeah, I bet you are," muttered Anna as she tossed her hair back over a shoulder and sniffed in disdain.

Dana just smiled indulgently at the younger girl as she continued to address her mother.

"Well there we have it, a confession straight from the source and an apology… of sorts."

She pursed her lips into a frown as if to say that she didn't think it was much of one as she added.

"And if it makes you feel any better, Janice, I don't mind telling you that I'm going to be painting Rhen's sassy little caboose bright red as soon as we get home today."

That got a squeak from Rhen, who knew she really shouldn't have expected anything less.

"Oooooh…"

Even though most, if not all, of her fellow students were no strangers to getting spanked themselves, the spectacle of one of their own having it so publically announced that they were in for one upon returning home was just way too juicy not to react to.

"Bunch of traitors," grumbled Rhen to herself as she folded her arms in front of her ruffle-covered chest and glared at her knees.

Apparently she hadn't grumbled quietly enough however, since the remark earned her a sharp, reprimanding look from her aunt, Sister Miller, and Anna.

"Watch it, missy."

The combined power of those three glares was enough to have Rhen sitting up straight, hands primly folded atop one another in her lap, as she swallowed hard and did her best to exude an air of total obedience and good behavior.

"Sorry!"

The adults kept up their scowling for a handful of heart-beats longer, before seeming to tune her out completely as they picked up their conversation as if nothing had just happened. Well, all of them except for Anna, who continued to smugly watch Rhen with the rest of the class while her mother spoke with the girl's aunt.

"Oh Dana, you're a peach," said Janice Miller with a satisfied nod as she cast a sidelong glance toward where Rhen was sitting. "Lord knows that girl definitely could stand to benefit from having to eat her lunch standing up today after the malarkey she's been spewing. Heck, if my Anna had said even *half* the things that Rhen has today, I'd have her chewing on a bar of soap until she had bubbles coming out her ears!"

That got a fresh round of snickers from the other kids in the room, and Rhen felt her stomach clench as she desperately hoped that her aunt wouldn't decide the other woman had a point.

"Oh, don't you worry," chuckled Dana, her face a mask of grim amusement. "By the time I'm through with her, Little Miss Sassmouth will *definitely* have learned a thing or two about controlling herself."

Well, at least she didn't say she was going to wash my mouth out...

Sister Miller let those ominous words hang in the air for several more long moments, enjoying the way they made Rhen squirm, before she spoke again.

"I'm sure you'll have no problem showing her the error of her ways, Dana, but uh... that's not actually the reason why I wanted Anna to come get you," she explained with a nod toward her daughter. "I was hoping I could get your approval to introduce Rhen to the Board."

Rather than more low whistles and excited exclamations, that question produced a round of shocked gasps and nervous titters among her fellow students. All of which were reactions that Rhen didn't like even a little bit.

"I know she's technically too old for it now," Sister Miller went on as she shrugged in a way that made it all too clear that she didn't mind in the slightest. "But I figured that since young Rhen here wants to be part of the lesson so badly, she could help demonstrate how the making amends portion of repentance typically works for little boys and girls who can't behave themselves during Sunday school. What do you think?"

Rhen wasn't sure why her aunt needed to be hauled in just so that she could give her permission to let her niece say she was sorry to a board of people, but at that moment she was totally alright with it. While having to apologize to what she assumed must be the head priest and his two assistants would be embarrassing, it was far from unbearable.

"I think that's a wonderful idea, Janice," exclaimed Dana with a pleasantly surprised laugh, her face brightening at the suggestion. "That'd certainly take her down a peg or two wouldn't it? By all means, feel free."

Uh-oh... thought Rhen with a grimace, resisting the urge to squirm her thighs together as she shifted uncomfortably in her chair. *I think I might have made a bit of a miscalculation here.*

"It's so nice to see that you're still a firm believer in training children up in the way they should go," crooned Sister Miller, still smug as ever as she moved to walk her friend toward the classroom door. "I'm sure this will be a very uplifting and edifying experience for Rhen as well. After all, the Board is a sacred tradition, and just because she's older than twelve now shouldn't mean she should be forced to miss out on experiencing it for herself. Frankly, if I had things my way, we'd keep it in use up until graduation. It just does such a wonderful job of curbing bratty behavior."

"Oh yes, you don't have to convince me there," snorted Dana, turning to glare past the other woman's shoulder toward her niece one last time before she went.

"I expect you to do as you're told and not give Sister Miller or Sister Anna any more trouble, Rhen," she said with a warning wag of her finger. "You do *not* want me to have to come back in here again before class is over. Is that understood, young lady?"

Once again being the center of attention, and not at all liking the direction things seemed to be headed, Rhen hastened to assure the sternly frowning older woman that she would be on her very best behavior from then on.

"I'll be good, Aunt Dana!"

She didn't care that her words brought about a fresh round of tittering from the other kids seated around her, at that moment she was in full-on damage control mode.

"You'd better be, missy," huffed her aunt with a frown, seemingly satisfied. "Because if I hear that you've been anything other than a perfect angel, I'll put you over my knee right in front of all your friends here before we go home and show them just how I handle smart-mouthed little girls who don't do as they're told. You got that?"

"Got it!" squeaked Rhen, face going beet red.

Nodding one more time, Dana at last turned to leave, calling over her shoulder as she went.

"You got everything handled here, Janice?"

"Sure do," answered the other woman easily, all traces of her earlier frustration having been replaced by smug satisfaction. "You just leave the rest to me and Anna. We'll have her ready and waiting for you to collect after class is over."

"Okay then," called Dana, waving casually behind her as she sauntered off toward a fresh cup of coffee. "See you later."

"Bye Missus Johnson," chirped Anna, waving after the woman in a transparent attempt to magnify her role as one of the no-nonsense adults, much to the unspoken amusement of her mother judging by the way her mouth twitched up at the corners.

After Rhen's aunt had left, a tense silence had descended upon the little classroom with its painted cinderblock walls and dusty blackboard once again. And for several long heartbeats, the only sound that could be heard was the faint ticking of the plastic clock mounted to the wall beside the door.

"Alright then, I'm going to go get the Board," declared Sister Miller, eventually breaking the pregnant silence as she dusted her hands off on the front of her dress and turned her attention toward her daughter with a brusque sense of purpose.

Anna was clearly doing her very best not to let on just how excited she was just then, and was failing miserably. But that didn't seem to bother her mother however, as she strode toward the open door that her friend had just left from.

"While I'm doing that, I want you to go ahead and get Little Miss Sassmouth here," she angled a stern nod toward Rhen before returning her focus back to her daughter. "In position and waiting for her punishment by the time I get back. Do you think you can handle that, Anna?"

"Sure thing, Mom," piped up the young lady, straightening up a little bit more where she stood as her mother flashed her an approving look.

"Good girl," she said as she turned to go again. "Oh, and feel free to toast her buns a little bit if she gives you any trouble. We all know she's going to be sleeping on her tummy tonight anyway, so a few extra swats here and there aren't going to make much of a difference in the long run."

"R-Right!" answered Anna again, barely-leashed excitement fully evident in her quavering voice. "You can count on me!"

With those parting instructions, Sister Miller bustled her way out of the classroom, leaving Rhen alone with Anna and the six other kids of her supposed age. All of whom had huge, anticipatory grins plastered across their faces.

Uh-oh…

Rhen could hardly blame them for their excitement though. She knew she would have had much the same look on her own face had she been in their position. Even so, she wasn't really given much of a chance to dwell on that though, as Anna wasted little time in getting down to business once she'd been left in charge.

"Okay Rhen, come here," she ordered, pointing to a spot a handful of paces in front of the blackboard in the center of the room. One that would put her directly in the middle of the semi-circle of chairs that everyone else was sitting in. "Right now."

Although Anna's "I'm the boss, and you'll do what I say!" voice still needed some work, it was still more than enough to get Rhen jumping up from her chair as if it had just tried to bite her. She wasn't sure what this whole "Board" business was all about anymore, but she was fairly certain that she'd been gravely mistaken earlier when she'd thought that it was merely some sort of half-hearted public apology.

Goddammit, I should have known that it would be something like this, she silently swore to herself, even as her non-verbal curse made her stomach roil with more butterflies. *Uh, sorry about that one, God… um, Sir.*

Approaching the place where Anna had indicated, she turned to face her with a sullen pout as she silently waited for her next order to come.

"Um…"

The Sunday school assistant floundered slightly and then cleared her throat, cheeks flushing as she tried to think of how best to phrase her next order.

"Ahem! B-Bend over and grab your knees," she snapped, folding her arms under the respectable swell of her breasts in

275

what was probably her best approximation of her own mother's "Do it now or you're going to regret it" stance. "Oh, and don't forget to keep your legs straight too. Mom likes the girls she paddles to have their butts angled up nice and high for the Board to land on. So no slouching, you hear me?"

Yeah, I bet you know all about that, don't you, Anna? mused Rhen darkly, not daring to voice that particular thought aloud, not when the other girl had been given carte blanche to spank her as much as she liked to if she didn't cooperate fully.

She turned to face the blackboard, deliberately putting her back to her eager audience as a shiver of morbid anticipation tingled its way down the valley of her spine. She gritted her teeth against the surge of embarrassment that roiled up inside her stomach as she bent at the waist, keeping her knees straight and her thighs pressed tightly together just in case things ended up going as badly as she feared they might. Dana was certainly a big believer in the merits of a bare bottom spanking, and she doubted that Sister Miller would be any different. There was no way she wanted to show off anything more than she absolutely had to to the gaggle of brats who were gearing up behind her to enjoy the upcoming show.

Her dire prediction proved to be at least a semi-accurate one as she felt Anna starting to fumble with the hem of her dress behind her, trying to gather up its billowy folds with just one hand as if she did things like that all the time. It was clear that she didn't though by the way she kept messing it up, but eventually she managed to get a proper grip on the garment with two hands, and a moment after that Rhen felt her dress being hiked up her legs and tossed over her hips to expose the seat of her panties to the classroom at large.

Well, at least I'm inside this time, she thought with a wobbly grimace, doing her best to try and find even a faint trace of a silver lining in the darkness of the hole she'd somehow managed to dig for herself. *That's got to count for something, right?*

It really didn't, and she knew it.

Oh crap, wait a minute…

As she had so often done since moving in with her, Dana had picked out her clothes for her that morning before church. And of course it was only *after* she'd felt seven pairs of eyes locking onto her rump followed by a chorus of faint snickering that boiled over into genuine cackles of delight behind her that Rhen remembered just what particular pair of underwear she'd been given to wear that day.

"Awww, I love Beauty and the Beast," cooed Anna, her voice positively oozing condescension as she ran a palm over the dancing Belles stretched snugly across the chubby curves of Rhen's bent behind. "I think I might have even owned a pair of panties like this back when I was your age too. Oh how *cute*!"

She gave Rhen's bottom a couple of tentative, exploratory pats, clearly testing to see how far she could push things with the minimal amount of authority her mother had left her with. Rhen grumbled grouchily at the way the other girl made her bottom jiggle in front of her friends, but all that seemed to do was give her more confidence, as she was rewarded with a little over a dozen enthusiastic (though not particularly well executed) swats to her upturned bottom.

SLAP! SLAP! SLAP!

"Uh-uh-uh," teased Anna, wagging an admonishing forefinger at Rhen while her other hand lay perched along the curve of the hip she had jutted out sassily to one side. "None of that now, missy, or else I might just decide that those panties of yours need to come down too."

"You wouldn't!" gasped Rhen, an electric shiver of terror arcing through her to dispel at her feet.

"Try me," warned the other girl, her voice a low growl now as she threaded the fingers of her right hand into the waistband of Rhen's Disney princess panties, snapping the elastic lightly against the tops of her arched cheeks. "Bad little girls like you usually only get the Board over their panties, but I'm sure my mom would be only too happy to make an exception if you keep sassing me."

"Um, no thanks," squeaked Rhen, doing her best to sound contrite as she began to verbally backpedal before Anna could change her mind. "Please! I'll be good, Sister Anna, I'm sorry."

"Well that's certainly an impressive improvement," interjected Sister Miller's amused voice from somewhere off to Rhen's left then, making everyone jump as she strode back into the small classroom unannounced and unhurried. "It's amazing how quickly misbehaving children change their tune once their bottoms are put on the line."

"It sure is," agreed Anna, clearly doing her best to sound like she too was well-versed in the ways of discipline, and not as if she'd just been caught with her hand in the cookie jar.

Her mother stepped up beside her and surveyed Rhen's panty-clad bottom and bent over position with a cool, critical eye, before nodding once in approval.

"Excellent work, Anna," she said with a tight smile, placing a hand on her daughter's shoulder and giving it a light squeeze. "A firm hand and a few swats on the tush are usually all you really need to get most bratty girls, like Rhen here, to fall into line. I hope you remember that the next time I need to leave you in charge."

"Thanks Mom," chirped Anna, positively glowing with the praise. "And yes, I most certainly will."

Rhen gritted her teeth at the sickly sweet tone the younger girl used, and vowed to herself that she'd never give her an excuse to try putting her mother's advice to the test in the near future or beyond. She had a feeling that Anna would be a very fast learner when it came to dishing out discipline, and she definitely didn't want to find out one way or the other if she could at all help it.

"You may take your seat with the others now, dear," her mother continued with a wave of dismissal a few moments later after she'd gotten her fill of admiring the sight of Rhen obediently presenting her Disney princess panties for discipline. Awaiting her punishment like the good girl she should have been acting like all along. "Unless, that is…"

She paused then and furrowed her brow in concern as she leaned in closer to Rhen and asked not unkindly.

"Would you like to have Anna help you stay bent over while you take your licks, Rhen? Your aunt mentioned to me in the hall that you're a bit of a squirmer whenever she has to spank you, and I would prefer it if I didn't have you dancing around and breaking position every time I pop your tush with the Board."

She took a moment to heft said Board in her hands as she went on.

"We've still got a lesson to get through today, you know. And as much as I'd enjoy showing you what a *proper* paddling feels like, one like the kind I give my Anna whenever *she's* been naughty, we really ought to be getting back to that as soon as possible."

The question and its accompanying light teasing were enough to give Rhen pause and convince her to tear her gaze away from the square-inch of worn carpet she'd been glaring at in front of her brightly-polished penny loafers for the last minute or two, pouting.

It wasn't like she squirmed *that* much, geez. At least, not enough to require someone else to help hold her in place for one little spanking from some dumb old board… probably.

"I'll be fine," she grumbled as politely as she could manage, trying to take solace in the fact that Anna's mother had so casually just mentioned her own spankings.

I guess Little Miss Perfectly-Mature isn't as well behaved as she likes to pretend she is.

It wasn't that much of a comforting thought at the moment, but it was better than nothing as Rhen tilted her head to the side, craning her neck back to see what it was that Sister Miller was brandishing at her that had prompted her to ask such a question in the first place.

And immediately she wished she hadn't.

The Board turned out to be a very scary looking wooden paddle with an extra-long handle and an even wider business end. Rhen had a sneaking suspicion that it might have actually started out life as some sort of tool for sliding pizzas in and out of an oven, but judging by the worn sheen it had on just the one side, it had clearly been put to use roasting butts for far, far longer. Some enterprising member of the clergy had even taken the time to lovingly engrave several verses from the Old and New Testaments that extolled the virtues of not sparing the rod and instilling discipline into the hearts of children from a young age and so on.

Rhen was honestly a little surprised at just how many scripture references seemed to apply to disciplining children, and how many they'd managed to fit onto the Board, especially given how large it was.

And the sight of them was starting to make her think that maybe she didn't like going to church so much after all.

Then again, she *had* been being a total brat all that

morning, so she supposed that it was only fair that she was about to be taken to task for it now. Besides, it wasn't like this was the first time someone else was going to watch her getting spanked.

At least my panties are up this time, she silently breathed in relief, feeling her stomach clench as the mental image of her underwear being tugged down to hang around her knees danced across her mind's eye. *Somehow though I doubt that Aunt Dana is going to be nearly so considerate when we get home...*

Rhen had a feeling that it was going to be a long, long afternoon for her.

Right at that moment though she knew that she had much more pressing concerns to worry about as she felt that massive paddle being tap, tap, tapped firmly across both of her cheeks at once.

"Holy crap that thing is big!"

"Why yes, yes it is," chuckled Sister Miller, pausing in her tapping to let the full weight of the Board rest ominously against the back of Rhen's panties. "Thank you for sharing that valuable bit of insight with us, dear."

Rhen's face flushed molten lava hot as her classmates snickered behind her. She definitely hadn't meant to voice that particular thought out loud.

"Now then, young lady," her teacher continued, derailing any attempts she might have made to rein in her embarrassment as that blasted paddle started to rub in a slow, lazy circle across her soft and yielding bottom.

Her voice easily cut through the snickering and snide comments her fellow classmates were sharing just as effectively as if it was *their* butts she was rubbing that paddle against.

"Seeing as you're a relatively new addition to our little

flock, I'll give you a brief explanation of how a punishment from the Board typically works."

Rhen found herself swallowing hard as she straightened her knees up a fraction, the gravity of the ritualized discipline she was about to receive sending the fluttering inside the pit of her stomach into overdrive.

God- I mean, gosh dang it! Why can't she just start whacking me already and get it over with? Geez! All of this standing around and waiting freaking sucks. At least with Aunt Dana it's fast and furious, and then it's over.

Thankfully though, this time she managed to not let any of those thoughts slip free as Sister Miller continued to explain.

"When we have little lambs that just can't seem to behave themselves during Sunday school, usually the younger ones around nine or ten mostly, and they refuse to listen to warnings, their teachers will often have them bend over for a few swats from the Board."

With those words she gave the Board a couple of light raps against the fullest part of her target.

"So that they can learn from the bottom up as it were. Typically these punishments are carried out over a naughty boy or girl's underwear, but as Anna said..."

At that she paused long enough to cast another tight smile toward her daughter, who at least had the good grace to squirm a little bit herself.

"In certain special cases, either egregious or repeated misbehavior, a bit of bare bottom discipline is called for."

Rhen squeaked, going so rigid in the knees that she nearly tipped over as she felt the paddle being pulled back from her tush. Her cheeks were clenched tight beneath the thin material of her princess panties, and she found herself fervently hoping and praying that they were going to stay where they were around her hips.

"And while it's certainly true that an argument could be made that a girl your age should *really* know better than to behave like a child, and therefore deserves to receive a more severe punishment with her panties down…"

The whole class drew in a collective breath of anticipation, the tension in the room skyrocketing.

"I think that we'll keep them up for today," chuckled Sister Miller, bringing the paddle back down in one final test swat as the gathered audience sighed with disappointment.

"Oh my gosh, thank you, ma'am," gasped Rhen, tension easing from her whole body as her legs wobbled.

She started to squirm in place just a little bit then, the sudden relief washing over her making her aware of just how badly she needed to use the bathroom right then.

Hold it in, Rhen, hold… it… in…

"You're very welcome, dear," replied the older woman with another low chuckle as if she could tell exactly what was going through Rhen's mind at that very moment as her voice darkened a shade and she added. "But I want you to know that this is your one and only free pass, young lady. If we *ever* have to do this again, you'd better believe that your panties will be coming down for an extra special session with the Board that will make today's lesson seem like patty-cake."

"It won't, I swear," Rhen hastened to assure her, falling into the usual refrain she adopted whenever she was about to be spanked. "I'm sorry, Sister!"

"Humph, we'll just see about that," huffed Sister Miller skeptically.

Rhen could practically feel the tension inside the room starting to build again as her teacher wound up for her first swat with the Board. Bringing it up to her shoulder and holding it there, poised to bring it down at any moment.

"Now hang on tight, Rhen, you'll be getting thirteen of these," she ordered. "One for each year of your age as a means to help you remember to act like it instead of being a little brat."

Rhen's ponytail bobbed in a silent nod of acknowledgement.

Well, at least it's not twenty...

"Oh, and I expect you to count each swat out loud and say thank you afterward. Is that understood?"

The question managed to elicit another two or three nervous titters from her classmates, though they were laced with far less mirth now.

Rhen was sure that most, if not all of them, were probably grappling with some rather unpleasant memories of what it had felt like to be in her position at some point in their past.

"Yes ma-" she began to answer, before her words were cut off in a squawk as the Board suddenly collided at full force with her bouncy bottom.

WOOSH-SMACK!

"Ah!" Rhen yelped, as an unexpected explosion of pain blossomed across both of her cheeks at once.

The sheer shock and sharp bite of the Board's impact caused her to immediately forget everything that she'd just been told to do as she shot to her feet. Her hands flew back to clutch at the seat of her panties where she was sure a fire had just been lit, and she hopped from foot to foot, moaning in agony.

Now *that* had hurt!

"Uh-uh-uh, Rhen," chided Anna, as she sprang from her seat and dashed over to her side. "You know that's not allowed, kiddo."

The indignity of being called "kiddo" by a girl who was only two years younger than she was on top of her already frayed nerves from trying to get a grip on the fury raging beneath her panties had Rhen acting before she had a chance to think.

Whirling to glare at the girl beside her, she spat.

"Oh my god, will you freaking just buzz off? I do *not* need your bullcrap right now!"

At the last minute she'd started to come to her senses and had managed to keep herself from swearing, but that was about the most she could do. She knew that she was probably in enough trouble as it was already for that little outburst. There was no sense in making it worse by potentially adding a bar of soap into the mix later on.

Rather than do as she'd been told however, Anna's face just set itself into a determined mask as she snatched up Rhen's still frantically rubbing hands in her own. With a firm shove, she tipped her forward until she was bent over again with her panties on display, and in the process pinned her wrists behind her back.

"Young lady, I am your elder and you will speak to me with *respect*!"

SMACK! SMACK! SMACK!

Anna punctuated each word of her impromptu lecture with as hard of a spank as she could muster, and whether it was from pure indignation or just being a quick learner, these particular spanks had Rhen gritting her teeth as her hips shifted from side to side in a futile attempt to get out of the line of fire.

"Okay, okay, I'm sorry, I'm sorry, I'm sorry!" she blurted out in between little yelps.

Her bottom was smarting something fierce from those

rapid-fire swats, and as the initial sting started to fade, she could feel her cheeks clenching with the fear that her panties might be about to come down.

"Well done, Anna," spoke up Sister Miller with an impressed little laugh, interjecting herself into the middle of their exchange as she cleared her throat and nodded approvingly at her daughter. "Just like I told you, a firm hand and a few swats on the tush will have even the brattiest girl falling into line in no time. Great work."

"Thanks, Mom," chirped the girl, one hand still pinning Rhen's wrists behind her back while the other rested warningly along the curve of her right cheek. "That was a lot easier than I thought it would be."

"Yes, it's not all that difficult once you understand the basics of it, and practice does tend to help in that regard," observed her mother dryly, her voice carrying a tight smile. "Speaking of..."

She hefted the board again, using it to shoo away Anna's hands from Rhen's bottom and wrists.

"Would you mind helping Rhen stay in position while we try this again?"

"Of course," agreed Anna without a moment's hesitation.

She then proceeded to adjust the folds of Rhen's dress across her back before laying her hands atop it there to help keep her bent over. With a smug smile on her face, she drummed her fingers against the small amount of exposed skin just above the white waistband of the girl's panties as she added with a bit more steel in her voice.

"Try and do your best to keep your hands on your knees this time, Rhen. If you don't think you can do it though, let me know and I'll hold them for you, alright?"

As much as the offer made her face flush with fresh heat,

Rhen couldn't help but nod slightly in appreciation for it.

"I will, um… thanks."

"No prob."

WOOSH-SMACK!

Again from out of nowhere came the sudden explosion of thick wood against soft and tender girl buns.

"Holy crap! Ow, ow, ow!"

"Easy there, kiddo," soothed Anna almost immediately, her voice mostly gentle now as she rubbed a hand in smooth circles along Rhen's lower back. "Just take a few deep breaths, and don't forget to count, alright?"

"R-Right," gritted out Rhen through clenched teeth as she hissed in air through them.

There was no way in heck she wanted to repeat any more swats from that godforsaken paddle if she could at all avoid it. (She already knew that there was no way that that first one was going to count.)

"I'm waiting, young lady…"

Rhen squirmed as she felt the heavy weight of the Board tapping impatiently against the seat of her panties again, and she breathed out a long, low groan.

"One. Thank you, Sister."

"There we go," cooed Sister Miller, sounding more than a little pleased with herself as she pulled the Board back up to her shoulder. "Only twelve more to go. Hang on tight now…"

WOOSH-SMACK!

Once more the paddle thundered down against Rhen's upturned bottom, rocking her up onto the balls of her feet as she hissed out a garbled mishmash of curse words and apologies through her clenched teeth. As the initial bite melted into a more manageable burning sensation, she shook her bottom up and down and side to side as much as she could in a desperate attempt to throw off at least some small portion of the harsh pain.

This time though she remembered what to say without being prompted.

"Two... owie, owie, owie! Thank you, oof-"

She sniffled.

"Thank you, Sister."

On and on it went, the seconds seeming to stretch out into hours as swat after, bottom-flattening, finger-clenching, teeth-rattling, swat crashed against Rhen's soft and yielding bottom cheeks encased in her still merrily dancing princess panties, clearly not bothered in the slightest by the raging inferno crackling just beneath their thin cotton surface.

Though the entire ordeal lasted just over three and a half minutes in total from start to finish, Rhen was left panting like she'd just ran a marathon when she was at last helped back to a standing position on wobbly knees by a smugly preening Anna.

"Am I going to have any more sass or backtalk from you, young lady?" demanded Sister Miller after she'd given her errant charge enough time to dance in place with her hands glued to the sizzling seat of her panties while her classmates looked on with varying degrees of morbid glee and snide amusement.

"No ma'am," Rhen answered immediately, not bothering to stop her squirming as the scalding heat in her bottom continued to throb on despite the lack of additional paddle swats landing against it.

Now that she had time to think and compare, Rhen had to admit that it hadn't been all that bad of an experience. It had certainly hurt, yes, and the humiliation factor of having all of her fellow students watch everything that had happened was nothing to scoff at either. But all in all it hadn't been quite as bad as a full-blown spanking from Dana when she was really steamed. It most definitely wasn't something she ever wanted to repeat again, but now that it was over, she felt oddly proud of herself for having endured it and as if she were now that much more a part of the group among her church friends.

She just wished they'd stop giggling at her.

"Good," sniffed Sister Miller, taking a step forward to grab Rhen by a handful of the scruff of her dress as she marched her over to face the blackboard.

She set the Board down to rest vertically upon the little metal shelf that held a pair of dusty erasers, with all of its bible verses facing out toward the other students, and then picked up a stubby piece of yellow chalk. With a quick flick of her wrist she traced out a small circle about two inches in diameter, a little more than a third of the way up the length of the blackboard.

Maintaining her grip with one hand still firmly entwined around the collar of Rhen's yellow and white, ruffled church dress, she was able to easily push her bright red face forward until her nose was pressing lightly against the dark slate in front of her.

"You see that circle?" she asked, even as she guided her face down until it was just below eye-level for her. "That's exactly where I want the tip of your nose to stay until your aunt comes to get you later. You got that?"

"Yes ma'am," came Rhen's muffled reply a moment later after she was sure that she'd gotten her head positioned just right.

"Good."

Sister Miller only let go of the repentant youngster's collar after she had her positioned just the way she wanted her, which forced her to arch her back and push out her simmering bottom toward the classroom as she rose up onto the balls of her feet and spread her legs about a shoulder's width apart to stay balanced. She then gathered up the loose folds of her dress that had fallen back down to cover her seat and pulled them up and out of the way once more. This time pinning them in place against the back of her dress with a pair of safety pins that Rhen hadn't known she'd brought with her until that very moment.

With her skirts now secured in place and no longer covering her yellow Beauty and the Beast panties and the faint splashes of dark pink peeking out from beneath their leg holes, Sister Miller then gathered up her wrists and arranged them too behind her back.

"There we go, perfect," she declared, taking a step back and surveying her handiwork with a little nod, her hands braced on her hips in satisfaction. "Now you be sure to keep those hands right where they are, Rhen. If I catch you rubbing before I say you can, I'll *really* give you something to whine about, you hear?"

"I won't rub, ma'am, I promise," Rhen squeaked against the blackboard in front of her, her hands tightening against her wrists where she was grabbing them.

"Very good... Now then, everyone," the older woman said, turning to face the rest of her class after a few more moments of letting Rhen stand hunched forward as the center of attention. "Shall we continue our lesson?"

"Yes, Sister Miller," was the immediate, angelic response from the six other students still sitting comfortably.

Not a single person dared to even *think* about sticking a toe out of line for the remainder of their discussion about the talking donkey from the Old Testament. And Rhen was left to wriggle and squirm, struggling to keep her nose in place inside that tiny chalk circle as the class continued on without her.

Well, at least today's lesson wasn't boring, she thought to herself with a wan smirk that was thankfully hidden out of sight from the ever sharp-eyed Sister Miller. *Although if Aunt Dana is really as mad as I think she is, I doubt that this little distraction will have been worth the price in the end.*

Rhen sighed then and blew a stray strand of black hair away from her face.

Oh well…

Chapter 16

Missus Hairbrush Returns

Shifting uncomfortably against the plush leather passenger-side seat of her aunt's SUV, Rhen winced as two bone-deep aches in the centers of her cheeks protested with the movement. She'd quickly found to her dismay that while sitting wasn't impossible for her, even the slightest bit of pressure on her well-paddled posterior was enough to send a twinge of discomfort radiating out from the twin bruises that had been left behind by the Board.

Well, she assumed that they were bruises, at any rate.

Rhen hadn't had a chance to properly inspect the results of her bout with the Board quite yet. Such things tended to require a good degree of privacy and access to a mirror, and while there hadn't been *that* many people still milling about the church building after services were over for the day, it still seemed profoundly foolish to risk pulling her panties down even a little bit until she was back at home and safely ensconced behind the dubiously impenetrable protection of her tightly-shut bedroom door.

At least there the only person who might walk in on her would just be Dana.

Sister Miller had left Rhen standing nose-first facing the blackboard until well after class had finished for the day, closing prayers had been said, and her aunt had at last come to collect her. Her adopted guardian had taken one good look at the back of her Disney princess panties, on full display thanks to the safety pins still holding up the back of her dress, and had let out a snort of wildly amused approval. And then had promptly left her right where she was while she and the self-satisfied Sunday school teacher made small talk.

As a result, she was forced to continue her inspection of the dusty slate in front of her while Sister Miller, Janice to her aunt, gave her the play-by-play of what had happened from the moment that Rhen had settled into her chair that morning for class, all the way up until when she'd been put into time-out post-paddling. She even went so far as to point out how she had her keeping her nose inside a much-too-small chalk circle while the paddle that had so thoroughly toasted her sore buns lay innocently right beside her. Just in case it was needed again.

"Oh now, Janice, that is *clever*," observed Dana with an appreciative chuckle, leaning in beside her diminutive girl-friend to eye where she had the tip of her nose pressed against, before tucking a loose strand of black hair back behind her ear for her and kissing her cheek.

"Hang in there, cutie pie, we'll go home soon," she murmured quietly enough so that only Rhen could hear her.

Straightening up, she popped the younger girl's pantied posterior lightly and then turned back to continue chatting with her friend.

"I do something similar with her at home by having her put her nose all the way into the corner after I'm done spanking her. It forces her to stick her tush out and really makes her adorable little caboose *pop*."

Unable to resist tormenting her pouting princess just a little bit, she gave Rhen's prominently presented cheeks a hearty swat.

SMACK!

"Ah!" squeaked the younger girl, fingers flexing as she

struggled to keep her nose in its circle.

"But I must say that this is pretty useful too, especially for those times when you just don't have a proper corner to work with. I'll have to remember it."

"It works just as well if you have her holding up a quarter or a piece of paper," replied her friend, folding her arms and looking on with pride at her handiwork.

"Maybe we'll end up putting that one to the test come report card time, huh, Rhen?"

It was a rhetorical question, Rhen knew, and she didn't deign to dignify it with anything more than a low murmur that managed to convey just how she felt about this whole arrangement; much to the amusement of the other adults watching her.

Anna was there too, of course, though she had little to contribute to the conversation outside of what her mother had already said. However, that didn't stop her from sharing all of the gory details from the short spanking she'd given Rhen as soon as the opportunity presented itself.

"I swear, you'd think she'd never been spanked before with how much she was carrying on," she crooned. "One little pop from Mom and then, *pow*, she was on her feet and hissing like a snake. I tried to help her get back into position, but then she started biting *my* head off like I was the one being rude or something, so of course I had no choice but to show the little sassy-pants who's boss. I'll tell you this much, she's *very* lucky that it wasn't just the two of us in the room, otherwise those panties of hers would've been coming down for a *real* dose of discipline!"

Rhen had been on the verge of opening her mouth to protest as Anna's recounting of events painted her as an unremorseful little brat, but quickly thought better of it upon hearing Dana and Janice laughing along with her. Deciding that she was already in enough trouble as it was, she instead chose to pout silently as her aunt and the Sunday school teacher heaped praise onto the younger girl for her fast thinking and decisive action.

"My, my, I had no idea you were so responsible, Anna," Dana said with what Rhen could only assume was a broad grin. "If you ever find that you have some free time during the summer next year, I might just have a job waiting for you at the daycare."

"Oh wow, really? Thank you, ma'am!"

"Of course, dear," the older woman laughed. "Anyone who can keep my Rhen in line is certainly someone I can trust to help look after a gaggle of little kids, I'd say."

Rhen had felt her teeth grinding together at that, and her hands had curled themselves into indignant fists where they lay held behind her back. But none of the other adults in the room paid her even the slightest bit of attention as she continued to grumble darkly to herself, the blackboard in front of her mercifully muffling several things that would have surely gotten her into even more trouble as their conversation wound down to a close.

Now though, she and Dana were on their way home, lunch time was just around the corner, and Rhen knew that a bruised ego and a little tenderness in her backside were about to be the least of her worries.

"So, um… Am I going to get my mouth washed out when we get home?"

The question had bubbled up and out of her before she had a chance to stop it, and now she sat there studiously facing forward, staring fixedly out of the front windshield of their car as she counted the trees on the median dividing the road ahead of them.

"No, no, not quite," answered Dana with a faint chuckle, laugh lines crinkling at the corners of her eyes where Rhen met them in the reflection of the rearview mirror. "While I suppose I probably *should* scrub out that sassy mouth of yours on principle alone, I know that you weren't actually swearing, so I'll let it pass. After all, it would be pretty cruel of me to deny a young lady such as yourself the chance to revel in some classic Bible jokes."

"Really?" croaked Rhen, scarcely believing her own good fortune as she felt a small spark of hope kindling within her.

"Yes, dear, really," her aunt confirmed with a good-natured roll of her eyes. "Janice really ought to have seen that one coming from a mile away, so I can hardly hold you entirely to blame for your, shall we say... indiscretion. But I'd also advise you not to push your luck in that regard again, either. Just because a word happens to be in the Bible doesn't mean that it's free game for you to bandy about as you please, and you know it."

"Um, right... Sorry."

Rhen felt herself wilting a bit under the stern glare she caught sight of in the older woman's reflection.

"So, uh... no punishment then?" she asked hopefully.

"Hah," snorted Dana in response, reaching over to pat her on the knee affectionately. "You wish, cutie pie. I told Janice that I was going to paint your caboose bright red when we got home, and I meant it, I'm afraid."

"Oh..."

Despite that dire pronouncement, Rhen couldn't help but feel a sizable measure of relief over the fact that she'd somehow managed to avoid another mouth soaping. That of course didn't stop her from crossing her arms in front of her with an unhappy huff either, lips angling down into a petulant frown as memories of awful, bitter soap bubbles replayed themselves across her taste buds.

After all, what was the point of getting into trouble if you didn't at least complain about it a little bit?

"But I already *got* spanked," she started to whine, exhaling her displeasure sharply through her nostrils as she drummed the heels of her penny loafers against the floor in front of her. "It's not fair if you spank me for it too. That's double jeopardy!"

"Technically, you got paddled, dear," Dana corrected, her amusement not waning in the slightest as she sent a side-long smirk toward the pouting girl beside her. "And while I certainly appreciate your attempts to appeal to my sense of justice, I'm afraid that this case has already been decided and your sentence passed."

She let the finality of that statement hang in the air between them for a moment or two longer as she flicked on her turn signal and made to pass a slow moving car in front of them.

"Besides," she added once they'd passed the bumbling minivan that had been going several miles below the speed limit, her voice growing deliberately frosty and ominous as she continued. "You'll just have to trust me when I say that a bright red bottom is going to be the least of your problems in just a little bit."

"Wh... what do you mean?" squeaked Rhen, feeling a fresh wave of dread starting to gnaw a hole in the pit of her stomach.

"Oh, you'll see soon enough, cutie pie," answered her aunt, her voice back to its usual warm and cheery self as she gave her an enigmatic little wink through her reflection in the rear-view mirror. "Suffice it to say that there is definitely more than one way to punish a naughty bottom and that by the time we're through today you will have learned a very valuable lesson in self-control that I doubt you'll want to repeat again anytime soon."

Rhen did not at all like the sound of that, not one bit, but decided that it might not be such a good idea to push for details just then.

Besides, she wasn't even sure she really wanted to know what the older woman had in store for her either. So instead, she just sniffed poutily and turned to stare out her window, trying not to dwell on whatever awaited her in the very near future.

Humph. Why couldn't I have just kept my big mouth shut?

—

Dana wasted very little time in getting down to business upon their arrival home from church. No sooner had the two of them walked through their front door, than she was giving her niece strict orders.

"Young lady, I want you to go straight to your room and change out of your church dress," she said, pointing toward the stairs. "And hang it up *properly* this time, please. After that, you can grab your hairbrush and meet me back here in the front room."

Rhen felt a good deal of the color drain from her face at the mention of the ever-dreaded Missus Hairbrush, and her steps faltered as she put one knee-sock covered foot onto the first stair.

It appeared that her luck had finally run out and that she and her fancy ebony hairbrush were about to have a long, and no doubt very painful, discussion.

"Go on now, we haven't got all day, you know," repeated Dana, stepping past her and giving the seat of her dress a hard pat to get her moving again. "Oh, and don't bother with putting on shorts or a skirt. You won't be needing them for a while, and they'd just be coming off anyway."

"Somehow I thought you might say that," answered the younger girl with a resigned, though not exactly dejected, sigh.

Figures.

"Hurry up now, cutie pie. You don't want to keep me waiting."

—

Sometime later, after making a quick pit stop in the bathroom to drain her nearly-overflowing bladder and then spending a moment or two thoroughly inspecting the marks left behind by the Board in the full-length mirror beside her closet door, Rhen padded her way back downstairs on bare feet. She'd been sure to hang up her ruffly, yellow dress back in her closet where it belonged this time, and after some debate had decided to keep the panties she was already wearing on, but had opted to change out of her camisole and into one of her more comfortable tops.

Wearing nothing but her childish panties and a t-shirt was hardly the same thing as being fully dressed, she knew. But since that wasn't really an option at the moment, Rhen was fully prepared to make do with what little she could as she made her way into her auntie's front room for her punishment.

It's better than nothing, it's better than nothing, it's better than nothing...

"Ah, there you are," cooed Dana, beckoning her over to where she was sitting in the middle of the couch situated between the two big bay windows that looked out onto their front lawn. "And don't you just look precious. Come here and have a sit on Auntie Dana's lap for a moment. We need to talk."

Rhen moved on jelly-like legs to do as she'd been told, her stomach a mess of butterflies as she perched her still tender tush atop the coolly preening older woman's strong right thigh, letting her bare feet dangle between her parted knees, just a few inches above the hardwood.

"Feeling a little sore, are we?" asked the Dana with a knowing look, smirking at the winces she was rewarded with as she bounced the smaller girl on her leg. "Though I doubt that's much of a surprise given what you went through earlier today, huh, cutie pie?"

"Yeah, kinda," admitted a sheepish Rhen with a shy half-grin. "That Board thing is definitely, um… very, uh… impactful."

"Hah! Yes, it most certainly is," agreed Dana with a snort of laughter, her right hand moving down to gently squeeze the side of her adoptive niece's soft hip, while the forefinger of her free hand playfully tapped the end of her nose. "Which is exactly why it's so effective for helping little girls learn to control themselves, instead of just acting on whatever silly little impulse pops into their head."

"Humph, I guess," conceded Rhen with a shrug, crossing her arms and pouting, not quite willing to admit out loud that she might still need to have that particular lesson drilled into her at her age.

"Oh, I think you *know*," countered Dana with a sharp look and a tight squeeze to her hip, locking eyes with her and silently daring her to deny it. "You're a very smart girl, Rhen, honey, but you *do* have a tendency to just do whatever you feel like whenever you think something is boring. Don't you?"

Swallowing hard, Rhen tried to match the older woman's look with one of her own. To just as silently convey that

that was in fact *not* the case, but she quickly found herself losing the staring contest as her cheeks flushed with warm embarrassment.

"Yes, Aunt Dana, I suppose I do..."

She could feel her lips twisting into a grimace around the words, tasting as sour as a lemon while rolling across her tongue, but unfortunately she also knew that they were very much the truth.

"There we go, a little bit of honesty and self-reflection, well done," cooed the older woman, nodding in approval at the admission and flashing her an encouraging smile. "And while I can certainly appreciate being bored and wanting to day-dream, that's still no excuse for derailing someone else's hard work just because you're not in the mood to listen, now is it?"

"No ma'am," answered Rhen with a sigh, unfolding her arms as she flopped her hands grumpily against the tops of her slim, bare thighs.

Oof. How the heck is she so good at this? she thought to herself with a silent harrumph, the heat in her cheeks seeming to coax all of the other butterflies that had still been sleeping inside her stomach back to life. *In less than three minutes she has me sitting on her knee like a ten year old and feeling just awful for my bad behavior today. Well, at least I'm going to be punished for it...*

Rhen felt the temperature in her face tick up a few degrees as that sobering thought crossed her mind.

Double oof. Now where the heck did that come from? I really am a bratty teen at heart, aren't I?

The look on her aunt's face sure seemed to say that she thought she was, and under the pressure of her knowingly raised eyebrows Rhen saw that it was pointless to try and deny it any further.

"I guess I really stepped into it this time, huh?"

"Just a little bit," conceded Dana with an amused twinkle in her eyes as she used her free hand to ruffle the top of her hair affectionately. "But that's okay. You're young and bound to make more than a few mistakes, which is exactly why Missus Hairbrush and I are here to help straighten you out when you do."

Rhen frowned at that, sticking her lower lip out in a half-hearted attempt at a pout.

"Gee, thanks."

"Anytime, hon."

With that, her aunt gave her a wink and then moved her right hand up from where it had been idly toying with one of the leg holes on her Beauty and the Beast panties, to rest along the dip of her lower back.

"Now why don't you go ahead and bend over for me, and we'll get started, alright?"

Letting out a long groan of trepidation, Rhen allowed herself to be tipped forward to lie across Dana's left thigh. This was a new variation on an all too familiar position for her, one that she had yet to experience in her many, many spankings over the last couple of months but also one that she quickly saw the value in. Once she was settled across the top of her thigh, her aunt moved her right leg around and over to pin the backs of her knees in place beneath it. And just like that Rhen found herself trapped and virtually immobilized across her left thigh, with her face and upper torso lying half-supported along the back and side of the couch in front of her.

Not exactly a comfortable position per se, but she suspected that a face full of throw pillow was about to be the least of her worries in just a moment.

"My goodness, I forgot just how *adorable* these undies are on you," Dana cooed, rubbing her right palm appreciatively across the back of Rhen's princess panties and giving the cheeks within a few light pats. "Did the boys and girls in your Sunday school class think so too, cutie pie?"

"I guess you could say that," Rhen growled into the throw pillow that she'd wriggled beneath her, making her aunt chuckle as she gave one of the dancing Belles a playful pinch. "Ow! Hey!"

Dana just ignored her though as she smoothed out the material where she'd pinched it.

"Well, at least you got to keep these on," she said with an unseen mischievous smirk, gripping the white waistband of Rhen's childish underwear and giving it a practiced tug that had them making the short descent down to mid-thigh. "I'm not so nice though, I'm afraid."

"It's not like they were doing that much good to begin with," grumbled the bratty sophomore turned teenager into her pillow, making Dana laugh despite only being able to half-hear her. "You could've just left them where they were, you know."

As she'd expected they would be, her complaints went completely ignored.

"My, my, would you just *look* at those marks," her aunt breathed, letting out an appreciative whistle as she traced a fingernail around the center of first one bare cheek and then the other.

The Board had left twin, oval bruises on each of them, both of which were stained a vivid shade of maroon around their edges and fading to a dusty almost-white in their centers.

"Janice is certainly no slouch when it comes to paddling bratty backsides, that's for sure. How many did she give you, thirteen?"

"Fourteen, actually," harrumphed Rhen, angling her head back so that she could rest her chin against her folded arms while rolling her eyes up toward the ceiling. "Since I stood up after the first one, she decided not to count it."

"Hmmm, that sounds about right."

Grinning from ear to ear, Dana poked at each bruise just enough to make the petite sophomore lying bare bottom up across her lap gasp and squirm a little bit.

She was just too cute not to.

"Well, if it makes you feel any better, *I* won't penalize you if you want to squirm and wiggle while I'm spanking you. I think you look rather adorable when you do so, actually."

As if to emphasize her point, she let her fingers wander down to tickle Rhen along her inner thighs, just barely grazing the base of her sex and sending her into a fit of frantic wriggling as breathy giggles escaped from her pouting lips.

"I'll be sure to k... keep that in mind," she managed to huff out once the older woman had finally relented enough to let her speak, trying not to let any of the embarrassment she was feeling at that particular moment leak into her voice as she surreptitiously rubbed her thighs together.

She was more than a little wet.

Oh god...

How on earth had the couch beneath her not caught on fire yet from all the heat radiating from her face?

"Yes, you do that," answered Dana with a good-natured sigh, giving each mostly-pale bun one final pat before scooping up the oval-backed hairbrush from beside her hip and bringing it to rest just below the outer curve of the bruise on her girlfriend's right cheek. "Now hang on tight, cutie pie. You're in for one heck of an unpleasant spanking, I'm afraid."

Tightening her grip on her pillow and burying her face against it, Rhen gritted her teeth as Dana started to bring her heavy, ebony hairbrush down against her unprotected rear end.

CRACK! CRACK! CRACK! CRACK!

Back and forth, side to side, and up and down it went. Her aunt smacked every available square inch of untouched bare bottom and thigh she could find, gradually filling in all of the whitespace around the marks left behind by the Board, painting them a bright shade of sizzling crimson.

"No, Aunt Dana, please! I'm sorry!"

Even though she'd known that it was going to hurt, Rhen had not been prepared for just how much that purely evil hairbrush that her auntie had bought for her was going to sting once she decided to get serious with it. That brief and brisk bedtime spanking she'd gotten with it the night they'd brought it home had definitely been unpleasant, but that was absolutely nothing compared to the blistering swats that were being hammered non-stop into her all too tender tush right then.

CRACK! CRACK! CRACK! CRACK!

Rhen liked to think that she'd gotten pretty good at taking a spanking without too much fuss over the last couple of months, she'd certainly had plenty of chances to practice at any rate, but any plans that she might have had to stay obediently stoic, or at the very least to not blubber like a five-year-old, went straight out the window less than a full minute into her hairbrushing.

Tossing her head back, she let out a frantic squeal of pain and began babbling out promises and apologies as the spanks began piling up far faster than she was able to handle them.

"Oh my god! I'll be good, I'll be good, I *swear*!"

Her pleas fell on deaf ears however. And worse still, no matter how hard she wriggled or thrashed, with her legs trapped beneath the weight of her implacable auntie's right thigh she was incapable of escaping from the fiery wrath being meted out across her helpless posterior. Left with no other recourse, Rhen found herself bursting into tears as her entire perception of the world around her suddenly shrank in to encompass only her shifting bottom and thighs as they were methodically set ablaze by Dana's relentless swatting.

CRACK! CRACK! CRACK! CRACK!

In no time at all, the sternly focused older woman managed to spread an all-consuming inferno across seemingly every possible spot she could find, beating out a tattoo of lava-hot pain that bored its way deeper and deeper into Rhen's tender flesh with each and every overlapping swat against her bouncing bare bottom.

"Young lady, we will have no more of this class clown nonsense at church, do you hear me? You will give Sister Miller the respect that she deserves and when she tells you to be quiet, you... will... be... *quiet*!"

On and on Rhen continued to yelp and cry, feet scissoring behind her as much as they were able to as she squeezed the pillow beneath her for dear life.

"Ow! Owie! Ack! Okay, okay, I'm sorry, I will!"

CRACK! CRACK! CRACK! CRACK!

Despite having already reduced her niece to tears in practically record time, Dana continued to keep her pace steady and unyielding for several more long and agonizing minutes.

She even went so far as to pull back first one cheek and then the other so that she could make sure that she made the extra sensitive places along the insides of where the younger girl's cheeks came together just as toasty red as the rest of her tush was. After all, she was nothing if not thorough, and since she was deliberately avoiding spanking over the marks left behind by the Board, she knew that she needed to get creative in order to evenly spread out the stinging heat from the hairbrush and not let it build up too much in any one particular spot.

She wanted Rhen's bottom to be bright red and aching, not battered and bruised.

—

Although it seemed like an unending eternity of pain for the one on the receiving end of it, Rhen's spanking was actually a fairly short one. Dana had been sure to keep one eye on the face of the old grandfather clock standing off to the side the whole time as she'd worked, watching as its hands gradually ticked round, until she'd confirmed that she'd seared her niece's seat for exactly ten minutes, and no longer.

Once the minute hand had ticked into place, she brought the spanking to a close with a half-dozen extra-hard zingers to the undercurves of Rhen's already well-roasted cheeks and then set the hairbrush aside with a long exhalation.

"Phew," she sighed, swiping the back of her hand across her sweaty brow before attempting to massage some of the stiffness out of her forearm with a wince.

Spankings like these were always a lot of hard work, but definitely worth it in the long run as far as she was concerned. And judging by the swollen, ruby red cheeks and thighs squirming against her left leg still, it was pretty clear to her that Rhen would be sleeping on her stomach that evening. Heck, she might even end up standing for breakfast the following morning if she were lucky.

Which was precisely the level of soreness that Dana had

been aiming for.

"There, there," she soothed, releasing the younger girl's legs out from under her own after a minute or two of letting her catch her breath.

She eased her over onto her back and then up so that she could sit on her lap again, this time perched on her other thigh.

"Deep breaths now, honeybuns… It's all over. Shhh…"

Despite the fresh agony that resting her relatively minor weight on her incredibly well-spanked bottom produced, Rhen nevertheless endured it as best she could as she buried her face against her aunt's soft bosom and sobbed. Heedless of the panties she still wore at half-mast around her knees.

Noticing those, Dana pulled away one of the hands that she'd been using to rub up and down along the valley of the crying girl's back long enough to slide them the rest of the way down her legs for her. A moment after that they slipped free from around her dangling feet, dropping onto the hard-wood floor just beneath them, abandoned. She smiled to herself at the sight of them there, and then leaned over to gather them up, tucking them away next to the hairbrush behind her right hip for safe keeping with a self-satisfied nod.

It wasn't like Rhen was going to be needing them any time soon, Dana mused. She fully intended on keeping the petite sophomore's naughty little bottom totally bare for the rest of the day as an added reminder to behave herself… and maybe also because she looked way too cute walking around in just a t-shirt with a freshly spanked caboose not to do so.

Either way, she continued to let Rhen sob and sniffle against her chest for another few minutes, rubbing her back gently and murmuring soft words of encouragement into her ear until she at last calmed down enough to the point where she only gave the occasional sniffle. Once the last of her sobs had come and gone, she disentangled the girl from around her chest enough so that she could look down at her and smile fondly.

"Alright, cutie pie, I think you know what comes next, don't you?"

Rhen did indeed know what came next, and she let out a tired sigh, feeling a measure of her usual brattiness starting to return to her now that she no longer felt like Dana was pressing hot irons against her bare bottom.

"Corner time?"

"That's right," sing-songed the older woman with a broad grin, her own usual playful sternness back in full swing as well. "You got it in one, you clever thing!"

"Lucky me..."

Moaning piteously at the ache that sliding off of her aunt's left thigh produced, Rhen offered very little in the way of resistance as she was helped back to her feet and steered by the shoulders over to her usual spot facing where the two walls opposite the big bay windows behind the couch met. Without needing to be told to do so, she raised her hands up and put them on top of her head, threading her fingers together before spreading her stance out a little bit and leaning forward to push her nose all the way into the corner itself.

"Good girl," cooed Dana, giving the scarlet seat presented to her an affectionate little rub before letting two of her fingers slip down between Rhen's parted thighs to confirm that she was indeed still soaking. "Now you just stay here for... oh I don't know... twenty minutes?"

She traced around the younger girl's opening with the tip of her middle finger for a moment or two as she thought it over, before finally slipping it in with a teasing snicker.

"Ah!"

"Yes, twenty minutes sounds good," she purred, pumping in and out of the panting girl a couple of times before extracting her hand just as quickly as it had entered. "And then we'll move on to the rest of your punishment, okay?"

Bringing her glistening fingers up to her smiling lips, Dana sucked them clean with a happy hum.

"The rest?" squeaked Rhen, a visible shiver running through her that made her swollen cheeks wobble in a most adorable way.

"Oh yes," confirmed Dana with an unseen conspiratorial grin as she moved to brace her hands on her hips. "Did you honestly think that a little sore bottom and some corner time were all that you were going to get after the way you were behaving this morning?"

"I was kinda hoping so, yeah," Rhen managed to answer back with something approaching her usual level of sass.

"Well think again, young lady," snapped Dana, not unkindly, as she leaned in to give her niece's jiggly cheeks a light swat that still nevertheless managed to draw out a hiss from her through clenched teeth. "Because I've got something extra-special in mind for you still that should *really* help you learn to exercise those self-control muscles more. Or, at the very least, should prove sufficiently embarrassing enough to make you think twice about smarting off to Sister Miller again next week."

Rhen did not at all like the sound of that one bit, but decided that it would probably be better not to argue just then.

"Yeah, yeah," she grumbled into the corner instead, grateful that it was able to at least mask the dirty look that was no doubt on her face right then.

She felt another tingling shiver trace its way down her

arched spine as she remembered that she was still standing half-bent over with her bare bottom within very easy swatting range and hastily added.

"Uh, ma'am."

"Twenty minutes," repeated Dana with a faint snort, only bothering to give her a light pat on each cheek as she moved to walk out of the room. "I'll see you then, cutie pie."

Chapter 17

Learning a Lesson in Self-Control

Some twenty minutes later, give or take a few extra minutes just for the heck of it, Dana returned to check on her naughty niece. Although much of the initial cherry red hue had faded from her cheeks, they still bore the unmistakable signs of having recently endured a rather lengthy and severe spanking, and the sight of that dusky red caboose poking out obediently from the corner that greeted her as she sauntered back into their front room immediately had the corners of Dana's lips twitching upward into a well-pleased smirk.

"Hmmm, still nice and pink, I see," she purred, her voice ringing with open amusement as she stepped up close behind the raven-haired girl.

Cupping first one cheek and then the other, she gave each of them a firm squeeze that produced a squeak from Rhen, causing her smirk to widen into a full-on grin.

"How're you feeling, cutie pie? Tired of staring at the dry-wall yet?"

"God yes," sighed Rhen with a barely suppressed grunt of discomfort.

Dana's kneading fingers weren't exactly unpleasant as she massaged her tender tush, but it was hard to keep from wincing or gasping either.

"Can I come out now, *please*?"

"Why of course," came the older woman's breezy response, giving the cheeks she'd just been tending to a light swat before taking a step back to make some room for her to turn around.

With a groan of relief, Rhen eased herself away from where her nose had been pressed between the walls in front of her, rolling her shoulders to shake off some of the stiffness that had been building up in them ever since she'd been put there. Part of her was tempted to tug down the front of the minty green t-shirt that she was wearing before she turned around, more so out of habit than any serious worries over preserving her modesty since it was just her and Dana in the house right then, but the relief that she felt as soon her hands found purchase against the swollen orbs of her scalded seat had her dismissing that idea without a second thought.

Instead she settled for angling her hips slightly to the side, half-turning to regard her auntie with a petulant frown over her shoulder so that she could avoid having to fully expose the silky smooth, pink lips of her hairless front for just a moment or two longer.

It was a futile gesture she knew, especially given who was responsible for said hairlessness in the first place. But try as she might, Rhen had yet to find a way to not feel herself being swallowed up in a sea of bashfulness whenever her panties or more were exposed as part of a punishment. Nor could she ever seem to find a way to tune out how much having her clothes so casually confiscated and her embarrassment put on such open display for anyone to see always seemed to further underscore the reality that she was just a naughty, bratty slip of a girl in need of some serious discipline in the eyes of seemingly everyone else around her.

"Awww, what's the matter, hon?" cooed Dana in faux-sympathy, matching the younger girl's scowl with a teasing half-grin. "Does somebody have a sore bottom?"

Rather than answer the mocking question directly, Rhen just stuck out her lower lip and glowered at her all the harder.

And was rewarded for her efforts with a fond ruffling of her hair and a playful tap on the end of her nose.

"Well, so long as you behave yourself, that'll be the last time I'll have to spank you today, I promise."

That was welcome news indeed for Rhen, who could feel her knees wobbling just a little bit from the relief it brought. Two spankings in one day was more than enough for her.

"But," her aunt added, leveling an admonishing forefinger at her with a stern frown that didn't quite reach her still-smiling eyes. "That isn't to say that we're quite through with your punishment yet either, I'm afraid."

Just as she'd been hoping it would, her petite girlfriend's cautiously optimistic face darkened into an adorably sulky scowl at that, but Dana remained unfazed by the dirty look being directed her way as she gestured toward the kitchen with a casual flick of her wrist.

"Now, now, no pouting," she chided gently, turning and beginning to make her way out of the room.

She didn't bother to wait and see if Rhen was going to follow after her as she moved off, confident that the younger girl would fall into step before she got too far. A well-spanked bare bottom was an excellent motivator for reluctant naughty girls, after all.

"Come along, dear, I've got everything all laid out and ready to go just in here."

Rhen spent another few moments grumbling and squirming as she faced the wall, before finally shifting her hands down to tug on the front of her t-shirt as she peeled away from the corner and sped off after Dana's retreating form.

"Hold on, I'm coming!"

Upon stepping into the kitchen however, she immediately felt her feet stumble and her stomach tighten with fresh worry as she caught sight of the chair that had been turned away from the big wooden table, waiting for her. Or more specifically, it was the presence of the most unwelcome of welcome mats that was laid out across its seat that had her moaning with frustration.

Oh god, not that stupid thing again!

Following the line of the younger girl's glare, Dana smiled knowingly as she reached out to wrap an affectionate arm around her shoulders, gesturing toward the sheets of notebook paper and the pen she'd also laid out on top of the table with her free hand.

"Oh yes, little girl, it's your old friend the punishment mat," she confirmed, letting her hand slip down from Rhen's narrow shoulders to rub lightly along the curve of her bare right cheek. "And you're going to sit your sore buns down on it right there at the table and write Sister Miller a nice, *long,* heartfelt apology letter for the way you were acting in her class today."

She let that all sink in for a moment or two, enjoying the way Rhen unconsciously nibbled at her lower lip as she no doubt tried not to think about just how unpleasant spending time sitting on the coarse and bristly mat could be, before she added with a light squeeze to her tush.

"And as you can see, I think it would be best if you wrote it out by hand. Handwritten letters are always so much more personal, I've found. Plus it'll give you a chance to work on your penmanship too, won't it?"

Rhen, still pouting, nevertheless nodded once at her aunt after she'd angled her head up to look at her. She was definitely not looking forward to spending however long it was that she was going to have to be stuck (literally) sitting on that gosh darn punishment mat. But then again, judging by the grimly amused twinkle she saw in the older woman's eyes, she had a sinking feeling that hand-writing a letter on an extra-sore bottom wasn't the worst thing that she had in store for her that afternoon.

As if reading her mind, Dana's smirk split into a full-on grin then as she began steering her toward the sink.

"But before you get to work on that," she purred. "There's one other thing we need to take care of first…"

Rhen could feel panic starting to well up within her as they drew closer and closer to the kitchen sink and the bone white bar of Ivory soap that sat freshly unwrapped and waiting for her there on the countertop.

"Wait, Aunt Dana, no please!" she began to protest, her feet dragging as her mouth twisted into a grimace at the far too recent memory of terrible tasting, soap being scrubbed relentlessly against her defenseless tongue. "You said you *weren't* going to wash my mouth out, remember? This isn't fair!"

"Oh honey, that soap isn't for your mouth," laughed Dana, bringing them to a halt just before the counter and gesturing toward the thing next to the bar of soap that her niece apparently hadn't noticed until right then. "It's for *that*, you silly goose."

"Huh?" asked a very confused Rhen, tilting her head first to one side and then the other, fixing the object in question with a tenuously hopeful stare as she tried to figure out what she was looking at.

Laid out on the granite countertop beside the bar of Ivory was a modestly-sized, empty bag made out of what appeared to be some sort of thick blue rubber. It had a sort of funneled opening on one end, and on the other had a coiled length of clear flexible tubing coming out of it that terminated in a white plastic nozzle about the width of her pinky and maybe twice as long.

"Um… and just what is *that*, uh… exactly?"

Whatever it was, Rhen had a sneaking suspicion that she wasn't going to like it one bit.

"Why, it's an enema bag, dear," explained Dana matter-of-factly, as if they were discussing the weather rather than some sort of creative new way that she was planning on using to punish the college sophomore turned thirteen-year-old brat standing in just a t-shirt and a nervous smile right beside her. "And judging by the look you're giving me, you've never heard of this specific method of attitude adjustment before. So, allow me to explain how it all works."

Tapping a forefinger lightly against the center of the bag, she said, "First thing's first. We fill this rubber bag here all the way up to just below the brim with some nice, warm, and most importantly *soapy* water. This one can hold about two quarts give or take, that's half a gallon if you're having trouble remembering your measuring conversions, which is about the average amount for something like this."

Rhen could already picture the two quarts of hot, soapy water in her mind's eye. And while she wasn't yet clear on what it was that her auntie planned on doing with them, the thought of it made her thighs squirm and her pussy ache as her stomach roiled with anxious tension, much to the other woman's clear amusement.

"After the bag is filled with water, I'll hang it up from one of the cabinets here, and then after that the water will start to flow down through this little hose."

Dana went on to trace her fingertip down to the bottom of the bag and then around the neatly coiled loops of the clear plastic tubing attached to it.

"But you don't need to worry about the water making a mess, dear. Thanks to this little clamp near the end here, it won't come rushing out until we're ready for it."

Smiling to herself at that, she at last tapped her forefinger against the base of the nozzle at the other end of the tubing, tracing it along its smooth surface all the way to its rounded tip.

"Finally, when the clamp is released the water will start to flow out of here, which will of course be situated neatly inside of your cute little tush."

The color had been steadily draining from Rhen's face all throughout this little explanation, horror slowly dawning on her as she tried to wrap her mind around what she'd just been told, and it took a supreme effort of will on her part to manage to croak out.

"M-My what?"

"Your tush, dear," repeated Dana just as casually as before. "For your punishment enema."

As if to make it even clearer for the fretting girl chewing on the end of her thumbnail as her eyes remained glued to the blue, rubber bag in front of her, she gave her a few firm pats right along the central divide between her cheeks, directly above the place where she intended to slide the nozzle of the enema bag into in just a few moments.

"Once we've gotten this little nozzle here *all* the way inside of you…"

Still grinning, Dana slipped her middle finger between Rhen's cheeks, gently stroking her intended target while keeping her voice brisk and business-like.

"I'll release the clamp and you'll slowly start to take in the full bag of soapy water over the course of a couple minutes. It's a very unique sensation and one that I don't think you'll be keen to repeat again anytime soon, but then again, that's rather the point, isn't it?"

With a low chuckle, she pushed on the stunned

sophomore's puckered anus, slipping her prodding fingertip into her up to the first knuckle.

"Eep!"

"Indeed," purred Dana, wriggling her fingertip tauntingly around Rhen's tight grip on it and leaning over to nip at her earlobe. "Then, once that's all taken care of, you'll hold *everything* in for ten minutes while you're back standing in the corner... and then that'll be that. Got it?"

"But... but..."

Breathless and unable to think of any viable excuses or arguments, Rhen just spluttered the word out over and over again as her face flushed almost as red as her bottom had been not too long ago.

"But... but why?"

Dana pulled her hand back from its teasing then, moving to rest it on her shoulder again and giving it a reassuring little squeeze.

"Honey, you are as cute as a button and smart as a whip, but like I told you earlier, you *really* need to learn how to control yourself better."

She paused, watching with satisfaction as Rhen swallowed hard, her lips opening and closing several times as she tried and failed to attempt to deny the truth they both knew.

"And since we've had to have this conversation, or one very much like it, more than a few times these last few weeks, I thought it was high time that we tried helping you learn in a slightly different way instead."

Her grin hadn't slipped at all so far as she'd spoken, and now she gave her a sly wink.

"You'll just have to trust me when I say that it'll all make a lot more sense in just a little bit when you're doing your absolute best to keep it all in."

"Oh… oh dear…"

Rhen had to admit that this new punishment made a sort of diabolically poetic sense to her, much like many of her aunt's other disciplinary tactics tended to, but that didn't mean that she hated it any less. Still though, she knew that this was going to happen whether she liked it or not. And while she was very much in the "not" camp in that regard, she also knew that there wasn't anything she could do about it either. So instead of running the risk of another spanking *and* an enema, she just nodded and gave an exasperated sigh.

She'd definitely earned this punishment, after all, hadn't she?

"Ugh, fine. Whatever… I guess," she conceded, folding her arms in front of her with a pouty huff.

"That's not exactly the attitude I would recommend you give me given your current predicament, young lady," replied Dana with a roll of her eyes, the corners of her mouth only dipping slightly. "But I think you'll be singing a different tune soon enough, so I'll forgive you. Now then, you just bend your bratty little butt over with your elbows on the counter here, and we'll get things started. Alright?"

Seeing little other choice than to obey, Rhen nodded once again and flopped forward with another disgruntled huff, glaring daggers at the backsplash of tiles only about a foot away from her face now as she shifted around into as comfortable a position as she could. But before she could truly settle into her groove attempting to bore a hole straight through the wall in front of her using only the power of her petulant indignation, she heard the water from the sink beside her turn on and she found her eyes being drawn inexorably toward the noise.

She watched with a mixture of curiosity and mounting dread as Dana gathered up her supplies, working up a bubbly lather on the bar of soap before holding it just above the top opening of the enema bag as she began to fill it up. Warm water cascaded down over the soap, carrying with it a steady stream of suds as it dribbled down into the waiting opening. Her aunt kept the flow of water to a medium trickle, and little by little the rubber walls of the blue bag began to bulge, expanding outward as they were filled from within by a milky white blend of soap and water.

Geez, if soap in my mouth was bad, I'm definitely not looking forward to finding out what it feels like going in the other end, thought Rhen with a shiver, clenching and unclenching her cheeks in time with the rhythm of the long, deep breaths she was forcing herself to take. *Ugh. This freaking sucks. Why couldn't I have just kept my big mouth shut? Everyone knows that Shrek jokes are old news anyway, darn it!*

All too soon Dana had finished filling the bag, and humming to herself, she reached out and turned off the faucet. She then hefted the sloshing, soapy mixture up a bit higher, eyeing it thoughtfully before nodding once in satisfaction and hanging it by its rounded, plastic hook from one of the cabinet pulls just above Rhen's head.

With that taken care of, she then took hold of the clear tubing, flicking it lightly a few times here and there to help push out the air bubbles as she uncoiled it until she was at last gripping the long, thin nozzle at its end in her right hand.

Holding it over the sink, she undid the little clamp at its base and let a small stream spritz from the end of it. Then, once the line was clear of anything other than milky white water, she nodded once more and cinched the flow on the hose shut.

After that, she picked up the bar of soap from where she'd left it on the countertop and began to rub it up and down all along the length of the nozzle, smearing on a thick coating of slick, bubbly residue.

"To help ease it in," she explained when she noticed Rhen's brows furrowing in confusion, lips pursed in a silent question.

Flashing her a grim half-smile, Dana turned slightly to give her a better view of what she was doing.

"Normally I'd just use some petroleum jelly for this part, but seeing as this is supposed to be a *punishment* enema and all, soap is a far more appropriate substitute. I think you'll find that it makes a much more... noticeable impression when it's going in."

Rhen let out a small squeak at that, rising up onto her tip-toes despite herself as she swallowed hard.

"Indeed," agreed her aunt with a light laugh, as if she'd just said something profoundly articulate and insightful.

"Now then," she went on, casually tossing the soap into the sink beside her and wiping her wet hand on the front of her blouse as she turned her full attention to the arched back and the very bare bottom thrust up and out before her. "You just relax and this'll all be over before you know it. Okay, cutie pie?"

"Yeah, sure, easy for you to say," groused a red-faced Rhen. "It's not *your* butt that's about to be pumped full of soapy water."

Choosing to ignore the whiney sass still wheedling its way out of her not-niece's pouting lips, Dana stepped around to her left side, giving her rump a little pat with her free hand as she passed. She then slid in snugly beside her hip, and resting her forearm along the groove of her spine and lower back, reached out with said free hand and parted the younger girl's cheeks just as wide as they would go.

"Well, hello there," she cooed in a teasing tone as her eyes locked onto their still clenching and unclenching target. "It's nice to see you too, friend."

"Oh god," moaned Rhen, burying her scarlet face in her hands as a molten wave of humiliation bubbled up to fill her from the soles of her feet all the way to the roots of her inky black hair. "This is *so* humiliating."

At least it's not the middle of the week, she silently told herself, not wanting to give the older woman any ideas for how to embarrass her even more in the future.

"Shhh... it's fine," soothed Dana, her voice carrying a broad grin as she let several excruciatingly mortifying seconds crawl by with her niece's cheeks spread wide and her puckered little rosebud on full display.

She'd caught glimpses of it here and there whenever she'd been spanking her in the past, but this was her first time seeing it up close and so clearly, and she had to admit that it was just as adorable as the rest of Rhen was.

"You have a *very* cute tush, honey, and that's nothing to be embarrassed about."

Smiling slyly, she added.

"Be a good girl for me, and I might just kiss it better after we're through here, alright?"

"Oh... oh really?" croaked Rhen, trying to sound coy, but not doing a particularly good job of it as Dana's teasing words made her clit positively *throb* with need.

"Really," confirmed the older woman, blowing an unexpected, cool stream of air against her puckered opening and making her squeak. "But only if you relax and let Auntie Dana take care of this naughty little tushy of yours. Deal?"

Snorting in spite of the monumental levels of shame-faced embarrassment and knee-knocking need she was experiencing just then, Rhen nevertheless made a valiant attempt to do as she was told. Unclenching her quivering backdoor, she did her best to let go of the tension in her cheeks as she shifted her feet awkwardly beneath her.

"Well, if you insist…"

"That's my girl," purred Dana sweetly. "Now you just take a deep breath and try to relax, here comes the choo-choo…"

Rhen let out a high-pitched squeak of surprise, jerking beneath her aunt's steady grip as she felt the hard plastic tip of the enema nozzle nudge up against her opening. It was a lot colder than she'd been expecting it to be, but at that particular moment that was about the least of her worries.

Closing her eyes, she forced herself to take in as deep of a breath as she could manage through her nose, holding it in for a five count, before letting it out slowly through pursed lips. Then, just as she was in the middle of exhaling, she felt Dana begin to push the nozzle into her. It slid home with next to no resistance thanks to the liberal coating of soap she'd worked up around its length and the rest of Rhen's breath escaped her in another squeak.

"Ah!" she gasped as she felt it slide in further still, pushing forward until it at last came to a stop somewhere around three or four inches deep inside of her.

Although at that particular moment, it felt a whole lot more like two or three *feet* as far as Rhen was concerned.

All things considered though, at least the nozzle was a narrow one, she tried to tell herself. While it was definitely not something that she could pretend *wasn't* lodged all the way inside of her from between her brazenly parted and well-reddened cheeks, it at least didn't feel like *that* much of an intrusion into one of her most delicate of places. Unfortunately for her however, the Ivory soap that it was lubricated with more than made up for any lack of girth on the nozzle's part as it began to mercilessly irritate her bottom from the inside out.

"Ack! Oh my god, Aunt Dana, please, it… it stings!"

"Yes, yes, I know, dear," replied the older woman, sounding not the least bit concerned as she twisted and turned the nozzle around inside of the petite sophomore's tush, holding her in place with the forearm she still had resting along the small of her back as she worked.

She kept this up for several long moments until she was confident that the little plastic nozzle wasn't about to slip free on its own, before at last letting go of it and the cheeks that she'd been holding apart, giving the younger girl a couple of brisk swats as her bottom jiggled back into place.

SMACK! SMACK!

"Now you hold onto that nice tight for me, and don't you *dare* let it slip free or else Missus Hairbrush will be making a return visit for round two before we try again. You got that?"

"Got it!" Rhen hastened to assure her, gritting her teeth at the marked increase in discomfort that clamping down as hard as she could around the soapy nozzle produced.

Given how narrow and slippery the darn thing was, it already felt as if it were on the verge of popping free at any moment and so she pushed past the urge to relax her cheeks and instead held on for dear life as she moaned and writhed with the effort of it all. The looming prospect of another spanking from her ebony hairbrush proved to be sufficient incentive to put up with the indignity of it all, and more to the point, she had a sinking feeling that a wildly unpleasant burning sensation tormenting the inner-walls of her delicate anus was about to be the least of her worries.

And oh how right she was.

"Very good," crooned Dana, grinning with wry amusement as she stood by and watched, waiting patiently for Rhen to get used to the sensation of holding onto the enema nozzle herself before she reached for the little plastic clamp near the end of the flexible tubing protruding from between her clenched cheeks and thumbed it open. "Now here comes the water…"

"Oh!"

Rhen let out a long, high-pitched squeal and rose up onto her tiptoes once again as she felt warm water start to gush into her, filling her insides up like a balloon as her eyes shot open and her mouth formed itself into a shocked little "o". The flow from the nozzle was a *lot* faster than she'd been expecting it to be, and as it rapidly pushed its way deeper and deeper into her, the soapy mixture began to make her cramp up in a most unpleasant way that had her dancing from foot to foot as she panted and moaned, heedless of the humiliating spectacle she was making of herself.

"Oh… oh god… Aunt Dana, please… it… it's too much. I can't take it!"

"Shhh… you can and you will," soothed the older woman in a gentle voice that nevertheless bore an unmistakable edge of steel to it that had her girlfriend's thighs squirming extra hard with the shiver it sent down her spine.

Dana idly rubbed the small of the younger girl's back with the pad of her thumb, tracing tight circles around the pale, smooth skin exposed by where her t-shirt had ridden up while she carefully monitored the flow of water through the tubing. Occasionally she would lean over her charge to check on how much was left in the blue, rubber bag hanging from the cabinet above her, before turning her full attention back to her struggling niece's flushed face and smirking.

"You have nobody to blame for this but yourself, you know, young lady, and I want you to remember that while the enema is doing its work," she chided. "Now do your best to focus on your breathing, and take your punishment like a good girl, alright? We're almost at the halfway point now."

With those scolding words she delivered a few light swats. Nothing all that terrible, really. They were little more than a few hard pats accentuated by a sharp flick of her wrist. But given Rhen's current distress and the state of her well-spanked bottom, they stung a whole lot more than they normally would have and were sufficient to get the flustered sophomore turned bratty teenager to yelp and squeal. And soon enough, promises to not only be good, but to be the very paragon of good behavior began tumbling free from her lips in droves.

"Oh my god, please, this is too much! I promise I've learned my lesson. I swear I'll be good. Please, Aunt Dana, I'll be an absolutely perfect super-duper-ultra-angel, I *swear*!"

"My goodness! An absolutely perfect super-duper-ultra-angel, you say?" teased the older woman with a faint snicker as she lightly tickled the delicate undercurve of Rhen's bare right cheek. "Hmmm… Well, while that *is* a tempting offer, I'm afraid I'm going to have to decline. You see, I much prefer the mostly-obedient, but still pretty naughty from time to time, version of you, dear. That one is a lot more fun to spank, you know."

As if to prove her point, she gave the cheek she'd just been tickling a hearty swat.

SMACK!

"No she isn't," protested Rhen with a high-pitched whine, knowing full well that she was not only fibbing, but playing directly into her snickering auntie's hands.

Even now with all of the humiliation and discomfort she was experiencing, she knew that she wouldn't ever want to trade her strict, no-nonsense life of love and discipline, rules and punishments, for anything.

Well, almost anything.

She definitely wouldn't have said no to a smaller enema bag and less-soapy water just then.

Neither was forthcoming though, and she was left with

no other choice than to pant and groan, wriggling in great discomfort as her insides slowly swelled and roiled with the water pouring from the nozzle. Not exactly burning per se, but most certainly cramping up and feeling a good deal more irritated than she would have preferred.

And it *sucked*.

Eventually though, about a minute or so later (which felt more like an hour to Rhen), the rubber bag had at last shrunk back to its original size, completely spent, and with that came a merciful end to the steady influx of water into her bowels.

"And... there... we... go," declared Dana, watching the last of the soapy water trickle its way down the clear plastic tubing before giving her niece a couple of congratulatory pats on either cheek.

"All done, cutie pie," she said as she thumbed the little clamp near the base of the nozzle closed, and smiled. "You took that really well, and I'm proud of you."

"Uh, thanks..."

"So..." asked Dana in a teasing tone, deliberately drumming her fingertips against the base of her captive cutie's spine and enjoying the grimaces it elicited. "How're we feeling?"

"Full," grunted Rhen, wincing against where she'd been resting the side of her face atop her folded arms.

Her brow was sweaty and furrowed into a frown as she did her best to focus on keeping her cheeks clenched together against the tide of water that she feared might escape from her at any moment if she wasn't careful.

"*Very* full."

"Hah, somehow I thought you might just say that."

Dana watched on with wry, self-satisfied amusement as her niece shifted her weight uselessly from foot to foot, dancing around in very clear discomfort and distress.

"Now then," she went on, bracing one hand against the sweaty small of the younger girl's back, while the other gripped the end of the nozzle still wedged snugly in between her cheeks. "In just a second I'm going to pull this out."

She gave the nozzle a little tap, tap, tap that had Rhen squeaking in an undeniably adorable way.

"And then you're going to go back into the corner where you'll stand and hold in your punishment enema for ten minutes while you think about how you're going to focus during Sunday school and control your actions better in the future."

"T-Ten minutes?" gasped Rhen, disbelieving.

She was pretty sure that she could handle *maybe* a minute at most without that nozzle where it was.

Oh god, this is the worst...

"Yes young lady, ten minutes," confirmed Dana with a good deal more steel in her voice this time around, before letting out a falsely-exasperated sigh. "And *please* don't interrupt me again. Not only is it rude, but the whole point of this little endeavor is to help you learn to think twice before you speak."

Releasing her grip around the base of the nozzle, she gave each of the tender backs of Rhen's thighs a hard smack to emphasize her point.

SMACK! SMACK!

"Understood?"

"Yes ma'am," yelped Rhen, her frantic shifting ratcheting up several notches thanks to the sudden, sharp swats. "I'm sorry!"

"Hmmm, we'll just see about that," mused Dana, not sounding all that convinced as she took hold of the nozzle once more. "Now then, as I was saying, I'm going to pull this thing out and then you're going to stand in the corner. But before we do any of that, you have a choice to make, little girl."

She let those words hang in the air for several long moments just to make sure that Rhen was fully paying attention before she went on.

"I know that this isn't going to be easy for you, I can tell already that the enema is doing its job pretty well given how wriggly and whiney you've been."

At that, her lips twitched up into an affectionate smile as she regarded her extra-squirmy sophomore.

"So, if you would like, you may wear a pull-up during your corner time. You know… just in case you think you might need it."

"Oh god," groaned Rhen, her face flushing hotter than it already had been at the very notion of such a thing, even as she began to give it some very serious consideration.

On the one hand, it would be beyond utterly humiliating to have to wear something like that, to actively *choose* to wear one no less. But on the other… it could end up saving her a *far* greater amount of embarrassment in the long run if things went horribly, horribly wrong.

She'd seen the pull-ups that her auntie kept stashed away under the sink in her bathroom, had actually gone snooping around looking for them the day after she'd had her pubic hair removed just to confirm that the older woman hadn't been bluffing about putting her into one if she didn't cooperate. There had definitely been a neat stack of them ready and waiting for her when she'd cautiously peered into the cabinet just after showering that night, and although she hadn't had the nerve to actually try one on, she knew that it was safe to assume that they would fit her perfectly.

Not that she had any interest in ever finding out for sure.

"Well?" prompted Dana, steering her out of her swirling thoughts with another casual tap on the end of the nozzle protruding from between her cheeks. "What's it gonna be, cutie pie?"

Rhen jumped, startled from her reverie and gritting her teeth at the decision she knew she had to make.

Huffing out a pout, she eased the pressure in her jaw and said, "Um… I'll uh, I'm fine without the uh…"

She swallowed hard, unable to bring herself to even *say* the word out loud lest she bring herself that much closer to finding herself wearing one.

"The uh… Um… No, I don't need any help, thanks."

Her obvious trepidation was not lost on the older woman though, it seemed, who found herself snickering again.

"Very well then, dear, have it your way," she said with a gentle roll of her eyes. "Now get ready, because this is coming out…"

Before Rhen had a chance to fully prepare herself mentally for what was about to happen, she felt Dana beginning to tug the nozzle free. Thankfully she'd already had her cheeks clenched, and while it was a bit of a fight, it nevertheless came free with a wet *pop*. Even better though, nothing else came with it, and she let out a small sigh of relief as she flopped out against the countertop.

I can do this, I can do this. No pull-ups, I can do this…

Her aunt gave her just enough time to catch her breath, carefully watching to make sure that she was actually as fine as she claimed she'd be, before nodding once in satisfaction and reaching out to help her up.

Even though the downstairs portion of their house had hardwood floors, she definitely didn't want to have to clean up any messes like that.

Or worse, humiliate her favorite brat in such a way.

"Alright, hon, let's get you back into the corner," she said after letting Rhen catch her breath, easing her away from where she'd been bending over and steering her back out into the front room.

She made sure to keep her pace nice and slow as the younger girl waddled awkwardly beside her.

"I know it's hard, but you can do it, I promise."

"Th-Thanks," Rhen managed to get out around the grimace of her hyper-focused concentration, several strands of her long, black hair plastered to her forehead with sweat.

Before she knew it, she found herself once again facing her least favorite corner of the house, though thankfully this time Dana didn't insist on enforcing her usual rules of hands on head and nose actually pressed up into the corner.

"Now you stay put right there and think about how you're going to behave better from now on," she scolded gently. "I'll be back in ten minutes to collect you, alright?"

"Right," answered Rhen in a breathy gasp, nodding her head just enough to show that she'd heard as she stared hard at the drywall in front of her, trying not to think about her roiling belly.

Leaving the younger girl to stew in her own discomfort, Dana pulled out her smartphone, set a timer, and then tapped the start button.

With that taken care of, she retreated back into the kitchen and began cleaning up her discarded enema supplies. After tossing the spent bar of soap into the trash can, she then rinsed out the rubber bag and tubing, hanging it all over the edge of the sink to air dry.

Throughout it all, she made sure to keep one eye on her slowly ticking timer, and an ear out to listen for Rhen's moaning and groaning as the seconds crawled by at a snail's pace.

Once she saw that there were only a handful of seconds left, Dana tiptoed her way back into the living room, moving over to stand just behind her thoroughly distracted niece just as the timer went off at last.

"Time's up, cutie pie," she declared with a congratulatory couple of pats across the central divide between the squirming girl's dancing cheeks. "Go on now, shoo!"

Not bothering to glower at the pats, Rhen shot from the corner and out of the room like a bat out of hell, both hands clamped tightly over her caboose as she babbled over and over again.

"Thank you, thank you, thank you!"

—

Rhen's punishment enema had indeed been a lesson that she would not soon forget, and she was resolved to be as quiet as... well as a church mouse during Sunday school next week.

She may not have totally mastered her self-control issues yet, but she felt that she was a lot closer to doing so by the time she at last flopped out onto her stomach for bed later that night, sore and totally spent as Dana planted a kiss on her lips as she settled Missus Hairbrush back into her customary position on the nightstand.

There would no doubt be more spankings, and possibly even an enema or two in her future when she eventually slipped up again, but that was just fine with Rhen.

Closing her eyes, she sighed as she cuddled up with her teddy bear and stuffed penguin.

Practice made perfect, after all. And that was good enough for her.

Chapter 18

TA Trouble

"Oh my god, Abby, Rhen, will you two *please* put a sock in it already?"

The two of them looking up from the not-so-murmured conversation they'd been having near the back of their classroom for the last ten minutes, Rhen and her former roommate from the dorms each flashed their irate TA a sheepish look.

"Sorry, Court," piped up Abby, bringing her hands together in front of her in a false gesture of apology even as she teasingly nudged her roommate turned study-buddy under their shared desk with the side of her knee. "We'll be good, I promise. So you know… go on, teach your thing, it's fine."

"Yeah," chimed in Rhen, emboldened by her friend's sass and flashing their TA an impish grin of her own. "There's no need to blow a gasket."

That managed to get a barely-stifled snicker out of Abby, while the older girl glowering at the two them from behind her podium at the front of the room just heaved out a long-suffering sigh and pinched the bridge of her nose in exasperation.

By some odd twist of fate, or maybe it was just her auntie's sharp eyes taking note of details that Rhen had missed while she'd been helping her rearrange her schedule for the fall semester, the TA for her introductory Physical Science course wound up being none other than Courtney Summers; Rhen's former RA from back when she'd been living in the dorms.

It had definitely been more than a little bit of a shock to see the tall, athletic girl already in the middle of writing out notes on the whiteboard that first time she'd walked into her lab. But other than a knowing smirk and the occasional swat on the butt hello, nothing too embarrassing had come of having one of the girls who'd been there to see Dana spanking her that fateful evening she'd moved out of her old room being in charge of her lab. In fact, Courtney was a remarkably good teacher, and now that they were well into late September, Rhen had come to look forward to their weekly labs together quite a bit. And not just because she couldn't wrap her head around chemistry or physics to save her life and heavily relied on the older girl to actually explain the things that her professor breezed past during their lectures.

At that particular moment however, Courtney was looking very much like she'd reached the end of her patience, and Rhen found her mouth going dry with the warning look she leveled at her and her friend.

Thankfully though, the silent tension didn't last for long.

"You know... you're lucky you're cute, Abby Jenkins," the TA admonished, her lips parting into a thin, enigmatic smile as she wagged a finger at the girl sitting next to Rhen with mock-sternness.

Abby returned the smile with a mischievous smirk and a wink, and Rhen felt her own mouth quirking to the side just a bit herself.

Before the two of them had been so rudely interrupted, Abby had actually been in the middle of filling her in on all about how she and Courtney had officially started dating only a few days earlier. And while this wasn't exactly shocking news to her, she'd been well aware of how they'd started seeing each other casually not too long after she'd moved out of the dorms, she was still nevertheless happy for them both.

They were an excellent match for each other as far as she could see, and it made her heart swell with warmth to see how the two of them looked at each other now.

That warmth quickly became a lead weight plunging down into the pit of her stomach however as Courtney turned her gaze away from her new girlfriend and leveled a hard, frosty glare at her partner in crime.

"And as for you, *Rhenny*," she snapped, her voice now carrying a steely edge that had its target sitting up straighter in her seat despite the snort of amusement she got from Abby for it. "You can see me after class, young lady."

For any other student that order would have been something to be casually laughed off, treated as just a funny joke among friends. But word of Rhen's spanking in the dorms last semester had spread like wildfire throughout their little group of twenty or so students thanks in no small part to Abby's penchant for gossiping, and that coupled with Courtney's naturally strong and commanding presence were enough to ensure that Rhen garnered no sympathy from her peers as many of them turned in their seats to smile condescendingly toward her.

"Uh-oh, busted," sing-songed someone from off to her right, much to the amusement of the other people sitting around her.

Rounding on the voice, Rhen glared, but all that seemed to do was coax out more snickering.

"Awww, look at her pouting. That's so cute!"

In their eyes she wasn't Rhen, the college sophomore, but rather Rhenny, the bratty (but bright) teenager, who for whatever reason had somehow wound up as part of their class despite looking like she'd barely started high school. Rather than a mature adult who didn't need telling twice to be quiet, she was someone who required a firm hand to keep her in line. And so while Abby's antics were met with good-natured dismissal by her fellow students, Rhen's were regarded as obnoxious and childish, and her being held after class for a good talking to was exactly what she deserved.

The worst part of all though, Rhen knew, was that they were right.

"Oh my god, *whatever*," she huffed, face growing warm.

"Excuse me?" demanded Courtney from behind her podium, her brows knitting together in annoyance. "Do I need to call your auntie, young lady?"

"No, no, that's fine!" Rhen hastened to assure her, doing her best to ignore the snickers her outburst elicited from the people around her as she shook her head quickly. "I'll meet you after class, uh… ma'am."

"You'd better, missy."

Courtney fixed her with a long, frosty look from across the room, silently daring her to say something else, but Rhen knew better than to take the bait and instead just har-rumphed, angling her blushing face down toward the notes she'd ostensibly been taking all lesson and further cementing her image as just another misbehaving teen being put in her place.

"Ahem."

With the matter now settled, Courtney cleared her throat, once again back to her usual easy-going manner as she gestured toward the PowerPoint presentation she had projected onto the whiteboard behind her.

"Anyway, so as I was saying…"

—

The rest of the lab that afternoon continued on uninterrupted by any more outbursts from Rhen or Abby. Now thoroughly embarrassed, she did her very best to lose herself in jotting down notes and throwing her hand up high to answer questions whenever the opportunity presented itself in order to try and ease some of the nervous tension making her heart flutter.

Unfortunately, it didn't help.

By the time class was over for the day, her stomach was a roiling mess of butterflies, and she could feel the faint heat of a blush coloring her cheeks a delicate shade of light pink.

I can't believe she's making me stay after class like some sort of middle schooler in detention. This is so not fair.

Rhen continued to remain seated after she'd finished packing up her laptop and textbook, never even considering trying to sneak away while her TA wasn't looking as she glumly watched the rest of her fellow students funnel out of the room.

The next thing she knew, it was just her and Courtney left.

Well, almost.

Abby was still there. She'd been loitering near the front of their tiny classroom ever since their lab had ended, chatting animatedly with her girlfriend.

"You planning on sticking around to watch the fun?" asked Courtney, wrapping her arms around the shorter girl's waist and pulling her in close before capturing her lips in a quick, but passionate, kiss.

"I wish I could," answered Abby with a short huff through her nostrils. "But I've got to hurry if I want to catch Doctor Baxter before his office hours are over."

"Bummer."

"Tell me about it."

Leaning her head in closer so that her smirking mouth brushed along the side of the other girl's ear, Courtney murmured something into it.

Rhen wasn't able to quite pick up what it was that she said, but judging by the breathy giggle it wrung from her friend and the way her right foot popped up in back as one of Courtney's hands ventured south to fondle her rump, she could hazard a guess that it probably had something to do with their plans to meet up later that evening.

Ugh. Get a room already, you two, geez.

"Alright, I'll see you tonight, babe," chirped Abby, rising up onto the balls of her feet to plant another quick kiss on her girlfriend's lips before stepping away and turning to speed-walk out the door.

Looking back over her shoulder as she went, she flashed Rhen an impish grin and winked.

"And I'll definitely be texting *you* later on as well... Rhenny."

Rhen's only response to that was to stick her tongue out at the retreating back of her friend and make a rude gesture under the table that would definitely have gotten her into major trouble with her aunt if she'd seen it.

Talk to you later too, you jerk.

"Now then," crooned Courtney, drawing Rhen out of her pouting as she eased the door shut behind her girlfriend and turned to regard her with a predatory grin. "I do believe that you and I have some business to take care of. Don't we, young lady?"

She arched a cool eyebrow with the question, and Rhen found herself swallowing hard as the older girl began to advance on her at an easy pace.

"Um... what do you mean?" she stalled with a hot blush, knowing full well what the other girl had in mind, but not daring to acknowledge it out loud just in case by some miracle it turned out that she was wrong.

"Oh, come now, Rhen," cooed Courtney, stopping only a few inches away from the younger girl so that she could loom over her, still grinning. "I know that I've been cutting you a lot of slack this semester, but did you honestly think that you could get away with wandering into *my* lab nearly ten minutes late and then be a disruptive little chatty Cathy all lesson without some sort of punishment for it?"

"Eep!" squeaked Rhen, feeling the heat in her cheeks radiating even hotter under the force of Courtney's implacable, smoldering stare. "But... but I...!"

Red-faced and starting to panic now, she attempted to bring to bear the only viable defense that she could think of just then.

"But you *know* how old I really am, Courtney," she protested, her words coming out a great deal more whiney than she'd meant for them to be. "This is total bullcrap! You can't just..."

But Rhen's short-lived burst of indignation fizzled out almost as soon as it had flared into life as she struggled to find the least embarrassing way to phrase things.

"Uh... you know..."

"Spank you?" offered Courtney helpfully, the corners of her mouth pulling back into a crocodile smile.

"Yeah... uh, that."

"Ah, but you see, that's where you're wrong, I'm afraid," countered the TA as if she were explaining an incorrect answer on a quiz, tracing a fingertip down along the curve of Rhen's pouting jawline and tilting her head back so that she was forced to make eye contact with her. "Your auntie already gave me permission to spank you whenever I feel like it back at the dorms, remember? And if you're going to behave like a little brat in my class, then you'd better believe that I'm going to treat you like one."

"But... but..." spluttered Rhen again, grasping at straws now. "But what about Abby? She was talking just as much as I was, you know!"

That wasn't exactly the truth, but at that moment she was prepared to massage the facts a bit if it meant avoiding what the wickedly grinning older girl had in mind for her.

"How come she gets to waltz out of here scot-free while I'm stuck getting uh... you know...?"

Again she couldn't bring herself to say the word out loud, and instead just waved her palm back and forth through the air beside her in a half-hearted pantomime of a swat.

"Oh, don't you worry your sassy little head about her," purred Courtney, smiling even broader now as she cast a side-long glance toward where the other girl had just left. "She and I will be taking care of *her* side of your little gabbing session later on tonight."

Oh really now?

Rhen felt her eyebrows arching questioningly at that last little tidbit of news.

You don't say...

"But we're not talking about Abby right now, are we, young lady?" interjected Courtney into her thoughts then before they could get too far. "No, we're talking about *you* and *your* behavior, and more specifically, what I plan on doing about it."

With those words her eyes grew a good degree or two colder as her face set into a familiar looking mask of determination.

"And that's to put you right over my knee and spank those bratty buns of yours until they're fire engine red and sizzling."

Crap! Why couldn't Abby have just kept her voice down

like I told her to?

Unable to think of anything to say that might earn her a reprieve from what was about to happen next, and knowing deep down that she fully deserved to be punished for the way she'd been behaving during her lab that afternoon, Rhen just glared at the smug TA; pouting at her and desperately hoping that the head-swooning mixture of anticipation and dread roiling around inside of her stomach just then wouldn't show too much on her face.

"Ugh, fine, whatever," she eventually huffed, breaking away from her TA's grasp and conceding defeat as she pushed away from her desk and rose to her feet. "You've made your point, Courtney, so let's just get this over with, alright? Just because I've got the rest of the afternoon off doesn't mean that I want to spend all day- Ah!"

Before she could finish her bratty tirade, Rhen found herself letting out a squeak of surprise that morphed into a yelp of pain as Courtney's right hand shot out like a viper and seized the top of her ear in a vice-like grip. Pinching it tight, she hauled her close enough so that she could feel the warmth radiating off of her torso, and was forced to angle her head back to look into the fiery, disapproving scowl of her TA.

"First of all, *little girl*," she drawled, her voice a low, dangerous growl as she fixed Rhen in place with a glare that made her knees wobble. "Until we're through here, you will refer to me as either Miss Summers or Ma'am, is that understood?"

"Ow! Okay, okay, geez…"

"Excuse me?" demanded Courtney, tugging up on the ear she had gripped between her thumb and forefinger and making Rhen squeak again as she danced around on her tiptoes, arms waving frantically out to either side of her.

"Ah, ah, ah! Courtn- I mean, Miss Summers, *please*, that hurts! I'm sorry, alright?"

"That's *better*," huffed the TA, easing her grip only enough so that Rhen no longer felt like her ear was about to come off.

Satisfied that she'd made her point for the moment, she began dragging her along, half-bent over by said ear, down the aisle between the desks of their little classroom, grabbing a chair to haul after them with her free hand as they went. Upon reaching the end of the rows of desks, she then swung her chair around so that it sat facing out about a foot or so in front of the little podium she usually stood behind during her lectures.

"Alright, kiddo, we're going to do this just the same way I do back at home with my little sisters," declared Courtney, releasing her hold on Rhen's ear and jabbing a finger toward a spot of carpet in front of her tennis shoes. "So I want you to go ahead and drop those jeans and panties right down to your ankles, now."

"Oh come on!" protested Rhen, her hands flying back to cover her soon-to-be-spanked behind as she took half a step back. "Do I really have to? Can't you just do it over what I'm wearing instead?"

"Young lady," warned Courtney, interrupting her with a hard glare that made it all too clear that she meant business. "If I don't see your naked ass ready for a spanking in the next three seconds, I'm going to blister your butt raw with my belt. You got that?"

"But!" whined Rhen again, even as her hands fluttered indecisively toward the front of her gray denim jeans.

"One..."

Courtney held up a single finger in front of her, drawing out the word as she counted it aloud.

"Cour- I mean, Miss Summers, come on, this isn't fair!"

The TA just raised another finger in response.

"Two…"

Oh crap!

Not wanting to find out just how hard her former RA turned disciplinarian could swing a belt, Rhen let out an unhappy groan as her hands flew to the front of her jeans, fumbling with the clasp and zipper there in a panic.

"Okay, okay, I'm going, I'm going! Just hold on a sec, would you?"

Dang it, where's that easy-pull waistband bullcrap when I need it most?

A moment later she had the front of her jeans undone and was shoving them down her legs, crumpling the bedazzled flowers stitched along the outer-seams of either leg as they, along with the pale purple panties that she'd been wearing beneath them, made the straight-line descent down toward her ankles in record time.

"Thre-"

"There, see? I did it!" gushed Rhen, shooting back up to a standing position and frantically waving her hands in front of her to stop the older girl from finishing her countdown.

"I do indeed," confirmed Courtney with a low chuckle, nodding in approval as her face once more broke out into a predatory grin that had Rhen swallowing hard as a knee-wobbling twinge of excitement throbbed from her clit, making her shiver.

Oh god, she moaned internally, straining not to rub her thighs together. *I think I see now what Abby meant by, "the look".*

Seeming to be in no particular rush to get her across her lap now that she'd so thoroughly exposed herself, Courtney slowly began to step around Rhen, circling her like a hungry shark as she carefully inspected every square inch of newly-revealed skin.

"Heh. I've gotta say," she crooned with a smirk, coming to a stop in front of her again and flicking a dismissive finger toward where her thighs were pressed firmly together. "I love the new look. It's very... you."

"Wha-? Oh crap!"

The comment elicited a mortified squeak from Rhen, whose wringing hands immediately shot down to cover her front as her face flushed a hot shade of crimson.

She'd gotten so used to being fully on display in front of Dana, that she'd completely forgotten about her auntie's little "haircut".

"Maybe I ought to have Abby do the same thing with hers," mused the older girl to herself, unperturbed by her depantsed student's discomfort as she rubbed her chin thoughtfully.

Courtney continued to stare off into space for another couple of moments, before apparently remembering what it was that she was supposed to be doing and shaking her head to clear it.

"Anyway..."

Face returning back to its mask of grim determination, she took hold of Rhen's upper arm, just above the elbow, and gave it a firm squeeze.

"Come on then, bratty buns, that butt isn't going to spank itself, you know."

With that, she led the two of them the short distance over to the chair that she'd set up in front of her podium, plopping herself down onto its seat and steering Rhen around to her right side. After letting go of the arm she'd been holding onto, she then reached around and laid her right palm along the small of the younger girl's back, guiding her gently, but firmly, forward across her waiting lap.

"That's right," she cooed. "Right across my knee, just like with your auntie."

"Oh god..."

A moment later, Rhen tumbled across the tops of her thighs, landing with a small grunt.

"Oof."

"Hands please."

"Huh?"

Looking around confused, Rhen craned her head back and to the left in an attempt to try and figure out what it was that Courtney, or rather Miss Summers, was asking her to do.

"Your hands, Rhen," she repeated, giving her own set a jaunty waggle in front of her. "I want you to put them behind your back for me."

"Oh, uh... okay?"

Not exactly sure where this was all going, Rhen nevertheless did as she was told. After some wriggling and squirming, she managed to bring both of her arms around behind her back, and was now drumming her knuckles near the very tops of her as yet unspanked bare bottom cheeks.

"Like this?"

"Precisely," confirmed Courtney, gathering her narrow wrists together in her left hand and shifting them up, pinning them in place against the small of her lower back. "I saw how much you liked to squirm when you were over Dana's knee that one time, and I'd just *hate* to accidentally hit something other than my intended target once we get going. So we're going to keep these nice and safe back here where they can't get in the way, alright?"

"Gee, how very thoughtful of you," deadpanned Rhen as she attempted to get more comfortable in this new position.

347

That was a lot easier said than done however, considering that with her feet already dangling above the floor she now had no way of gaining any kind of serious leverage. Trapped as she was with her jeans and panties tangled around her ankles, and Courtney's iron grip on her wrists immobilizing her arms, her options were limited to basically just crossing and uncrossing her ankles and rocking slightly to either side. It wasn't a particularly dignified position to be in, even for someone such as herself who was used to making regular trips over her auntie's knee at least once every two or three days for some sort of spanking or another, but Rhen suspected that that was probably the point.

"Ready?"

Courtney brushed her palm lightly across first one cheek and then the other, raising goose bumps along Rhen's bare skin as she spoke.

"Yeah, I guess," came the petite sophomore's huffy reply, still pouting.

SMACK! SMACK!

"What was that, young lady?" the older girl prompted sweetly, delivering two *very* hard swats to either cheek. "I don't think I quite heard you correctly. Could you repeat that for me?"

"Ack!" grunted Rhen, hissing in sharply through clenched teeth as her toes curled and uncurled inside of her tennis shoes. "Yes ma'am, Miss Summers, I'm ready."

Courtney's hand sure packed one heck of a wallop, that was for sure.

"Now see? That's what I *thought* you said," cooed the TA, lightly patting where she'd just swatted.

Geez, her poor sisters.

Rhen grimaced, blowing out a puff of air to shoo away a

stray strand of dark hair that had started tickling her nose as the last of the lingering sting from those two swats gradually started to fade away from her cheeks.

Well, at least Abby isn't here to see any of this.

That idea was of little comfort to her though at the moment as Courtney's left arm snaked itself tightly around her trim waist, pulling her in snugly against her strong abdomen just before she began bringing her palm down in earnest.

SMACK! SMACK! SMACK!

Conditioned by a lifelong love of competitive tennis, and clearly an old hand at delivering a world-class spanking to a sassy girl's backside, Courtney kept her pace brisk and relentless, pummeling Rhen's bouncing bare bottom with rock-hard, open-palmed slaps of her hand. They hit with a biting sting that took her breath away, and carried with them an even heavier ache that the TA knew would guarantee that she'd be feeling this spanking well past the time she was tucked in for bed that night.

I guess I'm sleeping on my stomach again, Rhen thought to herself with a resigned sigh, before letting out another series of high-pitched yelps as her feet flailed desperately behind her. *Oh my god, is her hand made out of rocks or something? Holy crap!*

But while the spanks that Courtney was delivering were no picnic, their accumulated impacts starting to overwhelm Rhen's reserves of endurance like a rising tide of lava threatening to swallow her up at any moment, it was the way she casually started chatting with her as she continued smacking her ever-increasing sore rear end that *really* made the whole experience a memorable one for the sassy sophomore.

SMACK! SMACK! SMACK!

"So, how's living with your auntie been treating you?"

SMACK! SMACK! SMACK!

"Awww, that's so great to hear! She really seemed like a nice lady when I met her back in the dorms..."

SMACK! SMACK! SMACK!

"Hey, you should totally come to the mall with me and Abby this weekend. We saw this sweater at the Disney store the other day that I bet would look just great on you..."

SMACK! SMACK! SMACK!

"Oh! Have you seen the trailer for the new Revengers movie yet? It looks pretty awesome..."

SMACK! SMACK! SMACK!

"Yeah, Abby is way more into all that superhero stuff than I am, but I'm still pretty excited to check it out. You should definitely come see it with us when it comes out next month. I bet Dana would even pay for you to go if you told her that we'll be there with you..."

SMACK! SMACK! SMACK!

"What? Of course I'm serious! I wouldn't want you trying to pull the ol' switcheroo and sneaking in to see Hammer: Origins or something like that instead. A growing girl like you can't afford to be kept awake all night just because she's afraid some scary pig monster might come to get her..."

SMACK! SMACK! SMACK!

It was a very surreal experience for Rhen to say the least.

Aside from the fact that she had her jeans and panties bunched up around her ankles, and her jiggly rump squirming frantically across the older girl's lap while she nonchalantly set it ablaze, their (mostly one-sided) conversation was in many ways just like it had been back when she'd been living in the dorms. Back then, Courtney would make her rounds every evening, stopping to chat with some of her favorites (Rhen included) as she went, which incidentally was how Abby had come to develop a crush on the athletic RA in the first place.

Unfortunately though, Rhen was a little too busy at that particular moment trying to will the tears pooling at the corners of her eyes to not start cascading down her cheeks to really appreciate the strangeness of it all just then.

"Courtney, please, come on, I'm sorry! Can't we stop now? I've learned my lesson, I swear!"

All her plea managed to do though was earn her a *very* hard burst of rapid-fire swats, spread out evenly across both of her sit-spots.

SMACK-SMACK! SMACK-SMACK!

"Remember, Rhen, right now it's *Miss* Summers," corrected Courtney with an affected sniff. "And no, we won't be stopping any time soon, I'm afraid. By the look of things, we're only about halfway done at the moment, so I'd buckle up and get comfy if I were you, kiddo."

It was about then that Rhen decided to abandon the last scraps of her dignity, scissoring her feet back and forth behind her for all she was worth as she let the tears begin to flow freely.

"Oh my god, you are *such* a meanie!"

"Hmmm, is that right?" purred the older girl, completely unconcerned as she continued to sizzle her sit-spots. "We could always start over if you'd like, you know."

"No, no! That's fine, I'll- Ack! I'll be good!"

"Heh. That's what I thought. So then, why don't you tell me about how your other classes have been going this semester…?"

—

By the time Courtney was at last finished with her, Rhen was a sniffling mess of a well-spanked little girl, with a bottom that was indeed fire engine red and felt as if it were hot enough to cook an egg on.

"Oh hey, that took way less time than I thought it would," observed the TA, barely even winded as she finally let go of the younger girl's pinned wrists and brought her watch up to check the time. "I thought for *sure* we'd be at it for another ten minutes at the very least before I finally started seeing some actual contrition out of you."

She shrugged then and snickered.

"I guess you're not so bratty after all, huh?"

"If... if you say so," panted Rhen, having let herself go completely limp across the other girl's lap.

As far as she was concerned, they could have stopped ten minutes sooner and she would have been just as sorry.

SMACK!

"Ah! Hey, watch it!"

"And just like that, it's gone," snorted Courtney, giving Rhen's right cheek a friendly squeeze before helping her back to her feet. "Oh well."

Following after her, she immediately began steering the pouting girl toward the whiteboard at the front of their class-room, hands guiding her by the shoulders as Rhen shuffled along, hands busying themselves with trying to massage some of the ache out of her throbbing backside.

"Alright, bratty buns, now that we've gotten all that spank-ing business out of the way for today, there's just one more thing left to take care of before I let you go," explained the TA in a stern, no-nonsense tone as she picked up an eraser and quickly began clearing the board of the various diagrams and notes she'd scrawled across it during the course of their earlier lab. "And that's to have you write out some lines."

"Lines?"

"That's right," she sing-songed. "Just like a proper detention, hehe."

Setting her eraser aside, she then picked up a red dry-erase marker and quickly wrote out a sentence near the top of the board, reading it out loud as she went.

"I will not disrupt Miss Summers's class, or I will be spanked."

"See that?" she asked, gesturing toward the phrase with her free hand. "I want to see that written out nice and neat one hundred times before I finish grading the last of my papers. You got that?"

"Oh my god, are you serious?" moaned Rhen, stomping one semi-trapped foot in protest as she eyed the sentence sourly. "That's going to take *forever*!"

"Well then, I guess you'd better get started, huh?" countered Courtney smoothly, taking hold of Rhen's right wrist and turning her hand palm up to deposit the marker she'd just been using into it. "After all, it sure would be embarrassing to have someone stumble in on you while you're still working, wouldn't it? Maybe I'll just text Abby and see if she wants to swing by and say hello before her next class..."

Grumbling something extra-bratty at that only-probably-half-joke, Rhen nevertheless nodded her head in understanding as she braced an arm against the board in front of her and leaned down to try and tug up her jeans and panties before she got started.

SMACK!

"Uh-uh, those stay right where they are until you're finished," chided her TA, delivering another heavy swat to the swollen cheeks in front of her that had Rhen shooting back to her feet as her hands flew behind her to clutch her scalded seat. "Now get to work."

"Yes, ma'am," she moaned petulantly, even as she moved to do as she was told.

While Rhen got busy writing, Courtney took her sweet time sauntering her way back over to the little desk she shared with the rest of the TAs that used the same classroom as her, pulling out a stack of papers from her backpack and settling down onto her padded swivel-chair to start grading them.

She began skimming her way through one, but most of her attention remained fixed on Rhen's waggling caboose as it shifted and wobbled with her movements as she began to slowly fill the whiteboard with the humiliating sentence she'd been given. Then, struck by a bolt of inspiration, the triumphant TA slipped her phone from out of her front pocket and quickly snapped a surreptitious picture of her girlfriend's former roommate hard at work writing her lines, stretched up onto her tiptoes to reach the upper part of the whiteboard, her tongue poking out from between her pursed lips in concentration as she did her best to keep her handwriting neat.

Smiling to herself, Courtney then sent that picture off to Abby along with a short message.

[Just finished up with Rhen. I'll see you tonite, hot stuff. Don't keep me waiting. xoxo <3]

Chapter 19

Halloween Havoc

Riding her bike home that afternoon on a well-spanked bottom was most definitely not a pleasant experience for Rhen, who by the time she reached her house had developed a very passionate dislike for any road or sidewalk that wasn't mirror smooth.

Freaking potholes, they should be illegal!

Worse still, any hopes that she might have had of keeping the spanking she'd received from her TA from her aunt flew right out the window almost as soon as she walked through the front door.

Stepping into their kitchen in search of a snack before heading up to her bedroom to catch up on YouTube videos and maybe do some homework, her eyes were immediately drawn toward the blue, rubber enema bag and the fresh bar of soap neatly laid out and waiting for her on the counter just beside the sink.

"Uh-oh…"

"Yes indeed, young lady," agreed Dana, looking very unimpressed as she strode into the kitchen and stopped to regard her with her hands braced on her hips in an all too familiar gesture of disapproval. "I just got off the phone with that lovely Courtney girl from your Physical Science class, and she had some *very* interesting things to share with me about your behavior in her lab today."

"Of course she did," sighed Rhen, running a hand through

her hair as she cast a weary, sidelong glance toward the punishment supplies arranged on the countertop beside her.

Two weeks huh? Man, I was really hoping that I'd make it a bit longer than that before this came up again, she silently lamented to herself with an embarrassed grimace.

Even though she knew that what was about to happen was fully deserved, that didn't make it any less unpleasant.

Oh well...

As she shifted nervously in place, face flushing with warmth while imagining what it was going to feel like having all of that warm, soapy water filling her up through her rear end and making her insides cramp in humiliating ways, another thought occurred to her, and Rhen found herself whipping her head back around to stare at her auntie in bratty accusation.

"Hey, wait a minute! How'd Courtney even get your number in the first place?"

"Why, I gave it to her, of course, you silly goose," replied Dana with a dismissive shrug, as if to say that that were obvious. "Back when I was giving her your forwarding address information when we moved you out, remember?"

"Oh..." harrumphed Rhen, mostly annoyed with herself for not having seen something like this coming sooner.

Not that knowing ahead of time that her RA turned TA could call to rat her out to her auntie whenever she felt like it would have really made that much of a difference anyway.

Still would have been nice to know, though...

Either way, Rhen knew that the important thing right then was to try and mitigate any possible damage that Courtney might have done by being... overenthusiastic... in her sharing of the whole truth of what had happened in class that day. And so, shaking her head to clear it of any lingering thoughts of the charismatic TA and her thigh-squirmingly-strong hands that had made her cry like a little girl not more than an hour earlier, she went on the offensive.

"Well, um… let me just say that in my defense, Abby was the one who started it," she said. "She and Courtney are *finally* an item now, you see, and she was filling me in on all of that stuff when we got called out for uh… talking too loudly."

She winced at the lame way those last few words came out, not sounding any better in her ears than they had in her head.

"Yes dear, I'm sure that you had absolutely no choice in the matter at all," replied Dana, not quite sounding convinced as she wrapped a stern, but affectionate, arm around her shoulders and began steering her toward the sink. "And trust me when I say that I can't wait to hear all about your friends' burgeoning love lives. But first you and I have something to take care of, don't we?"

"Yeah, I guess so," conceded Rhen with another exasperated sigh as she allowed herself to be led away, her fingers already in the process of undoing the front of her jeans as she dragged her feet.

They were going to be coming down anyway, she knew, so she might as well see if she couldn't at least avoid getting another spanking by showing that she was willing to accept her punishment like a good girl.

"Humph!"

Shucking her jeans and panties down to her knees with a huff, Rhen shuffled forward and plopped down onto her elbows across cold, granite countertop in front of her. Then, hearing water starting to flow from the sink beside her, she winced and looked over to watch as Dana began lathering up the bar of soap in her hands.

Oh boy, here we go again…

"Um… I don't suppose that now would be a good time to ask if I could go to the mall with the two of them this weekend, by any chance, um… would it?"

"Hah," snorted Dana, the soap shooting out of her hands and landing with a wet *plonk* in the sink in front of her as she turned to look at her with an indulgent smirk. "Yes, I think that definitely could be arranged, cutie pie. We'll talk about it after you've finished your homework, alright?"

"Yay!" cheered Rhen, wiggling her bare, and still very red, hips in celebration as she began planning out what she and the others would do that weekend while her cheeks clenched and unclenched in nervous anticipation of the less-than-fun punishment she had to deal with first.

—

Thankfully, that was the last time Rhen had to be taught that particular lesson about not paying attention in her classes for quite a while, but even so, it was far from the last time that Courtney found an excuse to spank her.

Every week after that fateful encounter with her tough but fair TA, Rhen routinely found herself being held after class for a sizable dose of extracurricular advisement. Advisement that invariably took the form of a lengthy, bare bottom spanking delivered at an easy pace across Courtney's strong, athletic thighs.

These spankings were followed afterward, without fail, by her being parked in front of the whiteboard at the front of their classroom with her pants down or skirt up and her panties around her ankles to write out some sort of relevant, and very embarrassing, sentence one hundred times before she was finally allowed to cover up her roasted rear end.

Unlike that first trip over Courtney's lap however, her

former roommate Abby always made sure to linger on after their lab was over to keep her naughty friend company while she received her oh so necessary (at least in hers and the TA's opinions) comeuppance. Watching on with wry, teasing amusement as she squeaked and squirmed across her girlfriend's broad lap while her cute little caboose was set ablaze, making the occasional snickering comment here or there about how adorable Rhen's outfit looked that afternoon, or else golf clapping whenever one particularly powerful swat or another found its mark. As before as well, while this was all happening, Abby actively participated in the nonstop stream of conversation led by Courtney as the three of them discussed their various plans for the weekend, caught up on what they'd been up to since last seeing each other in person, and just about anything else that happened to come to mind at the time.

It was undeniably a very surreal bonding experience for Rhen, but one that she wouldn't have traded for anything in the world.

Rather than be upset by these weekly after school detentions, she'd quickly adapted to the change in circumstances and had come to accept them as just another part of her life as a bratty twenty-year-old turned teenager. Plus it was pretty hard to argue with the obviously positive results that her regular butt blisterings from Courtney were getting.

Physical science had quickly become one of her best subjects, and she and the other two girls were now thick as thieves.

Back in the dorms, she and Abby had always been on fairly cordial terms with each other, but Rhen had always felt awkward around the vivacious chatterbox of a girl and hadn't really felt like they'd ever clicked. Now though, with this new and well-defined hierarchy in place, with her as the often misbehaving one squarely at the bottom, the chatty blonde and her girlfriend had rapidly become an odd combination of close friends, confidants, and doting older sisters all at once for her.

All of which were things that Rhen realized she'd desperately been craving only after she'd found them. Just like she had with her need for strict rules and discipline that she got from her Auntie Dana.

She just wished that the older woman wasn't such a stickler for her "punished at school, punished at home" rule.

Luckily though, her follow up punishments on the days that she had her lab detentions with Courtney and Abby usually only ever amounted to a light hand spanking over the seat of her pajamas just before bed. Which aside from reigniting some of the flames from earlier in the day, were little more than an excuse for the older woman to tease her some and pinken her buns just a bit before she tucked her in with a kiss goodnight.

Well, most of the time.

Apparently Missus Hairbrush also had some pretty strong opinions about her needing to do her very best in school. Opinions which Dana was only too happy to drill into Rhen's pre-tenderized bare bottom about once every two or three weeks.

Needless to say, her grades soon showed a rapid and marked improvement and in no time she was pulling in all A's in each of her classes.

Even if she did have a hard time sitting through most of them.

—

Just like that, September quickly gave way to October with

Rhen having found herself with a pair of closer than ever friends who had zero qualms about taking her to task and bossing her around whenever they felt like it, and before any of them knew it, it was already Halloween.

Aside from Christmas (for obvious reasons), October and the holiday of Halloween in particular were easily Rhen's favorite time of the year. She loved the cooling weather, the cascading umber hues of the changing leaves, and most of all the sudden influx of general spookiness that the season brought with it.

That year, the day itself happened to fall on a Thursday, and the morning of found her standing in front of the full-length mirror in her bedroom, making a few final adjustments to her outfit before heading off to campus.

Dana had spent the last two weeks tirelessly helping her put together her vampire queen costume from scratch in her free time, and it had turned out absolutely fantastic as far as she was concerned. Which was fortunate indeed, considering that Courtney had made the announcement just the week before that anyone who showed up to her lab wearing a costume on Halloween would get five free points of extra credit on the homework assignment they turned in at the start of class that day. And although her GPA was looking pretty bulletproof that semester, Rhen was still of the firm belief that she could never be too careful.

Sitting on a punishment mat with a thoroughly spanked bottom to finish overdue homework could sure do wonders for instilling a healthy respect for academics it seemed.

Even better though, since Dana had nobody to look after until school let out for the day, she had plenty of time to drop her off on campus herself, saving Rhen the hassle and embarrassment of trying to find a way to ride her bike without her cape and extra-ruffly petticoat getting in the way.

Examining her reflection in the mirror, and smirking to herself at the irony of being able to even see one given what it was that she was supposed to be dressed as, Rhen nodded in satisfaction. What she saw there wasn't exactly the super-hot crimson corset and tight, black leather miniskirt with fishnet stockings combo that she'd been aiming for originally, Dana had vetoed that idea almost immediately and spanked her silly for even suggesting such a thing, but the droopy sleeves, ruffled skirts, and high-collared cape that the older woman had sewn for her over the last two weeks sure did make her look and feel rather elegant.

Plus with her naturally black hair and pale skin, and a pair of red colored contact lenses for added spookiness, she looked the very picture of a cold and aloof ruler of an always-overcast kingdom of dread and evil.

"Okay, now say 'blood'," teased Dana in her best Count Dracula voice, squatting down onto one knee in front of her with her smartphone in hand as she snapped several pictures from various angles. "Oh you are just the *cutest*, I can't stand it!"

"Heh, thanks, Aunt Dana," chuckled Rhen, blushing in a very un-vampire like way as she spat out the fake plastic fangs she'd been wearing for their impromptu photo shoot and flashed the other woman a proper smile.

"You're very welcome, dear," she beamed, scooting over to take a selfy with her before climbing back to her feet and ruffling her hair affectionately. "Now go grab your backpack and let's get out of here. You're going to be late if we don't hurry!"

"As you command, oh matriarch of the iron hand!" decreed Rhen in her most noble-sounding tone, striding out of her bedroom with her back straight and her head tipped up imperiously. "Let us away to your horseless carriage and be gone from my castle that I might gain knowledge from the college of, uh… wizards… or something."

"Okeydokey, whatever you say, my princess of darkness."

SMACK!

"Bleh!"

———

Rhen's vampire queen costume proved to be quite the hit among her fellow students on campus that day. And as she made her way between classes, or as was the case around noon when she was standing in line in the food court waiting for her chance to order something from her favorite fast food place there, lots of people pointed her out to their friends and let her know how much they liked her outfit.

"Oh, hey look, isn't that the girl who graduated from high school super early or whatever?"

"Awww, it sure is, and just look how adorable she is. I love her costume!"

"OMG, me too, it's *super* cute. Did you see the little bats she has stitched down the front of it?"

"Hah, no, I hadn't noticed those. That's awesome!"

Rhen's face warmed considerably as she overheard the praise and adoration coming from the two girls waiting for their order numbers to be called next to her in the campus food court, and she smiled over toward them shyly.

"Uh… thanks, you guys," she said only a little awkwardly.

Then, feeling as if it would somehow be dishonest not to mention it, she added.

"My aunt actually made this costume for me."

"OMG that is *precious*," gushed the student who'd initially spotted her, clutching her friend's arm for support.

"So precious," agreed the other girl as she fished out her

smartphone from her purse. "Hey, can we get a picture of you real quick? Our sisters in Gamma Phi have *got* to see how cute you look."

Rhen's stomach fluttered at the request, but she knew that she was already too well known on campus for it to really matter anymore if anyone else mistook her for a young teen or not, and so she just nodded.

"Yeah, sure, that's fine, I guess. Um… you know, just tag me or whatever if you post it online, alright?" she requested with shy smile, tucking a lock of her black hair behind an ear and holding out her hand toward the two of them. "My name's Rhen Mathews, by the way, and my aunt would be super bummed if she didn't get a chance to see her hard work on display as well, uh… heh."

"Well it's a pleasure to meet you, Rhen," chirped the first girl in that way that adults often do when introducing themselves to children, seizing her hand in a firm grip and giving it a quick pump before gesturing toward her friend. "I'm Chelsea, and that's Veronica."

"Nice to meet you, kiddo," said the other girl, waving casually as she brought her phone up and centered Rhen in its focus, flashing her a teasing smile. "Say, does your mommy know that you're up past your bedtime? I thought you vampires were supposed to be asleep during the day?"

The pouting scowl that Rhen ended up with in the photo that was immediately taken after that question was very much on theme with the rest of her costume, and quickly became one of Dana's favorite pictures of her.

—

"Oh my god, her panties have little bats on them!" squealed Abby after their Physical Science lab was over for the day, dancing in place and excitedly pointing at the taut-ly-stretched seat of the panties that had just been exposed by her girlfriend.

"Um, uh… yeah… Aunt Dana said that they helped bring the whole outfit together," offered the younger girl with a wan half-smile from across Courtney's lap, wriggling in spite of herself as her former roommate reached out to trace a teasing fingernail along the undercurve of her left cheek. "H-Hey, watch it!"

Ever since she'd discovered how ticklish Rhen was back there, Abby had rarely missed an opportunity to take advantage of it.

"Well I definitely can't argue with her there," chuckled Courtney, batting away her girlfriend's wriggling fingers with a mock-scowl, before nodding her chin toward the tops of the still-squirming, chubby cheeks perched across her thighs. "But personally, I don't think it would at all be fair to subject these poor, sweet, innocent bats to *your* punishment."

"Yeah," agreed Abby with a mock-stern frown of her own, easily picking up on where the other girl was headed as she leaned forward and took hold of the pumpkin orange, elastic waistband right in front of her. "After all, *they* weren't the ones who were totally zoned out for half of the quiz review today, were they?"

"They sure weren't," confirmed Courtney just as gravely, wrapping an arm around Rhen's waist and hoisting her up off of her lap by a couple of inches so that her co-disciplinarian could slip their naughty student's panties off of her bottom and all the way down to her ankles with ease.

"Humph!"

Although she'd known that it was going to happen, Courtney always spanked bare without exception, Rhen still couldn't help but huff out a pout through her nostrils at the loss of her underwear, pursing her lips into a petulant grimace as she felt cool air caressing her now-naked cheeks.

"I don't think they would've minded staying where they were, you know..."

That managed to get twin snorts of amusement from the other two girls, but unfortunately no leniency.

"You know what? I think I'll just hold onto these until we're finished here," declared Abby as she crouched down behind her friend and began to work her panties free from around the maroon flats adorned with glittery bat wings that she was wearing.

Straightening up a moment later, she held out her captured prize before her, grinning from ear to ear at the obvious damp spot that was visible along its gusset.

"We wouldn't want to ruin these cute little panties of yours, now would we?"

"No, we most certainly would not," agreed Courtney, answering her girlfriend's teasing question before Rhen could come up with a sufficiently sassy retort.

Then, turning her full attention back toward the bare cheeks she was idly massaging, she felt her eyebrows quirk up as an amused laugh escaped her lips.

"Uh-oh, I think someone might've been in trouble once already today..."

"Hmmm, it sure does seem that way, doesn't it?" nodded Abby as she took in the lingering pink hue still coloring the lower half of Rhen's upturned bottom.

Taking the chance to point out just what it was that she and her girlfriend were talking about with a light wriggle of her fingers, she asked, "So what happened here, Rhenny?"

"N-Nothing," answered the thoroughly embarrassed girl in a breathy laugh, squirming madly as her friend's fingers sent spasming chuckles rippling up her sides.

"Are you *sure* about that, kiddo? It sure doesn't seem like nothing to me," pressed Abby, her grin growing even wider now as she shifted her tickling further in toward the central divide between Rhen's cheeks where she knew she was the most sensitive. "You'd better come clean soon, because I'm not going to stop until you do."

"D-Do your worst, I dare you!"

"Alright, have it your way…"

Rhen did her best to hold out for as long as she could under the interminable tickle torture of her best friend, but less than a minute later it became dangerously clear to her that she was going to lose control of her bladder if things kept going as they were for much longer.

"It was at breakfast, alright?" she finally gasped, throwing in the towel and squeezing her thighs together as tightly as she could to clamp down on any potential accidents, much to the amusement of her recently acquired older sisters.

Flushing scarlet with the memory of it all, to say nothing of her anxiety about possibly losing control if she wasn't careful, she quickly added in a jumbled rush, "I forgot to do the dishes last night and Dana spanked me for it before I got ready for school! There, are you happy now?"

"Very," answered Courtney and Abby together at the same time, the latter of who then took a step back and to the side behind her girlfriend's right shoulder so as to have the best possible vantage point for what was to come next.

"See how much easier it is when you just tell the truth, Rhenny?"

"Yeah, whatever," grumbled Rhen, letting herself go limp across Courtney's lap and not even bothering to pout as the older girl ordered her to put her arms behind her back for her.

What followed next was a fairly standard spanking from her TA, which meant that it left Rhen gasping and flailing her legs wildly behind her (unhindered by any sort of restraint this time) as the unyielding inferno Courtney casually stoked over the next fifteen minutes gradually overwhelmed her ability to not start sniffling and promising to be a good girl. In the meantime before that happened however, largely to distract herself from the humiliating inevitable, she busied herself with trying to make small talk with the two other girls.

SMACK! SMACK! SMACK!

"So um... Ack! Do you two- Ah! Have any pl- Oh! Plans for tonight?"

"Hmmm..." came Courtney's slow reply, mulling the question over for a moment or two before answering as she pounded her palm relentlessly against Rhen's bouncing bare buttocks. "I think the plan is to mostly just go bar hopping with a few other people and see what happens."

"That, and maybe see if we can't find a chill house party to go to afterward," added Abby. "Some of the girls from the dorms were talking about how Shauna Paulson's parents are out of town for the week, so you know, that could be fun. They've got a pretty sweet hot tub I hear."

SMACK! SMACK! SMACK!

"And a big-ass TV," piped up Courtney, her voice carrying an excited grin as she increased the tempo of her swats. "We could totally stream something scary on that! I think there's supposed to be a marathon of all the Hammer movies on tonight too."

"Ewww, gross," shuddered Abby. "I hate all that torture porn crap. Let's watch something with ghosts instead."

"Works for me," replied Courtney with a shrug, still swatting at a steady, nonstop pace.

SMACK! SMACK! SMACK!

"Awww- Oh! That- Ack! sounds like- Ah! fun…" Rhen managed to get out between yelps. "C- Owie, owie! Can I come?"

In response to her question, Courtney tightened her grip around her pinned wrists and zeroed in on the backs of her thighs, turning them molten lava hot as she delivered a rapid-fire volley of extra-hard smacks in the span of only a few seconds.

SMACK-SMACK! SMACK-SMACK! SMACK-SMACK!

"No you may *not*, young lady," she huffed with righteous indignation, before returning back to her normal pace and shifting her aim up to Rhen's frantically gyrating hips.

"That's right," scolded Abby, leaning over to deliver two sharply biting swats of her own to the thighs that her girlfriend had just abandoned.

SMACK! SMACK!

"Bar hopping and midnight house parties are completely inappropriate for a girl your age!"

"Yeah, what would your auntie say if she heard you were trying to sneak your way into bars, huh?" continued Courtney, punctuating the question with two more extra-hard swats to the centers of each cheek before smirking at the girl beside her.

SMACK! SMACK!

"We both happen to know for a fact, little missy, that she confiscated your license, and even if she hadn't, you'd still be underage."

"That's right, *Rhenny*, so don't you dare try telling us that she'd be cool with us letting you tag along unless you want me to go find some soap for you to chew on!"

"But… Ah! Ah! Ah! That's not *fair*!" protested Rhen, her

stomach-fluttering kicking into overdrive at the revelation that her two best friends were well aware of her confiscated "adult" identity and thought it was totally fine. "She let me go to that midnight premiere for Revengers with you guys last week, didn't she?"

"That's totally different and you know it," dismissed Courtney with a roll of her eyes. "Now quit your whining before I tell Abby to get me a hairbrush."

SMACK! SMACK! SMACK!

Rhen wisely chose to heed her disciplinarian's warning, but that did little to spare her bottom from feeling like it had swollen up to twice its original size by the time she was finished with her. Nor did it stop her from having to write out an extra-humiliating sentence on the whiteboard afterward either.

"I am too young to go bar hopping, but not too old for a spanking."

Over and over she repeated the words in her head as she copied them out onto the whiteboard in front of her, pouting all the while as she worked. But try as she might, Rhen couldn't bring herself to be upset with her friends for long, especially not when they showed her the king-size candy bar they'd bought for her.

"Since you can't come with us tonight," they explained with fond smirks as they sat together side-by-side against the edge of the front row of desks and watched her write.

"Awww, that's so sweet of you!"

And so, by the time she'd finished writing her punishment sentence out one hundred times, and had then posed for a picture in front of the neatly arranged lines so that Dana could see how cute she looked in her costume with a well-spanked bottom, all of her earlier frustration and annoyance at being left out of the older girls' plans for the evening had more or less evaporated.

—

Later, as the sun was just beginning to set, Rhen found that she no longer cared about missing out on going to a bunch of loud and overcrowded bars. Who needed all that crap anyway when there was free candy to be had? Unfortunately for her though, rather than being turned loose onto the neighborhood to collect as many sugary treats as she could, and possibly to play a trick or two if the opportunity presented itself along the way, her aunt had other plans in mind for how she would be spending her evening.

"No you are *not* going out on your own to wander the neighborhood until all hours of the night, young lady. I don't *care* what the other kids are doing, *you* are coming with me to the church's party, and that's final."

"But, Aunt Dana, it's *Halloween*!" moaned Rhen, her hands curling into cranky fists at her sides as she bounced them ineffectually against her dress's puffy skirts in protest.

"Yes, dear, I'm well aware of that fact," replied the older woman coolly, flashing her a warning look that told her to cut it out before she got another spanking for her trouble. "And I'd suggest you wipe that dirty look off your face. Things are not nearly so bad as you seem to think they are."

Not quite convinced yet, Rhen nevertheless calmed down enough to listen to what she had to say without completely flying off the handle, her nostrils flaring as she reined in her bratty temper. Her bottom still felt a bit tender from her time spent across Courtney's knee not too long ago, and the twinge of discomfort that shifting her weight from one hip to the other produced was more than enough to convince her that maybe respectful obedience might be the wiser course of action to pursue just then.

"Now then, if you'd have just let me finish what it was that I was *trying* to say before you started throwing your little tantrum, you'd know that what we're going to tonight is a trunk-or-treat party," Dana began to explain, one hand planted on her hip while she wagged an admonishing forefinger at her grumpy girlfriend with the other. "Instead of going door to door all night, you and your friends get to go from car to car in the parking lot and get your candy that way. It takes a lot less time than regular trick-or-treating does, and cuts out any chances for mischief or getting lost in the dark."

"Oh…" said Rhen, blushing slightly and casting her gaze down to study a particularly interesting looking knot in one of the floorboards at her feet as she realized that she might have jumped the gun just a little bit. "That doesn't sound that bad, I guess."

"Oh, don't be such a grumpy goose," teased Dana, her stern frown replaced now by an indulgent smirk as she closed the distance between the two of them and reached out to ruffle her hair affectionately. "You'll have plenty of fun tonight, I promise."

Then, leaning in close enough so that she could see the flecks of gold in Rhen's dark green eyes, she added in a conspiratorial stage-whisper.

"And just between you and me, it's pretty safe to say that you'll end up coming away with a *lot* more candy than you would've gotten going door to door. At least, if this year's party is anything like it usually is."

That certainly perked up Rhen, who suddenly found that she had a lot less interest in wasting her night with traditional trick-or-treating like some rank amateur. Hyper-concentrated candy distribution was clearly the way of the future.

"Well why didn't you say so?" she demanded with a broad grin, spinning on her heel to run off and grab her jack-o'-lantern pail from where she'd stashed it away in her bedroom. "Let's get going before all the good stuff is gone, come on!"

"Alright, alright," laughed Dana, holding up her hands to fend off her excited sassy sophomore as she all but barreled her over in her attempts to slip past and run up the stairs. "Let me just grab my keys and then we can go, alright?"

———

For as excited as she'd been on their drive over, much of Rhen's initial enthusiasm had dissipated by the time she and Dana found a place to park outside their church building among the other cars already there some twenty minutes later.

There were definitely a *lot* of people with their trunks popped open, strings of pumpkin lights or fake cobwebs connecting them together as their owners handed out what appeared to be great handfuls of candy while generic scary music played from a set of wireless speakers someone had rigged up to a tablet. The only problem was that it seemed like the vast majority of the costumed kids hurrying from car to car to collect their treats were much younger than she was.

"Um… are you *sure* that this is something teenagers are allowed to participate in?" Rhen asked hesitantly, carefully shifting her bright orange candy pail behind her back just in case someone saw her with it and got the wrong idea.

"Yes, dear, I am," confirmed the older woman with a gentle smile, laying a reassuring hand on her shoulder and stooping down to point toward a couple of kids further off in the distance who were currently in the process of receiving some rather sizable looking candy bars from Sister Miller. "Look over there, it's Jamie and Melissa from your Sunday school class, see?"

"Yeah, I guess," conceded Rhen with a nod, not quite sounding convinced as she puffed out her cheeks in an over-dramatic pout. "But it looks like they're just going around with their younger siblings, so I'm not really sure if that counts…"

Sensing that she'd need to try a different approach to coax her not-niece into letting down her guard and having fun that evening, Dana leaned in closer to murmur into her ear, "I'd be very careful if I were you, little girl, or else the switch witch might just come pay you a visit tonight."

"Psh, I'm not afraid of some candy thief and her healthy snack alternatives," countered Rhen with an impudent smirk.

"That's nice, dear," replied her aunt with a low laugh, sliding a hand beneath the folds of her cape to give her bottom a meaningful pat. "But the one I was thinking of likes to tan the hides of naughty girls who don't behave themselves on Halloween."

"Oh, well, um…"

Rhen swallowed hard at that, face flushing hot pink in the dwindling twilight.

"Then I suppose I ought to behave myself, huh?"

"I would say that sounds like a good idea, yes," agreed Dana with a sly twinkle in her eye. "Now why don't you go have some fun with your friends?"

And with that, she sent the younger girl scampering off to join the others already well into their trunk-or-treating with another firm pat to the seat of her swishy black skirts.

"I'll be inside if you need me, cutie pie."

—

Just as her auntie had predicted, Rhen did indeed end up coming away with far more candy than she'd been expecting to thanks to the various families participating in that year's trunk-or-treat party. There was clearly a disproportionate amount of adults handing out candy to kids collecting it, and she managed to double back for extras a couple of times by blending in with a few of the other kids from her Sunday school class who showed up after her.

After she'd finished filling her jack-o'-lantern pail to the point where nothing else would fit inside of it, she then made her way into the meeting house proper and quickly discovered that there was far more to this celebration than just wandering around a parking lot begging for candy.

"Oh man, they seriously went all out for this, didn't they?" she asked aloud to no one in particular as she gawked at the transformation that had taken place inside the modestly-sized indoor basketball court that the older teens usually met in for youth group activities.

"Yeah, Father Jacob really goes nuts for Halloween stuff," answered Anna with a broad grin as she stepped up beside her, hefting a massive and very tasty looking caramel apple in one hand and using it to gesture at the decorations and games lining the walls. "Love the costume by the way, Rhen. You look very spooky-cute tonight."

"Heh, thanks," replied the supposedly younger girl, feeling her face flush with warmth at the compliment.

Maybe Anna isn't so bad, after all? She certainly seems a lot less snooty now that we're not in Sunday school...

Shrugging at this revelation, Rhen flashed her a friendly smile.

"My aunt made it for me, actually."

"No kidding?"

Anna let out a low, appreciative whistle as she ran her eyes up and down her costume once again.

"Dang. Well, she did a great job. It sure beats the heck out of my 'costume', that's for sure," she laughed, tilting her head down just enough to draw the other girl's attention to the cat ears headband and black leather choker she was wearing.

Not quite sure how to respond to that, Anna not being a prissy bossy boots was really throwing her through a loop, Rhen just nodded shyly.

"Hey, where'd you get that caramel apple from?" she asked, hoping that changing the subject would help her feel less awkward.

"Right over there," replied Anna with a friendly grin, pointing off to where a small knot of kids were clustered around a rickety-looking card table where Father Jacob (with two, large Frankenstein-style bolts protruding from either side of his neck) was busy overseeing the mostly-orderly distribution of treats. "But I'd hurry up if I were you. Those apples tend to go fast every year."

"Thanks for the tip!"

Taking the advice to heart, Rhen immediately began skipping off toward the table Anna had indicated while attempting to juggle her heavy pail in both hands and keep her candy from spilling out of it as she went. She was in such a good mood, that even when the smug teenager playfully swatted her on the bottom as she passed her by, she didn't slow down in the slightest, and just threw her a pouty look over her shoulder and stuck out her tongue.

"Happy Halloween, kiddo."

"Thanks, you too!"

—

For the rest of the evening, Rhen and her friends threw themselves into the festivities with gusto. Drinking punch served from a bubbling witch's cauldron (packed with lots of dry ice), bobbing for apples, competing in no-hands donut eating races, and generally making a nuisance of themselves to all of the adults around them who were willing to look the other way for that one evening.

And it was, *awesome.*

She was still riding high on all the fun she'd had at the church's Halloween party by the time she and Dana finally got home later that night.

"It looks like you got a pretty good haul this year," observed the older woman as she tipped back the overflowing jack-o'-lantern Rhen had set down on the corner of the island in their kitchen enough to see that it was indeed packed to the gills.

"I sure did," chirped the petite sophomore happily, half-bent over and digging around in the back of their refrigerator in search of any cold cans of soda that Dana might have hidden there.

Caffeine-free ones of course since those were the only kinds she was allowed to drink this close to bedtime.

"Hey, what're you doing?"

Having turned around upon finding a drink, Rhen frowned as she watched her aunt putting her over-stuffed bucket of candy onto one of the high shelves in the cabinet above the sink.

"I'm putting your candy away, dear," she explained casually, shutting the door to the cabinet after she'd finished stashing her pail well out of her reach and turning to gesture toward the few pieces she'd left out on the island. "You're already hyped up on enough sugar as it is, so you can have these six pieces tonight, and then some more tomorrow, alright?"

"But that's not *fair*," whined Rhen, stomping a foot and turning her nose up at the meager assortment of chocolates she'd been allotted with a disdainful sniff. "I earned that candy fair and square, and I should be allowed to eat as much of it as I want!"

"Young lady, too much candy will give you a tummy ache and keep you wired all night," countered Dana firmly as she crossed her arms in front of her and fixed her with a no-non-sense frown. "And before you say it, I don't care that it's Hal-loween. A school night is still a school night, and bedtime is still bedtime, and I've made my decision. So tough tortellini."

Feeling her temper starting to boil over at being denied the opportunity to gorge herself on sugary sweets while she browsed the internet like she'd been planning to, Rhen's face flushed hot with indignation. With a huff, she slammed her can of soda down onto the countertop beside her and jabbed an accusatory finger at the cabinet where her (mostly) right-fully gotten candy had been locked away.

"This is such bullcrap!"

Rhen knew that it was a mistake even as she started yell-ing, but try as she might, she just couldn't stop herself once she got going.

"That's *my* candy, give it back right now!"

The hard look she got from her auntie at that however, took the wind right out of her sails.

Uh-oh...

"Um... please?"

Sighing to herself in exasperation, Dana just rolled her eyes toward the ceiling and began moving unhurriedly toward the refrigerator.

"I guess we're going to need one of these after all," she said, grabbing something from off the top of it that she'd apparently had hidden there. "Good thing I went ahead and prepared one while you were at school today, just in case. I had a feeling that it might come in handy before the night was through."

"Um, w-wait a second, hold on now… let's not get too hasty," squeaked Rhen, feeling her bottom cheeks clenching reflexively as she watched her aunt swish the long and supple switch through the air in front of her. "On second thought, I don't really need to eat all that candy tonight. You're right, it's fine!"

"It's a little too late to backpedal now, I'm afraid, cutie pie," replied Dana with a tight smirk, idly thwapping her switch against the side of her pants. "You're the one who decided to throw a fit when you didn't get your way just now. So be a good girl for me and get undressed to face the consequences, would you?"

Mentally kicking herself for getting into this predicament in the first place, honestly she could be such a child sometimes, Rhen let out a long, frustrated moan. Blushing with what she knew was fully deserved embarrassment, she turned and glared at the granite countertop in front of her and shifted her weight awkwardly from foot to foot with pent-up annoyance, before at last letting out a sulky harrumph and beginning to slowly disrobe.

"Humph!"

Pulling free the little knot holding her cape together around her throat, she slipped it off of her shoulders and took her time folding it up nice and neat before laying it out on the island in front of her. With that done, she then cast one last, pleading look over toward her frowning auntie.

"Are you *sure* I can't just have one more chance? Pretty please?"

Dana just cocked one incredulous eyebrow at that however.

"What do you think?"

"Yes?" ventured the younger girl hopefully.

"Rhen…" came the warning reply as her aunt took half a step closer.

"Fine, fine," she sighed in defeat, kicking off her bat-winged flats with a huff. "You can't blame me for trying, though."

"Uh-huh," was all she got in response as Dana rolled her eyes. "Quit stalling before I decide to move this little attitude adjustment out onto the back porch."

"Yes ma'am!"

Sufficiently motivated to hurry now, Rhen made short work of stripping off the black thigh-high stockings she'd been wearing, tossing them onto her folded cape with her dress and petticoat following shortly thereafter.

"Those too," ordered her aunt, flicking the end of her switch toward the fluttering bat panties she was still wearing when she started to falter, her fingers hovering nervously near their waistband.

"Oh come on," whined Rhen, hands cupping her rounded cheeks protectively as she turned her head to glare at her. "They barely offer any protection at all. Can't I just leave them on?"

"Young lady," warned Dana, drawing the words out into a reprimand all on their own as she remained standing right where she was and fixed her with a hard look. "I only switch over bare skin. So unless you'd like for this entire punishment to be delivered exclusively across the backs of your thighs, I'd ditch those panties. *Now.*"

"Okay, okay, I was just asking. Geez!"

Definitely not willing to call the other woman's bluff on that one, Rhen's hands yanked her panties down from her hips and sent them flying toward her ankles just as fast as she could get them to go. Leaving her standing there in just a plain black camisole that left her fully exposed from the waist down.

"Cami too," ordered Dana, her mouth twitching up into a teasing half-grin. "We wouldn't want to get it dirty, now would we?"

"Are you serious?" huffed Rhen, incredulous.

"I'm waiting," sing-songed her auntie, her stern mask slipping for a moment as she used the tip of her switch to tickle the younger girl's thigh.

"Okay, okay," giggled Rhen, squirming out of range before stripping off her camisole and tossing it onto the pile with the rest of her clothes.

"Ahhh, much better," sighed Dana in evident self-satisfaction before crooking a finger toward her with a hungry grin. "Now you get that cute little butt of yours over here and put your hands on top of your head."

"On my head?" asked a slightly confused Rhen even as she moved to do as she was told.

"Well, yes," answered Dana, not unkindly, as she sent a teasing smile her way. "These things tend to sting quite a bit you know, honeybuns, and I'd hate for you to end up with welts anywhere other than your tush and thighs just because your hands got in the way."

Thwip. Thwip.

With casual ease, Dana snapped her wrist twice in quick succession, lightly flicking the younger girl's rock hard nipples with the tip of her switch.

"Ah! Eep!"

"Well, except for there, maybe," she added with a snicker.

"I..." Rhen panted, fighting down a moan as her hands

automatically shot up to knead her naked breasts. "I, um… uh… I…"

Realizing that she'd completely lost the ability to form coherent sentences for the moment, she opted instead to just puff out her cheeks in a huffy pout, stepping in close to her auntie and raising her arms up to thread her fingers together on top of her head.

"Like this?"

"Precisely."

Nodding in approval, Dana moved around to stand near her left side, trailing a teasing hand across each cheek as she went.

"Now you just keep those hands right where they are and try not to move too much until we're finished here, alright?" she ordered, leaning over and beginning to tap, tap, tap the flexible length of wood in her hand against her girlfriend's wobbly bare bottom, testing her aim as she took a few practice swipes with the bendy, green branch.

Swallowing hard, Rhen felt an icy shiver trace its way down her back.

"R-Right!"

THWIP! THWIP! THWIP!

Almost as soon as the words were out of her mouth, Dana began whipping the switch down with lightning-fast flicks of her wrist, leaving bright pink, razor thin welts of sharp, hyper-focused pain all the way across her naked buttocks and thighs.

"Ah! Ah! Ah!"

Immediately Rhen's resolve to keep her hands where they were, to say nothing of her desire to not just hop over the island and run away for that matter, was put to the test as she frantically started shifting from one foot to the other and back again, dancing in place as little yelps and hisses sprang out of her mouth almost as fast as the nonstop swipes from the switch.

"Oh my god, that stings, that stings!" she squealed, unable to contain the thought in just her head alone as her hairless front bumped up against the cold, hard edge of the island in front of her, leaving her trapped with nowhere to go as her bottom all but burst into flames.

"It sure does, doesn't it?" replied Dana conversationally, not sounding the least bit sympathetic as she continued to paint thin lines of livid red across the majority of Rhen's frantically shifting bottom and thighs, watching in amusement as they gradually began to blend together into a mottled maroon as they overlapped.

THWIP! THWIP! THWIP!

"Aunt Dana, please, I'll be good!" the younger girl howled as tear tracks started tracing their way down her flushed face. "I'm sorry I threw a tantrum, I'll be good, I promise!"

"I'm glad to hear you say that, cutie pie, but I'm afraid we're not done quite yet," cooed her auntie, not slowing the constant flicking of her wrist in the slightest. "You see, a switching isn't over until the switch itself is completely worn out."

As if to underscore just what she meant, Dana ratcheted up the speed at which she was swatting by a few notches, pushing the petite sophomore's howls and squeals up several octaves in the process.

Oh my god, this is going to take forever! There's no way I'll even have a butt by the time she's finished!

THWIP! THWIP! THWIP!

—

385

In the end though, Rhen's bottom was far more resilient than she gave it credit for, and the supple, green branch that the older woman had selected to discipline her with only lasted for a few more minutes before it at last crumbled to pieces, totally spent.

"And there we go," sighed Dana with a sense of a job well done as she laid the remains of the ruined switch on the counter beside her niece's crumpled costume. "See? That wasn't so bad, now was it?"

Rhen's only response to this question was to hiss through clenched teeth, still dancing in place as her hands flew back to clutch at her scalded seat.

"If... if you say so..."

She couldn't see for herself yet, but her aunt had left it and the backs of her thighs a lovely shade of ruby red (that would probably have been quite enticing to a vampire, actually), with a great many long, thin welts, spidering out in all directions near the far edges of her hips and the sides of her legs.

"Oh come now, cutie pie," snickered the older woman, rubbing her soothingly between the shoulders as she leaned over to plant a quick kiss on her cheek, licking her lips and smiling at the strong taste of salt she found there. "I only used one switch on you. It could have easily been two or three if I were *really* trying to prove a point, you know."

Rhen felt her stomach lurch at that, and decided that maybe she had gotten off comparatively light after all as she felt her knees wobble just a bit.

"I uh... I hadn't thought of it like that," she admitted with a chagrinned look toward her smugly preening auntie. "Yeah, in that case, I guess it wasn't so bad."

"That's the spirit," laughed Dana, reaching up to ruffle the back of her untidy hair. "Now, your royal spookiness, I'd say it's about time for you to get that butt of yours upstairs and into the shower. Wouldn't you agree?"

"Can I still have my candy?" asked Rhen, eyeing the half-dozen or so pieces on the counter beside her hopefully.

She'd certainly felt like she'd earned them by now.

"That all depends," countered her aunt with a wry smirk. "Are you going to behave yourself?"

"Yes ma'am!"

"Well then, by all means, they're yours."

"Thank you," chirped the younger girl in a sing-song of her own, rising up onto her tiptoes to kiss the older woman on the lips and hugging her tightly for a brief moment before snatching up her candy and making a beeline toward the stairs.

"Anytime, cutie pie," laughed Dana with a dismissive wave toward the scampering girl's back. "I'll be up to tuck you in later, alright?"

""Kay!" came the barely audible reply from somewhere in the hallway upstairs.

With an affectionate huff of amusement, the switch witch moved to get out her broom and dustpan and began to sweep up the leftover debris from her sassy sophomore's well-earned punishment.

"God, I love Halloween."

Chapter 20

Road Trips and Overconfidence Do Not Mix

Life quickly fell back into its usual routine for Rhen after Halloween was over, and November flew by in a flash.

Over the next few weeks she went to school during the day while Dana ran her daycare, and on Thursday afternoons Courtney put her over her knee for a post-lab spanking while Abby cheered her on and made small talk. When she wasn't running around with the other kids her aunt looked after, she spent her free time hiding out in her bedroom bouncing between playing games on her computer and working on homework, and on Sunday mornings she went to church where she mostly resisted the urge to annoy Sister Miller.

In short, life was good for Rhen, and although she spent a lot more time than she would have perhaps preferred with her panties pulled down, getting her butt smacked silly for one bit of bratty behavior or another, she was undeniably happy.

Before too long the first major break of the fall semester had finally arrived, and the Wednesday before Thanksgiving found the college sophomore turned teenage troublemaker and her auntie taking a road trip south to visit her grandma for the holiday. She only lived about half a day's drive away by car, and now that Rhen finally had access to one in the form of Dana's bright red SUV it had been decided (mostly by the grownups and without any meaningful input from the younger girl herself) that it would be nice to have the two of them come down to spend the break with her grandma and the rest of the extended Mathews family. They would be staying in her old bedroom for a few days and would have Thanksgiving dinner with everyone, and then drive back Sunday morning so that there would still be plenty of time for Rhen to be in bed and ready for school to start up again the following Monday morning (even though she technically didn't need to be on campus until Tuesday).

Although she was definitely looking forward to getting to see her grandma again in person, Rhen still couldn't help but feel a little bit nervous about the notion of spending the entire Thanksgiving break with her since it would also be the first time that they'd be seeing each other face-to-face since she'd moved in with her "Auntie Dana".

They'd spoken to each other on the phone since then, of course. Rhen hadn't been able to stop herself from telling her all about how she and Dana had started dating, and had even admitted that her partner's no-nonsense approach to keeping her in line and doing well in school had been a huge help so far that semester. But even so, talking about things over the phone versus having them on display in person were two totally different animals.

Then again, she knew that Dana liked to keep in touch with her grandma as well, so she was probably way more aware of the details of their rather unique relationship than Rhen thought she was, and clearly she didn't mind. Heck, as far as she could tell, she wholeheartedly approved. But again, even so, it still felt more than a little awkward for her to imagine being back in the house that she'd grown up in as a teenager now that in many ways she'd been coerced into becoming one once again.

Was her grandma actually aware of how often she found herself getting spanked these days?

Would she approve?

Oh god! What if she decided to dust off that old leather belt she kept stashed away behind her closet door and put it to use again?

Would she *really* start spanking her again just because Dana did?

Up until then, with a couple of notable exceptions, Rhen had been able to justify the way others seemed to see her as just another bratty teenager in need of an attitude adjustment as being mostly due to her short stature and petite physique (to say nothing of the immature clothes that she wore day-to-day now), but her grandma actually *knew* how old she really was. Surely she wouldn't still treat her like a child now that she was a sophomore in college, right?

Maybe...

It was hard to tell.

Knowing how old she really was sure hadn't stopped Courtney or Abby from deciding that she fit the role of a smart-mouthed little sister better than she did a mature college student just on the cusp of turning twenty-one, after all.

There was also that initial phone call conversation that her grandma and Dana had shared at Papa Italiano's on the night she'd made the offer to let her move in with her to consider. Rhen had only been able to partially overhear what had been said between the two older women back then, but it sure hadn't sounded like her auntie had been shying away from sharing any of the nitty-gritty details of how she planned on keeping her new "niece" in line. And although she'd been unable to pick up any of what had been said on the other end of the line, Rhen was still pretty sure that her grandma had been agreeing emphatically with what she'd been hearing.

Which would certainly explain why she always took the time to pointedly ask if she'd been behaving herself whenever she called to chat with her on the weekends now.

Given the sheer amount of rather humiliating (albeit circumstantial) evidence that she'd managed to put together on the matter so far, Rhen could only assume that the cat was most likely out of the bag with regard to how often and in what ways she found herself being disciplined like the bratty child she truly was at heart. It wasn't a particularly heartening thought to consider, to be sure, but in the end what was the harm in having one more person know about the embarrassing aspects of her happy new life in the grand scheme of things anyway?

It wasn't like she would have been able to change things now, even if she'd wanted to.

She just hoped that her grandma wouldn't get to see first-hand just how routinely she wound up going over Dana's knee during the brief handful of days they would be staying with her.

She could behave herself for that long, couldn't she?

—

"Alright, cutie pie, you ready to hit the road again?" asked Dana as she finished signing the check for their meal and gathered up her purse.

They'd already been driving nonstop for several hours now, having left at the crack of dawn to avoid arriving in the wee hours of the morning the following day, and had decided to pull off at a mom-and-pop family restaurant for some lunch. Rhen had looked the place up on her phone before they'd settled on it, and they'd both been pleased to discover that the rave reviews the establishment had received online had definitely not been wrong.

"Yep," chirped the younger girl, sliding out from her side of their booth and stretching her arms up high over her head.

"Man, that pie was good!"

"It sure was," her aunt agreed with a sly grin, running an amused eye over the plate that had, up until recently, held a rather sizable slab of pumpkin pie with whipped cream on top of it.

There wasn't so much as a crumb left to be seen on its pristinely white surface now, and although she'd only gotten in a bite or two herself, Dana could safely say that it had indeed been excellent pie.

"Now then, why don't you go pop by the restroom real quick and then we can get going, alright?"

"That's fine," dismissed Rhen with an uninterested shrug of her shoulders. "I don't need to go."

"Um, excuse me, but are you sure about that, dear? You *did* have three glasses of soda with your lunch just now, you know," Dana pointed out patiently, nodding toward the trio of empty glasses on her girlfriend's side of the table that now only held a scant handful of half-melted ice cubes at their bottoms. "We've still got a long way to go before we reach your granny's house tonight, and there aren't going to be too many places to stop along the way. So could you please at least *try* and use the restroom for me before we go? It'll just take a minute, so you might as well, right?"

Feeling her face starting to grow warm with the way her auntie was treating her like a five-year-old in the middle of a crowd full of strangers, Rhen cut her off with an indignant huff.

"I... don't... need... to... go..." she repeated, drawing out each word and annunciating them with as much put-upon sass as she could muster.

She knew that she was playing a dangerous game in doing so, the dark look that she saw crossing the older woman's face as she spoke was evidence enough of that, but she just couldn't help herself.

"*God!* I think I know my own body just a little bit better than you do," she huffed, ignoring the fact that her partner had gotten pretty darn familiar with every nook and cranny of her petite frame over the last few months. "I'm a big girl, Aunt Dana, and I can take care of myself, alright? If I say I don't need to go, then I don't need to go."

Rhen winced internally as her bratty tirade tapered off with another huff, half-expecting Dana to seize her by the upper arm and push her over the edge of their table for an attitude adjustment right there and then, but thankfully she just sighed heavily and pinched the bridge of her nose with her thumb and forefinger.

"Okay, fine. Have it your way then," she finally said, straightening up and planting her hands on her hips as she fixed her in place with a stern glare. "But I'd better not hear any complaining from you when we're back on the road and you suddenly need to pee. You got that?"

"Yeah, sure, whatever, it'll be fine," snapped Rhen, scarcely believing her own good fortune as she began hustling toward the front doors of the restaurant.

She'd managed to avoid getting her butt swatted for being snarky, and she was eager to no longer be the center of attention. The sooner they were out of there and on to other things, the better, as far as she was concerned.

"Come on, let's go already. We're burning daylight!"

—

Despite her earlier assurances that she was fine, Rhen made it a grand total of fourteen minutes once they started driving again before the pressure in her bladder finally got to be too much for her to ignore.

"Um… Aunt Dana?" she piped up with a sheepish half-smile, shifting uncomfortably in her seat and trying to sound like the idea had just occurred to her and hadn't been all she'd been thinking about for the last several miles. "Do you think that maybe we could find somewhere to stop off real quick? I kinda need to go to the bathroom…"

"Oh you do, do you?" replied her partner, looking over at her with a sidelong frown. "I thought you said you didn't need to go?"

"Well, that's because I *didn't*," insisted the younger girl, squeezing her thighs together and blushing. "At least, not right then, at any rate. But I have to now though, so uh, you know… could we…?"

She made a vague gesture with her right hand, letting it finish the question for her.

"I'm afraid it's a little too late to be telling me all this now, hon," scolded Dana in response, rolling her eyes as she flicked on her turn signal and merged over toward the exit lane. "The next chance we're going to have to pull over won't be for another half hour, at least."

"What?" gasped Rhen in panicked disbelief, bouncing impatiently in her leather seat and then immediately wishing that she hadn't when doing so made the pressure in her bladder several times worse. "Can't you just like… find a gas station or something?"

"Well, I *could* have done that if you'd have said something about ten miles ago," countered her aunt with strained patience, snapping her head over to regard her in exasperation for half a moment before returning her full attention back to the road ahead of them.

Lifting a hand from her steering wheel, she gestured at

the thick walls of brush and trees stretching on for miles and miles to either side of them.

"But that was *before* we got onto the highway and started heading for the boonies. I'm sorry to say it, but we're pretty much stuck like this until we reach the next town."

"But...!" protested Rhen, hardly believing what she was hearing as she struggled to come to terms with the sobering reality of her situation.

"Sorry, cutie pie," cooed the older woman in a very "I told you so" sort of way as she reached over and gave her a conciliatory pat on the knee. "You're just going to have to hold it in until we get to the next exit, alright?"

"Ugh, fine, whatever! Just hurry the frick up, would you?"

That had not been a good idea, Rhen knew, but she was way too distressed to really care right then.

"Excuse me, little girl?" purred Dana, letting the hand still resting on the younger girl's knee slide up her thigh and give it a hard squeeze. "What was that?"

"Ah!"

Rhen let out a squeak of pain and her squirming increased tenfold as she felt the older woman's manicured nails dig in warningly against the soft flesh of her inner thigh through the thin material of her leggings.

"Please ma'am!" she hastily corrected herself. "Please just drive as fast as you can. I *really* need to go!"

"Of course, honeybuns."

Easing her grip, Dana gave her another little pat and then returned her hand back to its usual spot on the steering wheel, smiling wryly at how quickly her sassy sophomore could change her tune when it suited her.

"I'll get us to a rest stop just as soon as I can. So you hang in there for me, alright?"

Rhen just chewed on her lower lip and gave a strained nod, not trusting herself to say anything else at that particular moment.

She could already tell that it was going to be a long, *long* ride, and she forced herself to breathe out slowly, hoping to somehow ease the incessant pressure building up between her pushed-together legs by focusing on regulating her breathing.

It didn't work.

Sweat began to bead on her furrowed brow with the effort of holding her bladder in check. Wincing and gritting her teeth against each passing bump in the road, she tried (and failed spectacularly) to distract herself by counting the trees whipping by outside her window as she kept a desperate eye out for the billboards counting down the distance to the next rest stop.

Thirty miles…

Twenty miles…

Fifteen…

Ten…

"Come on, come on…"

Five…

Three…

"Oh, god, Aunt Dana, please hurry. I don't know how much more of this I can handle!"

"I'm driving as fast as I can, dear, but there's nothing I can do about this traffic. It's the day before Thanksgiving, after all," soothed the older woman, who couldn't help but smirk to herself just a little bit as she cast a sidelong glance toward her squirming niece.

She was simply too cute when she got all whiney like this.

"Just hold on for a little bit longer, alright? We're almost there, I promise."

—

"Oh thank god!" gasped Rhen as they finally pulled into a busy rest stop that was mercifully just off the highway.

No sooner had her aunt found a place for them to park, than the panicking girl was tumbling out of the tall SUV, frantically waddling toward the crowded entrance just as fast as she could.

"Come on... almost there..."

Unfortunately though, she only made it a few halting steps into the parking lot before the pressure finally became too much for her to handle and she at last lost total control of her bladder.

"Ah! Oh god... Crap, crap, crap! No, please...!"

But no amount of pleading could stop the flow of urine once it had been set into motion, and she was left with no other choice than to stand there and endure it as warmth began to spread out from between her legs, down her clamped-together thighs, and onto the concrete between her anxiously dancing feet.

"What's the matter, hon?" Dana began to ask as she emerged from around the back of their car, before cutting herself off as she got a good look at what was going on. "Oh dear, that's not good."

"Gee, you think?" demanded Rhen, red-faced and mortified beyond belief as she continued to wet herself.

"Shhh... there, there, it's alright," cooed Dana, stepping in behind her and rubbing her shoulders soothingly. "What's done is done. You just let it all out now, that's it... It'll all be over soon..."

"What the hell! Why's it still coming out?" Rhen moaned in abject misery as, despite her best efforts to stem the tide, her bladder continued to empty itself.

Surely it didn't always take this long for her to normally go, did it?

Probably... I guess I just never realized how long that really was until I had a whole bunch of random strangers standing around and watching me do it, she thought to herself with a sour grimace, desperately trying to come up with something else to focus on instead of the humiliating display she was making of herself. *Ugh. Why couldn't I have been born with a shy bladder or something? This is such bullcrap!*

In spite of her moaning and groaning however, urine continued to keep pouring out of her. Trickling on and on for the next half-minute, its warmth soaking through her panties, her leggings, and her skirt, dribbling down to puddle between her high-tops.

Dang it, dang it, dang it! Why did that stupid place have to have free refills on their drinks?

"Mommy, Mommy, look over there!" came the giggling squeal of a young girl a moment later.

Just when she thought that things couldn't possibly get any more embarrassing for her, Rhen chanced a peek through the gaps between the fingers she was using to cover her face and saw some little brat pointing at her and laughing.

"That girl wet her pants, hah!"

"Hush, Judy," scolded her mother, popping the small girl on the seat of her jeans and bustling her away into the big rest stop store after her father. "Don't you know that it's rude to point? Now come on before *you* have an accident as well."

"Oh my god..." Rhen moaned.

Yep. Things could definitely get worse.

With each thundering heartbeat pounding in her ears, she could feel her humiliation increasing tenfold until she was at last left standing there in the middle of the parking lot with all of her clothes below her waist soaked completely through and her face smoldering so hot that she was sure it would melt off at any moment.

"*Now* do you understand why I wanted you to use the restroom back when you had the chance?" asked her auntie once her little "accident" had finished running its course.

"God, yes," huffed Rhen.

Unsure about what to do with her hands just then, she opted to tuck them in under her armpits as she looked up from the puddle at her feet and scowled at nothing in particular.

"I'm pretty sure it would be impossible *not* to have learned my lesson by now."

One thing was for sure, she definitely wouldn't be skipping out on using the restroom during road trips ever again.

"Hmmm... we'll see about that," came Dana's cool reply, not quite sounding convinced.

With her still looming right behind her, gripping her shoulders, Rhen was unable to see the look on the other woman's face, but the way she'd murmured that last bit against the side of her ear in a low purr had her thinking twice about giving her any more attitude right then.

Uh-oh... This can't be good.

"Y-Yes ma'am."

Rhen swallowed hard, not quite sure what was going to happen next, but wanting very much for the parking lot to just crack open and swallow her whole. She had a feeling that that would be far more preferable to whatever her aunt had in mind for her.

Ugh. Why didn't I just go when I had the chance? What am I, five?

"Alright then, come along, cutie pie," cooed Dana brightly,

snapping her out of her moping as she stepped out from around her and took up her hand in hers, giving it a quick squeeze. "Let's get you cleaned up, shall we?"

"Wait, wait, wait! Hold on a minute," protested Rhen, dragging her feet as much as she dared to as she was pulled inexorably forward toward the automatic doors at the front entrance of the rest stop store. "I can't go in there looking like... like this!"

She sheepishly waved her free hand to take in the state of her clothes from the waist down and winced.

"Sure you can," countered her aunt smoothly, not slowing her pace in the slightest as she smiled smugly ahead of her.

"But... but..." spluttered the younger girl, cheeks burning and starting to panic as she struggled for a way to put her thoughts into words without embarrassing herself even further. "But people will *see*! Can't I just change in the back of the car or something?"

"People have *already* seen you, young lady. So it's a little too late to start worrying about that," chastised Dana in a tone that made it all too clear that she wasn't in the mood to argue as she wrinkled her nose. "And no, you may *not* go back to the car. I don't want your wet clothes dripping all over the seats in there. We're going to get you cleaned up and dried off in the restroom in here, missy, and that's that."

Frowning, Dana looked back at her petulantly scowling girlfriend, pursing her lips into a hard, thin line to quell any further whining as she bored her stern glare into the younger pouting face.

"They've got everything we need to get you changed in here, so quit your whining and come on before I decide to see if they have any souvenir paddles for sale as well. Lord knows you're in enough trouble as it is, and a healthy dose of wood to your bratty buns would definitely not be uncalled for."

"Trouble?" squeaked Rhen, bristling with indignation. "Why am I in trouble? I'm the *victim* here!"

That managed to stop Dana right in her tracks, but the way she rounded on her and brought the full might of her maternal ferocity to bear made it painfully clear that it wasn't because she thought she'd just made a good point.

"Young lady, the only thing that *you* are a victim of here is your own bad behavior," she scolded, tightening her grip on Rhen's wrist and wagging and admonishing forefinger only a few inches away from her face. "Did you, or did you not, pitch a fit and tell me that you didn't need to go back when we were leaving the restaurant?"

"Well, I…" stammered Rhen, caught off guard by the sudden lecture and unsure of how to answer the question without getting herself into more trouble. "I mean… I didn't have to go back then, you see…"

"That's a big fat load of bull patootie and you know it, Rhen. You didn't even *try* to go when I asked you to," snapped Dana, rolling her eyes in exasperation. "In fact, I believe your exact words to me were 'I'm a big girl, Aunt Dana, and I can take care of myself'. Well we both see how well *that* turned out, don't we, little girl?"

Rhen could feel the tips of her ears burning with shame, both from having her own sassy words thrown back at her and from being forced to direct her gaze down toward where her partner was pointing, getting her first really good look at the dark, wet stain glistening between her thighs, all the way down to her knees.

"But… but… That wasn't my fau-" she began to whine again, before being cut off by a sharp gesture from Dana.

"You hush up right now, missy!" she snapped, bringing the discussion to a sudden close with a jerk of her wrist as she resumed leading their march into the rest stop proper, continuing to lecture loud enough for everyone they passed by to get an earful as they went. "You *deliberately* chose to disobey me when I told you to use the restroom, being very rude about it in the process I might add, and in the end you wound up wetting your pants like a little girl because of it. Now those pants are coming down for a good, hard spanking, Rhen Elizabeth, and I don't want to hear another word about it. Is that understood?"

"Yes ma'am," squeaked Rhen, knowing that she was thoroughly past the point of no return now that her middle name was being used against her.

She'd screwed up royally, and now the only viable course of action for her was to allow herself to be paraded past all of the other smirking shoppers like the naughty little girl she was.

Well… At least I won't see any of these people ever again, she tried to tell herself, wincing as they passed by the mother and daughter who'd seen her in the parking lot earlier. *I guess it could always be worse…*

It wasn't exactly the most comforting thought in the world, true, but at that moment Rhen was willing to take just about whatever she could get as she waddled reluctantly beside her steaming auntie.

Pushing their way into the crowded women's restroom, Dana marched her grimacing girlfriend right up to the sink closest to the back wall of the little room and then jabbed a finger toward the tile floor.

"Strip," she ordered in a clipped, no-nonsense manner, heedless of the various onlookers watching them as they washed their hands or else waited for a stall to open up. "Everything below the waist, right now, young lady."

"Yes ma'am…"

Blushing scarlet, Rhen turned to face the wall so that she wouldn't have to look at anybody as she reached around to her side and slipped free the button clasp on her skirt. Weighed down as it was, it immediately fell away from her hips, landing in a crumpled ring around her ankles with a wet *plop*. Then, after staring at it miserably for a handful of heart-beats, she stepped out of it.

Humph. Would it kill someone to turn up the heat in here just a little bit? It's freaking freezing!

While Rhen busied herself with pouting, Dana bent for-ward and scooped up her discarded skirt. Shaking it out, she paused for a moment to examine the wet spot on it, clucking her tongue and frowning in disapproval before dropping the garment into the sink in front of her. She then reached out and turned on the water, letting it cascade down and soak into the material for a few long moments before gathering it up once again and wringing it out.

"Hurry up now, cutie pie, we haven't got all day, you know," she scolded gently, looking warningly over her shoul-der to get Rhen moving again as she continued to rinse and wring out the skirt in her hands.

"Right!" squeaked the younger girl, startled out of her grumpy survey of the uniformly white tiles in front of her as her partner reached out and landed a quick, wet swat to the uppermost part of her right cheek.

THWAP!

Doing her best to ignore the snickers and bemused looks she was being bombarded with from all of the other women in the restroom behind her, Rhen slipped her feet out of her high-tops and kicked them off under the sink where they'd be safely out of the way while she rubbed at her stinging nether cheek. She then gathered up the stretchy waistband of her dark leggings and began to peel them away from her damp skin, turning them inside out as she struggled to work them down to her knees. Then, using the wall in front of her for support, she braced herself with a hand on its cold, smooth surface and used her other to hold onto her bunched up and soaked leggings as she wrenched free first one calf, and then the other, before passing them over to her aunt so that they too could soak.

Thank god my top is still dry, she thought to herself with a little shiver, goose bumps sprouting up all across her now bare thighs. *I'll definitely pass on winding up completely naked in front of a bunch of random strangers, regardless of whether or not I'll see any of them ever again, thank you very much.*

"Ahem."

Dana cleared her throat, drawing her mind once again back to the task at hand.

"Do you need a hand there, hon?"

"No, I'm fine!" squeaked the younger girl, her face flushing far pinker than the hoodie she was wearing just then.

Letting out a long, low, mortified moan at what she knew had to come next, Rhen hooked her thumbs into the waistband of her sky blue panties and began tugging them down. Just like with her leggings though, they too clung to her clammy skin with a humiliating tenacity that made their descent a slow and awkward one.

"Grrr... come on, dang it..."

But before she could muster up the resolve to really get a good grip on them and shove them down, she felt one of Dana's strong hands pushing her forward between the shoulder blades while her other seized a great handful of the back of her waistband.

"I thought I told you to hurry?" she chided lightly, yanking the wet panties down in back and delivering two sharp swats.

SMACK! SMACK!

"Sorry, sorry!" babbled Rhen, dancing in place as she leaned against the wall in front of her for support.

Oh crap, swats on cold skin hurt way more than normal. That's definitely not good...

"That's okay dear," replied the older woman with a light chuckle, seemingly oblivious to the concerns running through her niece's mind as she squatted down behind her and wriggled her stubbornly stuck panties the rest of the way down to her ankles for her. "You aren't the first little girl I've had to clean up after an accident, you know, although you're definitely the oldest."

Dana let out an amused huff at that and lightly tickled the backs of Rhen's thighs as she added.

"Step out, please."

Biting her lower lip to prevent herself from giggling out loud as she involuntarily wriggled around, Rhen did as she was told while she remained resolutely facing forward, hiding her brightly blushing face from the rest of the people around her. Now that she was stuck standing there in just her long-sleeve top and a zip-up hoodie, she couldn't decide which was worse. Being bare bottomed in public and about to get a spanking, or being paraded around a store full of people after having just wet her pants.

Both, she decided a moment later, pouting with all her might at the wall in front of her as she listened to her aunt running her panties underneath the water from the sink before wringing them out. *Both are just the worst in their own special ways.*

A few moments later the flow of water was cut off again, and she shifted nervously in place as she heard Dana tugging a few paper towels out of the dispenser beside the mirror to dry her hands with.

"Okay, cutie pie, you stay put right there and I'll be back in just a bit, alright?"

Stepping up behind her girlfriend, Dana gathered up her hands for her and moved them up to her head as she normally did for timeouts and corner time. Once she had the girl's fingers threaded together on top of her inky black hair just the way she liked them, she then gently nudged the back of her head forward so that her nose bumped up against the cool tiles in front of it.

"Yes, Aunt Dana," murmured Rhen respectfully, the wall in front of her muffling her voice ever so slightly.

"It's not like I could freaking go anywhere now anyway," she added grumpily under her breath as her stomach churned with embarrassment and nerves.

"Good girl."

With a final parting pat to either clammy cheek, choosing to ignore the sass bubbling out of the petite sophomore for the moment, Dana spun on her heel and marched her way out of the restroom, whistling a nonchalant tune to herself as she went.

Left with little other recourse than to stand there obediently, knowing full well that she couldn't make a dash back to the car in just a hoodie and a smile, Rhen puffed out her cheeks and blew out an annoyed huff through her nose as she glared at the wall in front of her.

This sucks.

She did her best to ignore the idle chatter of the other women coming and going around her, but with nothing to distract herself with, she found herself unable to stop from absorbing every word they said.

"Uh-oh, it looks like somebody's in trouble," came the

unseen voice of a middle-aged woman as she click-clacked her way into the restroom on a pair of high heels.

"It sure does," crooned someone else trailing after her. "What's the matter, sweetheart, did your mommy get tired of you asking 'are we there yet?' while y'all were driving?"

Rhen could sense them approaching from somewhere behind her, but resisted the urge to turn around and let them see just how embarrassed she was right then.

That didn't seem to stop them from making it worse, however.

"Oh dear, would you look at what's soaking in the sink here…"

"Ahhh, now I see. She's that silly filly who had the accident in the parking lot that Martha was telling us about."

Shifting around uncomfortably with a sour grimace, Rhen gritted her teeth. She could practically *feel* the sneer on the unknown woman's face as she watched her from only a couple of feet away.

Yep. This really, really sucks.

"So what happened, dear, did you forget to go potty before y'all left?"

"Kinda…" mumbled Rhen noncommittally, hoping that the brief answer would be enough to satisfy the two strangers as the tips of her ears grew extra-hot.

"Probably figured she could hold it in," snickered the first woman again as she and her friend mercifully stepped away from Rhen and her pale, wobbly cheeks, moving off to find stalls. "My Jeffery used to have that same problem when he was a little boy, though a smacked bottom or two cleared that right up in a jiffy."

"Let's hope that this little cutie is so lucky. I bet she'd look just adorable with a red heinie," snickered her friend, before shutting the door to her own stall with a hard *clack*.

Dang it, dang it, dang it… This super-duper ultra-sucks! I definitely should have just gone back when I had the freaking chance.

Rhen let out a long, exasperated sigh and rolled her eyes.

Oh well, lesson learned… I guess. No use crying over spilled milk and all that other crap now, right?

—

Rhen continued to stand there maintaining her bare bottomed vigil for what felt like a very long time, but was in reality no more than ten or fifteen minutes. Either way though, she couldn't help but sag with relief when she at last heard her aunt's familiar gait marching up behind her, accompanied by the faint *swish-swish* of a plastic bag or two.

Oh thank god.

Rhen continued to remain where she was though however, not daring to budge an inch until she'd been given explicit permission to do so as she patiently waited while Dana dug around inside one of the bags she'd brought with her.

"Oh!"

Jerking up onto the balls of her feet, she let out a squeak of surprise as she suddenly felt a warm beach towel being swaddled around her chilly legs. She then eased back down with an involuntary sigh of relief, and did her best to keep her squirming to a minimum as her auntie quickly and efficiently dried off her cheeks and the sides of her hips with the thin towel.

"Turn around and spread your legs for me, please, hon," she ordered gently, even as she coaxed her to obey by steering her hips around herself.

Stomach churning with the command, Rhen nevertheless allowed herself to be repositioned, shuffling around to face the older woman who then squatted down onto her heels in front of her, towel in hand as she smiled fondly up at her. With her hands still clinging to each other for dear life on top of her head, and her face blushing about as red as a tomato, Rhen shifted her stance outward so that her feet were spaced approximately a shoulder's width apart.

"There we go, now let's just see if we can't get you nice and dry down here, shall we?" cooed Dana, leaning forward and patting down the front of her hairless groin with the towel a few times before doing much the same along either of her inner thighs and calves.

Mortified beyond belief, Rhen just tipped her head back and chewed on her lower lip to keep herself from letting out any embarrassing noises as her partner took her dear, sweet time toweling her off.

Then, just when she was sure that she was almost finished with this humiliating and humbling ordeal, she felt her eyes all but pop out of her head when suddenly Dana reached back behind her with her free hand, seized a great handful of soft cheek and tugged it aside so that she could get at all of the places in between her rounded chubs as well.

"Eep!"

Rhen squeaked again, and would have tumbled back into the wall behind her had it not been for her partner's steady hold on her caboose keeping her in place.

"Easy there, cutie pie, I need to make sure I dry you off *everywhere*, okay?" she cooed in response to her girlfriends groaning protest as she wriggled and squirmed ineffectually in her firm grip.

Grinning teasingly up at her from ear to ear, she let out a throaty little chuckle and winked.

"I'd hate for my favorite niece to be wandering around

with a pair of soggy buns, after all."

"F-Fine, whatever," Rhen forced herself to bite out, falling back on her usual sass to cover up just how embarrassed she felt right then. "Um… But could you hurry it up just a bit, please?"

"Awww, do you have somewhere to be, little girl? Don't tell me that you need to go potty again…" teased Dana, beaming mischievously up at her as she gave her one final, extra-firm rub between her splayed cheeks before letting her go and pushing back up to a standing position, towel in hand. "Okay then, have it your way, kiddo. You just go ahead and grab that sink there and we'll get your spanking out of the way right now. Sound good?"

Deciding that it probably wouldn't be a great idea to let the other woman know exactly what she thought about that particular plan right then, Rhen instead just nodded her hotly flushed face and shuffled over to stand where she indicated while doing her best to present the least amount of her bare front as possible to their gathered audience.

Oof.

Staring down at her thoroughly soaked and now drip-drying clothes in the sink in front of her, the smoldering in Rhen's face kicked up by several degrees. She found herself glaring at them for several long moments before finally forcing herself to look away as she brought her hands down from her head and used them to grip the far edge of the rounded porcelain before her in a death grip. This change in scenery wasn't all that much better though, unfortunately, since looking up meant that she had no other choice than to lock eyes with her own reflection in the mirror and watch as Dana moved around to her left side, positioning herself for her upcoming punishment.

Well, this is certainly new… mused Rhen with a wry grimace as she watched her auntie wrap a steadying arm around

411

her waist before bringing her right palm up to her shoulder, poised to strike at any moment.

"Ready?" she asked sweetly, matching stares with the petulantly scowling girl in the mirror and smirking as she leaned her shoulder against her back to force her to push her bare bottom out even further.

"I guess so..." mumbled Rhen as she shuffled her feet beneath her to accommodate her adjusted position.

"Alrighty then, let's make this nice and quick, shall we?" crooned Dana, her smirk growing even wider as she brought her right hand down to give her goose bumpy cheeks a couple of friendly rubs. "Like you said, we're burning daylight... although that's not the only thing that's going to be burning in just a second."

"Oh ha-"

SMACK! SMACK! SMACK!

"Ack! Hah..." answered Rhen, her deadpan retort quickly morphing into a yelp of pain as her spanking got underway without so much as a warning squeeze.

—

Keeping her pace smooth and relentless, and adding a little wrist-snap action to each impact, Dana focused on delivering sharp, crisp swats to her bratty girlfriend's chilly cheeks for the next three minutes straight.

She watched with grim satisfaction as Rhen's grip instantly tightened on the sink in front of her, her knuckles going white and her eyes screwing themselves shut as her ponytail bobbed from side to side.

"Ah, ah, oh!" she gasped and hissed through clenched teeth, clearly doing her best to keep as quiet as she could as her bare feet took turns stomping out her protests on the hard tile floor beneath her.

Not that it made much of a difference.

The staccato reports of a hard palm striking soft flesh reverberated off of the tile walls and floor of the little restroom, magnified enough to let everyone outside of its thin walls know exactly what was happening within.

Dana knew too how much more a well-deserved spanking on a cold and clammy caboose could sting, and she wasn't holding anything back as she continued to thoroughly drive that lesson home to her favorite brat.

"What are you going to do the next time I tell you to use the restroom, Rhen?" she demanded, deciding that it was about time to start peppering in some lecturing with her swats.

"Use it, use it, use it!" the younger girl squealed, tossing her head back before dipping her chin forward again and letting out a great, long moan to make room for more yelping.

"Good," sniffed Dana, keeping her swats rhythmic and unrelenting as she continued to scold her squirming niece. "You need to learn that when I tell you to do something, it's not because I'm trying to boss you around, mostly, but because I know something that you might not. Like for instance that there won't be any stops for over half an hour while we're driving. You see?"

"Yes, Aunt Dana, I do- Ah! I do!"

SMACK! SMACK! SMACK! SMACK!

"That's right, little girl!" she growled, delivering four extra-hard swats to punctuate each word before continuing. "If you'd have just listened to me and done as you were told in the first place, you wouldn't have wet your pants in front of all those people and you wouldn't now be getting this spanking, would you?"

"No ma'am!"

That definitely brought a satisfied twinkle to the older woman's eyes and she knew that she'd just about finished with her niece's punishment. Still though, she mused as she shifted her aim a bit lower to Rhen's largely-untouched sit-spots, it would be better if she at least heard an actual apology or two before she brought this spanking to a close.

SMACK! SMACK! SMACK!

Suddenly upping the tempo and force of her swats without any build-up or warning, Dana began going to town on her naughty niece's naked thighs, painting overlapping red hand-prints all across their desperately squirming, creamy backs for a solid minute of uninterrupted agony.

"Oh! Oh! Aunt Dana, please, I'm sorry, I'm sorry. Owie, owie, *owie*!"

"I should hope so, young lady," she huffed, expressing her dissatisfaction with several more hard swats. "You're very lucky that they don't sell any bars of soap here, or else you'd better believe that you'd be chewing on one right now for all that fibbing you did about not needing to go potty earlier."

"Oh my god, I'm sorry!" squealed Rhen through gritted teeth, stomping her feet over and over again and making her burning bottom bounce and wobble. "I didn't think it was going to be that big of a deal. I'll never do it again, I *swear*!"

"See that you don't," sniffed Dana with every ounce of matriarchal disapproval that she could muster. "We've still got a long way to go before we're done driving today, and I want you to know that I have absolutely no problem pulling over and toasting your bratty buns some more if you give me a reason to. Is that understood, little girl?"

"I won't, I promise!"

"Good."

With that, the older woman slowed her pace once again, and then shifted her aim back up to the fullest, most jiggly parts of her girlfriend's caboose. She delivered another two dozen extra-hard and sizzling swats to really make sure that the message had sunk in, and then just as quickly as it had begun, Rhen's spanking was suddenly over.

—

"Am I going to have any more attitude from you today, young lady?" demanded Dana, grabbing a handful of swollen, dark pink cheek in her right hand and squeezing hard.

"No ma'am, I'm sorry ma'am," squeaked Rhen in response, feet dancing beneath her as her hands let go of the sink and waved animatedly to either side of her as if she could somehow fly away from her richly deserved punishment.

"Well, I'm very happy to hear that," cooed her partner, immensely satisfied.

Releasing her cheek and smirking at the adorable way it wobbled back into place, she guided the panting girl back to a standing position and turned her away from the sink in order to wrap her in a tight embrace.

"There, there, cutie pie. We're all done now, it's okay, shhh…"

Relieved beyond belief to hear that the slate had once again been wiped clean for her, Rhen let out a long sigh and melted against her auntie's sturdy form. Feeling lighter and more at peace than she had all day, she buried her face against the warmth of her sizable bosom, holding onto her for support and reveling in the back scratches she was giving her as she fought to get her blushing and wincing back under control.

She knew that it had been a pretty light spanking all things considered, and now that the initial fiery fury had faded to just a dull tenderness, she found herself once again growing all too aware of her current state of undress in the middle of this very public restroom.

"Um… you wouldn't happened to have bought me some dry clothes while you were out there by any chance, um… would you?" she asked hopefully, murmuring the question against the soft material of Dana's cardigan as her stomach flip-flopped around a particularly boisterous swarm of butterflies.

"Why, as a matter of fact, I did," she confirmed with a reassuring pat on her back and another fond rub of her bare cheeks, before disentangling herself from her and leaning over to snatch up one of the plastic bags she'd brought with her from off of the tile floor at her feet.

Letting out another small sigh of relief, Rhen watched with barely restrained patience and both hands doing their very best to shield her naked front from view as her aunt dug around in the bag for a moment, before dropping it to the floor again upon finding what it was that she'd apparently been looking for.

What the…?

It took her a few moments to fully grasp what it was that she was looking at, but as she continued to stare her confusion gradually gave way to flabbergasted horror as realization suddenly dawned on her. A great yawning chasm then opened up in the pit of her stomach, draining all of the color from her disbelieving face as she stood there and watched as Dana tore open a hole in the plastic wrapping of the crinkling package and extracted from it a bright pink pull-up.

"Wait, Aunt Dana, no. You can't be serious…" she began to protest, her voice caught somewhere between pleading and unhappy acceptance.

Taking half a step back, she unglued one of the hands she

had pressed between her legs, holding it out in front of her as if it could somehow fend off what the other woman held in her hands.

"I'm way too old to be wearing something like... like that... Come on!"

"Oh hush now, don't make such a fuss," chided Dana in response, unfolding the padded pair of training panties with practiced ease, one corner of her mouth quirking up in smug amusement as she got her first good look at the design printed across their front. "I even made sure to get you the Disney princess ones, see?"

She turned the humiliating garment around in her hands so that Rhen could see the design as well.

"Look, it's Beauty and the Beast. Didn't you say that that one was your favorite?"

Grrr... I don't know why I ever told you that, Rhen growled to herself in silent indignation.

Although aloud, she said, "But... but why?"

She already had a pretty good idea about what the answer to her question would be, and she knew that asking it didn't really do anything to help her "I'm way too old for this" argument, but she just couldn't help herself as she stomped her foot and let out a frustrated moan.

"You mean aside from the fact that I'm the adult in this relationship and what I say goes?" asked her aunt coolly, cocking one eyebrow at her and making her knees wobble slightly with the look she gave her.

"Um... yes?" squeaked Rhen, knowing full well that she was potentially courting another spanking with her reply.

Thankfully though, it seemed that her aunt was still in a forgiving mood, because she just smiled frostily at her and went on to explain.

"We've already had one accident from you today, *little girl.*"

She made sure to put a great deal of extra emphasis on those last two words as she stared down hard at Rhen, silently daring her to deny it. She then let the tension build between them for a few more heartbeats, satisfying herself that she wasn't about to be interrupted before she continued.

"And I think we'd both prefer it if you didn't end up wetting your pants again during the rest of our trip. Wouldn't you agree?"

"I mean... I guess so," conceded the younger girl with a pout, no longer caring about her nudity as she folded her arms in front of her and glared daggers at the bright pink monstrosity in her partner's hands.

She knew that she'd already lost this argument, that she'd lost it before it had even begun, but she just couldn't help herself as she tried to postpone the inevitable.

"But... but, um... Are you sure they're even going to fit?"

It was a flimsy excuse, she knew, but it was the best she could come up with on such short notice.

"They're the same size as the ones we have back at home," answered Dana with a shrug and a tight smirk that said she knew exactly what she was up to. "So, yes."

"Oh..." was Rhen's only response to that, deflated slightly by the knowledge that the sizable stack of pull-ups she'd spied hiding in the cabinet underneath the sink in her bathroom were indeed meant for her.

Shifting her gaze to stare at a point just past her auntie's shoulder and frowning in consternation, she struggled to find some last bit of hope to cling to, but unfortunately came up empty.

"But I mean... Couldn't we just... like, um...?"

"What's the matter? Do you not like these ones, cutie pie?" teased the older woman, her face a mask of mock-concern as she added facetiously. "If you want, we can go back out and take a look at the other designs they have here in the store. I think I saw some Barbie ones if you'd rather have those..."

Horrified, Rhen watched as Dana made as if to turn and lead the two of them back out into the thoroughly crowded rest stop store.

"No, no, no, these ones are fine!" she reassured her quickly, scurrying around to block her path as one hand again shifted down to cover her hairless front while the other tried to stop her smirking partner before she could get too far.

"Oh, are you *sure*?" cooed Dana, drawing out the last word and grinning triumphantly from ear to ear at her niece's adorable antics.

"Ugh, yes," snapped Rhen, her nerves and embarrassment suddenly getting the better of her.

Crossing her arms in front of her with a huff, she stomped a foot and scowled impotently at the smiling older woman. If she was going to be strong-armed into wearing something as humiliating as a pull-up at her age, then she wasn't going to pretend to like it.

At least, not in public.

"Can we just get this over with already, *please*?"

"Of course, dear," chirped Dana as if she hadn't just been given a whole heaping helping of sass.

Dropping down onto one knee in front of the delightfully pouting younger girl, she held open the pull-up for her to step into.

"Here you go."

Of freaking course she doesn't just let me put the stupid thing on myself. Ugh.

Taking the invitation with as much attitude as she could safely get away with without running the risk of having her pull-up pulled down for another spanking before she'd even had a chance to get used to wearing it, Rhen slid first her left foot, and then her right, into the leg holes offered to her. She could feel that her face was glowing far redder than her bottom was at that particular moment and she chewed on her lower lip in quiet humiliation as Dana took her time sliding the training panties up her narrow legs, settling them snugly in place around her hips.

True to her prediction, they fit her like a glove, and she hated it.

"Awww, now don't you just look precious," cooed the older woman, smiling up at her and reaching out to fondly pat the padding between her legs. "What do you think, honey-buns, are they comfy?"

"I guess so," grumbled Rhen, not quite willing to concede the point just yet.

Catching sight of her reflection in the mirror beside her however, she had to admit that she did indeed look pretty darn cute standing there in just a zip-up hoodie and her bright pink pull-up. Not that she would have ever admitted anything like that out loud voluntarily.

At least they're not super bulky, she tried to tell herself, twisting her hips from side to side to see how she looked from different angles. *Nobody should be able to tell what I'm wearing once I've got something on over them. Speaking of...*

"Um... Can I at least have that towel to wrap around my waist so that nobody has to see me in this... *thing*?"

She couldn't even bring herself to say the word out loud quite yet.

God, this sucks.

"Sorry, cutie pie, but I'm afraid not," replied Dana with a dismissive shake of her head, climbing back to her feet and proceeding to wrap up her wet clothes in said towel before cramming the whole soggy mess into a plastic bag. "Try not to sweat it too much though, okay? You look absolutely adorable in that 'thing', and everyone else has already either seen you walking through the store in your soaked leggings and skirt, or else heard you getting your spanking just now anyway. The sight of a well-spanked naughty girl wearing a pull-up after having had an accident will hardly be that much of a shock to any of them, I'm sure."

"Not really what I meant, you know…" grumbled Rhen in response, rolling her eyes but deciding not to push the issue any further as she stooped down to retrieve her high-tops, slipping them back onto her still chilly, bare feet.

"I know, dear," snorted Dana, playfully swatting her padded posterior before draping an affectionate arm around her shoulders. "Now come along, let's go pick out some snacks and then we can get back on the road, alright?"

"Sounds good to me," answered Rhen, only half-lying as she allowed herself to be steered out of the restroom.

Truth be told, she wished that they could just teleport back to their big red SUV and cut out her embarrassing walk of shame altogether, but she knew that that wasn't an option and instead resigned herself to a fresh round of well-deserved pointing and snickering.

"Now that you mention it, actually, I *am* kind of hungry…"

"Hah! What else is new?" teased Dana with a tinkling laugh as they at last stepped out of the restroom. "Don't you worry though, cutie pie. I saw that they have some of those chips you like, and I'll be happy to buy you a bag and something to drink to tide you over until we get to your granny's house. Sound good?"

"Oh heck yeah!"

On a whim, Rhen stepped in closer and wrapped her arms around her partner, rising up onto the balls of her feet and planting a quick kiss on her cheek.

"Thanks, Aunt Dana."

"Anytime, kiddo," the older woman chuckled. "Anytime."

Chapter 21

Reunited and Back to Basics

"Wake up, cutie pie, we're here…"

"Huh?" slurred Rhen, tumbling out of a blissful doze with a sudden start as she was gently shaken awake by a hand on her shoulder.

Confused and not quite sure where she was just then, she whipped her head up and around from where she'd been drooling on her seatbelt, blinking in bewilderment.

"Aunt Dana? Wha-? What's going on?"

Reaching up, the dazed girl rubbed absently at her bleary eyes with the back of her hand, before opening her mouth as wide as it would go and letting out a prolonged yawn.

"Where are we?"

"Why, we're at your granny's house, of course, silly goose."

Rhen continued to just stare blankly at the older woman for a few more moments, not quite comprehending her words as the disjointed memories of some fanciful dream about flying around in space in a cake-powered robot continued to clog up the gears in her mind. But, as she blinked again and shifted up from her huddled slouch, the world around her started to come back into focus once again and she at last remembered what it was that she and her auntie had been doing before she'd fallen asleep.

"Oh… yeah, that's right," she mumbled drowsily, head still catching up with her as she unbuckled her seatbelt and stretched her arms above her head in the SUV's spacious interior. "We're here already?"

"We sure are," confirmed Dana with a fond smirk, reaching out to gently tap the end of her nose with a forefinger. "So shake off those cobwebs, sleepy head, and let's go say hello."

Turning to look out her window, Rhen couldn't help but grin. The sun had long since set by then, but even in just the faint glow of the porch lights in the distance she was still able to immediately recognize the familiar sights of the old gravel driveway they were parked on and the even older (but still incredibly well-maintained) farm house out in the middle of the country.

"Huh… That didn't take nearly as long as I thought it would," she observed with another stretch, rocking her head from side to side and popping her neck, before sighing in satisfaction.

"No kidding. It's amazing how quickly time flies on a long drive when you're fast asleep for most of it," agreed her aunt with an amused snort. "By the way, I just want you to know that you are *very* lucky that your snoring is cute, little girl, or else I'd have been poking you awake every few minutes at the rate you were sawing logs."

"I don't *snore*!" denied Rhen vehemently, one hand pressed to her minimal breast in mock-outrage and blushing slightly at her partner having just called her cute.

That never got old.

She was just about to open her mouth and deliver a suitably scathing retort when she felt something crinkle beneath her.

Wait a minute… What happened to my skirt?

Still a bit drowsy, she looked down and frowned in confusion at the bare legs she saw idly kicking back and forth in front of her, and then immediately felt her heart leap into her throat as she was suddenly reminded of the dramatic shift in wardrobe that had been foisted upon her only a few hours earlier.

"Oh crap!"

No longer feeling even the least bit sleepy, Rhen sat bolt upright in her leather seat and hurriedly started yanking down on the front of her zip-up hoodie in a frantic attempt to try and hide the Disney princess smiling sassily up at her from between her clamped-together thighs.

"Aunt Dana, quick, I need pants!"

"Oh hush, you," dismissed the older woman with a disapproving cluck of her tongue, reaching over and gently undoing her girlfriend's white-knuckled grip on the hem of her hoodie. "And stop that! You're going to stretch out your pretty new sweater if you keep tugging on it like that, you know."

"But…" protested Rhen, letting out a piteous moan as fresh warmth rushed into her cheeks, painting them a noticeable shade of strawberry red even in the dim glow of the car's interior lights.

"You look *fine*, dear," soothed Dana, giving her a reassuring little pat on the knee, but making no move to pop the hatch on the back of their car. "If you didn't need pants back when we left the rest stop, then you most certainly don't need them now, either. Besides, we're only going to be hanging around your granny tonight anyway, and I know for a *fact* that she's already seen your bare buns on enough occasions to not be phased by seeing you running around in just your undies. So try to relax, alright?"

Hearing those words, Rhen huffed out an indignant snort through flared nostrils and then opened her mouth to contest everything that her auntie had just said.

As far as she was concerned, putting on some pants was

of vital importance to her very existence at that particular moment. And more to the point, she wanted to make it abundantly clear to everyone involved that the padded pink monstrosity that she'd been forced into wearing was *not* her underwear. It was an embarrassing punishment and *maybe* a cute and somewhat-necessary precaution against over-hydrating, and nothing more. Moreover, she didn't *care* that her grandma might have seen her naked butt before. That was then and this was now, and despite her outward appearance and the way everyone around her seemed dead set on treating her, she *was* (technically) an adult, gosh darn it!

But the twinkling look of amusement and silent challenge in Dana's dark eyes was more than enough to get her to pause and think twice about saying any of those things out loud right then.

Humph.

Forcing herself to take a deep breath and relax before she could say anything that she might regret, Rhen instead pursed her lips together into a silent scowl, grumbling her grievances internally instead.

This is such bullcrap! Just because I look like a naughty teenager and maybe sometimes act like one, doesn't mean that I should have to be treated like one too. We're on vacation, darn it! Shouldn't that count for something?

"Hmmm… Oh dear, it looks like someone is still a bit cranky from her nap," observed Dana a moment later, taking in the glower on her face and arching an eyebrow in only semi-serious warning as the right corner of her mouth twitched toward a smirk. "You know, I could always warm your caboose back up before we get out of the car if you'd like to just get that temper tantrum out of your system now, cutie pie. Would you prefer to greet your granny with a freshly-spanked, *bare* bottom instead of with your pretty panties on?"

"No, no, that's fine," squeaked Rhen, backpedaling as fast as she could as she reeled in her sulking to only a slight pout. "I'll be good."

"Oh, I'm sure you will, dear," answered her partner with just a hint of sarcasm, reaching out and ruffling the younger girl's hair before turning away and removing her keys from the ignition. "Now then, let's get going, shall we?"

Rhen continued to remain seated right where she was for another couple of heartbeats as Dana pushed open her driver's side door and moved to step out of the car.

Ugh. This sucks.

She had *planned* on using the remainder of their drive down to her grandma's house to formulate some sort of plan that would help her avoid getting mixed up in a situation just like the one she found herself in at that very moment, but alas, something had gone terribly awry.

Gosh darn it. I never could stay awake on long car trips.

Between the soothing monotone of their SUV rumbling down the highway, the warmth of the pull-up swaddling her along her hairless front and over her rounded cheeks, not to mention the cozy heat radiating into her tender tush from the passenger-side seat warmers that Dana had set to full power to combat the chill November air, she'd fallen asleep almost immediately. No sooner had they pulled out of the rest stop and gotten back underway again than she'd completely zonked out, drifting off before she'd so much as even finished her preliminary brainstorming session.

Now they were parked outside of her grandma's house and it was too late, *far* too late, to do anything about her state of undress. She could already see the shadowed form of the spry old woman who'd raised her ever since she'd been a small child ambling her way down the path winding away from the farm house's front porch to greet them, and she knew then that she was all out of options.

"Crap, crap, crap!" she swore to herself, venting her frustrations by stomping her feet against the rubber floor mat beneath her before slumping back against her seat with a huff, arms folded and brows knitted together into a dark scowl. "Well, I guess the cat's definitely out of the bag now. If Grandma wasn't already aware of how Aunt Dana handles disciplining me, she sure will be in just a second or two. Freaking... awesome."

Deciding that the best course of action for her right then was to just bite the bullet and face her impending humiliation head-on, Rhen heaved out one last put-upon sigh of resignation and then pushed open her own car door. Plopping down onto the gravel beneath her, her high-tops crunching it underfoot, she tried to ignore the sudden swell of butterflies in her stomach as she took in a deep breath and forced herself to smile.

Okay... I can do this. They're just pull-ups. It's not that big of a deal, right?

"Hi Grandma!" she called out in greeting, trepidation only dampening her enthusiasm a little bit as she waved her hand high overhead.

"Well bless my stars, if it isn't my favorite little Rhen," exclaimed her grandma in a thick southern accent, increasing the speed of her stiff gait as she hastened to close the distance between the two of them. "Lord, is it ever good to see you again, child."

"You too," answered Rhen with genuine delight, meeting the woman who was almost as short as she was halfway and wrapping her up in a huge bear hug. "I've missed you *so* much!"

"Me too, child, me too," wheezed the old woman, patting her granddaughter's back and wincing as she felt a couple of her ribs creaking with the strength of the embrace she suddenly found herself caught up in.

They continued to stay locked in place like that for several more moments, the raven-haired girl breathing in deeply the scent of her grandma, before finally letting her go with a contented sigh.

Stumbling back with a light chuckle, the old woman straightened out her clothes and then took a moment to get her first proper look at her granddaughter.

"Well, well, well… what do we have here?"

"Um… well, I…" hemmed Rhen, reflexively bringing her right thumb up to her lips to chew on her fingernail as she struggled to find the words to explain away her current state of dress, or more to the point, lack thereof.

As she'd known they would, her grandma's sharp eyes had immediately snagged on the bright pink-pull up secured around her narrow hips. But rather than be put off by the sight of it, she instead fixed Rhen with a knowing half-grin that wasn't all that far off from the one Dana was wearing as she appeared from around the front of their car a moment later, waving hello as well.

"Well howdy there, Melinda," she called out, stepping up behind Rhen and laying her hands affectionately on top of her shoulders, giving them a firm squeeze. "As you might've guessed from our Rhen's adorable choice in undies, we hit a bit of a hiccup on our way up here."

"That's one way of putting it," grumbled Rhen, causing both women's grins to grow just a bit wider.

"You see, *someone* here decided that she didn't need to use the bathroom after lunch, refused to go even, only to discover that her bladder wasn't quite as big as she thought it was. Can you believe that?"

"You don't say?" drawled Melinda Mathews, folding her arms in front of her and shifting her weight over to one hip.

Letting out a mock-exasperated sigh, Dana pulled the younger girl in a bit closer against the warmth of her front, kneading her upper arms with her strong fingers.

"I'm afraid so," she confirmed with a melodramatic shake of her head as she cast her eyes skyward. "I managed to get her to a rest stop eventually, but traffic was pretty bad on the interstate and it took us a while to get there. And unfortunately, Rhen couldn't quite hold it in and ended up wetting her pants right there in the middle of the parking lot."

"Oh dear, is that so?" came the old woman's scandalized reply, looking aghast at her granddaughter and then back up at her partner for added effect.

Blushing scarlet, Rhen could only give a strangled nod as her auntie continued for her.

"Yep. She managed to soak through pretty much everything she was wearing below the waist by the time she was finished. Luckily, since we were already right there, I was able to just march her straight into the bathroom and get her cleaned up without too much of a delay. I got her clothes soaking in one of the sinks, and then after toweling her off, I warmed her caboose up for a bit for fibbing about not needing to go and for giving me so much attitude about it earlier."

Dana snorted at that and then sighed again, wistfully.

"My goodness, you should have seen the way she was carrying on in there. You'd have thought I was taking the brush to her for swearing in church or something. But no, it was just a quick hand spanking to keep her on her toes and to remind her to behave herself for the rest of the drive. However, since we'd already had one unexpected accident today, I decided that it would probably be better if I went ahead and put her into something a bit more... *appropriate*. You know, just in case."

Positioned as she was with the back of her head resting against the soft mounds of Dana's generous breasts, Rhen was unable to see the wink she gave the woman standing in front of her, but there was no missing the broad grin that split her grandma's face a moment later.

"Hah!" she exclaimed, shaking with barely-restrained mirth as she threw her hands up into the air before planting them on her hips and nodding once in approval. "Dana, you're a genius. We used to have to make stops *all* the time back when I'd take Rhen on road trips when she was younger. Had a couple of close calls too if memory serves. I can't believe I never thought to just pop her in some pull-ups and be done with it. It sure would've saved me a whole heap of hassle if I had, that's for sure."

She lightly slapped her palm against her forehead as if she'd just remembered she'd left the oven on then and sighed good-naturedly.

"Oh well. Live and learn, I guess," she said with a shrug, before once again running an appraising eye up and down her blushing granddaughter's slim form. "Gotta say too, she sure does pull 'em off pretty well, doesn't she? You'd never be able to tell just by looking at her that she's any older than thirteen or fourteen tops. Goodness me, what an adorable little girl she is."

"You can say that again," chuckled Dana in agreement, squeezing her girlfriend's shoulders one more time before coaxing her to turn around so that her grandma could get a good look at her padded backside as well. "She looks even cuter from behind, wouldn't you say?"

"Definitely," cawed the old woman in unabashed amusement as she reached out and gave the cheeks presented to her a friendly swat.

SLAP!

"Eep!" squeaked Rhen, the noise escaping from her pouting lips before she could stop herself as she jumped in surprise.

That managed to draw twin smiles from both of the older women.

"Awww, is someone still a little tender from her spanking?" cooed her grandma in a false-sympathy, stepping in closer and pulling back on the waistband of her granddaughter's pull-up to take a peek at the cheeks hidden within.

Snorting in derision, she let them go with a scowl.

"Oh come now, you're not even pink back there anymore. You'd better can the theatrics, you silly girl, before I give you something to *really* whine about."

The old woman decided to punctuate her admonishment with a much more firm swat this time, but landing as it was against the padding on the younger girl's behind, it mostly just impacted with a muted *THWUP* that didn't actually produce any noticeable sting.

It was still more than enough for Rhen to get the message loud and clear however.

Spankings were indeed very much back on the table for her as far as her grandma was concerned, and she'd need to make sure to watch her behavior around her very carefully from then on lest she end up getting reacquainted with the feel of her lap in the days to come.

On the bright side though, Rhen reasoned to herself with her hands still clamped firmly to her padded posterior, if that were the case, then that also meant that she no longer needed to worry about being on her absolute best behavior anymore either. If her grandma already knew all about how she got spanked by her partner, then there was no longer any need to try and keep her from finding out. And so, feeling empowered by the knowledge that everyone was at least on the same page and that there were no longer any embarrassing secrets to worry about hiding, Rhen curled her hands into tight little fists at her sides, stomped back around to face her grinning grandma and stuck her tongue out at her, pouting for all she was worth.

"Meanie."

The two women just laughed, and laughed, and laughed.

"Oh lord, I've missed you, child."

—

As soon as her grandma had shown the two of them up to the bedroom that she and Dana would be sharing while they were staying with her, Rhen's old one as it so happened (though now with an extra cot set up in its middle for her partner to sleep on since her own bed was unfortunately way too small to share), the younger girl immediately set to work digging around inside the small suitcase she'd hauled up the stairs after her in search of some actual clothes she could wear below her waist. While thankfully for the moment it was just her and the two older women in the house, her cousins and their families wouldn't be showing up until the following morning and would only be staying the one night, Rhen was still very eager to put the whole business of her "accident" behind her just as soon as she could.

Apparently though, Dana had other plans.

"Uh-uh, I don't think so, cutie pie," she tut-tutted when she turned from her own unpacking and noticed what it was that Rhen was up to.

Swooping in behind her in two quick strides, she plucked a pair of moderately-frilly panties out of her hands and then seized her upper arm in a firm grip before delivering half a dozen quick swats to the backs of her bare thighs.

SMACK! SMACK! SMACK! SMACK! SMACK! SMACK!

"Ow! Oh! Hey! Come on, Aunt Dana. What the heck?" Rhen protested, dancing from foot to foot in her auntie's steely grip as she pouted over her shoulder at her. "We're not driving anymore, so can't I change out of these stupid things now?"

"No you may not, young lady. I bought an eight pack of those pull-ups, and we are *not* going to waste them," Dana scolded sharply, letting go of her arm and tucking the confiscated pair of panties back into the suitcase where they'd come from. "Once you've shown me that you're responsible enough to not need them anymore and have finished off the rest of the ones in the pack, then, and only then mind you, may you go back to wearing your big girl panties. Is that understood?"

"But... but...!" spluttered Rhen, looking desperately from her suitcase, down to her bare legs, and then back up at her frowning partner again. "But what if someone *sees* me?"

"It's a little too late to start worrying about that now, wouldn't you say?" her aunt asked with a snort, rolling her eyes. "Besides, your granny has already gotten a pretty good look at them, so I think it's pretty safe to say that there's no un-ringing that particular bell anymore, kiddo. And as for the others..."

Dana paused for a moment then and flashed the younger girl pouting in front of her a teasing half-smirk.

"I believe you already know perfectly well how to avoid having any of them find out what you've got on underneath your britches. Don't you, little girl?"

As if to underscore just what she meant, she gave the padded posterior of the petulant princess in question a couple of meaningful pats and then supplied the answer for her as she slipped her hand beneath her pull-up to fondle her cheeks.

"You just have to behave yourself."

Dana's half-smirk widened into a full on grin then as she slid two fingers between her cheeks, teasing at what she found there and making Rhen swoon.

"Or don't."

Shrugging, she gave the panting sophomore a quick kiss on the cheek and then retrieved her hand from its teasing before turning back to her own unpacking.

"I don't mind taking you to task if you end up being a little too naughty while we're here, and I'm sure that everyone else would just *love* to see how cute your caboose looks in those pull-ups… right before I take them down and spank you silly."

Humph, yeah right, grumbled Rhen to herself as her face twisted into a mortified grimace at the very notion of being spanked in front of any of her extended family. *There's no way in heck I'm going to let that happen. Just you wait and see. I'm going to be the world's best, most perfectly-behaved little angel come tomorrow.*

"Ugh, fine, whatever," she finally harrumphed a moment later, accepting that this was likely the best deal that she was going to get and not really feeling like falling asleep in her old bedroom with a freshly-spanked rear end that night for being argumentative.

Instead she returned her full attention back to the suitcase in front of her and set about fishing for a loose-fitting skirt that would hopefully obscure even the faintest hint of padding around her hips. She'd save her jeans for tomorrow when she knew that she'd be running around and playing in the back yard, knowing that they'd do a much better job of keeping her from inadvertently flashing anything that might give away her shameful secret to anyone.

Finding a knee-length skirt that would suit her needs for the evening, she shook it out and then smiled in grim satisfaction, the wheels in her head already starting to turn as she fought to come to terms with this new predicament she suddenly found herself thrust into.

Although things could have certainly stood to be far better than they were right then, all in all they weren't nearly so terrible as she'd initially thought they were either, she decided after mulling the issue over for a bit. Staring off into space, she fiddled with plucking off stray bits of lint from the layered ruffles in the dark gray garment she held in her hands, feeling a tenuous sense of cautious optimism starting to swell within her as she did some quick mental arithmetic.

She only had seven pairs of pull-ups left in that stupid package her aunt had bought for her, and then she'd be free of them for good. That really wasn't all *that* many in the grand scheme of things, right? How hard could it be to behave herself around any potential witnesses to a punishment for just one, measly week?

Hmmm… come to think of it, all I really have to do is watch myself around everyone else tomorrow and Friday morning. Once they're gone, it'll just be me, Grandma, and Aunt Dana in the house again, and they've both already seen me in these things, so there's no worry about keeping them hidden from either of them. Right then… So it'll just be the three of us Friday afternoon all the way through Saturday night, and then we drive back home on Sunday morning, so there's nothing to really worry about there either. As far as I can tell, the only real potential chance that someone I know might see me in these freaking things is during my weekly spanking from Courtney, but I won't be seeing her, or Abby, until Thursday, so...

Tossing her skirt down onto the mattress in front of her, Rhen took a few moments to count out the days on her fingers as a plan slowly began to coalesce in the back of her mind.

Let's see... Monday is five, Tuesday is six, and Wednesday makes seven...

Smiling to herself, she breathed out a small sigh of relief and then discreetly pumped a fist in triumph, feeling as if she'd somehow just gotten away with something major.

Which in a very real way, she supposed she had.

Her "older sisters" could be absolutely ruthless with their teasing when they thought that she was wearing something cute or they happened to stumble upon something that made her blush. And Rhen would've gladly taken a week's worth of bedtime spankings from Missus Hairbrush if it meant that neither of the two college coeds who looked after her on Thursdays would ever find out about her brief foray back into training panties.

Okay, yes. I can totally do this. I just have to be on my best behavior tomorrow, and then not push things too much around the daycare kids next week until Thursday, and then bam! I'm golden. Heh... Rhen Mathews, you sly devil.

Deciding that it might seem odd to literally try patting herself on the back just then, Rhen instead made due with nodding smugly. Half a heartbeat later however, something far more humiliating than simply having to hide some slight-ly-padded panties underneath her clothes suddenly sprang unbidden to her mind, and she shivered.

Wait a minute...

Looking down at what she was wearing, she gave the crinkly waistband hugging her hips an experimental tug, frowning.

How long are these things supposed to last for again? Surely she's not expecting me to...

Face heating up considerably, she shook her head to clear it of the horrifying mental images that her line of thinking had started to conjure, before twisting half-around toward her auntie to regard her with a worried look.

"Um, say... Aunt Dana?"

"Yes dear?"

Her partner looked up from her suitcase, fixing her in place with a slight upward quirk of her right eyebrow.

"You're uh... you're not expecting me to actually, you know..."

Pausing for a moment, Rhen waved her hand vaguely in front of her as if it could somehow pluck the right words out of the air for her.

"*Use* these things by any chance, um... are you?"

She let the question hang in the air then, gesturing down toward her hips with one hand and hoping that the scarlet blush sizzling her cheeks at that moment would be enough to convey what it was that she meant without her actually having to say anything more.

"No dear, they're just a precaution for in case you have another accident," clarified Dana with a twinkle of wry mirth in her dark eyes. "But if you'd really prefer something like that, I'm *sure* I could find some diapers that fit you the next time I'm out shopping..."

"No thanks, that's fine!" squeaked Rhen as she hastened to assure the older woman that that would most definitely *not* be necessary, furiously waving her hands in front of her in an attempt to chase away the idea before it could take root.

"Okay then..." replied her auntie a little too slowly,

drawing out the words and pretending to sound like she wasn't entirely convinced as she leveled another teasing smirk at her.

She let the idea play out in the younger girl's mind for a few more mortifying moments, before finally flopping the cover on her suitcase closed and moving around her cot to drape an affectionate arm around her shoulders, turning to guide her out of the mildly-cramped bedroom.

"Come on, kiddo. Let's go see what your granny is up to, shall we? I think I smell dinner cooking."

Jerking out of her worried reverie, Rhen sniffed the air once and then gasped in delight, face breaking out into a sudden, luminescent smile.

"Oh my god, you're right!" she squealed. "She's making her homemade Sloppy Joes. Oh heck *yes*. Let's go!"

Not sticking around long enough to see if the older woman was actually going to follow after her or not, the eager brat sped out of the room, completely forgetting about the skirt she'd left abandoned on top of her suitcase or the fact that she was running around in just a long-sleeve shirt and a pull-up just then.

"Huh. Well then…"

Shrugging to herself and quickly tidying up the mess of crumpled clothes and charging cables that her girlfriend had already managed to make of her side of their bedroom, Dana shoved her hands into her pockets and followed after her at an easy pace, whistling to herself as she went.

Somehow she got the distinct impression that it was going to continue to be a *very* fun holiday break for her and her favorite sassy sophomore. Though at the rate things were going, she suspected that Rhen probably wouldn't be sitting so comfortably on their return drive home by the time it was finally over.

"Oh well… she knows how to avoid that," Dana sighed. "We'll just have to see if that girl can stay out of trouble for more than a few hours at a time while we're here."

Saying it out loud, she couldn't help but roll her eyes as she snorted.

"Yeah, and maybe pigs will learn to fly."

Chapter 22

Turning up the Heat on Some Holiday Cheer

While Rhen and Dana might have been the first to have arrived at the old, country farm house that Wednesday evening, come Thursday morning, her grandma's house was soon packed to the gills with her extended family and their children.c

Her cousin Brian and his wife Maureen had been the first to arrive not too long after the breakfast dishes had been cleared away, bringing along with them their three girls (all of whom were under the age of twelve) in tow. Then, only a few minutes later, her other cousin and his wife, Eric and Jessica, had pulled up with *their* twin daughters as well. And just like that, Rhen's adolescent home had suddenly gotten a whole heck of a lot more cozy.

Or cramped.

She found that her views on the matter tended to vary depending on what kind of a mood she was in at the time.

And how long it had been since she'd last had her bottom swatted for something.

—

"Hello there, everyone, I'm Rhen's Auntie Dana. It's a pleasure to meet you."

Rising gracefully from her seat at the kitchen table, Dana gave a pleasant wave to the group of adults who'd just entered the kitchen while her girlfriend remained preoccupied with beating her high score on the game she was playing on her phone, stepping in and setting the tone for their relationship before Rhen even realized what was happening.

"Oh no, no, we haven't met before at any reunions. I'm actually a somewhat recent friend of the family who's been looking after this little cutie pie while she's been going to school up north. We met over the summer when she came to help out at my daycare, and we hit it off almost immediately. Or rather, I suppose it would be more accurate to say that she decided to test me right away after showing up nearly an hour late on that first day, and my hand ended up hitting it off quite a bit with her bare butt until she was ready to behave herself."

That last tidbit managed to draw out a round of amused snickers from everyone gathered in the kitchen, instantly endearing Dana to the other adults as her cousins and their wives turned their mildly condescending half-smirks on the girl in question, still engrossed in her game and only half-listening.

It was only after their laughter had died down that it occurred to Rhen that she'd somehow become the center of attention all of a sudden.

Wait a minute... Did she really just say what I think she said?

Looking up from her phone with the beginnings of a blush staining her cheeks a soft pink, her stomach starting to tighten itself into a hard knot, she cast a furtive glance toward her grinning auntie for confirmation; not liking at all what she saw there.

Oh yeah. She definitely did. Freaking, awesome.

Dismissing her with a roll of their eyes, the adults in the room once again resumed their conversation, acting as if she weren't right there in front of them.

"Oh Dana, that is *precious*," cooed Maureen, before pursing her lips into a puzzled frown. "Although…"

Tilting her head to the side and tapping a thoughtful forefinger against her cheek, she regarded Rhen quizzically for a brief moment, seemingly trying to decide something based solely off of the girl's physical appearance and the context clues that the other woman had provided about their relationship so far.

"Isn't she a little too old to still be getting spanked?"

"You would think so, wouldn't you?" mused Dana with an enigmatic smirk, eyes sparkling with undisguised mirth. "But it could also just as easily be argued that a girl her age really ought to know better than to behave the way she does in the first place. Unfortunately though, our dear, sweet, Rhenny here just can't seem to help herself a lot of the time."

Reaching over, she ruffled the indignantly scowling girl's inky black hair and then shrugged at Maureen and Jessica while Rhen continued to pretend to play her game, the flush in her face now bright red.

"I don't really mind though. You see, some girls simply need a firm hand to provide them with the structure and discipline they crave, even when they're older, and Rhen definitely fits that description to a T. Luckily though, she's easy enough to handle. All you really have to do is pop her across your lap and warm her caboose for a few minutes whenever she's being naughty, and then she goes back to being right as rain. In fact, she's usually a total sweetheart most of the time, even if she *does* tend to procrastinate doing her homework and chores, and has a sassy streak a mile long."

"Oh, I see," replied Maureen with a thoughtful nod, her husband and the two other adults joining her, evidently satisfied. "That *does* make a lot of sense… I think. And in that case, I'm glad that she has you to keep her in line."

"More like she's there to keep me across her knee," grumbled Rhen with a half-smirk half-pout, unable to stop herself despite knowing that it would only serve to further prove Dana's point.

"Only when you deserve it, cutie pie," chirped her partner brightly, not missing a beat as she and the other adults in the room shared a knowing look.

Then, realizing that they'd gotten off topic, Dana cut herself short before she could continue to further pontificate on her views on child rearing and discipline. Clearing her throat, she returned back to what she'd been saying before she and the others had gotten sidetracked.

"Ahem. But yes, anyway... As I was saying, I'm a friend of the family who's been looking after Rhen while she's going to school up north. Last semester she told me that she needed a place to stay before fall started. I offered to let her move in with me, though on the condition that I was going to be keeping a *very* sharp eye on her, she said yes, and the rest is history."

Smiling at the pouting girl beside her, Dana leaned down and planted a quick kiss on her cheek before straightening up again and blushing slightly.

"Oh, but where are my manners? I've been standing here chewing your ears off this whole time and I haven't even gotten your names yet!"

Clearly not bothered in the slightest by this apparent lapse in manners, the younger girl's cousins and their wives each took a turn shaking hands with the affable older woman, exchanging polite greetings and introducing themselves one by one.

And just like that, before she'd even realized it had

happened, Rhen's Auntie Dana had suddenly become just another part of the family.

"I think you've had enough screen time for now, Rhen, honey," Dana prompted after the last of the pleasantries had been exchanged between the adults, plucking the girl's smartphone from her hands and ignoring her indignant protests as she stowed it away in her front pocket. "Come say hello to everyone. It's rude to ignore your cousins, you know."

"Yeah, yeah, I hear you…"

Pushing away from the kitchen table with a barely-restrained harrumph, Rhen moved around from the far end of it to greet her cousins properly, waving at their children and awkwardly returning the hugs she got from the adults.

"Hey, how's it going? Uh, long time no see and all that… How's, like, life… and stuff?"

Aside from her grandma, Rhen wasn't particularly close with any of her extended family members. Both of her cousins were well over a decade older than she was, being closer in age to Dana than they were to her, and she hadn't really spoken much to either of them outside of the occasional comment on the odd social media post here and there in nearly just as long. As a result, she was practically a stranger to the two of them and their families.

Heck, come to think of it, she wasn't even sure if they actually knew how old she really was. It wasn't like she could've guessed *their* ages outside of a vague "fortyish" herself.

Between their not ever talking and the unassailable awkwardness of trying to ask someone their age when you were supposed to already know it, Rhen was hardly at all surprised to find herself quickly being lumped in with the rest of the "kids" instead of being treated like the highly-intelligent college sophomore that she actually was.

Yeah, well, what else is new? she thought to herself with good-natured resignation after Maureen had finished asking her how she'd been enjoying school so far that semester. *I guess I should be glad she isn't offering me candy or something.*

Her cousins and their spouses already had their hands more than full with juggling their own kids, all of whom were wound up and bursting with energy after a long car ride with not much more to do than watch the trees pass them by. And it soon became all too clear to Rhen that they were content to simply follow the lead of Dana and her grandma with regard to how they should treat their pipsqueak of a younger cousin. Therefore, it didn't come as too much of a shock to her when after everyone else had gotten settled in and all of the requisite hugs and kisses had been exchanged, that she found herself being dismissed with the rest of the Mathews's pre-pubescent brood to go play in their grandma's spacious back yard while the rest of the adults visited and ostensibly finished preparing Thanksgiving dinner.

"You too, cutie pie. Go on now," her aunt insisted when Rhen tried to linger behind after the others had gone, attempting to quietly re-insinuate herself back into the conversation about the drive down that her grandma was currently in the middle of having with her cousins and their wives. "Why don't you go show Riley and the others that tree house you were telling me about yesterday? I bet they'd love to see it."

"But Aunt Dana," she started to protest, defaulting to whining before she could stop herself and immediately regretting it when she saw the annoyed eye-rolls from everyone else around her. "I don't *want* to go play with a bunch of dumb little kids!"

"You'd better watch that mouth of yours, Rhen Elizabeth," her grandma suddenly cut in across her brewing tantrum.

Descending upon the unsuspecting twenty-year-old turned teenager before she'd even realized what was happening, she spun her around by the shoulder and cracked her hard palm down several times in quick succession against the seat of her dark blue jeans.

SMACK! SMACK! SMACK!

"That is no way to talk about your family, little missy!"

Between the thick denim of her jeans and the bright pink padding hidden beneath them, Rhen could barely even feel the swats. But they were still more than enough to get her hopping forward out of range of her grandma's itchy palm as both of her hands flew back to shield her vulnerable caboose.

"Now go on and *get*, before I decide to pull those britches down and teach you some proper manners, girl."

"Okay, okay. Freaking *sorry*, geez…" grumbled Rhen, hands still hovering behind her backside as she fled from the kitchen at a rather undignified speed-walk and made her way out into the back yard, the amused smirks of her cousins and their wives chasing after her all the while as she went.

I guess I'll just go babysit the brats then…

—

While the adults inside the house toiled languidly away at preparing Thanksgiving dinner, in between tall glasses of wine and gossiping about each other's lives, Rhen and her younger cousins busied themselves with running around like madmen among the grasses, trees, and shrubbery that comprised the whole of her grandma's spacious, half-acre field of a back yard.

After rejoining the group, she'd immediately led them over to the massive oak some twenty yards away from the porch and had then taken great delight in showing off the robust treehouse that her grandpa had built for her back before he'd died. And much to her surprise and delight, she'd even found that her grandma had taken the time to restock the plastic cooler she kept stashed away in there with fresh snacks and sodas for them all to share.

Oh Grandma, you old softie, you...

Riley, Sally, and the rest of her cousins were all suitably impressed by her "secret fortress" as she'd always liked to call it back when she was younger (and still did now as a matter of fact), and she and the older tweens had a blast whiling away a good portion of the late morning and early afternoon within its timber walls. Mostly playing cards and talking about the TV shows they'd been watching and what they wanted for Christmas that year.

Much to her own chagrin, Rhen fit right in with them, just like she did back home at her auntie's daycare.

At first that was a little embarrassing for her to think about, especially after the way she'd been practically chased out of the house to come join them in the first place, but she managed to get over those feelings quickly enough as she and Riley started talking and discovered that they happened to play several of the same video games.

In the end, it turned out to be a very fun afternoon indeed.

—

When at last it was time to come back inside and wash up for dinner, Rhen wasn't at all surprised (but still very much annoyed) to find that she was apparently expected to sit at the kids table with rest of her cousin's children.

At first she'd tried to argue that she belonged with everyone else at the adults table, although she deliberately chose not to mention that that was because she was a twenty-year-old college sophomore, lest she inadvertently humiliate herself even further by tempting Dana to demonstrate that as far as she was concerned she was just a thirteen-year-old brat who needed her attitude adjusted right there in front of everyone. Instead she'd just let the implied understanding that she was the oldest of the "young'uns" (as her grandma liked to call her and the other kids) speak for itself, and pointed out with a pout that they could easily make enough room for her at one of the corners if they all just squeezed in a bit and watched where they put their elbows while they ate. She'd even promised not to drink any of the expensive-looking wine that Brian and Maureen had brought with them, but alas, she'd been denied out of hand.

"Sorry, kiddo," crooned Maureen with a smug smirk as she cozied up next to her husband, holding out her glass for him to fill. "Maybe next year, okay?"

Incensed by the casual dismissal, Rhen had tried to press the point further, but all that she'd gotten for her trouble were three hard swats from Dana as she spun her around and sent her scrambling back over to rejoin the other snickering tweens and little kids at their own table.

"Quit being so fussy, Rhen, or I'll give you something to fuss about. You hear me, little girl?"

"Humph! Yes ma'am..."

Cowed for the moment, Rhen made the short trip back to her abandoned folding chair at the somewhat-rickety card table set up a few feet away from the sturdy mahogany one that Dana and the rest of the adults were situated at, grumbling darkly under her breath all the while as she went.

We should've just stayed home and gotten Chinese food instead. Turkey is gross, anyway. Who needs it? Humph.

After that, dinner had passed by in relative peace, and although her pride still smoldered at the indignity of having to use plastic silverware and eat off of a paper plate instead of using proper utensils and the fine china like all of the other adults in the room, Rhen soon forgot about her embarrassment as she began stuffing her face with her grandma's absolutely delicious home cooking.

Okay, okay, I take it all back. Turkey is pretty delicious. And I don't know what these tan carrot looking things are, but they are totally rocking my world right now...

Once everyone had had their fill, they'd each taken turns going around the room sharing some of the things that they were grateful for that year. And when it was her turn, Rhen had said without a moment's hesitation that it was Dana and the kindness that she'd shown her in taking her in and really giving her a sense of stability and structure that was what she was most grateful for.

"I don't know what I would've done if I hadn't met her. She's been *such* a good influence in my life ever since that first day at the daycare. And although it seems like I can't go more than a few days without a trip across her lap for one bit of sass or another, I know that she only wants what's best for me and is trying to help me be a better person. So uh... thanks, and I love you, Dana."

So touched had her partner been by the gesture, that she'd immediately teared up, slid her chair back from the table, and all but tackled the younger girl in a bear hug.

"Come here you adorable little cinnamon bun. I love you too!"

After that, she'd swept Rhen up under her arm like she sometimes did when she wanted to deliver a quick spanking, and carried her back over to the adults table, explaining that she was going to make her wish come true as she once more sat down in her chair. And so, just like that, Rhen suddenly found herself cuddling together with her adopted auntie, perched on her lap for dessert at the adults table; much to the amusement of everyone else around them.

And for once, she didn't mind the smirks in the least.

Several slices of pie and scoops of ice cream later, satiated and feeling sleepy, everyone had wound up going their own separate ways to either catch a quick nap or else watch some football while they digested everything that they'd just eaten. Rhen for her part decided to stick by Dana's side after dinner, and had fallen asleep almost immediately after cuddling up with her in a recliner in the living room while she and her cousins watched TV.

All in all, aside from the earlier bumpy start, she had to admit that so far it had been a very good day.

—

A few hours later, the sun had once again set in the sky, and the college sophomore turned teenage troublemaker found herself being roused from her peaceful nap by a gentle shake.

"Wake up, child. It's time to get ready for the Trail."

"Mmmm… just give me five more minutes," mumbled Rhen, rolling over under the blanket that Dana had laid across her while she'd been sleeping and waving groggily to shoo away her bothersome grandma.

"No can do, sweet pea. It's time to get up," repeated the old woman, this time with a touch more steel in her voice.

Tugging away the fuzzy blanket from around her granddaughter's shoulders, she rolled her back over to get her attention, jostling her enough to help shake off some of the dream dust. She was well-used to rebuffing her attempts to avoid getting up on time, and knew just how to deal with her if push came to shove.

"Come on now, up and at 'em. Don't make me tell you again, young lady."

Scowling grumpily, Rhen cracked one eye open just wide enough to see her grandma standing there looming over her with her hands planted firmly on her hips and a no-nonsense scowl painted across her face. And although it had been a long, *long* while since she'd been awoken to such a sight, she still remembered all too well the times that she'd been rolled over onto her stomach for a far ruder wakeup call back when she'd still been in high school.

The more things change, the more they stay the same, I guess…

Deciding that it probably wasn't a good idea to try testing her luck with so many people still hanging around inside the house, Rhen huffed out an annoyed harrumph through her nostrils and then did as she was told, retracting the footstool on her chair and unhurriedly climbing back to her feet with another yawn.

"Alright, alright, I'm up," she grumbled, rolling her eyes and stretching. "No need to get all bent out of shape about it, geez."

Unfazed by the younger girl's sass, Melinda Mathews just rolled her own eyes in return and scoffed.

"I've still got your granddaddy's belt hanging up in my closet, you know. Am I going to need to go get it?"

She paused for a moment then, her lips quirking up into a knowing grin as she added.

"Little girl."

Rhen gulped, swallowing hard.

"I uh… I see you and Dana have been trading pointers," she replied with a slight blush and a chagrinned pout.

"You could say that," crooned her grandma in response,

still grinning as she turned and pointed out of the room. "Now go and wash up before I decide to remind you what a well-smacked bottom from your grandmother feels like, you sassy malassy."

Sassy malassy? Geez. I don't think I've heard her bust out that old chestnut since I was in middle school...

That thought didn't do much to help Rhen's confidence right then, and she quickly decided that it would probably be better if she put some distance between her and her grandma before she started doing anything more than just calling her by one of her old pet names from when she was younger.

"Yes ma'am!" she squeaked, the color in her cheeks deepening as she scurried past the smug old woman, racing toward the stairs at Mach speed in search of an empty bathroom to hide in.

"Humph, that's what I thought."

More than a little amused by her brief encounter with her bratty granddaughter, Melinda shook her head and then set about tidying up her living room while she waited for the rest of her family to get ready to leave.

"I swear, that girl just doesn't know when to keep her mouth shut sometimes."

Shaking out the still-warm blanket from the chair that Rhen had been sleeping on and inhaling deeply the familiar scents of the girl she'd raised since she was a small child, she shrugged.

"Oh well," she chuckled to herself. "At least she's cute when she's being a brat. No wonder Dana keeps her on such a short leash."

—

Hmmm... Well this freaking sucks.

Staring petulantly at her reflection in the mirror, Rhen splashed some cold water onto her face and gurgled out a sigh against her cupped hands.

She was already groggy and grumpy from having her nap so rudely interrupted, and to make matters worse, she was about to be dragged out for nearly three whole hours of absolute *boredom*.

Every year on Thanksgiving, after eating dinner and spending the requisite amount of time either napping or watching sports, Rhen and her grandma piled into her old station wagon and drove into the nearby town of Redberry to walk along the downtown streets, taking in the first official lighting of the town's Christmas lights.

Truth be told, the displays organized by the local business owners on Main Street, and the intricate Santa's Village that was set up out front of the dusty old courthouse were all quite impressive, whimsical even. There was also hot chocolate and freshly-baked treats available from little stalls that Rhen couldn't get enough of, and some of the more elaborate light shows were even synced up to music and pulsed in time with carols being played from unseen outdoor speakers.

It was all quite fun, and an excellent way to usher in the start to the Christmas season.

The only problem was that Rhen had already walked the Redberry Trail of Lights nearly a dozen times by now. And while it was true that the displays were different every year, she was still confident that she'd more or less seen all that the town had to offer, and the prospect of spending all that time wandering around in the chilly night air ogling a bunch of twinkly lights on strings while her cousins' kids took forever moving from set piece to set piece seemed to her like just the absolute worst.

"Ugh. Would it freaking kill Grandma to just go see a

movie or something instead for *once*?" she huffed, groping blindly for one of the towels beside her as her face continued to drip into the sink below. "This sucks."

Finding one, she let out an exasperated groan and then buried her face against it to dry herself off while she continued to grumble several more things into its muffling folds that would most definitely have gotten her mouth washed out if anybody had been around to hear her.

Growling in annoyance and venting her frustrations by scrubbing her face extra-vigorously with her towel, Rhen suddenly stopped as the beginnings of an idea began to take shape.

Wait a minute...

Looking up at her reflection in the mirror and taking in the slightly flushed hue of her cheeks from where she'd just been rubbing at them, her face split into a devious grin.

"Of course!"

Dana and her grandma would *never* think of dragging her off to the Trail of Lights if she was sick. And what better way to show that she was under the weather than with a flushed face and a warm forehead?

All I've gotta do is give a couple of coughs, maybe a sniffle or two here and there, and then bam! It'll be three whole hours of completely uninterrupted private time all by myself to do whatever the heck I want, she mused, mind already racing ahead with the possibilities of having the house all to herself. *It'll just be me, a few slices of pie, and my laptop. What could be better?*

Grinning from ear to ear now, she buried her face in her damp towel once again and started scrubbing for all she was worth.

Rhen Mathews, you adorable genius!

—

With her plan firmly in place and all of her lines memorized, Rhen at last emerged from the bathroom next to her old bedroom, wiped the smug grin off of her face, and took a deep breath.

"Okay... It's show time!"

Padding her way down the stairs as quietly as she could, and starting to feel just the faintest hint of butterflies swarming around inside of her stomach, she gritted her teeth and steeled her resolve.

It's too late to chicken out now, girl.

Reaching the foot of the stairs, she leaned around the banister and quickly spotted Dana chatting away with her cousin Brian and his wife, along with her grandma, all in the living room.

Let's do this!

Stepping out onto the entryway landing, she schooled her features into a mask of misery and fatigue, and then began moving toward the living room, sniffling all the while as she went.

"Aunt Dana..." she whined, coughing into her loosely curled fist and dragging her feet as she slowly strode over to stand in front of the woman that she knew she would need to convince the most. "I don't feel so good."

"Awww, honey, I'm so sorry to hear that," cooed Dana, adopting a look of worried concern as she dipped her chin down to regard her mopey girlfriend. "What doesn't feel good on you, exactly?"

"Um... well, uh... you know..." stalled Rhen, her stomach lurching at the question.

Crap.

She had *assumed* that her performance and the general flush in her face would be obvious enough to not need to give any more specific details about what was wrong with her, but apparently not. Fighting hard to clamp down on the sudden urge to panic that reared its ugly head within her chest, she left her auntie waiting for several thundering heartbeats as she frantically tried to come up with something plausible sounding.

Running through and rejecting every major illness she could think of, she eventually swallowed hard and rallied her response in her head.

Okay, okay. I can still make this work. I just need to keep my cool...

Coughing into her hand again, she looked up at her partner with a miserable expression.

"My nose is all runny and my throat keeps tickling me and making me cough. I uh... I think I might've caught something earlier while I was playing outside with everyone."

Yeah! It was cold outside, so now I've got a cold. Perfect.

"Hmmm... you don't say?" questioned the older woman, one eyebrow quirking up skeptically as she frowned. "It's a bit odd then that you're the only one reporting these symptoms since everyone else was out there for just as long as you were and they're all fine, wouldn't you say? Are you *sure* you don't just have a case of 'I don't want to go out tonight'-itis, little girl?"

"W-What?" demanded Rhen, thrown off balance by the accusation and trying to sound wounded.

Forcing herself to give a great, snotty sniff, she grimaced when her nose sounded like it was barely even clogged, but continued to press on determinedly.

"No really, I mean it! I think I might even have a bit of a

fever or something."

Deciding to play her trump card and end things quickly before they could get any further out of control, Rhen held her hand to her forehead to confirm that it was indeed still nice and warm, and then eased up onto her tiptoes so that Dana could feel for herself.

"See?"

Eyes narrowing suspiciously, her aunt nevertheless reached out and laid her palm across her forehead.

"Well, you're definitely pretty toasty up here, that's for sure," she conceded, before tracing her palm down along her jawline to cup one of her cheeks, rubbing her thumb across its smooth surface. "Same here too, it seems. Not to mention that your cheeks are looking *awfully* red right about now..."

It took a lot of hard work to stop herself from smirking right then, but somehow Rhen managed to keep her face a mask of put-upon weariness as she pouted.

"See? I told you that I wasn't feeling good. So can I *please* stay home while the rest of you go out to look at the dumb old stupid Christmas lights?"

"Hmmm..." her partner replied slowly, her lips quirking into an enigmatic little smile as she mulled the question over, continuing to idly stroke her cheek with her thumb.

Checkmate, declared Rhen internally, the tension in her stomach easing as triumph flooded in to replace it. *I think I'll start with the apple pie, and then see whether or not I'm more in the mood for pumpkin or chocolate next...*

"You know, Dana," came her grandma's voice out of the blue just then, stepping up to the older woman's side and looking about as convinced as she'd been as she eyed her. "There's a very easy way to check whether or not she's really sick, you know."

What? No, Grandma, get out of here!

"Why, that's an *excellent* point, Melinda," agreed Dana, her smile taking on a decidedly dangerous edge to it now as she half-turned to face the woman who'd just spoken. "You wouldn't happen to have a more *traditional* one lying around by any chance, would you?"

"As a matter of fact, I do," she confirmed with a matching upward twitch of her lips. "They're a little bit slower, yes, but they tend to get the most accurate results in these sorts of situations, I've found. Why don't you go ahead and take her to the kitchen, and I'll meet y'all there in just a minute, okay?"

Uh-oh, thought Rhen, eyebrows knitting together in sudden worry. *I'm not sure I like where this is headed...*

"That sounds like a plan to me," nodded Dana, letting go of her girlfriend's frowning face and taking up her hand in hers, giving it a firm squeeze. "Come along, cutie pie. Let's go check your temperature."

Crap. Yeah, this is definitely not good.

Rhen wasn't exactly sure *why* her grandma and auntie were so insistent on checking her temperature in the kitchen when they could just as easily do it right there in the living room, but she quickly decided that she had much more pressing concerns to worry about as she was led away from her cousin and his wife.

They probably just don't want me around the kids in case I really am sick, she tried to tell herself, mind racing as she scrambled to come up with some way that she could possibly fool a thermometer. *Maybe I'll get lucky and she'll have one of those fancy digital ones that you just swipe across a person's forehead?*

Looking over at the VCR and small shelf of VHS tapes still nestled underneath her grandma's equally ancient TV as she and Dana passed it by, Rhen grimaced.

Or... maybe not.

—

Rhen and Dana weren't left waiting for too terribly long in the kitchen. After a couple minutes of awkward silence, with Rhen occasionally coughing or sniffling in a perfunctory attempt to keep up her ruse for as long as possible, her grandma finally came bustling in to join them.

"Found it!" she declared, triumphantly holding up a digital thermometer with a yellow rubber duck on the end of it for them both to see.

Striding over to join them by the edge of the table, she held it out to Dana.

"Here you go, Miss Dana. I figured that you'd probably want to take care of this yourself."

"Awww, thank you, Melinda," replied Dana, one hand pressed to her heart as she accepted the device with a grin. "I know that we're in a bit of a hurry, so thank you for indulging me."

"Oh no, not at all, hon. Please, feel free to take all the time you need," answered the other woman with casual ease, aiming a stern frown toward her granddaughter as she added. "You don't need to convince *me* about the importance of handling these kinds of situations in a certain way. If something is worth doing, it's worth doing right, after all. But, speaking of being in a hurry... if it turns out that our patient here is really just suffering from a case of the Lazy Bone Blues, I think I might have just the thing to help tide her over until a more thorough treatment can be applied later on tonight."

"Oh really now?" crooned Dana, arching a curious brow.

"Yep," confirmed Melinda with a wink, taking her gaze

away from Rhen. "Nothing too fancy, just a little home remedy that ought to get the point across for us."

"Well in that case, I'll leave her in your capable hands should the need arise."

"Of course, dear."

Not quite following the conversation between the two older women, but still feeing her stomach brimming with anxiety and nervous anticipation nevertheless, Rhen decided that the best course of action for her right then was to just remain silent and exude as much of an "I'm sick" aura as she could while she furiously rubbed her tongue against the backs of her gums in an attempt to warm them up enough to deceive the thermometer in her auntie's hand.

It's better than nothing, it's better than nothing, it's better than nothing…

Thankfully, this time the full flush in her face and the slight shortness of breath she was experiencing from her rapidly beating heart would at least help her sell her fib. She just hoped that her mouth would register as being even a fraction as hot as her cheeks felt right then as Dana turned on her with an impish gleam in her eyes.

"Okeydokey, cutie pie, let's check that temperature. Shall we?"

"Uh, yeah… Sure, no problem," answered Rhen, hoping to sound nonchalant and at the same time drained and sickly.

She did her best to sniffle again, not succeeding particularly well this time either, but she chose to ignore that as she tilted her head back and opened her mouth wide.

"Ahhhh…"

But the twin snorts of amusement she got from both her partner and her grandma a moment later had her quickly closing her mouth and looking between the two of them in confusion as butterflies suddenly began performing aerial acrobatics inside of her stomach.

"Wha-?"

"Wrong end, sweetie," said Dana with a half-smirk as she pointed toward her waist with the metal tip of the thermometer in her right hand. 'This is the kind that goes inside your tush."

And while Rhen's mouth fell open once again, her grandma added helpfully.

"It's the most accurate way to check if a little girl is telling fibs about being sick or not."

"That's right," agreed Dana, drawing out the words in a sing-song as her half-smirk blossomed into a full-on grin then. "Now you go ahead and bare those buns for me, and we'll get this taken care of in a jiffy, alright?"

"But… but…" spluttered Rhen, face glowing crimson even as she turned and slowly began to do as she was told, hands moving on autopilot as they fumbled awkwardly with the front clasp of her jeans while her head tried to process the impending humiliation that she was about to endure.

"Yes dear, that's right. It's going in your butt," teased her partner as she watched the younger girl's lily white, bare bottom come into view as she pushed her jeans and pull-up down to her knees at the same time.

"Oh *hah-hah*," grumbled Rhen, shuffling forward a couple of awkward steps and flopping across the mahogany tabletop in front of her with a harrumph.

Shifting around with nervous, pent-up energy, she readjusted the position of her elbows and forearms beneath her in an attempt to get more comfortable.

It didn't help.

"Can we just get this over with already? I thought you said

we were in a hurry."

"Well, would you look at that? It seems like our patient is already experiencing a miraculous recovery," observed her grandma wryly.

"It sure does," agreed Dana, sliding in along her left flank and giving her bottom a light rub. "But I still think that we'd better wait and see what the thermometer has to say on the matter before we decide anything. You know, just to be safe."

"Oh, I couldn't agree more."

Well, at least we're out of sight for all of this, Rhen tried to tell herself, scrabbling desperately for any silver lining that she could cling to as she crossed her fingers beneath her, naked cheeks clenching and unclenching in the warm kitchen air. *Aunt Dana said that this would only take a couple of minutes, so if we hurry then I'll only have to worry about the others possibly overhearing a spanking later on tonight... I can live with that.*

"Uh-oh... Has our bratty little Rhen finally sassed herself into some serious trouble?" asked a deep male voice, rich with amusement as its owner casually strode into the kitchen to see what all the hubbub was about.

Oh god. You have got to be kidding me.

Hearing Brian snicker, Rhen instinctively tried to push herself back to her feet, but was held firmly in place by Dana's strong hand pressing against the small of her back. Deciding that it was probably a very bad idea to try pushing her luck just then, she instead let out an annoyed growl, but otherwise didn't move. She knew that the damage had already been done, and was determined to avoid compounding her embarrassment any further by allowing him, or anybody else for that matter, to get a good look at her totally hairless front.

Or God forbid, what had been covering it up only a few

moments earlier.

"Maybe. We'll know for sure in just a minute or two, I suspect," answered her grandma for her, sounding not the least bit concerned. "Are Maureen and the girls ready to go yet?"

"Yes Grandma," piped up a polite twelve-year-old voice from somewhere behind Rhen.

"Oooh, is Rhen gonna get a spankin'?" added her eager sounding younger sister.

"Probably," answered the mortified college sophomore's auntie for her with a shrug, making her girlfriend's naked cheeks wobble as she gave them a couple of light pats. "But if she is, it'll have to wait until bedtime since we don't want to be late for the Trail. Isn't that right, Rhen?"

"Yes ma'am," bit out a furiously blushing Rhen through gritted teeth, before grumbling under her breath. "All those freaking lights can go to hell for all I care."

SMACK! SMACK!

"Watch it..." warned Dana, showing off once again that she had far better hearing than the younger girl gave her credit for.

"Sorry!" squeaked Rhen, much to the amusement of the gathered onlookers as her feet danced on reflex beneath her, set to moving by the sudden burning sensation that had blossomed in the centers of each of her bottom cheeks.

Then, feeling her jeans starting to shift a bit further down her legs with the movement, she suddenly froze.

Oh god... please no...

But it was far too late for any help from the divine now.

"See, Melody? Even big girls sometimes have to wear pull-ups," pointed out Maureen, gesturing toward the waving Sleeping Beauty who had remained resolutely in place around Rhen's knees after her jeans had slipped down to her ankles.

"I guess so…" answered the ten-year-old, not sounding all that convinced even as she grinned wickedly at her cousin's predicament. "But I still don't think it's fair that I have to wear them at bedtime."

"As soon as you can prove to your father and me that you can go three whole weeks with dry sheets, then we can talk. Okay, honeybunch?"

"Fine…" harrumphed Melody with a grumpy sigh, clearly this was a discussion that she and her mother had had many times before, adding under her breath. "I still think it's stupid, though."

"Yes dear, so you've said," chirped Maureen with only a little bit of strained patience evident in her voice. "Now why don't you and your sister go play with the others while we finish up in here, alright?"

"Ahhh," whined the two girls at once.

"But I wanted to watch!"

"Can't we stay, Mommy?"

Maureen remained resolute however.

"*Now*, girls," she repeated sternly. "Unless you want *your* butts getting spanked at bedtime too."

"Yeah, whatever…"

"Fine…"

Sounding more than a little sullen, Brian and Maureen's daughters nevertheless did as they were told, and Rhen let out a small sigh of relief once they were gone.

"I swear," sighed Maureen to herself in exasperation. "Those girls can be *such* a handful…"

"Little brats," grumbled Rhen under her breath in agreement, making sure to keep quiet enough to avoid more swats from Dana this time.

She wasn't sure if she particularly liked being labeled as a "big girl" since she knew for a fact that Dana had informed her cousin's wife while they'd been cleaning up after dinner that she was actually a sophomore in college, but she wisely chose to keep her mouth shut for the moment.

Ugh. Why did I ever think that this stupid plan was going to work? Three hours isn't all that long, and those gingerbread donuts are pretty good too. Dang it, dang it... Crap!

"Now then," declared Dana, derailing her train of thought as she cleared her throat, bringing everyone's attention back to the task at hand.

She wetted the tips of her thumb and forefinger with her tongue, before giving them a quick couple of twists around the metallic end of the thermometer.

"You just relax that tush of yours, Rhen, honey, and this'll all be over before you know it. Okay, cutie pie?"

"Yes ma'am..."

Fairly certain that steam was about to start shooting out of her ears at any moment, Rhen nevertheless tried her best to do as she was told.

Oh god, here we go.

She let out a long, low, pitiful moan of embarrassment as she felt the fingers of her auntie's left hand walk themselves slowly down along her lower back and to the midpoint of the central divide between her bare cheeks, before parting them as wide as they would go.

"There you are," cooed Dana, as she and everyone else gathered around inside the cramped kitchen got a totally unobstructed view of her puckered rosebud. "Now take a deep breath, hon, here comes the choo-choo train..."

Gritting her teeth against every curse word that was struggling to come flying out of her mouth just then, Rhen did her best to keep her bottom as relaxed as possible, which was a lot easier said than done given the half-dozen or so pairs of eyes all watching her in self-satisfied delight. Despite her best efforts to stay quiet and dignified under the circumstances however, she still couldn't help but let out a high-pitched squeak as she felt the ice-cold tip of the thermometer press itself insistently up against her rear opening.

"Eep!"

Rather than take things nice and slow to ease the darn thing in, Dana instead just chuckled softly to herself, and in one smooth motion, suddenly slid the entire saliva-lubricated length of the rubber ducky thermometer into her all at once.

"Ah!"

"There we go…" she cooed, still sounding totally unconcerned as she released her adorable girlfriend's cheeks and gently flicked the yellow duck at the end of the thermometer poking out from between them with a teasing forefinger.

Rhen managed by some miracle not to make any noise at that, other than to hiss in a sharp breath through her teeth as her eyes shot wide open.

Aunt Dana, you freaking meanie pants. Come on!

"I think we'll leave that right where it is for… Oh, let's say… two minutes, just to be on the safe side," explained the older woman to nobody in particular as she set the timer on the thermometer's digital display with a couple of quick button presses.

Still holding onto it with one hand to keep it in place, she gave Rhen's jiggly buns a couple of affectionate pats.

"Unless, of course, there's something you'd like to share with us, young lady?"

Unable to bring herself to cop to fibbing out loud, Rhen just shook her head and kept her jaw clamped tight against any more embarrassing squeaks that might try to escape from her as a small, irrational part of her mind clung to the paper-thin hope that she might actually be running a bit of a temperature after all.

Come on... come on... she thought desperately, grinding her teeth as she willed some of the flaming heat in her face to make its way south to between her pale cheeks.

Two minutes later though, the thermometer beeped, signaling that it was finished taking its readings, and to nobody's surprise it registered a totally normal temperature for the bare bottomed girl still pouting in place where she lay bent over across the kitchen table.

Gosh darn it.

"Well, well, well," drawled Dana in false-surprise. "What do you know? No fever."

Rhen just groaned, bouncing her bottom once with a huff as she glared daggers at the pitted, wooden tabletop beneath her.

"So then I suppose that means that *someone* here was telling me a fib when she said that she wasn't feeling good. Wasn't she, *Rhen*?"

Setting the thermometer aside, Dana pushed her back down against the table along her shoulder blades, arching her back and thrusting her bottom out as she proceeded to give her cheeks a few quick, hard swats that sent them bouncing and got her hopping from foot to foot in surprise.

SMACK! SMACK! SMACK! SMACK! SMACK!

"Yes ma'am, I'm sorry ma'am!" blurted Rhen in a hurry, not daring to deny it now that she'd been so thoroughly proven to be lying.

"Well you and I are going to be having a nice, long chat about the importance of honesty when we get back home tonight," snapped her partner as she made her displeasure known with four more hard swats to the backs of her thighs. "You can count on that, little girl."

SMACK-SMACK! SMACK-SMACK!

"So I'd enjoy being able to sit down on this sneaky seat of yours while you still can, if I were you."

"Yes ma'am," squealed Rhen again before slumping in defeat against the table beneath her and resting the side of her sizzling face against its cool surface.

Why oh why did I ever think that this was a good idea? she thought to herself miserably as she felt Dana move behind her and start to readjust her clothes. *This sucks...*

"Whoa now, hold on there just a sec, Dana," spoke up her grandma then, staying the other woman's hand before her furiously blushing granddaughter's pull-up could be tugged up more than an inch or two past her knees. "Leave those undies right where they are for a minute, would you? I've got a little something here that ought to help Little Miss Sneaky-Pants remember to behave herself while she's out walking the Trail with everyone tonight."

Oh crap. What now?

Rhen couldn't see what it was that her grandma held in her hand as she glided over and slid into place against her right hip, opposite her auntie, but one thing that she knew for sure was that she *definitely* didn't like the delighted laugh of surprise it got from both her and Maureen.

"I thought that it would be nice and fitting that since Rhen here has been telling us lies," the old woman went on to explain, her voice brimming with grim mirth as she brought her free hand down to pat her granddaughter's right cheek with a low chuckle. "That she should at least spend the evening *feeling* like her pants are on fire."

"Oh, Melinda, that is genius!" declared Dana as she too

patted the cheek closest to her. "She'll definitely be running around with a temperature back here with *that* keeping her company."

"Um... with what now?" the younger girl finally managed to muster up the courage to ask, squeaking out the question as she twisted around to crane her head back to see what all the fuss was about.

"Oh, nothing to worry about, child, it's just a bit of ginger root," answered her grandma blithely, beaming down at her with a fond, tight smirk.

It was a smirk that was tinged with the silent promise that Rhen was going to be a *very* sorry little girl before she was finished with her, and one that said sorry-little-girl-to-be hadn't seen on her grandma's face in several years now. Not since the last time she'd truly been taken to task for misbehaving, sometime back in her early days of high school.

Oh... crap.

As if she were able to read her mind, her grandma's ill-omen smirk widened by another tooth or two as she continued.

"It's a good thing that Maureen had a few fingers of this stuff left lying around from those parsnips she made earlier, because it's the *perfect* thing for putting some heat directly into the seat of naughty little girls who like to tell fibs about being sick."

"Agreed," said Dana with a firm nod as she eyed the peeled and pared root in the old woman's hand with a cool, professional eye, matching her smirk with one of her own. "Although personally, I prefer to use soap sticks for teaching a lesson like this, I'll still be the first to admit that there's definitely something special about ginger roots that really get a naughty girl to sit up and take notice."

She patted Rhen's quivering caboose then, chuckling quietly.

"You did an excellent job with carving that thing, by the way, Melinda. It looks fantastic."

"Awww, well thank you, dear," replied the other woman, smiling from ear to ear. "I don't think I've had to actually peel a ginger root like this since Rhen's daddy was a boy, but it's nice to know that I've still got the knack for it."

Although Rhen was far from being an expert when it came to such things, she was still able to tell just by looking at the stomach-clenchingly long and bulbous root that her partner had been spot-on in her assessment. And even worse still, although she'd never actually experienced whatever it was that was about to happen to her before, she still knew enough from the punishments that she'd been subjected to over the last few months to be able to make an educated guess about just where that root was about to go and what it would be doing once it got there.

Uh-oh... somehow I don't think that this is going to be fun... Double crap.

Her grandma had expertly stripped away the outer layers of the finger-length piece of ginger root she now held, exposing the moist and porous material beneath its surface. The tangy juices coating its length glistened in the light of the overhead fan, and Rhen could feel them tickling the insides of her nostrils even from her spot face down and bottom up across the table

Squinting closer, she felt her stomach do several more flip-flops in a row as her worst fears were confirmed for her. Her grandma had clearly taken the time to carve out a small divot near the root's curved base, one that would prevent it from slipping out of her rear end unexpectedly once it was in place.

Lucky me... she deadpanned to herself with a grimace and

a harrumph that made her naked cheeks wobble again.

As if she too could read her thoughts, Dana smirked and then slipped back in against her left hip, perching her own much wider rump along the edge of the stout table behind her.

"Alright then, that's enough dilly-dallying, I'd say. You just relax that tush again, cutie pie, and we'll have Missus Ginger right where she needs to go in no time. Alright?" she cooed, leaning over and parting her girlfriend's cheeks with both of her hands, spreading them as wide as they would go and fully exposing her to the room at large once again.

"Humph. Fine..."

Ugh. Why does this part never get any easier? You'd think I'd be used to it by now, but no....

"My, my, such an attitude on that one," snickered Maureen from a few feet away.

"Yes, she certainly is a *handful*, isn't she?" agreed Dana with a mock-exasperated sigh and a roll of her eyes, before her face broke out into another smirk and she winked at the other woman. "But that's alright. I don't mind keeping her in line. If you think she's cute now, then just wait until she's sniffling in a corner with a red caboose. Now *that* is a sight to behold."

"Heh. I'm looking forward to it."

"I think we all are, dear," chimed in Melinda Mathews, nodding at both women knowingly before turning her full attention back to the target that had just been exposed for her. "Now let's just see if we can't change Little Miss Grumpy Goose's tone just a bit..."

Mortified beyond belief, but knowing that she was powerless to stop what was about to happen to her, Rhen chewed on her lower lip and silently debated with herself about whether or not taking a full-on spanking there and then wouldn't be far more preferable to what her grandma had in store for her.

Burying her scorching face in her hands, she let out another long, low moan, and then arched her back and pushed her bottom out even further for her grandma and the ginger root she held poised only a few inches behind her. She hoped that by showing a bit of submission and acceptance for her punishment right then, that maybe she might earn herself a reprieve from the spanking (and probably mouth soaping) that she knew she had coming later.

"Yeah right," she grumbled into her hands before sighing heavily, her groin aching with need in spite of herself. "Ugh. This is *so* not fair."

At least it can't be any worse than an enema, right?

It was.

It was *much* worse.

Somehow it felt to her as if the ginger, that when last she'd looked only seemed to be about the width of her thumb, had suddenly just doubled in size as its cold, juice-slicked tip pressed insistently up against her puckered rear opening.

"Oh god, oh crap!" Rhen gasped, eyes shooting open wide as her hands clenched themselves together into little fists beneath the twin swells of her breasts, inadvertently pawing at her rock hard nipples and making herself groan.

"Easy now, child, easy… No need to make such a fuss, it's just a bit of ginger," soothed her grandma, taking her time pushing and twisting the root further and further into her, seemingly only a millimeter or two at a time.

"E-Easy for you to say!" snapped Rhen in response, letting out an involuntary squeak as a particularly knobbly bit forced its way through her back door, much to the amusement of the two older women administering her punishment and her gathered audience of cousins and their wives.

Eventually, mercifully, somehow, the root finally finished making its glacially-slow journey all the way inside of her, and Rhen blushed scarlet and grit her teeth against another squeak as she felt her rosebud cinch in tight around the divot at the base of the ginger, exhaling out her displeasure through her flared nostrils.

Then, a moment later after taking some time to admire the sight of it fully in place and only barely protruding out of her girlfriend, Dana let go of her cheeks, watching with a chuckle as they wobbled back into place.

With that, Rhen let out a long sigh of relief, beyond grateful that the deed was finally done, before letting her arms turn to jelly beneath her as she sagged against the sturdy table. Her moment of peace was short-lived however, as she almost immediately jerked her head back up again with a panicked yelp as it suddenly became all too clear to her just why her aunt and grandma had been laughing earlier.

Uh-oh.

Aside from the monumental humiliation of having her grandma feel that she needed to take the time to carve up and then shove a rather sizable piece of ginger root into her tush, the burning sensation that its oils produced as they soaked into her rosebud and the insides of her opening left Rhen feeling like she was suddenly being flooded from the inside out with boiling magma!

Or... maybe just hot sauce.

Either way, it was definitely *not* a pleasant experience to say the least, and she began to gasp and squirm as her now-plugged bottom shifted and wriggled frantically behind her.

"Oh my god, oh my god, oh my god!" she squealed, the words coming out all at once in a jumbled mess as her arms flailed animatedly out to either side of her. "I'm sorry, I'm sorry, I'm sorry."

"Hah! Well now, that was certainly faster than I'd been expecting," observed Dana with undisguised amusement as she once more stepped around behind Rhen and squatted down onto her heels.

Moving at an easy, unhurried pace, she began to tug up her bright pink pull-up, restoring it along with her jeans back in place around her gyrating hips, before then giving the center of her now-covered seat a fond pat.

"I can see that you're already starting to feel the effects of the ginger. Good."

"Oh yeah, I'm not surprised," chimed in Maureen from beside her smirking husband. "I've had those roots ripening in the fridge for a while now, so it's pretty safe to say that they're definitely more than a little, uh… *flavorful*."

"No freaking kidding," hissed Rhen through gritted teeth, not bothering to wait for her partner's permission before she sprang back to her feet and began dancing around in front of the gathered adults in a futile attempt to somehow ease the roiling inferno raging inside of her. "Oh come on, Aunt Dana, you can't *seriously* expect me to keep this stupid thing in the whole time while we're out tonight!"

"I can, and I do," was her auntie's iron-hard reply as she and the old woman beside her each planted their hands on their hips and glared at their misbehaving charge with mirrored frowns of disapproval. "That root is going to stay right where it is until it's time for bed. And it's not coming out until *after* you've had that naughty, lying mouth of yours washed out and you've taken a trip across my knee for one heck of a spanking, little girl."

"Oh yes, someone is definitely going to be sleeping on her tummy tonight," agreed Melinda Mathews with a firm nod. "I cannot *believe* that you'd try pulling a stunt like this after I'd literally just finished telling you to behave yourself not more than ten minutes earlier. You should be setting a better example for your cousins, Rhen Elizabeth!"

"Brian and Eric are fine," growled Rhen, glaring at the wall ahead of her and refusing to meet anyone's gaze just then. "They don't need my help."

SMACK! SMACK!

"Keep it up, little girl, and see what it gets you," growled Dana after seizing the pouting sophomore by the upper arm and landing two lightning-fast swats to the backs of her thighs.

"Okay, okay! I'm sorry, geez," whined Rhen, petulant fists flopping around uselessly at her sides.

"Oh, you are going to be *very* sorry if you keep on testing me, child," harrumphed her grandma in response. "It's pretty obvious now that I've been cutting you way too much slack lately. Well, that all changes starting tonight. If you so much as poke one more toe out of line while you and your auntie are staying with me, you'd best believe that I'll be tanning your hide raw with your granddaddy's belt. You hear me, girl?"

Mortified beyond belief to be dressed down in such a way in front of everyone, Rhen could only moan indignantly and cling to her bubbling seat as she continued to hop around in place.

"Ugh, fine, I'm *sorry*! I'll be good, alright?"

"We'll just see about that."

Dana let those last few words hang in the air for several more excruciatingly embarrassing moments, before she at last cleared her throat and gathered everyone's attention again.

"Ahem. Now that we have that settled…"

With those words she gave her girlfriend's padded rump a light pat, ignoring the temper tantrum that she knew was still brewing just beneath the surface as she dusted her hands off.

"Who's ready for some hot apple cider and Christmas lights?"

Everyone joined in with the chorus of acknowledgements, even Rhen despite the flush still staining her cheeks bright red.

"Oh! Me, me, me!"

The initial, overwhelming burning from the root's insertion had started ebb away to only a mildly-intolerable throbbing by then, and at that particular moment she was desperate for something, *anything*, to take her mind off of the firm, bulbous mass nestled snugly between her cheeks.

"Great, then let's get going," declared her grandma, moving over to grab her keys from off the counter. "If we hurry, we can still find a good parking spot."

Leading the charge, reinvigorated with a newfound sense of holiday cheer, Rhen was the first one out the door.

"I call shotgun!"

Chapter 23

Another Taste of Discipline

Although walking the Redberry Trail of Lights proved to be about as slow an endeavor as Rhen had been expecting it to be, she was at least happily proven wrong about it being boring. Walking down the somewhat crowded main thoroughfare of the little town hand in hand with Dana, the sassy sophomore found herself genuinely "Oooh"-ing and "Aaah"-ing right along with everyone else at the captivating displays of twinkling lights arranged outside of the local businesses in between sips of a very tasty hot chocolate and a massively oversized gingerbread pastry that was most definitely giving her one heck of a sugar rush.

It was almost enough to make her forget all about the bulbous length of ginger root wedged finger-deep inside of her backside, still quietly sizzling away at her insides and making her wince with every other step.

Almost.

In the end though, Rhen was glad that she went. Even if it *had* come at a highly humiliating (and totally self-imposed) cost, she knew for sure that she'd always look back fondly on the pictures that she and her partner took together that night and smile.

Even the photo of her jumping nearly a foot in the air with a squeal after Dana had goosed her.

Actually, that one was secretly her favorite.

—

Upon arriving home however, it became all too clear that her brief reprieve from further punishment was over. She and the rest of her family had had their fun, and now it was time to get down to business. After all, lying about being sick was seriously naughty behavior no matter how you tried to spin it, and there was no way that her auntie nor her grandma was going to let her off the hook without being thoroughly chastised for it.

Oh well… You win some, you lose some, I guess. Can't say I haven't totally earned what I've got coming, at least…

While Dana slipped away to help Maureen and Jessica with settling their kids down for bed in various spots in the farm house's guest room, Rhen's old play room, and even the second-floor loft that was usually reserved for Christmas decorations (or pretending to be a pirate if you happened to be in the mood for such things), Rhen was passed off to her sternly scowling grandma for the first part of the reckoning she'd been promised.

"Alright, you just come with me, young lady," the old woman huffed, her right hand shooting out to snatch up her granddaughter's earlobe in an iron grip between thumb and forefinger. "We're going to see if we can't scrub away some of those fibs from that tongue of yours."

"Wha-? Oh! Owie! Grandma, come on. No please, not so hard…"

"Oh, hush up with all that fussin', you big baby."

"Ah! Alright, alright, I'm coming, I'm coming! Geez. Slow down at least, would you? You're going to yank my ear off!"

Ignoring the younger girl's further petulant complaining and protests, Rhen's grandma marched her by the ear at a brisk pace that had her scrambling to keep up.

"Now is definitely not the time to be giving me an attitude, little girl," she growled, dragging her through the house and into the spacious bathroom adjoining her master bedroom on the first floor.

After pausing just long enough to flip on the overhead lights, she led Rhen across the cool tile floor and over to the far edge of the room, where she unceremoniously pushed her over the edge of the counter running along the wall beside the sink. Without a single moment of hesitation, the petite sophomore's grandma then pounced, pinning her torso against the smooth countertop beneath her and proceeding to deliver two dozen hard smacks to the seat of her dark blue jeans.

THWAP! THWAP! THWAP! THWAP! THWAP!

The individual spanks themselves didn't register as much more than a firm pat that jutted her forward slightly thanks to the padding she still had protecting her round rump, but they nevertheless had Rhen apologizing profusely long before the dull reports of the old woman's small palm exploding against her wriggling caboose finished echoing off of the bathroom walls.

"Please, Grandma, no, I'm sorry. I'll be good!"

SMACK!

"It's too late for sorries now, missy," snapped Melinda Mathews, putting all of her displeasure and righteous indignation into another swat, that despite the padding she was still wearing had Rhen gasping from the force of its impact as it bounced the font of thighs roughly against the edge of the counter in front of her. "You've been acting like a spoiled little brat all day, Rhen Elizabeth, and it's about time that you were reminded what happens to naughty girls in this house!"

At that, Rhen opened her mouth to deny the accusation, but unfortunately she also knew that it was true. So instead she just let out a frustrated harrumph and stomped her feet, glaring balefully at her grandma through her reflection in the mirror only a few inches away from her nose.

"I think I remember just fine already, thanks," she snapped, sounding very much like the disobedient thirteen-year-old she was at heart. "Ugh. This is *so* not fair."

"Is that right?" deadpanned her grandma, rolling her eyes in exasperation. "Okay then, let's see how sassy you're feeling after *these* come down then, shall we?"

"No, wai- Eep!" Rhen began to plead before her whining was cut short by a mortified squeak as she felt her grandma's surprisingly nimble fingers slip beneath her and begin undoing the front clasp on her jeans.

"You've been getting way too big for your britches lately, young lady," she scolded, giving said britches a well-practiced yank that sent them falling down to her ankles, along with her stomach. "And it's about damn time they came down."

"Oh, come on!"

"Not feeling like such a big girl now, are you, darlin'?"

As if to underscore her point, Rhen's grandma then gave the crinkly seat of the bright pink pull-up still snugly fastened around her granddaughter's hips a meaningful pat.

"And as cute as these are, they're comin' down too."

"No, Grandma, wait! Please, you can't!" whined Rhen, ponytail bobbing frantically from side to side as she shook her head, but she was quickly proven wrong as her training pant-ies followed after her jeans without so much as a whisper of resistance.

Then without warning, two dozen more brisk and power-ful swats suddenly began to explode against her now unpro-tected, bouncy buns, making her squeal and whine as she began wriggling like an eel across the countertop.

SMACK! SMACK! SMACK! SMACK! SMACK!

"Oh my god, oh my god, oh my god. I'm sorry, I'm sorry!"

"What was that, dear? Did you just say that I *couldn't* spank my *naughty... bratty... fibbing... disobedient* grand-daughter on her *bare...* bottom?" demanded her grandma, emphasizing several of her words with exceptionally hard spanks that had Rhen tossing her head back and squealing with the heat of their impact.

"Owie, owie, *please-* Ah! I'm sorry, alright?"

"Are you going to keep being a sassy malassy instead of taking your punishment like a good girl?"

"No ma'am!" squealed the willful twenty-year-old turned teenager, thoroughly chastened.

She'd forgotten just how hard her grandma could spank a naughty bottom when she was in a mood to. All of that time spent raising crops and baling hay before she'd retired had granted her some *very* strong arms that hadn't lost any of their oomph since she'd last had a chance to demonstrate them for her granddaughter, and the breathless brat couldn't help but sag with knee-quaking relief when she at last stopped pummeling her rump with punishing blows.

At least she hasn't gone for the belt yet, she thought to herself with a silent sigh.

As if reading her mind, her grandma harrumphed and then gave her one final swat.

SMACK!

"Ack!"

"Young lady, I have half a mind to go grab your grand-daddy's belt and *really* go to town pre-heating this tush of yours before Dana gets a crack at it," she growled, planting her hands on her hips and glaring at her granddaughter's pouting reflection in the mirror. "But I promised that I'd let her take care of you, and I'm a woman of my word, so those patty-cake swats are all you'll be getting from me tonight.

Assuming of course that I don't catch any more lip from you, that is."

"No ma'am, you won't, I promise," Rhen hastened to assure her.

"Is that right?"

Once again without warning, her grandma surprised her by stepping in close and seizing hold of a great handful of pinkened cheek. Then, squeezing hard, she dug her nails in deep enough to make Rhen squeak out several more hurried and frantic apologies and promises to be good.

"Ah! Ah! I'm sorry, I'm sorry, I'm sorry! I'll be good, I *swear*!"

"Oh, you'd better be, sweet pea," the old woman replied in turn, far too calmly for Rhen's liking as she gave the cheek in her grip a rough shake. "Because I'm going to be watching you like a *hawk* for the rest of the weekend while you're here, and I won't hesitate to whoop this behind of yours raw if you give me a reason to, believe you me. You got that, little girl?"

"Yes ma'am," squealed the breathless sophomore in turn, gasping in relief when her left cheek was at last released, and only blushing a little bit as she felt it wobble back into place.

"Good," sniffed her grandma, seemingly satisfied for the moment, before softening quite a bit as she sighed wearily. "I hope you know that I don't *want* to have to discipline you, Rhenny, hon. Really, I don't. But when you act this way you really don't leave me with any other choice, and I *will* take you task if you're going to be naughty. I understand now how much you need a firm hand to keep you on track thanks to Dana, and I'm going to be doing my darndest from now on to make sure that you get all of the *strict* love and support that you need from me. Okay, sweet pea?"

It was a mostly rhetorical question, Rhen knew, but she

still couldn't help but nod along anyway. It seemed like the smart thing to do in any case, and truth be told she was actually rather touched that her grandma clearly cared so much about her and her wellbeing. Even if that also meant that she was fully onboard the whole "Let's treat Rhen like she's a bratty thirteen-year-old" train.

Oh well, I guess it's not so bad...

"Thanks, um... I uh... I really appreciate that, Gran-Gran."

She flashed the old woman a sheepish grin, feeling fresh embarrassment bubble up inside of her as she inadvertently slipped back into using the old nickname for her grandma, but she shrugged it off just as quickly as her heart swelled at the tender smile she got in return.

"Of course, child."

SMACK!

Unable to resist giving the captivating bare cheeks in front of her just one more swat, Rhen's grandma popped her sharply right in the middle of her rounded rump and then took half a step back.

"Now you stand up and give your granny a hug before I decide to you need some more of that."

"Yes ma'am!"

Rhen readily obeyed, heedless of her nudity for the moment as she pushed away from the counter and all but tackled her grandma, wrapping her arms around her thin shoulders in a fierce hug. She squeezed hard then, though not hard enough to make her wheeze like the night before, and silently worked to fight down the butterflies whirling around inside her stomach, doing her best to avoid thinking about the actual punishment she still had coming.

"I'm sorry I was being such a brat today. I love you, Gran-Gran."

The more she said it, the better the name tasted on her tongue.

"I love you too, dear," cooed the old woman, moving one hand up to scratch the spot just between her shoulder blades that she knew never failed to make her melt.

As it always had in the past, scratching their made Rhen gasp and then sigh, going limp in her supporting embrace as she moaned contentedly.

Oh god, I've missed this…

"But I'm afraid that doesn't mean that I'm going to be going any easier on you," added Melinda with a low chuckle, patting her granddaughter's bare bottom affectionately. "You know that, don't you?"

"Yeah… I do," grumbled the younger girl against her grandma's shoulder, listening to the soothing rhythm of her breathing for several more moments before she huffed grump-ily. "I guess we should probably get to it then, huh?"

"Yes, we probably should," agreed the old woman with another chuckle, disentangling herself from the pouting prin-cess in her arms and flashing her a teasing smirk. "But first, how about you go ahead and bend that bratty butt of yours over one more time for me and I'll get that root out of you? I know Dana said that she wanted to leave it in until after she was done with you, but I don't think she'll mind all that much if we take care of this now. It's done enough sizzling for one night, wouldn't you say?"

"Heck yes it has!" exclaimed Rhen, practically throwing herself across the countertop and rising up onto her tip toes as she arched her back and pushed her bare bottom out as far as it would go behind her.

Although in this position her jiggly cheeks were already naturally parted, exposing the bulbous, unpeeled head of the root lodged deep inside of her (along with just about every-thing else between her legs for good measure), that didn't stop her grandma from taking it upon herself to compound her humiliation even further by deliberately parting her cheeks all the wider still before she finally, mercifully, began to extract the thing that had been making the incorrigibly sassy sopho-more squirm around like she'd needed to pee all night.

Holy crap! I swear I'll never complain about getting another enema ever again for as long as I live, Rhen thought to herself with a wince as she felt the stupid root finally start to come free. *At least those are over relatively quickly and nobody has to know why you're suddenly walking around like a penguin.*

Her cousins had taken great joy in teasing her about the ginger root that had been stuck in her bottom that evening and the way it made her walk, asking her several times if she needed to go "potty" while they'd been out on the Trail that night.

Often they'd accompany their factious questions with a knowing pat to her padded posterior and an invitation to just go ahead and relieve herself if she was feeling so uncomfortable.

"It's not like you need to worry about getting your clothes wet, you know."

"Yeah, honeybunch, we can just change you when we get home."

"Why wait until then? I bet that drug store over there has pull-ups in her size."

"Oooh, that's a very good point. In that case, go ahead, Rhen, honey. I'm *sure* Dana won't mind waiting a few minutes while your Auntie Maureen and Auntie Jessica take you in back there to get you all sorted out. Right?"

"Of course not," her partner had snickered. "By all means, go for it."

Needless to say, Rhen had needed to work *very* hard to avoid biting back with anything too sassy that evening, and for the most part she'd done a good job.

Mostly.

She'd had a good amount of success with grumbling scathing retorts under her breath as she'd walked, letting the noise from the milling crowd around them and the Christmas carols playing from unseen speakers swallow up her sass, but her luck had finally run out when she'd lagged behind to stick her tongue out at everyone's backs and blow raspberries. Doubling back, her auntie Dana had swooped in behind her and smacked the mostly unprotected backs of her thighs a good half-dozen times for that one.

It had still been *so* worth it as far as she was concerned, though.

"Oh my god, *thank you*," gasped Rhen when the root was at last pulled free of its sheath, its passing seeming to take far less time than it had going in.

Slumping against the spotless countertop beneath her, she sighed long and hard, her limbs going jelly-like as she sagged against its cool surface.

"I swear I'll *never* pretend to be sick like that ever again."

Or if I do, I'll be sure to say that I have a tummy ache instead, she couldn't help but add silently.

Now that she was free of that damnable ginger root, she could already feel her reserves of disobedient daring starting to refill again.

"I should hope so," snickered her grandma, patting her lightly trembling tush fondly before turning and beginning to walk out of the spacious bathroom to dispose of the no longer needed hunk of vegetable, calling over her shoulder with a snort as she went. "It usually only takes being figged once to ensure that the lesson sinks in permanently, I've found."

"Yeah, no kidding," groaned Rhen in response to that as her grandma left her alone.

Reeling her panting back in, she steadied her wobbling knees and got her feet underneath her as she pushed herself back up to a standing position.

"Yeesh."

She turned her back to the mirror then, and hunching forward, reached behind her and parted her cheeks one more time.

Craning her head back to look at her exposed nether regions in the mirror, she huffed.

"Well, everything *seems* to be normal back there still," she observed with a pouty grimace, before letting go of her cheeks and crossing her arms in front of her with another harrumph, straightening up and stomping a foot for good measure. "I'll definitely skip out on having that happen ever again though, thanks."

Rolling her eyes, she snorted to herself.

"Yeah right. As if I even have a freaking choice."

Despite her attempts to stoke the fires of her petulant outrage however, she just couldn't bring herself to be all that upset about the punishment she'd just endured, and a moment later she gave up trying to resist the small, contented smile that tugged up on the corners of her mouth.

"Oh well…"

Between the relief of not having that darn ginger root making its presence undeniably known with each and every step she took, and her grudging acceptance that her grandma had indeed already seen her naked plenty of times before, Rhen didn't bother with pulling up any of her clothes as she instead yawned loudly and stretched her arms up over her head.

Standing there on full, brazen display with her jeans and her humiliating "undies" bunched up around her ankles, she rolled her shoulders a couple of times and then pulled her long, black hair free of its ponytail, dragging her hands through its soft tresses and shaking it out as she sighed happily.

"Hmmm... I think Dana *might* just have a point about all that 'needing a firm hand' stuff after all... Heh."

"I couldn't agree more, sweet pea," quipped her grandma then, startling her out of her reverie as she walked with purpose back into the bathroom.

"Oh! Uh... Hi Grandma..." squeaked the mortified twenty-year-old turned teenage troublemaker, raising one hand up in awkward greeting more out of habit than anything else.

Crap! I hope that doesn't get back to her. There's no way she'd ever let me live it down if she heard what I just said...

Unfortunately though, Rhen had far more immediately embarrassing things to worry about just then, as she'd forgotten all about the *other* change that her auntie had mandated for the lower half of her body.

Something which her grandma's sharp eyes had absolutely no problems picking out almost immediately.

"Awww. Now would you look at that? You're as bald as a butternut squash down there, aren't you?" she cooed with a genuine smile as she closed the distance between the two of them and casually dragged her fingertips along the smooth skin just above the younger girl's folds to feel for herself. "Oooh, that's nice. The look *definitely* suits you, hon."

"Y-Yeah... wh-whatever," stuttered a red-faced Rhen, one hand moving to belatedly shield her front as she took half a step back and tried to as nonchalantly as possible stoop down and grab the pull-up from around her calves.

At least it'll cover my front, she tried to tell herself as she fumbled blindly for her training panties.

Her grandma had other plans for her though, unfortunately.

"No, no, you just leave those right where they are, missy," she countermanded in a no-nonsense voice, batting away her questing hand just as she'd managed to get a grip on the elusive waistband of her pink padding. "In fact, I think we'll go ahead and have you take off the rest of your clothes too while we're at it."

"What, why?" demanded Rhen, her blush deepening along with her pout before letting out a surprised squeak as her naked rump butted up against the cold edge of the countertop behind her, cutting off her retreat.

With another harrumph, she straightened herself up to her full height, both of her hands covering her front now.

"I thought you said that you were just going to wash my mouth out? How come I've got to get undressed for that?"

"Because I'm your grandma and I said so?" countered the old woman archly, planting her hands on her hips and fixing the girl in front of her with an unimpressed look that had her swallowing hard despite her attempts to be obstinate.

"But that's not *fair*," whined Rhen, mostly succeeding in stomping a foot even with the jeans still tangled up around her ankles.

"Well that's too bad, little girl, because it's happening whether you like it or not," snapped her grandma, her tone making it crystal clear that the discussion was over. "Besides, it's for your own good. As I'm sure you're well aware by now, mouth soapings tend to be a bit... dribbly, and no granddaughter of mine is going to run around *this* house in sopping wet clothes. So off with 'em!"

"But… Couldn't we just like…?"

But Rhen's grandma just fixed her with a hard glare when it became apparent that she wasn't about to start moving anytime soon, and growled.

"*Now.*"

"Ugh, fine, whatever," the younger girl at last conceded with a put-upon huff, beginning to slowly do as she was told even as she continued to pout.

"Good girl."

Hooking a thumb casually over her shoulder while her other hand remained braced on her hip, her grandma smirked and then added wryly.

"Now don't you fret none, sugar plum. Your auntie already handed off your jammies and a fresh pull-up to me when I passed her in the hall coming back from the kitchen just a minute ago. Snow White and your dreamy clouds are ready and waiting for you on my bed, and I'll be happy to help you get dressed after we're finished here, alright?"

"Do I even get a choice?" huffed Rhen, abandoning all pretense at attempting to shield her humiliating haircut in favor of crossing her arms in front of her chest again as she glowered adorably.

"Nope, 'fraid not."

Deciding to underscore just how much she meant that, Rhen's grandma stepped in even closer and then took hold of the hem of her long-sleeve shirt.

"Alrighty, sweet pea, just like we used to do. Raise your arms up over your head, and Gran-Gran will help you get undressed, okay?"

Blushing furiously, Rhen nevertheless complied.

"Whatever," she sighed, putting all of her mortified embarrassment into that single word and drawing it out long enough for it to be muffled by her shirt as it was turned inside out and drawn up over her head while she rolled her eyes.

"That's my good girl," cooed her grandma, carelessly tossing the no longer needed shirt onto the countertop beside her. "Okay, the cami is next. As adorable as you happen to look in it, I'm afraid that when I say I want you to take off all of your clothes, I do mean *all* of your clothes."

"Ugh."

I'd forgotten just how good she was at all this.

Rhen could feel a hot blush creeping its way up her neck and working its way across her face, an unstoppable attack on her composure.

She could already tell that it was going to be a long, *long* night.

"Yes ma'am…"

Chapter 24

A Teachable Moment

"Night, Gran-Gran, love you."

"Love you too, sweet pea. Sleep tight and I'll see you in the morning."

Padding her way out of her grandma's master bedroom some fifteen or so minutes later, having just finished enduring a mouth scrubbing that she wouldn't be forgetting anytime soon while she stood there in her birthday suit before being dressed once more like a small child in her sky blue pajamas and a fresh pull-up by the same old woman who'd raised her since she actually *was* a small child, Rhen began to slowly make her way down the first floor's main hallway in search of her auntie and the spanking that she knew she still had coming.

Ugh. Yuck...

It took a lot of willpower to resist spitting onto the floorboards just then, but somehow she managed not to, and with another huff she forced herself to swallow her mouthful of slightly sudsy saliva.

How can something that smells so nice taste so gosh darn awful? It's freaking witchcraft, I say.

Scraping the top of her tongue across the underside of her two front teeth, Rhen scowled and then decided to veer off toward the kitchen in search of something that would hopefully help mask the residual taste of soap still clinging stubbornly to the insides of her cheeks and along her gums.

Spanking or no, I have got to do something about this mouth feel, she reasoned to herself, doing her best to ignore the frisson of excitement that such rebellion stirred in her lower abdomen. *Aunt Dana can wait just a little bit longer... probably.*

Despite having been out of practice for nearly a decade now, her grandma had nevertheless demonstrated that she was still more than capable of delivering a world-class mouth soaping when she put her mind to it. And worse still, after she'd finished scrubbing Rhen's tongue and teeth raw, she'd set the bar of soap she'd used aside with a dire warning that it would still be there waiting for her should she need a refresher course on telling the truth in the days to come.

Rhen had done her absolute best to make it crystal clear that that would *not* be necessary.

Shivering, the grouchy girl swallowed hard and winced at the bitter taste that doing so elicited as she tiptoed along the quiet hall. The whole experience had been so unpleasant that she was now seriously considering taking up a vow of silence for the rest of the weekend, just to be on the safe side.

Hah. Yeah right.

Despite the twinge of worried panic that even so much as *thinking* about that evil, evil bar of red soap produced, Rhen knew that sassing was far too easy (and fun) for her to ever give it up. And so she dismissed the idea out of hand in favor of just grumbling about how unfair it all was that she'd gotten in trouble in the first place while she was still well out of earshot of anybody who might be inclined to swat her for expressing such opinions out loud.

Totally not dragging her feet at all in the slightest just because she knew she still had a spanking from Dana to get through before her slate would finally be wiped clean for her earlier bad behavior, the anxious girl who'd been so thoroughly thrust back into her adolescence set about making herself a snack.

Better late than never, right?

She knew that she was just putting off the inevitable as she flipped on the overhead lights in the kitchen and started digging around inside the refrigerator, but she just couldn't help herself. What was the point of being treated like a naughty thirteen-year-old all the time if you couldn't at least indulge yourself in a little bit of petulant procrastination every now and then? Besides, she was already going to get her bare bottom spanked silly before she turned in for the night anyway, so what was the harm in an extra bit of brattiness before she had to face the music?

It's a good thing we left Missus Hairbrush back at home, she thought to herself with a wry smirk. Somehow *I doubt that she'd be too happy with my behavior today.*

After downing a sizable slice of chocolate pie and two tall glasses of ice cold milk, Rhen loosed a resigned sigh and then harrumphed.

Oh well, I guess I might as well get this over with...

"Or not," she murmured aloud after giving the matter a bit more thought, idly sucking a stray bit of whipped cream from the tip of a finger. "After all, it would be awfully rude of me not to clean up this mess I just made..."

And so, moving with deliberate care and slowness, she went about killing a bit more time by dumping her dirty dishes into the sink with a clatter before rinsing, scrubbing, and then drying them off by hand. Just to be an obedient and tidy girl, of course. And then at long last, when there was no longer anything left that she could reasonably justify distracting herself with, she reluctantly began making her way back toward the living room of the old farm house where she'd been told her partner would be waiting for her.

True to her grandma's word, there she found Dana and Maureen standing off to one side near the dusty old TV, casually chatting and laughing with one other while working their way through the remainder of the bottle of wine they'd opened at dinner, clearly enjoying the peace and quiet that had descended upon the nervous girl's childhood home now that the kids had been settled down for the night.

Well, all of them except for Rhen, that is.

At least the peanut gallery is in bed already, the sassy sophomore tried to tell herself with a brittle upward tilt of her lips that didn't do much to quell the swarm of butterflies that stirred to life inside her stomach the moment she locked gazes with her auntie and saw the twinkling promise of a *very* sore bottom dancing in her dark eyes.

"Uh… Hi, Aunt Dana," she greeted tentatively, approaching the two older women but deliberately remaining just outside of grabbing distance in case her partner too felt like she needed to set the mood with a sudden flurry of sharp swats before they got into her actual punishment.

Dana didn't *seem* particularly upset or angry right then, but after the appetizer she'd gotten from her grandma in the bathroom before her mouth soaping, Rhen was hardly in the mood to rush headlong toward the main course if she could at all help it.

"Well, hey there, cutie pie. You all finished up with chatting with your granny?" asked Dana in the same tone of voice that she used whenever Rhen had just gotten home from school, beaming fondly down at her as she turned away from her discussion with Maureen.

"Uh-huh," smirked the younger girl sheepishly. "I guess you could say that."

"Good, good. How about you show me those chompers then?"

"Uh, okay…"

Shrugging, Rhen tilted her head back and flashed the other woman the biggest smile that she could muster under the circumstances.

"Hah. I see someone decided to stop off for some pie on her way here," teased Dana, playfully rapping the end of her nose with a forefinger after she'd closed her mouth with a pout. "Chocolate, right?"

"Yeah…" admitted Rhen, looking only slightly guilty.

As far as she was concerned, her little detour had well been worth the risk of a more severe punishment.

After the awful bitterness of her grandma's soap, that pie had tasted absolutely *heavenly*.

"Somehow I thought that might be your go to after munching on some soap," snickered her aunt, sweeping in beside her and wrapping an affectionate arm around her shoulders. "So then, are you ready for your trip across my lap before you hop aboard the Beddy-Bye Express?"

"I guess so…" grumbled Rhen, her face taking on a shade of red similar to that of the bar of soap her grandma had just finished using on her as she allowed herself to be steered toward the antique and somewhat sagging couch at the other end of the room.

However, before they'd taken more than a few steps, they were held back by a tentative voice calling out after them.

"Um… Say, Dana… would it be alright with you if I stuck around to watch how you deal with her?" asked an abashed Maureen, gesturing vaguely toward Rhen and looking very unsure of herself just then.

"Well, of course it's alright with me! The more the merrier, I say," answered Rhen's partner readily, waving the other woman over to come join them as she took a seat in the middle of the couch. "Come on over here and find yourself a good spot where you can see all the action. You're not going to want to miss this. Rhen gets to be just about the *cutest* thing you ever did see once she starts kicking up a storm over my knee."

"Oh! Well, um… thank you," squeaked out the other woman in obvious relief, tension visibly easing from her shoulders as she scurried over to hover beside the armchair that Rhen had been napping in only a few hours earlier. "I was actually hoping to see how it was that you, um… you know, how you… handled doing all of *this*."

Again, she gestured vaguely with her right hand as she spoke, taking in Dana's waiting lap and the blushing girl standing just in front of it; twisting a stray lock of her inky black hair around a finger as she chewed nervously on her lower lip.

Seeming to summon up all of her courage with a grimace, Maureen forced herself to press on.

"I mean, I know that Rhen's not, you know… *actually* a child, but you see, Brian and I have been talking a lot recently about maybe switching over to spanking for our girls since all grounding them ever seems to accomplish is to make them grumpier and us miserable," she began to explain, fidgeting awkwardly with one of the sleeves on her blouse.

"Tell me about it," commiserated Dana with a tight smirk and a knowing roll of her eyes that seemed to set the other woman more at ease. "A sore bottom definitely tends to get the message across a lot more effectively, I've found."

"Yes, exactly! That's what I was hoping I'd hear you say," replied Maureen excitedly. "As far as I can tell, it *seems* like the right move for our girls as well, especially after how I've seen you and Melinda handling Rhen today."

At that, both women turned their attention briefly toward

the scowling sophomore just long enough to confirm that she was indeed still pouting, but nevertheless standing obediently awaiting her well-deserved spanking.

"Humph!" Rhen huffed, if for no other reason than to vent some of the anxious anticipation roiling around inside of her stomach.

"Be patient, cutie pie, we'll get to you in just a minute, I promise," teased Dana, before turning her attention back toward the woman standing beside her. "Please, go on."

Clearing her throat, Maureen blushed ever so slightly.

"Well, you see… the thing is that while I *think* that spanking is the right call for my girls, I've still been hesitant to actually try disciplining any of them that way since I've never actually, you know… *spanked* anyone before."

She shrugged then, flashing Dana an embarrassed half-grin before pressing on.

"Truth be told, I'm not really even sure where to begin in the first place, and I didn't want to just throw caution to the wind and see what happens either in case I end up screwing things up so badly that it completely ruins my image as 'Mommy the Authority Figure', you know?"

"Oh, absolutely," nodded Dana, her face breaking out into an even wider grin as she beckoned the other woman a bit closer. "But don't you worry, hon. Spanking a naughty girl, of any age, is actually a *lot* easier than you might think it is once you get the hang of it. I know it might *seem* really daunting at first, but trust me when I say that once you've gotten some practice under your belt, you'll have those little darlings of yours thinking twice about being bratty in no time."

"Thank goodness," sighed Maureen, clearly more than a little relieved to hear that her concerns weren't as monumental as she'd originally feared they were. "That's very reassuring to hear."

"Of course, of course," dismissed Dana with a nonchalant wave of her hand, before frowning. "Hmmm… in fact…"

Pausing for a moment or two, she tapped a thoughtful forefinger against the side of her cheek, staring off into space and appearing to be mulling something over before she suddenly sprang back to her feet and turned to gesture at the seat she'd just abandoned in the middle of the couch.

"Why don't *you* spank Rhen tonight, and I'll coach you through it?"

"What?" squeaked her petite girlfriend, stomach plummeting to her ankles as she whipped her head back and forth between the two women in stunned disbelief. "Aunt Dana, no, you *cannot* be serious."

"Hush, dear," chided her partner, brushing away her protests with another casual wave while she kept her attention locked on Maureen with a sly grin. "So what do you say, Maureen? Think you're up for it?"

"Uh… I think so, yes… But are you really sure that you don't mind?" asked the other woman tentatively, taking half a step forward even as she cast a sidelong glance toward the glowering college sophomore turned teenager just beside her.

"Of course I don't mind!" boomed Dana with a boisterous laugh. "You'd hardly be the first person other than me to have taken her over your knee since I started looking after her, and I'd be more than happy to show you the ropes before you try springing them on your own kiddos."

Hearing that, Maureen's face lit up with an eager smile.

"Well, in that case, count me in!"

"Great! Now you just sit right here," Dana leaned over and patted the spot she'd just abandoned on the couch and nodded invitingly. "And we'll get started."

"Oh, come on!" protested Rhen, stomping a foot as she glared at her auntie and them Maureen while they moved to take their places. "Don't I at least get a say in this?"

"No," they both said in unison, before snorting in amusement.

"Ugh, whatever."

Folding her arms in front of the happy, pastel rainbow emblazoned across the minimal chest of her pajama top with a huff, Rhen rolled her eyes and tried not to let on just how embarrassed (not to mention knee-wobblingly excited) the idea of her cousin's wife spanking her made her feel.

I mean... I guess I'm just another little kid in the family and all that as far as she's concerned, but still... Humph!

"Alright now, first thing's first," declared the bratty girl's partner with an eager clap of her hands once she'd finished swapping places with Maureen on the couch, hovering just off to her right and grinning excitedly. "Once you've decided that it's spanking time, you need to make sure that it's *very* clear that your decision is final. There will be no more second chances, and no delays. When Mommy says that it's time for someone to take a trip across her knee, that's the end of the discussion. Make sense so far?"

"Uh-huh," nodded Maureen, licking her lips nervously. "Consistency is key in these sorts of things, right?"

"Exactly," agreed Dana, her grin growing even wider. "So then, once it's time for a bottom blistering to actually happen, the first thing you'll want to do is tell that naughty miss you're about to spank in no uncertain terms to get her little butt over to you right away. If you can pull this part off just right, you shouldn't ever have to repeat yourself more than once, or have to go chasing after your little darlings to make them take their medicine. But remember though..."

At that Dana held up a warning forefinger and her grin turned grave and serious.

"You're aiming for commanding and in control, *not* angry and terrifying. You got that?"

"Got it," confirmed the other woman, looking just as serious.

"Good," nodded Dana, lightening up again. "Now then, why don't you give it a shot with Rhen here? Show me your best 'Come to Mommy' voice."

"R... Right!"

Screwing her face up into a mask of grim determination, Maureen turned a fiery glare on the younger girl awkwardly fidgeting with the hem of her pajama top only a few steps away from her and jabbed a painted fingernail down toward a spot of carpet just in front of her bare feet.

"Young lady, you get over here this instant!"

Despite knowing that she was (mostly) just practicing, Rhen still couldn't help but let out an involuntary squeak as her stomach lurched and her feet scrambled to obey automatically.

"Eep! Yes ma'am!"

Oh crap.

Swallowing hard, she barely managed to suppress a shiver as she came to a sudden stop only a few inches away from her would-be spanker's knees.

I think she just might be a natural at this...

"Well done, Maureen," exclaimed Dana, clapping the other woman on the shoulder with a surprised, but happy, laugh. "That was *perfect*."

"Oh! Um, well, uh... thank you," answered a bashful Maureen a moment later, blushing a bit and looking more than a little shocked that her command had been so effective.

Watching her little niece (because despite her age and the way their family tree was actually laid out, she just couldn't help but think of her as anything else), standing there squirming in front of her, waiting obediently to be hauled across her lap for a good, hard spanking, she smirked.

"Heh. You know, I've got say that this is rather fun."

"Isn't it though?" agreed Dana with a knowing twinkle in her eye as she spared an amused glance toward her girlfriend who was busy cupping the seat of her pajama bottoms, looking worried. "There's nothing quite like the feeling of satisfaction that comes from putting a bratty little girl in her place, is there? Especially when she's so *cute*."

She heaved out a contented little sigh at that and then winked at Maureen before getting back to business.

"Now then, are you ready to move on to the next part?"

"Definitely," confirmed the other woman with a keen nod, her confidence growing by the moment.

"Great. In that case, let's talk about clothing. Now you can spank a naughty girl over her panties if you really want to, but personally I only ever like to do that when I'm in a rush or need to just deliver a quick attitude adjustment. When it comes to actual *punishment* spankings, like the one you're about to give Rhen, you always want to stick to working with a bare bottom."

"Really?" questioned Maureen. "Why's that? Wouldn't a spanking over her panties be just about the same as one on her bare bottom?"

Pausing for a brief moment, she eyed Rhen's slightly-padded hips and then added with a wry smirk.

"Well, most of the time, I mean."

"*Technically*, yes," conceded Dana, smirking too at her niece's adorable choice in underwear. "But there are a few very key differences that make spanking a bratty girl directly on her bare bottom the far superior choice in my opinion."

Holding up a hand, she began ticking off points on her fingers.

"Hmmm, let's see... First of all, it creates a very important headspace that lets the naughty girl in question fully grasp that she's being *punished* and not just taken to task briefly because you didn't like her tone or something like that. Second, it's always nice and embarrassing, *especially* for older girls, to be stripped below the waist like a child. That alone can really help further enhance their punishment without you having to do anything more than yank their undies down for them."

She grinned briefly at that, sharing another knowing look with her student.

"But more to the point, spanking on a bare bottom undoubtedly packs more of a sting, and not just emotionally, since there's nothing standing in the way between the naughty girl's cheeks and your palm or implement. Moreover, spanking on a bare tush allows you to see *exactly* where you're swatting, as well as the spots that you might be neglecting as the case may be, and gives you a much clearer idea of how effective your individual spanks are at getting your point across. Plus not having any clothes in the way while you're working also helps highlight the spots where you might need to focus more on, as well as the ones that you might be going a little *too* hard on. Which honestly, is even more important in the long run."

Sweeping her palm to the side and beaming, Dana concluded by saying.

"In essence, spanking on a bare bottom not only humbles a naughty girl, but also gives you the best possible vantage point to make sure that you're delivering *exactly* the kind of punishment that she needs. Not too soft, but never overly harsh either. Understand?"

"Hmmm... I think so..." murmured Maureen thoughtfully, dragging out the words as she attempted to digest everything that she'd just been told while she frowned at her lap.

Then, a moment later, she looked up at her mentor and smiled.

"Yes. Yes, actually, that makes a *lot* of sense. Thank you for explaining that so thoroughly for me, Dana. I never would have thought of even half of those things before you mentioned them, and I'm glad that you were able to set me straight before I could make a mistake I might regret."

"No problem, hon. Going bare for punishments is definitely one of those things that you either have to just learn through experience, or be lucky enough to have someone explain to you," shrugged Dana with a wistful smirk. "It took me a good couple of years of trial and error before I finally managed to figure that one out for myself, actually. So I'm glad that I'm able to help you sidestep that."

Then, grinning mischievously she added.

"Plus now you'll get to see how Rhen's face just about bursts into flames every time she has her panties pulled down for a spanking. It's so darn adorable, I almost can't stand it."

"Oh, *you* can't?" mumbled Rhen with a disgruntled huff and a roll of her eyes, going completely ignored in spite of her sass.

"Awww, that's so cute," cooed Maureen, eyeing the blushing girl in front of her with a tender smile tinged with just a hint of something more predatory. "I'm definitely looking forward to that."

"Hehe, me too," giggled Dana, plucking her wine glass up from where she'd left it on a side table and taking a long sip.

"It's honestly one of my favorite parts of punishing her. Plus it never fails to make her super we-"

"Aunt Dana!" interrupted Rhen with an indignant squeak before her partner could elaborate further on how her punishments tended to affect her body, glaring daggers at the two slightly wine-drunk women who were toying with her. "Don't you think that maybe you're starting to get a *little* off topic?"

"Hmmm... I suppose maybe just a bit," conceded the older woman, completely unfazed by her girlfriend's embarrassment as she took her time swallowing the remainder of her drink before planting her hands on her hips and clearing her throat.

"Ahem. Now then, why don't you go ahead and pull Little Miss Rhen's jammy bottoms down for her, Maureen, and we'll get on to the next part of our lesson?"

"Oh, are you sure that's alright?" double-checked Maureen, sounding slightly worried. "Isn't she a little too old for me to be doing that for her? Wouldn't it be better if she just undressed herself instead?"

I think it would be "better" if I didn't have to get undressed at all in the first place, thought Rhen sourly, wisely choosing to keep that particular bit of sass locked up tight in her head.

"Of course not," snickered Dana, patting the other woman reassuringly on the shoulder and rolling her eyes. "If she was willing to act like a naughty little girl and earn a spanking in the first place, then she can most certainly take her punishment like one as well. Besides, Rhen *technically* being a 'big girl' just means that you baring her bottom before you turn her over your knee for a spanking will be all the more embarrassing and effective as a punishment for her. Isn't that right, cutie pie?"

Rhen felt her stomach flip-flop at having the question directed at her, but as much as she might have wanted to deny it, she just couldn't bring herself to fib again. Especially not with the taste of soap still fresh in her mind.

So she didn't.

"Yes ma'am," she harrumphed, face glowing a hot shade of crimson as she crossed her arms in front of her with a surly pout.

"See, what'd I tell you?" pressed Dana with a fresh smirk, reaching out to ruffle her not-niece's hair. "Her jammies haven't even come down yet and she's already been reduced to a bashful little brat who's clearly knee-deep in regrets about her bad behavior. Aren't you, hon?"

Again, Rhen wanted to deny it, but her auntie had pretty much hit the nail right on the head. She was indeed very much wishing right then that she'd just sucked it up and went along with everyone else to the Trail of Lights without trying to pretend that she'd been sick.

"I guess so…"

"Perfect."

Turning her full attention back to Maureen, her partner went on.

"But to answer your other question: Yes, sometimes it is better to have the girl about to be spanked undress herself. Like again for instance, if you're in a hurry and just want to make a quick attitude adjustment, there's nothing wrong with having your daughters just drop their jeans or flip up the backs of their skirts for you. But generally speaking, I think it really helps set the right tone if you as the spanker do it for them, *especially* for formal punishment spankings."

"Ahhh, gotcha."

Nodding once again, Maureen fixed her face back into its earlier mask of grim determination, making the butterflies inside of Rhen's stomach go wild with worry.

"Alright, little lady, you heard your Auntie Dana. These are coming down."

Suiting actions to words, she leaned forward and pulled free the loose knot that had been tied with the drawstrings holding up the younger girl's fluffy-cloud-covered pajama bottoms. She then took hold of their stretchy, elastic waistband on either side of her hips and gave them a sharp tug that sent them sailing down to her ankles in one fell swoop.

"Oh god," groaned Rhen, her face flaring up with another flash of heat as she felt the cool living room air rush in to tickle the backs of her exposed thighs.

I guess this is really happening after all, she moaned silently, forcing herself to keep her eyes fixed squarely on a spot of wall just above Maureen's dark brown hair while her hands fidgeted nervously at her sides.

"Awww, what's the matter, honeybunch?" cooed the woman in front of her, leaning back against the couch she was sitting on and grinning smugly. "Not feeling so big and clever now that you're about to go over Auntie Maureen's knee for being a naughty little fibber?"

Rather than say no and risk further teasing questions, Rhen just harrumphed.

"You know I am."

"Excuse me?" demanded Dana then, raising a single eyebrow in silent warning.

"Eep!" squeaked Rhen in response to that, hastening to correct herself. "I mean, yes ma'am!"

"Well, good," sniffed Maureen, clearly pleased with the sudden upswing in politeness from her niece but not quite willing to let the flustered girl off the hook just yet.

"Big girls who act like little brats *ought* to feel embarrassed when they're being punished," she scolded, even trying out wagging an admonishing forefinger at Rhen before looking over toward Dana to check how she was doing.

"That's right," agreed the other woman, folding her arms and grinning from ear to ear. "See, Maureen? You're a natural! So many people overlook how important it is to take your time to scold and lecture during a punishment spanking, but look at you! You're doing it without even thinking about it. Great job!"

"Oh, well, um… thanks," replied a suddenly bashful Maureen, her own cheeks coloring ever so slightly from the praise.

"Ahem."

Seemingly as if to distract herself from her nerves, or maybe just to reassert her stern matriarch persona once again, she cleared her throat and turned her focus back on Rhen, smiling tightly at her with a mixture of fondness and amusement.

"Boy oh boy, Dana, there really is just no getting around how adorable she looks in these things, is there?"

Gesturing at the Snow White pull-up secured in place around Rhen's hips, she chuckled.

"Yes," agreed the other woman with a wistful sigh, before turning a similar smile on the younger girl as she purred. "Like I was telling you this morning, I hadn't really *planned* on putting her into pull-ups back when she agreed to come live with me last summer…"

Rhen's frown deepened incredulously at hearing that, and she let out a disbelieving harrumph.

"Well, not for any extended period of time, at any rate," Dana amended with a wink at her pouting girlfriend. "But they really are just too cute when paired with her jammies, aren't they?"

"Absolutely," confirmed Maureen with a fervent nod as she

snickered. "I guess you could say that her wetting her pants yesterday while y'all were driving ended up being a *happy accident* after all, huh?"

"Hah!" snorted Dana, cracking up and laughing hard for several long moments before finally managing to get herself back under control, wiping away a tear from her eye. "How did I not think of that earlier? 'Happy accident', oh dear, that's hilarious, Maureen."

"Yeah, yeah... hardy-har-har," groused Rhen, tossing her loose hair over a shoulder with a disgruntled shake of her head. "Just remember that this is only a onetime thing until we're done with that pack you bought Aunt Dana. So don't get used to them or anything!"

"Oh, is that so?" prompted her partner with an arched brow, still chuckling.

She was smiling, but the way she'd purred the question had Rhen's knees suddenly feeling like jelly and her very grateful that she was wearing something absorbent as her bladder threatened to betray her again.

Still though, it wasn't like she could back down now.

In for a penny, in for a pound, I guess...

"Yeah," she sniffed, putting all of her considerable sass into that single word as she planted her hands on her hips and tossed her hair again for good measure. "Humph!"

"I see her attitude just about matches her undies," commented Maureen dryly, stern disapproval sobering much of her earlier mirth.

"Yes..." agreed Dana with a pensive frown of her own. "That it does."

They continued to let the bratty not-teenager stand there stewing in her own petulance for several more excruciatingly long moments, watching as her glowering and grumbling gradually gave way to anxiety and uncertainty as her momentary burst of sass-fueled defiance sputtered out under the combined weight of the two women's withering glares.

Finally though, Dana cleared her throat, breaking the tension as she spoke up again.

"Hmmm… You know what? I think you might've just given me an idea, Maureen."

"Oh really?" asked the other woman, looking bemused. "And what's that?"

Leaning in and leveling a single, commanding forefinger at her girlfriend, Dana bored a hard stare into the younger girl's sparkling green eyes that made it crystal clear that what she was about to say was not up for debate.

"Since you seem to be having *such* a hard time behaving yourself, cutie pie, even when you're standing there with your jammies around your ankles and about to be turned over someone's knee for a good, hard spanking, we're just going to have to up the ante a little bit and see if that can't help straighten your attitude out."

Uh-oh… I don't think I like where this is headed, thought Rhen to herself with a worried grimace, feeling her stomach perform several flip-flops in a row. *Dang it. Why didn't I just keep my big mouth shut?*

As if reading her mind, Dana's lips quirked upward just enough to show that she meant business and knew *exactly* how much her girlfriend was going to hate what she had in store for her. While at the same time keeping her eyes soft enough to show that she wasn't actually trying to be cruel, but rather was just providing her with an extra dose of the tough love that she knew she craved and responded to so well.

"From now on, I think we're going to make pull-ups an official part of your bedtime attire. Which means that when

I tell you to go put on your jammies, I'll be expecting to find you wearing one of those underneath them as well. You got that, little girl?"

"Wha-!" Rhen began to splutter indignantly, being cut short before she could really get a good tantrum going by a sharply upraised hand from her aunt that forestalled any further complaining just then.

"They fit you perfectly, and we've got plenty of them back at home that are just sitting there collecting dust under the sink in your bathroom, so we might as well put them to use. And besides, I think it'll do you a world of good to start your mornings off by eating breakfast on a padded caboose. It'll help you remember to act your age throughout the rest of the day."

Grinning from ear to ear at the dumbfounded look of horror that this announcement had produced in her adorably obstinate niece, Dana couldn't resist adding.

"Not to mention the added benefit of not having to worry about you wetting the bed anymore."

At that insinuation, Rhen's cheeks puffed out indignantly and she looked like she was about to explode with mortified outrage, but her auntie's smile turned placating then and she waved her down.

"Easy there, cutie pie, no need to bust out the big frowns now," she soothed with a low laugh. "I'm just teasing you a little bit. I know that you haven't *actually* done that before. But then again, you hadn't ever wet your pants with me before yesterday either. So, you can never be too careful, right? Plus, like I already told you, you're as cute as a button when you're wearing a pull-up, and as far as I'm concerned, that's practically reason enough all on its own."

"You won't get any arguments from me on that account," chimed in Maureen with a sly smile. "And I can't tell you too how much it would mean to Melody to know that she's not the only one who has to swap out of her panties every night when it's time for bed. I don't know if you were able to pick up on it or not at all today, but she actually looks up to you quite a bit, Rhen."

Rhen hadn't known that actually, and the knowledge that one of her cousin's kids thought that she was still someone to admire even after no doubt overhearing her humiliating temperature taking and figging earlier that night, took most of the edge off of her indignation.

"She does?"

"That's right," confirmed Maureen with a broad grin that suddenly turned playful. "Although I really do wish you'd set a better example for her."

"Oh, uh…" murmured a once again flustered Rhen, blushing and looking ashamedly down at the crumpled heap of her pajama bottoms around her ankles. "Sorry, Aunt Maureen."

"That's okay, dear. I forgive you."

To her own chagrin, Rhen actually sighed with relief upon hearing that.

Geez. I really am just a bratty little teenager at heart, aren't I?

"Oh honey, I am *so* proud to see you taking responsibility for your behavior," cooed Dana with a twinkle in her eye, moving half a step closer to ruffle her hair before returning to Maureen's side and planting her hands on her hips with a brisk air of finality. "But I feel like we're getting a bit off topic now."

Oh now you think we're getting off topic? thought Rhen with an internal roll of her eyes. *How convenient.*

As if picking up on her silent sassing, Dana leveled a hard frown at her that didn't quite reach her eyes.

"We're here for a *spanking* after all, not to discuss how cute you look in your jammies. So, Maureen," she paused to nod encouragingly at her student. "Why don't you go ahead and finish pulling down those pretty pink padded panties for Little Miss Rhen here, and then take her across your knee so that we don't keep her up all night?"

"Sounds like a plan to me," agreed the other woman, scooting toward the edge of her seat and leaning forward again.

She quickly sent the furiously blushing sophomore's pull-up south to join her pajama bottoms around her ankles and then casually patted the tops of her thighs.

"Alrighty, honeybunch, come here and show me how you lay over Dana's lap when she spanks you."

"Humph! Fine…"

Still a bit miffed and more than a little grumpy about her sudden bedtime wardrobe adjustment, Rhen nevertheless did as she was told, managing to somehow half-shuffle half-stomp her way over to Maureen's right side despite the clothes still bunched up around her ankles. Blowing out a resigned sigh through her nostrils, she then levered herself awkwardly up onto the couch cushions beside her and shuffled forward on her knees a bit, before stretching herself out across the older woman's waiting lap.

She then spent another couple of stomach-clenchingly embarrassing moments after that wriggling her bare bottom around from side to side as she fought to get comfortable, eventually shifting her knees forward and positioning her naked hips directly atop Maureen's firm thighs, before grabbing a throw pillow from the far end of the couch and burying her burning face into it as she at last settled down to await her punishment.

"I'm ready now, ma'am…"

"Heh. I can see that, darling."

"Yeah, I freaking bet you can," harrumphed Rhen into her pillow with a self-pitying pout.

Maureen just ignored her however, rolling her eyes with a barely-suppressed chuckle.

"Ahhh, this is nice," she cooed instead, giving the bare cheeks presented to her a couple of tentative rubs and then a more confident pat when Dana nodded encouragingly at her to keep going.

"Yes, over the knee is definitely my favorite position to spank a naughty set of buns in," agreed Rhen's auntie, reaching down and giving her girlfriend's right sit-spot a quick tickle that sent her squirming. "Plus it gives you easy access to all the ticklish spots."

"You don't say?" laughed Maureen, following her mentor's example and gently wriggling her fingertips along the pudgy undercurve of Rhen's left cheek, producing much the same result. "Hah! I think I see what you meant about her being extra-cute once she starts squirming over your lap."

"Told you," snickered Dana, before giving the giggling girl a couple of light pats and straightening up, once again switching back to being all business as she planted her hands on her hips and frowned down at her disobedient niece. "Now then, are you ready for your punishment, little girl?"

"Ugh. You'd think that would be readily apparent by now," grumbled Rhen against her pillow, wiggling her hips sassily to emphasize her point before heaving out another put-upon sigh and looking up sullenly. "Yes ma'am."

Rather than immediately start swatting away like her partner typically did at that particular point in her punishments however, Maureen instead just let her answer continue to hover awkwardly in the air for several more moments, until she at last broke the silence by asking.

"So, um…. Now what do I do?"

"Now you start spanking," replied Dana matter-of-factly, miming smacking a bottom and flashing her an encouraging smile. "Go on, just jump into it and show me what you've got. I'll stop you if I see something you need to change."

"Oh, okay."

Maureen laughed nervously to herself and sat up a little bit straighter then, frowning in concentration.

"I can do that… I think."

Taking a long, slow, deep breath, she began tentatively slapping the naked cheeks stretched out across her lap.

Pop… Pop… POP…

"No, no, no, you're going to have to spank a *lot* harder than that if you ever plan on getting through to her," interrupted Dana after only a few weak slaps, shaking her head and holding up a hand to stop her student. "See how she's barely even responding?"

Leaning in, she then swatted her niece's upturned bare bottom, *hard*.

SMACK!

"Oh!" squeaked Rhen, drumming her feet animatedly against the couch cushions behind her as her lips formed a surprised, little O.

"Now *that's* the kind of reaction you're looking for," declared the older woman with a self-satisfied smirk.

"I see…" replied Maureen slowly, nodding thoughtfully at the bright pink handprint that Dana had just left behind on the younger girl's right cheek.

"Don't worry, you'll get the hang of it soon, I'm sure," she encouraged. "Come on now, keep going. Try again."

"Right!"

Squaring her shoulders, the novice spanker started once again bouncing her palm against Rhen's naked rump with gusto, moving in a herky-jerky fashion and grunting with the effort of each swat as she pulled her hand up high overhead before slamming it back down with seemingly as much force as she could muster.

POP! POP! POP!

"Take this, and this, and this you naughty girl!" she huffed and puffed.

POP! POP! POP!

Still though, despite demonstrating a slight improvement from her first attempts at dishing out discipline, Maureen's smacks continued to fail to elicit much more than a perfunctory grimace and the occasional slightly uncomfortable shift from Rhen with their impacts.

I think I see now why she was so worried about ruining her reputation as a disciplinarian with her kids, thought the bratty sophomore to herself with a silent snicker. *I'd be running riot over her in no time if this was all I had to worry about.*

"Not bad," interrupted Dana again after spending a few more moments observing the other woman's efforts, before reaching out and gently touching Maureen on the shoulder to get her to pause. "You're doing better, but your technique still needs some work. Here, let me show you a couple of things…"

Stepping around from her perch at the other woman's shoulder, she squatted down onto her heels just in front of her and then began to slowly guide her through the basic motions of delivering a properly punishing spank.

"See, you've got the basic idea right, but you're tensing

up way too much when you start bringing your hand down. It's robbing your swats of all their power. What you need to do instead is keep your shoulders nice and loose the whole way through your downswing and focus on aiming for *speed*, not power," she explained while demonstrating just what she meant by bringing her own palm down in a fluid arc that landed gently against Rhen's right cheek, making it jiggle. "If you do that, then the strength will come naturally as a result."

"Hmmm... So like this?" asked Maureen, visibly relaxing as she adjusted her movements to match those of her mentor, gently slapping her palm against Rhen's left cheek in time with the girl's partner.

"Exactly," confirmed Dana. "But make sure you remember to keep your hand rigid and your fingers straight and together too. No, no, don't cup your palm, that'll just make a lot of noise without actually accomplishing anything. Keep it flat like this... There you go!"

"Heh. I think I'm starting to get the hang of this," chuckled Maureen, brows knitting together in concentration as she worked to incorporate everything she'd just been told into her own spanking technique.

After copying her mentor's slow motion example a couple more times, she then brought her palm sizzling down at full force without any warning.

SLAP!

"Ah!"

"Yes, that's it!" cheered Dana. "Your technique on that last swat was perfect. The only thing you need to work on now is remembering to follow through."

"What do you mean?" asked Maureen, frowning slightly at the far less vivid handprint her smack had left behind before starting to practice moving her palm up and down again, sending small ripples jiggling through Rhen's bare bottom with each experimental pat.

"You stopped short," elaborated the girl's aunt, using her hands as a visual aid to demonstrate what she meant. "Your swat was excellent, but you stopped it as soon as your hand came into contact with her rump. Instead what you need to do is pretend that you're aiming for a spot just a couple of inches *past* where her tush actually is so that you impart the full force of your palm with each spank. Once you start doing that, then you'll *really* have her squealing like the naughty girl she is, trust me."

"So... like this?"

Shaking out her shoulders to loosen them up one more time, Maureen pursed her lips together in concentration and took a firm grip around Rhen's trim waist with her left hand. After taking a couple of deep breaths to steady herself, she then brought her right hand up to just past her shoulder and then sent it crashing back down hard and fast, dead-center against the younger girl's bare left cheek.

SMACK!

"Aieee!"

"Yes, yes, yes!" cheered Dana. "That's it *exactly*. Now try again on the other side."

SMACK!

"Ah! Owie, owie, owie!" howled Rhen, arching her back as she half-pushed herself up and hissed in a sharp breath through clenched teeth before sagging back down across Maureen's lap.

Crap! Why does she have to be such a fast learner?

"Way to go, Maureen. That was perfect!" praised the gasping girl's auntie as she stood back up and snickered. "She *definitely* felt those ones. Didn't you, cutie pie?"

"Ugh," huffed Rhen, turning her head to glare petulantly at her partner. "Yes."

"Awww, yay!" cheered Maureen with a little clap for herself, partially breathless from the adrenaline rush of delivering two back-to-back successful swats. "You were right, Dana. Those last two felt *so* much better."

"Told you," crooned the other woman, flashing her a big thumbs up. "Believe it or not, most of the time your hand is all you'll ever really need to reduce a bratty girl to a sniffling, red-bottomed mess. It just takes time, patience, and a little bit of elbow grease is all."

"Is that right?"

Maureen couldn't help but stare at her palm with a newfound awe and respect.

"I never would have thought it would be this easy."

"Yep, it really is," agreed Dana with a good-natured shrug. "Welcome to the Bossy Mommy Club."

"Thanks," smirked Maureen.

Nodding in acknowledgement, Dana then raised a cautioning forefinger.

"But don't forget too that just because she's crying after you're finished with her, doesn't mean that she won't need another spanking sooner rather than later. Like I was telling you this morning, some girls just can't help themselves and simply *need* a firm hand to keep them in line. So don't sweat it if you find that you have to spank your girls more often than you might have thought you would, or even for the same things multiple times. It's totally normal for rambunctious girls to want to push their boundaries, and not something that you need to worry about."

At that, the spanking veteran flashed her novice learner an encouraging smile and patted her on the shoulder.

"And some girls are just naturally naughty and need lots of attention, so try not to let it bother you, alright? It's not a reflection on you as a disciplinarian, I promise. It's just the way the good lord chose to make them. You just focus on making sure each trip over your knee is a memorable one, and the rest will sort itself out over time. Oh, and above all else, be *patient*. Spankings aren't silver bullets that'll instantly transform your children into perfect angels overnight. It takes time and lots of consistent and swift consequences to effect a major change in attitude, especially when you're looking after a willful and sassy girl like Rhen here."

Unable to resist, the girl's auntie reached out and gave her rounded rump a teasing pinch that managed to get an adorable squeak of surprise out of her.

"But if you stick to it, you *will* start to see a gradual improvement in behavior over time. So don't stress if you find one or more of your girls needs to take multiple trips across your lap in a week. Their bratty buns are more than well-equipped enough to handle it, trust me. Heck, that's totally normal, really. Little Miss Cutie Pie here for instance can hardly seem to go more than a couple days without having *her* caboose painted bright red for one bit of sass or another, and she's totally fine."

"I do not…" groused Rhen with a huff, her face flushing far pinker than the two handprints still visible on her backside.

"Sure you don't, honey," teased Dana, drawing out the words with another pinch and a snicker. "Sure you don't."

"Humph! Meanie."

"Silly goose."

SMACK!

"Ah!"

That time the girl's partner decided to punctuate her reply with a sharp swat that made her jump.

"Hmmm… I think I'm starting to see what you mean about the whole 'needing a firm hand' thing," piped up Maureen then, smiling fondly at the loving exchange between the two women. "I'll be sure to keep that in mind when I start reining in the girls tomorrow, thanks."

"Of course," nodded Dana, patting the other woman encouragingly on the shoulder again. "I'm sure it'll go wonderfully. You're definitely a natural at this, trust me."

"Awww, well thanks! That means a lot coming from you, Dana," gushed Maureen, her face lighting up with the praise.

"Anytime, hon. Us mommies and aunties have to stick together, after all."

Dana flashed the other woman another smile and a thumbs up, before clearing her throat.

"Ahem. Now then, since you've clearly got the basics down, let's talk a little bit more about the target areas you should be focusing on, and then I'll let you get to work putting all of this into practice. Alright?"

"Sure, sounds great."

"Great. So then, when you're spanking a naughty girl's bratty buns, you want to spend most of your time working on the lower half to lower third of her cheeks, right where it's the most jiggly," explained Dana, leaning forward over her girlfriend once again and tracing a downward-sweeping arc along her bare and barely pinkened cheeks before giving each one a light slap to highlight the exact spots she was talking about. "Those areas can take pretty much anything you can throw at them without any problems, and unless you're *really* swinging for the fences, which you shouldn't be by the way, you don't need to worry about actually hurting her. Most girls have

527

plenty of padding back there and can take a *lot* more punishment than you might think they can. In fact, most of the time Rhen's rump goes back to being lily white only two or three hours after I'm through spanking her."

She paused for a moment then and shared a wry smirk with Maureen.

"On the one hand it's a little annoying to see all of that pretty, pretty red I worked so hard to color in back there disappear, but on the other, it just means that she has no excuse to avoid any further trips across my knee that might come up later that day if she decides to give me more attitude. So I suppose it's a fair enough trade in the end."

"Heh. Good to know," crooned Maureen, giving the naked cheeks in front of her a couple of hard squeezes. "I guess that means I don't need to worry about holding anything back then."

"Lucky me," deadpanned Rhen, flopping her face sullenly against her throw pillow and scowling.

This sucks.

"Oh Maureen, I'm so glad to hear you say that!" cooed Dana, ignoring her niece's sass. "That is *exactly* the kind of attitude you should be approaching a spanking with. No half-measures, no token punishments, and no going easy. If the little miss in question was willing to misbehave and earn herself a spanking in the first place, then you owe it to her to provide her with the consequences that she deserves as well."

"Yes, that makes sense," agreed Maureen, nodding seriously. "If I'm going to punish her, then I need to do it right or not at all."

"Exactly," confirmed Dana. "And speaking of doing things right, if you really need to get her to pay attention to a particular point you're trying to make, or you just want to leave her with something that she'll be feeling for a while after you've finished with her, all you have to do is shift your aim a bit lower and really let her have it right along that crease where her bottom and thighs meet."

Again, she paused to trace out the area that she was talking about, eliciting another round of involuntary laughter and squirming from her now very nervous niece in the process.

"That's where she rests most of her weight when she's sitting down, and since it's not quite as padded as the rest of her tush is, getting spanked there *really* packs an extra punch that'll have her wincing for quite a while after you're done."

"You don't say?" drawled a bemused Maureen, squeezing the center of Rhen's left cheek experimentally before repeating the process with her sit-spot and nodding.

SMACK-SMACK!

"Oh! *Owie!*"

Again without warning, she brought her palm cracking down twice in rapid-fire succession against the false-teenager's bare bottom, aiming for the spots she'd just been groping and grinning in self-satisfaction at the distinct escalation in yelping that the latter swat had produced.

"Ah yes, I think I see what you mean now."

"I should freaking hope so," growled Rhen darkly, looking up from her pillow and folding her arms beneath her chin as she glared at the worn stitching of the armrest in front of her.

SMACK! SMACK! SMACK!

Three more boulder-heavy smacks found their marks then, causing the bratty girl to flail her legs behind her as she buried her face in her arms and squealed into her throw pillow.

"What was that, *little girl?*" demanded Maureen, leaving her rigid palm poised just above Rhen's bare right cheek as she waited patiently for a response.

"Nothing ma'am," squeaked the younger girl, all of her earlier sass having boiled out of her for the moment thanks to the fresh rush of heat to her face that was giving the warmth in her lower cheeks a run for its money. "I'm sorry!"

"That's better," sniffed Maureen, letting her palm relax again as she began to drum her fingertips against where she'd just swatted. "Now, what was it you were saying before we were so rudely interrupted, Dana?"

"Nice."

Her mentor flashed her a broad, approving grin.

"I think it's pretty safe to say that you're just about ready to go now. The only bit of advice I can still think of to give you is that if sit-spot swatting just isn't doing the trick for you, you can always try smacking the backs of her thighs as well. Now *those* definitely sting something fierce when they get popped, believe you me."

Frowning slightly, she added with a warning forefinger.

"But make sure you're extra-careful with those. A naughty girl's thighs don't have anywhere near the same amount of padding that her caboose does, so you can't go too crazy on them or else you might end up leaving bruises or really hurting her, and that's not what we're aiming for at all, is it? We want tough but fair, not abusive."

"Understood," answered Maureen with a serious nod of her own. "So then, should I get started?"

"No thanks," squeaked Rhen at that, making both women laugh and snapping loose the taut silence that had started to build in the room. "You *really* don't have to, I promise."

Unsurprisingly though, she went completely ignored.

"Go for it," chuckled her partner with a casually dismissive wave of her hand as she took half a step back and positioned herself to get a better angle for the upcoming festivities.

And so she did.

SMACK! SMACK! SMACK!

Eager to prove that she could actually spank a naughty girl properly, Maureen set to her task with a gusto that made Dana proud. In a matter of moments she made it very clear that not only was she a fast learner when it came to the act of disciplining a naughty bottom, but that she also had a natural talent for judging where and how hard to spank a girl for the best possible results once she had her over her lap, and she quickly had Rhen kicking and scissoring her legs behind her.

"Oh my god, I'm sorry, I'm sorry! I'll never lie about being sick again, I *promise*!" the twenty-year-old turned thirteen-year-old brat squealed out around several yelps and gasps of pain.

SMACK! SMACK! SMACK!

But unfortunately for the squirming sophomore, Maureen was just as good as her aunt was when it came to ignoring her pleas for leniency and her vows to be good. And so, Rhen was left with no other choice than to buck and squeal, writhe and yelp, trapped in place across the broad expanse of her new auntie's lap as her bare bottom was set ablaze with no regard for her crying.

SMACK! SMACK! SMACK!

The sternly frowning mother of three was absolutely relentless in the application of her rigid right palm against the naked cheeks trapped across her lap, encouraged ever onward by Dana who stood just off to the side occasionally making a suggestion or comment here and there that kept her technique razor sharp and furiously powerful. With her help, she kept up a steady stream of rapid-fire spanks that soon had the naughty, black-haired girl in her clutches wriggling fruitlessly against the vice-like grip of her left hand as she was reduced to a sobbing mess like the little brat that she'd been behaving like all day

"There will be no more fibbing, and no more sassing your elders. Is that understood, young lady?" she demanded, punctuating her question with two extra-hard swats to the backs of her thighs for good measure.

SMACK-SMACK!

Rhen just sobbed out something incoherent in reply that made both of the adults in the room look at each other and smile fondly.

She was just too cute when she started crying.

Almost as much as she was when she was squirming and kicking her legs like she could somehow swim off of the lap she was trapped across.

SMACK! SMACK! SMACK!

—

For the next ten minutes straight, Maureen focused on nothing but fanning the flames she'd kindled in Rhen's bare, bouncy bottom into a raging inferno as she gradually painted her cheeks dark pink, then strawberry red, and then finally an angry shade of crimson that was hot to the touch and carried with it a noticeable swelling around the younger girl's compact caboose.

At an eventual nod from Dana, she at last began to slow down the pace of her swats, and then stopped altogether, slightly winded but otherwise very pleased with herself and what she'd been able to accomplish.

"Have we learned our lesson, young lady?" she demanded, not unkindly.

"Yes ma'am!" moaned the thoroughly punished girl into her soggy couch cushion in between sobs.

"Good. I'm glad to hear it. I'm going to be holding you to

that, you know."

Again, Rhen just sobbed out a muffled, watery response. "Yes ma'am…"

Then, just like that, all of Maureen's implacable sternness evaporated like dew in the morning sun and she began to gently sooth the poor girl's battered buns with soft rubs and gentle, reassuring caresses along the silky smooth column of her back.

"There, there, honeybunch… That's it, let it all out… We're done now… It's okay, shhh…"

She and Dana let Rhen continue to sniffle and cry into her throw pillow for a few minutes longer, waiting patiently as the younger girl caught her breath and regained her composure at her own pace.

"Wow. If her butt feels anything like my hand does right about now, I'm pretty sure that she's going to be on her very best behavior for at least a week," laughed Maureen, shaking out her aching palm before blowing on it theatrically and smirking.

"Hah," commiserated Dana with a snort of her own. "Yes, I know exactly what you mean. It's not quite a 'this is going to hurt me more than it hurts you' kind of thing, but a prolonged hand spanking definitely takes a toll on your palm, that's for sure."

Both women shared a laugh at that, and Rhen grumbled something sour to herself in an attempt to not snicker right along with them as she continued to pout into her pillow. She managed to keep quiet for the most part however, and instead contented herself with basking in the radiating warmth of her *very* well-spanked bare bottom as it washed over her in waves, making her sleepy.

"Don't worry about it too much though," her auntie

continued to say, clapping the other woman on the shoulder with a broad grin. "You'll build up some more endurance as time goes on, I promise."

"Thank goodness!" laughed Maureen, flexing her fingers and frowning melodramatically. "I think my poor hand might just fall off if I had to spank all three of my girls back-to-back like this."

"It's definitely a concern," agreed Dana, the sparkling mirth in her eyes belying the serious grimace she had painted across her face. "But you can always use something other than your hand to dish out discipline if you need to, you know. There's absolutely nothing wrong with that. In fact, I'd start keeping an eye out for an implement or two to have on hand for just such an occasion if I were you. You can definitely get a lot done with just a hand spanking, but sometimes it's better to not wear out your palm when you could just as easily accomplish the same results, if not better, with far less effort using an implement instead."

"Yes, that does seem rather useful," mused Maureen, idly drumming her fingers across Rhen's swollen right cheek as she mulled over what she'd just been told.

"Personally, I'm a big fan of hairbrushes and wooden spoons for when it comes to *really* driving a lesson home. Rhen even has a special one that we bought for her that's just for spanking her naughty buns that we keep on her nightstand so that it's close by whenever it's needed at bedtime," Dana went on to explain with an eager nod. "And from what I've heard, Melinda has an old leather belt that she's rather fond of using for when she needs to have a more serious talk with our favorite little cutie pie."

"That's definitely one way of putting it," groaned Rhen, unable to resist making the joke and being rewarded with a few light-hearted swats and snickers for her trouble.

"See, what'd I tell you?" laughed Dana. "It's not even been ten minutes since she finished crying, and she's already back to sassing. Some girls are just so incorrigible, I tell you!"

"Awww, I think it's cute," cooed Maureen with another fond pat.

"Oh, no doubt," agreed the pouting girl's partner. "But yes, as I was saying. Look around your house for a bit and see what sticks out to you. I'm sure you'll have no problem whatsoever finding something that you feel comfortable with using. Also, if you're ever not sure about something, you can always give the front of your thigh a couple of test swats. That, or rope one of your daughters into a quick attitude adjustment with it… just call it maintenance."

Dana winked at that.

"Oooh, very clever," replied Maureen, nodding eagerly.

"You'll find that I'm full of all sorts of fun and interesting ideas for when it comes to keeping naughty girls in line," snickered Dana with a self-deprecating shrug. "And of course, you already have my number, so feel free to call or text if you need any advice. Alright?"

"Thanks Dana, I really appreciate that a lot."

"Of course! I'm always happy to help out a fellow spanker. Now then, I think our little cutie pie has had enough time to let her buns cool off. So are you ready to learn about corner time?"

"Oh yes, *absolutely*," answered Maureen, clearly having caught her second wind.

"Great. Then help her back up to her feet, and follow me."

—

Twenty minutes later found Rhen with her still somewhat sniffly nose jammed into a dusty corner next to her grandma's equally dusty TV, with her hands on top of her head and her pajama bottoms and pull-up long since abandoned on the arm of the couch behind her.

Although her bottom still throbbed and ached with a lingering heat that she knew would be keeping her warm as she fell asleep later that night, she'd long since gotten over her earlier crying. And despite the humiliation she'd just been forced to endure, she bore neither Maureen nor her auntie any ill will.

She'd been a naughty girl after all, and she'd fully deserved everything that she'd gotten from the two of them, and then some.

When her Auntie Maureen's phone at last started to beep insistently, signaling the end of her stint in timeout, Rhen felt herself sag with relief as she loosed a grateful sigh.

Thank god! It's finally over...

At that particular moment, the sore sophomore was fairly certain that she'd have gladly taken a second spanking from her aunt right there and then if it meant that she'd no longer have to put up with the interminable boredom that came with standing in the corner.

"And that's twenty minutes right on the dot," declared Maureen, silencing her smartphone and climbing back to her feet from off the couch.

Slipping it back into her front pocket, she then padded her way over to where Rhen was continuing to remain obediently in place facing the wall.

She'd long since learned the lesson that it was best to just stay right where you were when you were doing corner time until you were given explicit permission to move, lest you get another spanking for your trouble.

"Okeydokey, honeybunch, you can come out now," cooed

the woman looming behind her, punctuating her permission with a friendly pat to her naked caboose. "All is forgiven."

Thoroughly chastened and in dire need of a reassuring cuddle just then, Rhen peeled herself away from the corner she'd been sniffling into for the better part of the last half hour and let herself be wrapped up in Maureen's warm embrace.

Although the older woman's scent was different from that of her partner's, made up of a strange blend of different perfumes and soaps than those she was used to, Rhen found that the warmth of her soft breasts and the steady rhythm of her heartbeat were more than familiar enough for her to get lost in as her newly-declared Auntie Maureen gently caressed the back of her hair and murmured softly against the top of her head.

"There, there, little one… Shhh… I've got you."

After what felt like a very long time, but was in reality only a couple of minutes, Rhen at last pulled away from the embrace and smiled.

"So, uh… I'm sorry I was being bad earlier, but um… can I *please* get dressed now?" she begged, her gaze turning to fix longingly on her pajama bottoms, and yes, even her pull-up.

"Well, of course you can, cutie pie. Come on over here and I'll get you sorted out in a jiffy," agreed Dana, beckoning her over as she scooted to the far end of the couch and snatched up her girlfriend's discarded clothes.

"Thank you!" breathed the younger girl, sighing in exasperated relief as she skipped over to her aunt and endured the comparatively minor humiliation of having her re-dress her like the small child she so often acted like.

"You took your spanking very well, dear," praised Dana as she finished retying the drawstring around Rhen's pajama bottoms.

She then reached up and tucked back a loose strand of inky black hair behind her left ear.

"Are you ready for bed?"

"What? But Aunt Dana, it's not even ten yet!" her not-niece protested, just barely managing to stop herself from stomping a foot. "Can't I *please* stay up for a little bit longer since we're on vacation?"

"You've had a long day and have been more than a little bratty tonight, missy," countered her aunt firmly. "Going to bed early with a ruby red rump seems like a pretty fitting way to cap things off and remind you to behave yourself tomorrow, wouldn't you say?"

"I guess so," grumbled Rhen, arms folded sullenly across her chest as her cheeks puffed out with a mighty pout. "I think I've learned my lesson enough already, though…"

"Yes, clearly," observed Maureen with a dry smirk.

"Uh-oh, it's a grumpy goose!" teased Dana, grinning impishly. "Quick! Someone call the tickle monster!"

She then proceeded to smother her naughty niece's impending tantrum with a thorough assault on her sensitive sides and armpits with her wriggling fingers that quickly had the younger girl squirming and dancing and forgetting all about her earlier annoyance about being sent to bed early.

"No! Stop, stop!" she squealed, only half-meaning it as she writhed and giggled.

Eventually Dana relented, just when she knew that the younger girl was on the verge of wetting herself, pulling her hands back and letting her catch her breath.

"Okay, fine. I'll tell you what," she offered with her hands still planted firmly on either side of Rhen's hips, drinking in the warmth radiating out from beneath her pajama bottoms with her fingertips. "If you go brush your teeth right now and *promise* me that I'll find you under the covers with your eyes shut and doing your best to fall asleep when I come to check on you at eleven, I'll wave the early bedtime. Deal?"

"Deal!" agreed Rhen immediately, beaming brightly from ear to ear.

Then, eager to make the most of the limited amount of time she'd just been allotted, she stepped in close and threw her arms around her auntie in a quick hug, before pulling back just far enough to plant a kiss on her lips. She then rounded on Maureen, pouncing on her and repeating the entire procedure, though with a kiss on her cheek this time, much to the amusement of the two older women.

With that taken care of, Rhen shot out of the room like a rocket, her feet stomping loudly on the staircase as she fled up to the bedroom she was sharing with her partner and the laptop that she'd been dreaming about all evening. However, before she'd gotten much more than halfway up the steps, she scurried back down, and leaning around the banister called out.

"Goodnight Aunt Dana. Goodnight Aunt Maureen. I love you both!"

"Night-night, honeybunch."

"Love you too, cutie pie."

In the end Rhen supposed that it had indeed been a pretty good day after all.

Chapter 25

Christmas Fun and Battered Buns

The rest of the fall semester, what little of it there was left after the Thanksgiving break was over, passed by uneventfully for Rhen. Aside from the new and profoundly humiliating addition of having to change into a pull-up every night before bed, life went back to being much the same as it always was for her and her bossy boots Auntie Dana, and the next few weeks flew by in a blur. The temperature continued to plummet as the days grew shorter, and trudging through blankets of fluffy white snow soon became the norm. Finals week came and went, with Rhen passing all of her classes with flying colors due in no small part to Courtney's and her aunt's relentless application of bare bottom encouragement whenever they caught her starting to slack off, and before she knew it, Christmas was right around the corner.

—

DING-DONG!

"Rhen, honey, could you get that for me?"

"Sure thing, Aunt Dana," called the twenty-year-old turned teenager from inside her bedroom.

Pushing away from her laptop and the idle web browsing she'd been occupying herself with for the last couple of hours, she sprang to her feet and scrambled out of her bedroom. Taking the stairs two at a time, she came skidding to a stop a few inches away from the front door (her socks sliding her along the last few feet of the journey) just as whoever it was on the other side rang the bell again.

DING-DONG!

And again.

DING-DONG!

And again.

DING-DONG! DING-DONG! DING-DONG!

"Okay, geez, hold your horses! I'm coming, I'm coming…" she chided the unseen visitor without any real annoyance in her voice, running a quick hand over her hair a couple of times before turning the lock and throwing the door open.

"Oh hey, guys. What're you doing here?" she asked by way of greeting, grinning at the unexpected surprise of finding her two best friends standing hand-in-hand on her doorstep. "I thought you were going upstate to visit Abby's family for the holidays?"

"Oh, we're still doing that," answered Abby with an unconcerned shrug, before beaming giddily. "We're flying out tomorrow, as a matter of fact. But *today* we're… your… babysitters!"

As she said it, she threw her hands into the air and let out a very excited "Whoo!"

"My what?" demanded Rhen, taken aback. "Why the heck would I need a freaking babysitter?"

"Tsk, tsk. Such language," chided Courtney with a playful smirk. "Careful there, bratty buns, or else you might just end up over someone's lap for that kind of potty talk."

"Yeah, Rhenny," chimed in Abby with a wicked grin of her own. "Watch your fucking mouth."

SMACK!

"Oh!"

"That goes for you too, hot stuff," admonished Courtney

with a wink, leaving her hand right where it had landed on her girlfriend's backside. "You're supposed to be setting a good example for her, remember?"

"Oh yeah," giggled Abby, clearly not bothered in the least as she wagged a finger at the petite girl in front of her. "Do as I say, not as I do, missy."

"Psh, whatever," huffed Rhen, trying (and failing spectacularly) to affect a sense of nonchalance as she suddenly straightened up where she stood and ran a hand down the back of her skirt, smoothing it out across her backside with a shiver.

It hadn't been *that* long since the last time she'd been put across Courtney's knee, after all.

"Hey now, I'm not paying to heat up the whole neighborhood, you know," chided Dana, seeming to materialize from out of nowhere then as she clapped an affectionate hand on Rhen's shoulder, making her jump.

Much to the amusement of the two coed lovers still standing on their doorstep.

"Stop blocking the door and let your friends in already, cutie pie."

Steering the younger girl aside and ignoring the mounting series of protests that she knew were brewing just beneath the surface of her indignant pout, she waved the others inside.

"Thanks for coming on such short notice, you two. Now get in here before you freeze to death out there."

"Yes ma'am!"

"With pleasure."

Graciously accepting the older woman's offer, Courtney and Abby quickly set about stomping off the last bits of snow still clinging to the soles of their boots and then made their way into the invitingly warm two-story house.

"Thank you for having us, Missus Johnson," spoke up Courtney as she breezed past Rhen, breathing into her cupped hands and rubbing them together.

"Yeah, we're totally happy to watch Rhen whenever you need us to," added Abby with a broad grin.

"Oh, that's such a relief to hear," sighed Dana, hand to her chest. "You girls have *no* idea how hard it is to find a good sitter at the last minute."

"I'm glad we could help you out then," replied Courtney with a fervent nod.

"But... but..." Rhen continued to splutter oh so eloquently, refusing to accept the reality of her situation as she watched her friends shrug off their winter coats and hang them up on hooks by the front door. "But why are they *here?*"

"Because I invited them over, of course," answered her partner with a shrug as if to say it were obvious. "I needed someone to keep an eye on you while I went Christmas shopping this afternoon, and they were the first to come to mind."

Courtney and her girlfriend each flashed the dumbfounded sophomore an identical grin at that.

"That's right," sing-songed her (now former) TA.

"Oh, we are going to have *so* much fun today!" cooed Abby.

"Hooray..." deadpanned Rhen, crossing her arms in front of her and rolling her eyes. "Lucky me."

—

Despite her vehement protests that she didn't *need* a babysitter, let alone two of them, and her insistence that she was fully capable of staying home alone without accidentally burning the place down in the process, Rhen soon decided to just let the matter drop entirely. While it was definitely embarrassing to have the unexpected time she got to spend hanging out with her two best friends labeled as a "babysitting playdate" by her auntie, she was honestly happy for their company that afternoon and managed to get over her initial indignation surprisingly quickly once it was just the three of them.

Plus the offhanded way Courtney just pushed her over the arm of the couch in the front room, flipped up the back of her skirt, and then proceeded to lay into her with two dozen hard swats to the seat of her panties after Dana had driven away had a remarkable way of getting the sassy sophomore to change her tune in a hurry.

"Are Abby and I going to be getting any more attitude from you while we're here, young lady?" she demanded, one hand pinning Rhen in place with her feet suspended several inches off the floor while the other began tugging on the waistband of her panties.

"No ma'am! I'm sorry, ma'am! I'll be good, ma'am!" promised the TA's petite "little sister" in a hurried jumble, scissoring her feet frantically back and forth behind her in a desperate attempt to convey just how serious she was in her convictions to behave herself.

"Hmmm... I don't know, Court," purred Abby, standing just beside her girlfriend and watching the exchange between the two of them with a hungry grin. "I personally think that maybe you ought to confiscate her skirt and panties just to be absolutely *sure* that she'll be on her best behavior today."

"Wait, what?"

"You know, that's not a bad idea," agreed Courtney, tugging her captive's panties down another inch or two.

"Oh come on, that is *so* not fair," whined Rhen, face flushing far warmer than her bottom felt right then. "I haven't even done anything yet!"

"Well, you *were* just sassing us a minute ago," pointed out Abby helpfully.

"Humph," she groused in reply with a flip of her hair. "That hardly counts as anything and you know it."

"Is that so?" crooned Courtney, drumming her fingertips along the divot just above her charge's semi-bared cheeks as her grip tightened on her waistband.

"Um, yes?" supplied Rhen hopefully, toes curling and uncurling nervously behind her.

"Hmmm…"

Courtney pretended to give the matter some serious consideration for several more embarrassing moments, before finally easing the pressure on Rhen's lower back and tugging the waistband of her panties back up to its proper place just above her hips.

"You're skating on some very thin ice, you know, kiddo," she admonished, offsetting the lecturing tone in her voice with a gentle tickle along one pale, silky smooth inner thigh before affectionately patting the rainbow polka dots stretched taut across Rhen's rounded cheeks. "But, I'll tell you what. If you promise me that you won't be a Whiney Wanda while we're making gingerbread cookies today, then I'll let you keep these on. Deal?"

"Deal!" exclaimed Rhen, ready to promise just about anything right then, before perking up as the rest of Courtney's words caught up with her.

"Wait a minute… did you just say *gingerbread* cookies?" she pressed, forgetting for the moment to sound petulant as she broke away from her inspection of the couch cushions in front of her to eye her two best friends quizzically.

"That's right!" confirmed Abby, shrugging off her back-pack and holding it out in front of her triumphantly. "We stopped by the store on our way over here and got everything we need to make them from scratch."

She then fixed a dubious look of concern on her face and added worriedly.

"And boy oh boy, it sure would be such a shame if we didn't get a chance to make them just because someone was being a little brat and had to spend all afternoon standing in the corner with an exceptionally well-spanked, albeit cute, bare bottom. Wouldn't it?"

"Okay, okay, I get your point," conceded Rhen with a good-natured harrumph. "You win. I'll be good. Now can we *please* make some cookies? That sounds super awesome right about now."

SMACK!

"Hell yeah we can!" exclaimed Courtney with one final, hefty swat dead center between the younger girl's cheeks before helping her back to her feet. "You just go ahead and drop that skirt and we'll get right to it."

"What?" squeaked Rhen in outrage, hands flying back to cup her cheeks protectively. "But you said-"

"I *said* that you could keep your *panties* on," interrupted Courtney with a sly grin. "I never said anything about your skirt, did I?"

"I…" Rhen began to protest again, before rolling her eyes and sighing in exasperation. "Ugh. Okay. I guess not. But I want you to know that that's a dumb technicality and I'm going to be lodging a formal complaint with the Babysitters Union once we're through here today."

"Tough luck, kiddo," countered Courtney, folding her arms beneath her firm breasts and fixing her little sister in place with a predatory grin that made her stomach flutter pleasantly. "They're off for the holidays, I'm afraid. Now lose that skirt before I decide to have Abby do it for you."

"Hehe," giggled the other girl, making over exaggerated grabby-grabby motions with her hands as she took a step forward. "I'd be more than happy to help you with that if you'd like me to, cutie."

"No thanks, I've got it!" the youngest among them hastened to assure her two smirking babysitters, proving her point by yanking down the zipper hidden along the side of her hip in a flash and letting her black, pleated skirt drop to the floor around her in a crumpled heap. "See?"

Abandoning the garment where it had just fallen in front of the couch, Rhen made an immediate beeline toward the kitchen before either of her friends could change their minds about confiscating her panties too, calling over her shoulder as she went.

"Dibs on licking the spoons!"

"Hah! Yeah right, pipsqueak!" shouted Abby, chasing after her.

Rolling her eyes and sighing in false-exasperation, Courtney stooped down to pick up the backpack that her girlfriend had completely forgotten to bring with her and followed after her two friends at an easy pace.

"Oh yeah, this is going to be *so* much fun."

—

The next couple of hours proved to be a chaotically fun mix of impromptu food fights, singing along to cheesy Christmas music at the top of their lungs, eating lots of very tasty raw cookie dough, and occasionally even actually baking something. Luckily enough for the three of them, Courtney happened to be a seasoned veteran when it came to crafting baked goods, and so despite Rhen and Abby's best attempts to derail her efforts by eating all of their yummy materials before they could actually go into the oven, in the end they came away with three cookie sheets worth of adorable little gingerbread men and women.

"Awww, they're so cute," cooed Abby, hovering over the latest batch to be pulled from the oven.

"And they smell *delicious*," added Rhen, practically drooling.

"Back! Back I say!" cried Courtney, playfully snapping a dish towel at her two friends before picking up a rubber spatula and beginning to scoop their fresh-from-the-oven confections out onto a set of wire cooling racks they'd found stashed away in one of the cabinets.

"Ahhh, you're no fun."

"Spoil sport."

"And you two are a couple of brats," retorted the oldest of the three of them with a mock-growl, turning her spatula on each of their rumps for a couple of token swats.

SLAP-SLAP! SLAP-SLAP!

"Eep!"

"Rude!"

Setting her impromptu paddle aside, Courtney then popped one of their more malformed cookies into her mouth with a smirk.

"Hey!" protested Abby and Rhen simultaneously.

"Deal with it," snickered the TA, sticking out her tongue.

"Oh, I will," promised Abby with a wink, shoving her hands into the pockets of her apron with a harrumph that made Rhen proud. "I know where you sleep, babe."

Deciding to follow the other girl's example, even though she had no real plans to do anything other than pout, Rhen crossed her arms in front of her petite chest and glared petulantly. It *felt* like a good glower as far as she could tell, but unfortunately the effectiveness of it was diminished somewhat by her being stuck in just a pair of panties and a t-shirt.

Even so, it still at least managed to make Courtney laugh.

"Meanie."

"Cutie."

"Humph!"

After spending a few more minutes idly chatting among themselves while they waited for their cookies to firm up enough to be handled without falling apart, it was unanimously decided by the three college coeds to forego decorating them in favor of just dipping them in the cream cheese icing they'd been chilling in the refrigerator. And so, after piling a plate up high with their creations, and then pouring out three extra-tall glasses of milk to go with them, they retreated up to Rhen's bedroom to hang out while they stuffed their faces with gingerbread people and ate the various bits of candy that had originally been intended to serve as their clothing.

It was definitely the right call they all agreed after they'd finished demolishing most of their plate of cookies, and with contented sighs, they each found somewhere comfy to settle down in while they let their inevitable food coma run its course.

You know what? mused Rhen to herself with a half-suppressed yawn as she settled back in front of her laptop and pulled up her Twitter feed. *Being babysat really isn't so bad, after all...*

—

None of the college coeds paid much attention when they eventually heard the front door open and close downstairs sometime later that afternoon, although Rhen did at least bother to call out a perfunctory hello to her partner before resuming her game while her friends watched on lazily from their spot cuddled up on her bed.

All three of them jerked upright and took notice however, when less than a minute later they heard Dana Johnson's voice thundering for them from the foot of the stairs.

"Rhen Elizabeth Mathews, you and your friends had better get your butts down here this instant, little girl!"

"Yes ma'am!" squeaked her niece, all but leaping out of her chair and scrambling for the stairs without pausing to see if her babysitters were actually following after her or not. "I'm coming!"

"Uh-oh..." drawled Courtney, stretching out her arms over her head before pushing off of Rhen's surprisingly comfortable mattress and climbing back to her feet. "Better go see what that's all about."

She winked and then held out a hand to help Abby up after her.

"Yeah," snickered the slightly shorter girl, shaking out her loose blonde curls and following after her girlfriend as she led the way out of their friend's bedroom. "I wonder what could have *possibly* put her into such a crabby mood..."

"Only one way to find out," purred Courtney with a wry smirk, planting a quick kiss on the other girl's equally amused lips. "This is going to be fun."

"Totally."

—

To neither girl's surprise, they quickly found Rhen and her aunt waiting for them in the kitchen.

"Hey there, Missus Johnson," chirped Courtney, waving as she and Abby stepped into the room and only faltering for the briefest of moments at the annoyed look she got in return from the older woman. "What's up?"

"Hello dear," answered Dana in a clipped tone of voice that still somehow managed to sound warm and inviting despite the scowl that had drawn her lips into a thin line of stern disapproval. "I was just asking Rhen here to explain to me why it was that I came home to find my kitchen in a total state of disarray."

"It's not *that* bad-" the younger girl tried to protest, before being cut off by a sharply upraised hand from her auntie while she kept her eyes focused on her two ostensible babysitters.

"You hush your mouth, little girl. The *adults* are trying to have a conversation here."

It took a supreme effort of will just then for Courtney not to smirk, even more so when she caught the glint of amusement in her employer's dark eyes. Forcing herself to keep her face a neutral mask of puzzled concern, she took in a slow breath through her nostrils and then made a show of casting an appraising eye around the kitchen.

Pretty much every available spot of the once pristine countertops was now covered in a dusting of flour and brown sugar, half-empty bags of candies and other ingredients had been left lying about all over the place, and there were multiple mixing bowls, whisks, and wooden spoons with thick dollops of icing or sticky batter clinging to their sides strewn about willy-nilly.

In short, it was a mess.

A *big* mess.

Shrugging apologetically, Courtney flashed the frowning older woman a sheepish grin.

"I'm sorry, Missus Johnson. We uh... kind of got distracted after we finished baking the cookies, you see, and it just sort of slipped our minds to clean up, I guess."

"Is that right?" asked Dana skeptically, hands planted firmly on her hips as she narrowed her eyes at the two coed lovers fighting down grins behind her worried looking niece.

"Yes ma'am," confirmed Abby, doing a mostly passable job of sounding contrite beside her girlfriend. "Just completely slipped our minds. Poof."

She blew out a breath and wiggled her fingers in front of her face for added emphasis then.

"We'd be happy to clean it up now if you want," finished Courtney, taking a tentative half-step forward and making as if to pick up a discarded mixing bowl.

"Oh, you most certainly *will* be cleaning all of this up," agreed Dana with a haughty sniff, catching on to the little game that her girlfriend's friends were playing and feeling her lips twitch up into a sly smirk of her own that she did her best to keep angled away from Rhen. "But not until *after* all three of you have taken your spankings for leaving this place in such a mess to begin with."

"What?" demanded the petite sophomore then, ignoring for the moment that she was still in just a t-shirt and an adorable pair of polka-dot panties as she rounded on her aunt and stomped her foot indignantly. "Aunt Dana, no. Come on! You can't spank us for this. We just forgot to clean up a little bit, is all. It's not a big deal. We'll do it right now, I promise!"

"*Excuse* me, little girl?" replied Dana in a low, dangerous purr, dipping her chin down to regard her with one imperiously quirked eyebrow. "This is far more than just a 'little mess', and I think it's pretty safe to say that you know by now that I'm more than capable of spanking a naughty girl's bottom, let alone three of them at the same time."

"But... Like... Well, okay... *yeah*, I guess so. But, I

mean…" fumbled Rhen, much of her earlier petulance having withered away under the force of her auntie's hard stare as she grasped desperately for any viable defense she could think of, before giving up and smiling feebly. "I was, uh… hoping you wouldn't?"

"Hah," snorted Abby at that, earning a disapproving side-long glance from Rhen's partner and a surreptitious elbow to the ribs from Courtney.

"Well, that's just too bad. Now isn't it, missy?" answered Dana with a roll of her eyes and a shake of her head to cover up her own smile. "Because it's going to happen whether you like it or not, I'm afraid."

Deciding that it would probably be best to keep control of the initiative and not let her girlfriend have another chance to rally a defense, she jabbed a finger out to the side and snapped.

"Clear some room on the island there, and then all three of you bend over. *Now*."

"Yes ma'am!" came the three naughty girl's immediate replies in unison as they scrambled to do as they were told, pushing aside cooling racks and cookie sheets as they hurried to line up side-by-side facing the wide edge of the island in the center of the kitchen.

Taking a moment or two to eye the three rounded rumps being presented to her, Dana felt her face break out into a wide grin as she watched their respective owners clear off a spot on the granite countertop in front of them.

"Tsk, tsk, tsk…" she clucked, "What on earth am I going to do with you three?"

"Spank us, probably," guessed Courtney.

"Seems likely," agreed Abby.

"Oh, very clever," conceded the older woman with a snort,

before adding with a touch of steel in her voice. "Now bend over."

Whether it was on purpose or not, it was hard to tell for sure, Dana couldn't help but notice that Courtney and Abby just so happened to have positioned themselves to either side of her niece, effectively trapping her in place between the two of them and ensuring that she was forced to follow their lead as they leaned forward and settled down onto their elbows on the island in front of them without any protest.

"You know, cleaning up after yourselves really isn't that hard, girls," she started to lecture, casually bracing her hands on her hips and taking her time to savor every moment of her pre-spanking scolding. "I don't mind that you used the kitchen while I was gone, or even that you made a mess. In fact, from the nibble or two I had before calling you down, I have to say that you did an *excellent* job on your cookies. But that's still no excuse for your lack of follow through. Honestly, I just cannot believe that you three would be so, so…"

She paused for a moment then, fishing around for the right word that would convey her annoyance while also making it clear that she wasn't actually all that upset with any of them.

"So *neglectful*."

"Sorry ma'am."

"Sorry Aunt Dana."

"Uh, yeah… sorry."

Chorused the three girls from their humbling position with their backs arched and their bottoms pushed out to await their punishment, each putting their own special spin on their apology and knowing full well that it was far too late for mere words to save their rumps now.

"Uh-huh…" replied Dana, not exactly sounding convinced.

Stepping up behind Courtney, drawing in close enough to

feel the warmth radiating off of the older girl's firmly toned body, she leaned over her and let her hands snake around to the front of her hips, deftly undoing the button clasp on her tight, denim blue jeans. She then took half a step back, and with deliberate slowness, wriggled them down to her knees.

"I especially expected better from *you*, Courtney, dear," she chided lightly, giving the mostly bare cheeks exposed by the girl's skimpy thong underwear a friendly pat that helped to dull the stern disapproval permeating her voice. "You're the oldest, after all. You really should be setting a better example for these two."

"You're right, ma'am, I'm sorry," replied Courtney dutifully, looking over her shoulder and smirking at Rhen's aunt as she gave her hips a saucy wiggle.

Dana smirked right on back at her and pinched her left sit-spot.

"Oh, you will be by the time I'm through with you, young lady. Trust me."

She then winked and sent the TA's panties down to join her jeans around her knees.

"Yes ma'am…" sighed the now bare bottomed girl, propping her chin onto her hands and smiling dreamily before remembering that she was supposed to be pouting.

Moving over to Rhen next, Dana smirked as she felt her jump as she lightly traced her fingertips over the seat of her panties. But other than a quick tickle along her sit-spots to get her squirming, she skipped over her entirely as she set her sights on Abby instead.

"The same goes for you too, young lady," she scolded, repeating the process of lowering the blonde girl's jeans down to her knees, along with her slightly more modest panties. "You were supposed to be keeping an eye on Rhen, not letting her run riot all over you."

Her lecturing was met with another saucy hip wiggle, and a mostly sincere sounding.

"Yes ma'am. I'm sorry ma'am."

"Humph. We'll just see about that."

The curvy blonde sophomore did a mostly good job of suppressing a nervous giggle at hearing that.

"And as for *you*, little girl," Dana growled next, at last turning her full attention on her niece and taking hold of the waistband of her panties on either side of her hips. "You know better than to leave the kitchen looking like this after you're done cooking. Don't you?"

"Yes Aunt Dana," answered the younger girl quickly, stomach roiling with the all too familiar contradictorily wonderful-awful sensation of anxious anticipation as she shifted her weight from foot to foot, nervously chewing on her lower lip.

"Eep!"

Despite being well-used to the sensation by now, she still couldn't help but let out a mortified little squeak as she felt her panties suddenly being yanked down off of her hips, making the descent to her ankles without any resistance.

"Gosh dang it! Why didn't it we just clean up?" she grumbled under her breath, mortified beyond belief.

"Sorry hon," murmured Abby, flashing her adoptive little sister an encouraging half-smirk as she reached out and clasped her right hand in her own.

"Try not to sweat it, kiddo," added Courtney just as softly, taking up her other hand and giving it a reassuring squeeze. "It's just a little spanking. You'll be fine."

"I guess so..." mumbled Rhen, her initial embarrassment gradually giving way to chagrinned acceptance as her cheeks flushed hot pink. "This still sucks though."

"Oh yeah, *totally*," agreed Abby, not quite managing to sound as sincere as she had just a moment ago.

"You'll live," snickered Courtney with a roll of her eyes.

Dana left the three of them to their quiet chatting as she set about in search of a wooden spoon to use on them. But, much to her annoyance, she soon discovered that *somehow* Abby, Courtney, and Rhen had managed to use every single one of them over the course of baking their delicious gingerbread cookies.

"Hmmm…" she mused aloud as she contemplated the seemingly carefully orchestrated mess in her kitchen.

Fixing Courtney and then her girlfriend each with a suspicious glare, she made a show of scooping out the heaviest wooden spoon in her arsenal from an abandoned mixing bowl that had been hidden just a little too well out of sight to be a coincidence, and then took it over to the sink and began washing it off.

"Today is your lucky day, ladies… and Rhen."

The two older coeds couldn't help but snicker at that, even more so when they caught sight of the sour grimace it evoked from their adorable little sister.

"Why's that, ma'am?" questioned Courtney, the very picture of polite curiosity.

"Oh yes, do tell," cooed her girlfriend innocently, idly waggling her bare hips from side to side.

"Well, that's because you're all about to find out just how much more than normal a spanking from a wet wooden spoon stings on a naughty bare bottom."

"Oh joy of joys…" droned Rhen dryly, while her two best friends just giggled to either side of her.

"Fair enough, ma'am," conceded Courtney.

"I guess you could call it poetic justice for us making a

mess," her girlfriend shrugged. "Makes sense to me."

"Couple of freaking goodie-goodies," grumbled the middle brat under her breath, making both of her friends giggle all the more.

"Yes, indeed they *are* 'goody-goodies'," snapped Dana, rounding on the three of them and making each girl jump as she fixed her niece in place with a hard stare. "And I for one think that you could stand to follow their example just a little bit better, missy."

Despite the mostly-concealed twitch of her partner's lips, the fiery look in her eyes still had Rhen's cheeks clenching on reflex and an electric thrill tracing itself along her undeniably moist folds.

Oh god, how can she do that with just a look?

Forcing herself to swallow hard, she straightened up on her elbows and nodded for all she was worth.

"Yes ma'am!"

"Good."

Looking down on her naughty charges with grimly amused self-satisfaction, Dana rapped the head of her damp wooden spoon against her palm and then began to slowly advance on the three bare bottomed girls, moving with the languid ease of a predator descending upon captive prey.

"Now then, I think we'll start things off with you, Court-ney," she declared in a cool, matter-of-fact voice, menacingly tap, tap, tapping her spoon against the leftmost girl's leftmost cheek.

"If you say so," answered back the TA with just a bit more flippancy than Dana was hoping to hear.

THWAP-THWAP! THWAP-THWAP!

"Pardon me, young lady?" pressed Dana just as noncha-lantly as before after she'd finished painting four vivid pink ovals across the sassy girl's firm cheeks.

"Um, n-nothing, ma'am," hissed Courtney through clenched teeth, flexing her rump and bouncing on her heels as she struggled to ride out the near-overwhelming stinging sensation that Rhen's aunt had just brought to bear against her bare bottom.

"Ah, then I must have just misheard you," replied the older woman with a friendly rub of each scalded cheek before taking one step over to the side and lightly tapping her spoon against her niece's backside next. "And how about you? Do *you* have anything to say for yourself, Rhen, dear?"

"No, Aunt Dana," the youngest of the three bratty coeds hastened to assure her.

THWAP-THWAP! THWAP-THWAP!

"Ah! Owie!"

"You don't say?"

Finally, Dana turned her sights on Abby, repeating the same tap, tap, tapping movements as before.

"I don't have anything to say for myself other than 'I'm sorry', ma'am," the curly blonde sing-songed before Dana could even ask.

THWAP-THWAP! THWAP-THWAP!

"Good girl."

Taking two steps back, she spent a few very enjoyable moments surveying the results of her efforts so far, admiring the three unique, and equally adorable in their own special ways, sets of bare cheeks arrayed before her.

"Are we starting to learn our lesson, girls?"

"Kinda…"

"Definitely!"

"I guess so…"

Dana smirked at the three responses she got to her question and silently resolved to get all three of the naughty girls she was disciplining to start singing the same remorseful tune by the time she was through with them.

"Good. Then in that case, I shouldn't hear any complaining from the three of you while we continue on with the rest of your punishment."

Although she couldn't see their faces, Dana was still fairly certain that her remarks had just been met with three near-identical eye-rolls.

"Alright now, from the top…"

Stepping up beside Courtney again, laying a steadying hand along the small of the taller girl's back, Dana began beating out a rhythm against the TA's well-toned cheeks with a half-dozen vicious swats.

THWAP-THWAP! THWAP-THWAP! THWAP-THWAP!

"Oof!" groaned Courtney in response, hands balling themselves into tight fists throughout the course of her punishment, before relaxing as she let out a long, slow breath and chuckled. "I think I'm starting to see now what you meant about the whole wet wooden spoon hurting more thing, ma'am."

"I thought you might be a fast learner, Courtney, dear," crooned Dana, giving the girl's once again relaxed cheeks a couple of light pats as she stepped to the side. "Now let's just see if Rhen can spot the difference."

THWAP-THWAP! THWAP-THWAP! THWAP-THWAP!

"Oh my gosh, oh my gosh, *ow*!" yelped the petite sophomore, her loosely pulled back hair whipping about to and fro as she danced in place against the countertop.

"Well?" prompted her auntie with just the hint of a smirk.

Rhen, who liked to think of herself as something of an expert when it came to wooden spoon spankings by now, couldn't help but agree that her partner had been onto something. There was undoubtedly something about the heavy spoon's slick, wet surface impacting against her unprotected and jiggly rump that made it sting that much more than usual. And on top of that, the additional (albeit probably minor) weight added to the head of the spoon thanks to the water that had been absorbed into its wood fibers made sure that each swat packed one heck of an extra punch.

Basically, it *sucked*.

"I'm waiting, little girl..."

Tap. Tap. Tap.

Going beet red in the face, Rhen let out a mortified groan, bouncing her hips in annoyance before finally grumbling.

"Yes, okay? It *does* hurt more. You were right."

About a million times more as a matter of fact, she added to herself silently.

"Ahhh, how gratifying," sighed Dana. "There's nothing quite like having your hypothesis being born out in real world testing. But then again... we really ought to see what Miss Abby here has to say on the subject before we start drawing any major conclusions. After all, the best studies *are* peer reviewed."

"Don't I know it," snickered Courtney, who'd been compiling research data for her faculty advisor for what felt like the better part of the last two years.

Slipping in beside the buxom blonde on Rhen's right, Dana wasted little time in getting to work setting her cheeks to dancing with her wooden spoon.

THWAP-THWAP! THWAP-THWAP! THWAP-THWAP!

Abby did a remarkable job of managing to stay stoic for the first half of her swats, but by the time the last of them had found their mark, she was crying out with each one's impact just as Rhen had.

That didn't stop her from giggling and managing to say coyly after she'd caught her breath.

"I don't know, Missus Johnson... It's hard to say for sure one way or the other. I think maybe you should give Courtney and Rhen some more data points to work with while I compile my own findings."

"Cute."

Dana punctuated her remark with two lightning-fast, sharp cracks of her spoon against the backs of the snickering sophomore's creamy thighs.

THWAP! THWAP!

Now that definitely got her attention.

"Oh! Ow!"

"I'll leave you to edit your abstract then, young lady."

"Yes ma'am," harrumphed Abby, only sounding slightly put out as she surreptitiously reached back to sooth her scalded thighs.

"And no rubbing," added Dana sharply, not even bothering to look behind her as she moved back down the line of bratty bottoms.

"Sorry, sorry!" squeaked the blonde girl, snatching her hand back before it had had a chance to travel more than a few inches.

"Hmmm... Now where were we?"

Setting her sights back on Courtney and her caramel colored cheeks, Rhen's partner closed in on her. After giving each bun an exploratory squeeze and deciding that she was still getting far too much sass from the three bare bottomed brats who were supposedly very contrite and resolved to be good, she took a firm grip around the long handle of her wooden spoon and set about lighting into the athletic girl with two dozen sizzling smacks in the span of about thirty seconds.

THWAP! THWAP! THWAP! THWAP! THWAP! THWAP!

"Holy crap!"

This time her efforts were met with a *lot* more hip wiggling and barely restrained yelping. She even got an (admittedly, rather flimsy) promise to be good after the girl had managed to catch her breath.

"Yikes! Alright… Okay…. I'm sorry!"

"Better."

Grinning smugly, Dana gave the now significantly warmer cheeks another pair of firm squeezes.

"You know, I think we're finally starting to get somewhere."

"Oh god…"

Letting out another groan, Rhen huffed and then rolled her eyes as she forced herself to relax her own nervously clenched rear end in preparation for her upcoming turn with the spoon.

"This is so freaking humiliating."

"Oh, it's not so bad," dismissed Abby with an airy wave, giggling again as her little sister began to squeak and yelp as Dana tore into her vulnerable rump with another two dozen merciless swats.

"Yeah, well… Let's just see how much you like it," countered Rhen with a put-upon harrumph after she'd finished panting and moaning, turning to stick her tongue out at her former roommate while her aunt took up position beside her.

Abby stuck her tongue right back out at the provocation, and then proceeded to yelp and squeal just as much as her friend had as the older woman behind her proceeded to lay into her own naked nates with righteous fury.

"Ah! Oh! Ow, ow, ow, *owie*! Oh my fu- I mean *freaking* god, I'm really sorry ma'am! I'm sorry!"

"Ahhh, music to my ears," cooed Dana, smiling broadly and tracing lazy circles with the head of her spoon around Abby's still squirming backside. "Now let's just see if we can't get a proper chorus going, shall we?"

This time she was met with three identical groans as three heads of hair dipped down at the same time in exasperation and more than a little worry.

"Yes ma'am," they all droned in unison.

Waving her wooden spoon in front of her like a conductor's baton, Dana stepped up beside Courtney again.

"Once more from the top now, girls."

—

In the end it took six more rounds of two dozen swats each before Dana was finally satisfied that all three of her kitchen mess culprits had been served their just desserts. By then, Courtney, Rhen, and Abby were each sporting a matching pair of angry red and rather swollen bare bottom cheeks that pulsed hotly with each heartbeat, and had taken to sniffling and making very heartfelt apologies and promises to be good.

It was absolutely adorable, and Dana's fingers itched to pull out her smartphone and snap a quick picture or two before she let them up.

"Maybe next time," she muttered to herself with a quiet huff.

"Alright, you three, I think that's enough spanking for one afternoon, wouldn't you say?"

The sighs of relief that greeted her announcement were enough to make Dana laugh out loud.

They really were just too cute.

After taking a moment or two longer to bask in the self-satisfied glow of a job well done, she then schooled her features back into a mask of vaguely stern disapproval and planted her hands on her hips.

"Courtney, Abby, you two may stand up now. Pull up your pants and then come give me a hug, alright?"

"Yes *ma'am*!" the two lovers echoed simultaneously, springing back to their feet and not bothering to adjust any of their clothing before they swung around and all but tackled the older woman.

"Thank you for that," murmured Courtney.

"Yeah, that was *so* much fun," added Abby, just as quietly.

"Any time, girls," cooed Rhen's auntie, patting each of them fondly on the back before giving their sizzling rumps one hard squeeze each. "Now you'd better pull those panties and jeans back up before I decide to take them being down as an invitation to start over."

Despite the grins on their faces, both girls were very quick to redress that time around.

"No thanks!"

"I'm good!"

While the two of them took to fixing their wardrobes and scrubbing the few remaining tears they'd shed from their faces with the backs of their sleeves, Dana approached her adorable adoptive niece and helped her back to her feet.

"Come here, cutie pie. I've got you," she cooed, wrapping her up in a firm embrace and rocking her gently.

Looking over the younger girl's frazzled mop of inky black hair and inhaling the fruity scents of her shampoo, she couldn't help but smirk a little as she watched the other two girls also find solace in each other's arms.

"No more messes?" Dana asked with a faint snicker against the top of Rhen's hair, reaching down to grab her still sizzling caboose with both hands, hoisting the shorter girl up onto her tiptoes in the process as she squeezed.

"No more messes," she agreed with a half-groan half-gasp as she too breathed in deeply against the generous swell of her partner's bosom, reveling in the familiar and comforting fragrances of her perfume while also doing her best to ignore the fact that her bottom cheeks were spread wide apart and that her back was directly pointing toward her two best friends.

Whatever. It's not like they haven't seen it all before anyway, she decided after a moment's contemplation, before sighing contentedly. *Let them look all they want. I don't care. Heh. It's kind of fun, actually...*

Dana and Rhen continued to stay like that for several long and face-explodingly warm moments before the older woman finally eased her grip on her swollen caboose and Rhen was at last able to pull herself free from the humiliating embrace.

"Uh-uh-uh," her aunt chided without much in the way of actual sternness as she made to reach down for her panties, gently batting away her hands before seizing hold of her upper arm in a firm grip. "You know the rules, cutie pie. Any little girls who get their bottoms spanked in *this* house have to stand in the corner afterward. Don't they?"

"But... but..." protested Rhen ineffectually as she was frog-marched past her smirking friends, who waved to her as she passed them by. "But how come I'm the only one stuck with corner time? That is so not fair!"

"It's *fair* because I say it is," chided Dana with a friendly, but unyielding, grin, before leaning in to purr against her ear. "Plus we can all see how wet you are, honeybuns, and I like to watch you squirm."

"You... you don't say?" stuttered Rhen, swallowing hard as one hand drifted on reflex between her thighs.

She nearly tripped over her panties then as her fingers came into contact with her sopping folds, and it took a supreme effort of will to pull them back and not start attending to the aching need that she'd suddenly become aware of down there.

"Oh my god, you are *so* mean," she harrumphed, doing her best to ignore the flash of heat that had just rushed up her face.

"That's right I am," snickered Dana nipping her girlfriend's ear playfully before straightening up and returning to being all business. "Now quit your fussing before I give you something to fuss about."

"Yeah, *Rhenny*," Abby called after the two of them with a giggle, dragging her girlfriend after her to watch the fun. "Act your age, little girl."

Courtney and Dana both couldn't help but snort at that one.

"Very cute, Abby, dear."

"Oh my god, you guys suck," grumbled Rhen, unable to quite stop herself from smiling along with everyone else as she was guided into her usual spot facing the corner in the front room that pointed her thoroughly-reddened bare bottom toward the big bay windows that looked out onto her auntie's front yard. "I am so going to get you back for this. Just you wait."

"Oh yes, I'm sure you will," replied Courtney condescendingly, not sounding the least bit intimidated.

"Yeah, there's definitely no way that could possibly backfire," agreed Abby, miming a bottom swat. "Maybe I'll have Courtney let me be the one to teach you some manners next time around. Now, wouldn't that be fun?"

Deciding that the best course of action for her right then was to not dignify that embarrassing question with a response, Rhen instead just clasped her hands on top of her head and shoved her brightly blushing face into the corner.

"Humph!"

Once her partner was satisfied that she wasn't going any-where anytime soon, and had taken the time to adjust her panties so that they hung evenly around her ankles, she then turned her attention toward the two broadly beaming college coeds lingering smugly just beside the couch where Rhen's skirt still lay abandoned in a wrinkled heap on the floor.

"Alright, you two, while she's busy with inspecting the cor-ner, would you mind helping me out with unloading the car and moving all of her Christmas presents up to my room?"

"Sure, no problem," agreed Courtney with an easy shrug.

"Oooh, presents!" cheered Abby, clapping excitedly. "I can't wait to see what you got her!"

Suddenly feeling a *lot* less grumpy about being treated like a bratty thirteen-year-old who'd been left to stand in the cor-ner while the adults went about their business, Rhen straight-ened up a bit and tried angling her head ever so slightly to the side.

SMACK!

"You get that nose back in the corner right this instant, missy!" warned her aunt with a firm swat that made the already sore girl jump. "And I'd better not catch you trying to peek again, or else I'm going to tear that cute little tush of yours up with Missus Hairbrush. You got that?"

"Yes ma'am," answered Rhen with a harrumph while flex-ing her scalded seat, her buoyant mood only slightly damp-ened by the sudden resurgence of heat in her left cheek. "I won't peek, I promise."

"That's better."

—

Rhen was left to stew in her own embarrassment with only her glowing bottom for company for the better part of the next fifteen minutes. Standing there staring at the all too familiar painted drywall in front of her with a bored pout on her face, she listened to the steady rhythm of the old grandfather clock ticking away behind her as her partner and two best friends "busied" themselves with unloading the various gifts and fun things that Dana had purchased for her while she'd been out shopping that afternoon.

At least, that's what she assumed they were up to, at any rate.

In the bratty twenty-year-old's opinion, it sure sounded a lot more like they were just taking their dear sweet time moving a dozen or so bags from one spot to another one at a time. Apparently too, one or more of them suffered from some sort of pathological need to drag their feet and pause to make idle chitchat between each and every trip back and forth from the car, which in turn prolonged the entire experience exponentially. Little by little though, her corner time *did* crawl by, and through it all Rhen couldn't help but smile as she listened to the three most important people in her life setting about stashing away her Christmas loot.

Oh gosh, I sure hope she decided to get me Bonestorm, after all. The commercials made it look so rad...

Thankfully, there was at least one unforeseen benefit to neither her aunt nor her friends seeming to be in any particular hurry. While they chatted in between trips, they tended to leave the front door to the house open for long stretches of time. This allowed frosty bursts of early evening winter air to occasionally gust in to cool Rhen's sizzling seat, which honestly was well worth the added boredom in her opinion.

In the end it took a ton of willpower on her part to fight down the urge to try and maybe sneak just a *tiny* peek at what Dana might have bought for her. Having to wait almost an entire week to find out what she had in store for her was going to be pure torture, but the looming threat of a visit from Missus Hairbrush was more than enough to keep her suffi-ciently motivated to rein in her gnawing curiosity before it could get her into any more trouble.

By the time the last of the items had been secured away behind the near-impregnable protection of her auntie's closet door in her master bathroom, Rhen was starting to rethink her fondness for the chilly winter air as it started to make her teeth chatter. And so, when she at last she felt the kneading caress of Dana's strong hands massaging her goose bump cov-ered cheeks behind her, she practically melted into her grip.

"Ahhh, that's nice," she sighed, drifting out of her aimless reverie and looking back with a lazy smile.

"I'm glad to hear it," purred Dana with a firm squeeze and a wink. "Now why don't you come out of that corner before you freeze to it? I think you've learned your lesson by now."

"You better believe I have," breathed Rhen with a chuckle, rolling her eyes heavenward in gratitude as she waddled back a couple of steps and turned to face her aunt before beginning to pull up her panties over her thoroughly cooled caboose.

She'd just about managed to get her polka-dots situated back into place around her hips when Dana's sharp gasp of righteous indignation had her looking up with the sudden worry that they were about to come right back down again.

"Young lady, what on *earth* happened to your clothes?"

"Huh? My Clothes? What about them?" asked Rhen, gen-uinely confused as to what all of the hubbub was about as she glanced down at the black and pink t-shirt she was wearing and frowned.

Seeing the state that it was in however, she felt her stomach clench as the butterflies that had been frozen up until that point immediately thawed and began fluttering around in a panic.

"Oh..."

"'Oh' is right," agreed her aunt with a haughty sniff, planting her hands on her hips as she settled back into lecturing mode. "I thought you were baking cookies today, not rolling around in a bag of flour!"

"What? Come on! It's not *that* bad," Rhen tried to argue, self-consciously batting at the front of her t-shirt and wincing as a rather sizable cloud of all-purpose flour puffed free from it. "Er... Well, I mean..."

"Not that bad?' echoed Dana in exasperation. "Rhen, you have bits of cookie dough batter stuck in your *hair*. And... is that brown sugar all over the front of your legs? Honey, you're a mess! Didn't you at least wear an apron while you were cooking?"

"Um... I was planning to," the younger girl offered with a sheepish shrug. "But Courtney and Abby only brought two of them."

At that, Rhen looked over toward where her two best friends were standing off to the side and watching the unfolding drama with naked amusement. Clearly, they weren't going to be any help at all just then.

Traitors.

"And you couldn't just wear mine?" pressed Dana with a raised eyebrow, drawing the younger girl's attention back to the situation at hand.

"Well, I was *going* to," she began to explain again, before losing her nerve as she saw the incredulous look in her partner's eyes. "No really, I was! But uh... you see, the thing is... I kind of got, you know... distracted, and maybe... sort of...

forgot?"

"Uh-huh," deadpanned Dana, not sounding the least bit convinced. "Well, I certainly know one young lady who is in desperate need of a bath and a change of clothes right about now."

Rhen was just about to nod and say that she'd get right on that, relieved to say the least that her auntie hadn't decided to toss another spanking into the mix for good measure, when she felt a ball of ice suddenly form in the pit of her stomach as she watched the older woman look over toward the two smirking coeds beside her and flash them a conspiratorial grin.

"Abby, sweetheart, would you please be a dear and give Rhen a bath for me while Courtney and I take care of cleaning up down here in the kitchen?"

"Wha-?" Rhen began to splutter.

SMACK! SMACK!

Before being cut off by a casual pair of heavy swats that temporarily knocked the sass right out of her, making her grip her flaming backside as she hopped from foot to foot, hissing through clenched teeth.

"Of course, ma'am," agreed Abby, completely ignoring the adorable rendition of the spankee dance that her best friend and former roommate was currently in the middle of performing. "Come on, Rhenny. Let's go get you into a nice, hot bubble bath."

"But... but..." the younger girl continued to protest feebly, her face glowing scarlet as she was taken by the hand and led away.

"Oh, and once you're done getting her squeaky clean, will please make sure you put her into a fresh pull-up?" Dana added as they went. "You'll find them in the top drawer of her dresser. Pick out whichever one looks the cutest to you, and then find her something nice to wear for dinner tonight, alright?"

"Sure thing, ma'am, no problem," sing-songed Abby, grinning from ear to ear and practically buzzing with barely restrained excitement as she pulled Rhen after her.

"Thanks hon," Dana called out as they mounted the stairs, before adding just as they were about to disappear out of sight. "And just so you know, you and Courtney are also totally welcome to come join us for dinner tonight too if you'd like to. It's me and Rhen's six month anniversary, actually, and we'd love to have you along to celebrate. We're going to Papa Italiano's, and it'll be my treat if you decide to come."

"That sounds great," replied Courtney, answering for her and her girlfriend. "Count us in."

"Wonderful!" exclaimed Dana, clapping the older girl on the shoulder and moving off toward the messy kitchen. "We're also going to be stopping by the mall afterward for some pictures with Santa, and again, you two are more than welcome to tag along if you want."

"Awww," sighed Courtney, starting to gather up the various bowls that she and Abby had strategically left strewn about the counters. "There's no way we'd miss that. We'll be there!"

Chapter 26

Just Another Day in Love

Christmas morning found Rhen waking up just after sunrise like she had pretty much every other morning for the last few months since she'd moved in with Dana. As she stared up at her ceiling fan with one foot still firmly planted in dreamland, she considered just rolling over and going back to sleep for a few more hours. But the mental image of the massive pile of presents under the tree in their front room that she'd sneaked a peek of late last night just wouldn't get out of her head.

"Eh, screw it."

Sitting up, she kicked her blankets off into a pile at her feet, let out a long yawn as she stretched, and then rolled out of bed.

She could always take a nap later. Right now there were presents to open!

—

"Aunt Dana, wake up!" Rhen sing-songed at the top of her lungs, throwing open the bedroom door across the hall from her own and making a beeline toward where her auntie was still sleeping. "It's Christmas, it's Christmas!"

"Huh? Wazzat-?" slurred the older woman groggily, only just beginning to stir beneath her sheets before letting out a yelp of surprise as another body suddenly flopped down onto the queen-size mattress next to her, making her bounce.

"Wake up!"

Again.

"Wake up!"

And again.

"Wake up, wake up, wake up," chanted Rhen, jumping up and down on her knees, before descending upon the startled red-haired woman and shaking her insistently by the shoulders.

After all, fair was fair, right? Why should she be the only one in their house who had to put up with being dragged out of bed earlier than she wanted to?

Worst case scenario, I get a spanking, she thought to herself wry smirk. *I can live with that.*

"It's Christmas!"

"Alright, alright," laughed Dana, rolling over and pinning the overexcited college coed beneath her, very much awake now. "Come here you!"

Grinning wickedly, she then proceeded to tickle her trapped not-niece senseless in retaliation for interrupting her beauty sleep.

"Hey, Rhen, did you hear?" she teased, slipping her hands beneath the younger girl's sky blue pajama top and mercilessly attacking her sensitive belly and sides. "It's Christmas, it's Christmas!"

Stuck as she was with the older woman's weight straddling her hips, Rhen was left with little other choice than to buck and grind her pelvis ineffectually against her partner's, gasping and chewing on her lower lip in between bursts of involuntary laughter. She did her best to try and outlast the relentless assault on her armpits, but she knew that it was a losing battle, and unfortunately her bladder wasn't quite up to challenge as she was. After only a minute or so of tickle torture, she was forced to throw in the towel before she gave Dana something to *really* tease her about.

"Okay, okay! Oh my god, you win!" she gasped out in between giggles, arms flailing out to either side of her as if she were making snow angels in the bed sheets. "Aunt Dana, *please*, I'm going to wet my pants if you keep this up."

"Oh?" pressed the other woman coyly, ceasing her tickling in favor of cupping the younger girl's breasts, idly pinching and rolling her erect nipples between her thumb and forefinger and savoring the warmth radiating out from her silky smooth skin.

Shifting around on the mattress, she forced a bare thigh between Rhen's pajama-clad legs, flashing her an impish grin as the top of her leg butted up against the padding she knew was hidden there.

"Well then, I guess it's a good thing you're wearing a pull-up, huh?"

"Oh come on!" whined the younger girl, squirming some more in protest as her face flushed a bright shade of red. "You know that's not playing fair."

"So?" asked Dana breezily, grinning even wider now as she leaned down to purr into the adorable twenty-year-old's ear. "Did you ever stop to think that maybe I *want* to make you wet your pants, honeybuns? To send you so far over the edge that you lose all control just like you did a few weeks ago? I could even spank you afterward too just like last time and then wash your mouth out since you told me that you don't ever wet the bed. I bet you'd just *hate* that, now wouldn't you?"

"Um…" countered Rhen, quite undone by the older woman's stern tone and completely incapable of thinking of a rebuttal just then as her face all but burst into flames, eradicating rational thought for the moment as her hips moved of their own accord to grind themselves against Dana's firm thigh.

"Humph!"

"Awww, don't pout," she cooed, her face mere inches away from Rhen's now as her grin grew steadily more predatory.

Leaning in, she planted a quick kiss on the tip of her nose and then pulled her hands free so that she could smooth back a few unruly strands of dark hair from her rosy forehead.

"I was only kidding…"

She leaned in for another kiss then, capturing Rhen's lips with her own and running the tip of her tongue across her teeth before pulling back, making her moan in frustration as she winked.

"Mostly."

With that, she rolled off of her and then out of bed entirely, pulling the sassy sophomore up after her as she went.

"Now why don't you run along and wait for me downstairs? I'll be there in a few minutes and then we can open presents, alright?"

"Yay!" cheered Rhen, all petulance and lingering butterflies forgotten about for the moment as she crushed her partner against her in a tight hug.

Sure, the knee-quaking *need* still throbbing between her thighs was enough to drive her crazy, but she'd gotten used to being wound up and then turned loose by Dana by now and was able to (mostly) shrug it off. After all, she knew that it would end up being resolved one way or the other eventually if she just stayed patient and didn't press the issue.

Besides, whining about it now would just be admitting defeat.

Rhen let go after just a quick squeeze and then scampered off toward the open bedroom door with a twirl. However, she stopped short after only a few steps and turned back to stick her tongue out at her bossy boots auntie, determined to get one final bit of attitude in.

"Don't take too long, or else I'm starting without you!"

"You'd better not, little girl," growled Dana, half-chasing her out of the bedroom, before coming to a stop at her door and sighing in amusement as she listened to her thunder down the stairs, giggling up a storm as she went.

"Oooh, that girl is just *begging* to get her butt beat."

Shaking her head with a low chuckle, Dana moved off to go get changed.

"What a sweetie."

—

True to her word, Dana only spent a few minutes brushing her teeth and restoring some semblance of order to her hair before she threw on some comfortable clothes and made her way downstairs. There she found Rhen ready and waiting for her in their front room, parked in the middle of the couch and bubbling with barely restrained impatience. She'd already picked out a promising looking present from near the front of the pile at the base of their tree, and was currently fiddling with the ribbon bow on its top while she kicked her feet back and forth in front of her.

"See?" teased the older woman, sweeping in to sit down beside her and wrapping an affectionate arm around her waist in a sidelong hug. "That wasn't so bad, now was it?"

"Humph. I guess not," conceded Rhen with a pout that didn't quite manage to chase away the grin on her face. "So *now* can I start opening my presents? Pretty please?"

"Almost," replied her partner with a shake of her head.

"But-" the younger girl started to protest, before being

silenced by a gentle fingertip pressed to her lips.

"Shhh… There'll be plenty of time for that in a minute, cutie pie," she cooed with a wink. "First thing's first though, we need to take some pictures to commemorate our first Christmas together. Plus I'm pretty sure that your granny would kill me, and probably spank you silly, if I didn't at least get a shot of you in front of the tree, you know."

"Okay, yeah, I guess that's fair," snickered Rhen with a theatrical shiver.

"Good girl. Now stand up."

Setting her present aside with a melodramatic sigh, Rhen hopped up off of the couch and sashayed her way over to stand in front of the elaborately decorated fir situated opposite her usual punishment corner.

"How's this?" she asked, striking a pose.

"Perfect," answered Dana, fishing out her smartphone from her pocket and swiping open her camera app. "Now say, 'Santa'."

"Santa!"

Beaming from ear to ear, Rhen let her auntie take as many pictures of her as she wanted to, occasionally turning to strike a different pose or else moving around so that her presents or the Christmas tree were more in frame. Then, after snapping probably way more pictures of her than she actually needed, Dana moved in to join her in front of the tree, and cuddling up together they took several more selfies that Rhen knew she would treasure always.

With the all-important picture taking finally out of the way, Rhen was at last turned loose to start opening her presents.

A task that she took to with reckless abandon.

"Come to momma!"

Practically diving headfirst under the tree, she began

ferreting out packages for her, and ones for Dana. (She had done a little bit of shopping herself with Abby and Courtney earlier that week, and her grandma had sent a few gifts for her as well.)

"Okay so, uh… how about I open one and then you?" she asked, plopping down amidst a palisade of presents and clapping eagerly. "Sound good?"

"Works for me, cutie pie," answered Dana with a thumbs up. "Go for it!"

And so she did.

—

Rhen spent the better part of the next half hour riding high on a wave of surprise and delight as she went through the process of reading out who a present was from, and then tearing the wrapping paper off of it to see what was inside.

"Oh my god, Aunt Dana, thank you!" she squealed upon opening a box to find a super cute sweater that she'd been eyeing for a while inside, only to explode into a fit of cheering when she noticed the copy of Bonestorm that the older woman had hidden away within its folds.

Springing to her feet, Rhen threw herself at her aunt, squeezing her as tight as she could and peppering her face with kisses.

"Thank you, thank you, thank you!"

"Oof!" groaned Dana as the black-haired missile collided with her chest, knocking most of the air out of her.

"Y-You're welcome, cutie pie," she managed to wheeze once she'd caught her breath, gently disentangling herself from her adorable not-niece and ruffling her hair fondly.

Turning her back toward the tree with a self-satisfied grin, she sent her along with a pat to her padded caboose.

"There're a few more fun things hidden away in those boxes, you know. You'd better get back to unwrapping, or else we're going be here all day."

"Good point!"

Plopping back down amid her dwindling fort of presents, Rhen snatched up another one and read off its tag.

"Oh, nice! This one's from Gran-Gran."

Giving it an investigatory shake and hearing the tell-tale rattle of candy within, she snorted out a laugh.

"I knew she wasn't actually serious about sending me coal!"

—

Despite the countless number of spankings she'd received over the last few months, Rhen was pleased to find that she'd apparently still been well-behaved enough to get much of what she'd asked for on her Christmas list.

Dana and her grandma definitely hadn't skimped out on spoiling her that year, and apparently now that she was being routinely disciplined like a child, Santa Claus had even decided to deliver a few presents to her as well.

Although Rhen couldn't help but notice that he and her auntie happened to have *very* similar handwriting.

Heck, even her auntie Maureen and auntie Jessica had decided to get in on the fun, each sending her gift cards and a couple of cute tops.

"Awww, these are adorable!" Dana had cooed upon inspecting the frilly items of clothing. "I'm so glad I thought to send them your sizes."

"Uh, yeah... good thinking," deadpanned Rhen with a sheepish smirk, not quite sure if she liked the idea of her extended family shopping for her in the juniors section.

Then again, the tops they'd sent *were* pretty cute.

Oh well... she thought to herself with a silent sigh and a roll of her eyes. *I guess I can put up with perpetually being treated as just another little kid in the family if it means more presents on Christmas, heh.*

—

When finally the last of Rhen's and Dana's presents had been opened and shown off, and what remained of their shredded wrapping paper had been swept into a mostly neat little pile in one corner of the room, the younger girl heaved out a satisfied sigh and moved to flop down on the couch again.

"Thanks for everything today," she said, turning where she sat to thread her arms around her partner and leaning in to plant a heartfelt kiss on her cheek. "You really didn't have to go all out like this, you know."

"Awww, it was my pleasure, hon," replied Dana, returning the kiss with one of her own before reaching over to haul the younger girl up onto her lap for some proper cuddling. "I'm always happy to spoil you."

"Is that right?" snickered Rhen, wriggling around to get more comfortable before laying her head against the crook of her auntie's neck. "I'll be sure to keep that in mind come Valentine's Day, then."

"Oh don't you worry, cutie pie," reassured Dana, nuzzling the top of her head with a sly grin. "I've got some *very* special plans in store for you for that night."

She leaned in closer then, bringing her lips right next to her girlfriend's ear to murmur conspiratorially.

"Courtney and I have been brainstorming, and let's just say that an enema nozzle and a ginger root aren't the only things that I can think of that can fit inside your tush."

Chuckling quietly, she nipped at the smaller girl's earlobe, making her squirm oh so delightfully, as she added.

"I've got a certain something all picked out for you, and I think you'll find that it's *very* age inappropriate for bratty little girls... and that you're going to love every single second with it inside of you."

That managed to bring a fresh burst of scarlet to the bratty sophomore's cheeks, one that only intensified as her partner slipped her hand down the front of her pajama bottoms to tease at her moist lips.

"I, uh..." she managed to croak out only after swallowing hard as an electric thrill arced across her aching lips at her lover's caressing touch. "I'm looking forward to it."

"Mmmm... me too," purred Dana, kissing the top of her hair before plunging two of her fingers into Rhen's smoldering sex.

"Ah!"

"Now be a good girl and come for me."

"Y-Yes ma'am!"

Ever eager to please, Rhen gave herself over to her partner's thrusting fingers entirely, parting her thighs and letting her take her. Her squirming hips soon fell into rhythm with the digits working their way in and out of her, riding them for all she was worth as they fucked her silly.

"I'm waiting..." Dana growled into her ear after they'd been at it for a while, increasing the force and speed of her pumping as she nipped at her earlobe. "Don't make me tell you again, little girl."

Rhen, who had already been a hair's breadth away from tipping over the edge as it was, was then shoved off of it entirely by her partner's implied threat.

"Oh god!"

Eyes rolling up into the back of her head, she let out a high-pitched moan of ecstasy as she contracted around Dana's still-thrusting fingers, losing herself in the bliss of oblivion as she finally came.

And came.

And came.

"Good girl," purred Dana when she had at last regained some semblance of control over her own body, panting and sweaty as she lay limp in her arms.

"I knew you could do it."

"I…" Rhen huffed, still partially out of breath and unable to think of anything sassy or witty to say just then. "I… yeah…"

"Heh, you just take your time to recover now, cutie pie," cooed Dana, kissing the top of her head again and rubbing her back. "I've got you."

The two of them continued to stay cuddled up together like that for several more, extremely comfortable minutes, neither of them really feeling the need to say anything in particular, content to just bask in the warmth of their embrace for a while longer. Eventually though, once the afterglow of Rhen's orgasm had finally faded away, Dana broke the silent spell they'd fallen under when she snaked a hand down to cup her girlfriend's caboose, making the padding hidden beneath her pajama bottoms crinkle adorably as she squeezed.

"You know, I think you might've missed a few presents back behind the tree there," she said, pointing with her free hand toward a trio of neatly wrapped packages hidden just out of sight against the wall behind a couple of low-hanging branches.

"Oh hey, you're right!" exclaimed Rhen, having now

caught her second wind.

Jumping to her feet, she all but dove underneath their Christmas tree, kneeling on the hardwood floor and flopping onto her belly as she fumbled around trying to grab the just out of reach packages.

"Get over here, you sneaky sausages..."

While the younger girl busied herself with doing that, Dana casually slipped her smartphone out from her front pocket again and snapped a few more surreptitious photos of her adorable cloud-covered caboose as it waggled back and forth behind her.

"Need a hand there, cutie pie?" she teased after stowing her phone away, leaning forward and reaching out to pat the tempting pair of cheeks being presented to her.

"No thanks, I've got it," came Rhen's muffled reply from beneath the tree, squirming her hips in self-satisfaction as she sent first one, and then another, of her hidden presents skidding across the floor toward the center of the room.

At last she scooted back on her knees, making the seat of her pajama bottoms bob up and down amusingly as she did so, and emerged with a triumphant exclamation as she held her final gift aloft over her head.

"Ta-da!"

Dana golf-clapped appreciatively for her, smirking to herself at the mess of little green needles sticking out at odd angles from her girlfriend's hair.

"Well? Don't leave me in suspense, dear. Who's it from?"

"Hmmm... Let's see," answered Rhen as she slowly rotated the smallish box around in her hands, producing a faintly metallic-sounding rattle from whatever was inside of it as she searched for a label. "Ah, here we go. Oooh, this one's from Gran-Gran."

"Is it now?" purred Dana, working very hard to keep her face a mask of polite curiosity as she scooted toward the edge of her seat for a better view and watched as her niece began to pull at the tape on one corner of the box. "I could've *sworn* that she said she was only sending those three presents in the mail when I talked to her earlier this week. I wonder what else she could've possibly gotten for you."

Yeah, I'm sure you're totally in the dark here, Aunt Dana, mused Rhen to herself with a silent snicker, picking up on the older woman's playful tone. *Fair enough. I'll play along.*

"Only one way to find out," she said with a shrug, trying to ignore the faint stirrings of butterflies in her stomach as she proceeded to tear the wrapping paper off of the box in her hands with wanton glee. "Maybe it's some bracelets or something?"

"Maybe," agreed the other woman with a mysterious smile.

"Huh…" said Rhen when she at last pulled open the lid of the thin, white cardboard box that had been hidden inside the wrapping paper, dumping its contents out onto her lap. "It's a… belt?"

At least, I think it's a belt.

Tossing the empty box aside without a second glance, she scooped up the weighty coil of dark leather and clinking silver and examined it thoughtfully.

Without even having to try it on, she could already tell that it was way, way too big for her narrow waist. In fact, as far as she could tell, it looked more like something you'd wear to hold up heavy tool bags or one of those fancy cowboy holsters she'd seen in movies, not a cute pair of jeans.

Not that most of her jeans these days could even accommodate a belt, thanks to their easy-pull waistbands.

Hmmm... Maybe I was wrong about Aunt Dana messing with me?

"What the heck?" she demanded. "This thing doesn't even look like it can fit through regular belt loops. Did she accidentally send me something meant for Brian or Eric instead?"

She was pretty sure that the label had said "To: Rhen" on it, but now that it was in shreds all around her, she wasn't so sure anymore.

"Gee, I hope I didn't just open up someone else's Christmas present by accident."

"No, that one's definitely for you," her aunt reassured her, leaning down to pluck up a handwritten note that she'd completely missed in all of the excitement of opening her gift. "It's just that that belt isn't meant for your *pants*, cutie pie."

"Wait, it's not?"

"Nope," crooned Dana, grinning mischievously and holding up the note so that she could read it aloud. "To my favorite grandbaby. I hope this belt helps you remember to behave yourself this year. Love, Gran-Gran."

"Oh..."

Rhen's face had grown hotter and hotter with each word as she'd sat there fidgeting and listening to her partner read.

"How uh... how thoughtful."

I guess I really shouldn't be surprised, she mused with an internal eye-roll. *I suppose it was only a matter of time before I felt the belt on my bare butt again, after all. Oh well...*

"Isn't it though?" cooed Dana sweetly, extending a hand toward her not-niece, palm up. "Here, let me take a look at that."

Passing the belt over with a grimace, Rhen felt the butterflies in her stomach swirl into full flight as she watched her auntie roll out the thick strip of leather and then double it over, giving it a couple of quick test snaps.

SNAP! SNAP!

"Eep!"

Rhen could feel her cheeks clenching on reflex as the sharp cracks of leather on leather echoed throughout the house.

"Oh yes," declared Dana, flexing the stiff belt between her hands and beaming brightly. "This is definitely a *very* nice belt. We'll have to call your granny later and thank her for giving you such a thoughtful present."

"If you say so," harrumphed Rhen, the pout on her lips doing very little to hide the look of masochistic hunger in her eyes as they remained glued on the belt in the older woman's hands. "Or we could just pretend it was lost in the mail."

"No way, cutie pie," shot back Dana with an amused grin. "This beauty is going straight onto a hook inside your closet when we get the chance."

Rhen just rolled her eyes and nodded obediently, doing her best to keep her thighs from squirming too much.

"Oh, well… um… okay."

Dana let her stew like that for a bit longer then, drinking in the mixed feelings of embarrassment and intrigue plain on her face, before waving casually at the two other packages still on the floor beside her.

"There're still two more gifts to unwrap, you know," she pointed out with a snicker. "No more dawdling, now. Show me what else you got!"

"Right!"

Eager to put the thought of the embarrassing gift from her grandma behind her, Rhen snatched up the closest box she could reach and hurriedly searched for the label on it.

"Okay, so… this one's from Courtney and Abby," she said, hefting the long, rectangular box in her hands and giving it a couple of investigatory shakes. "Which is kind of a surprise, actually... I thought we'd agreed that we weren't going to get each other gifts this year and instead just go out for brunch when they came back from Abby's?"

"I guess they must've had a change of heart," shrugged Dana, not bothering to hide her smirk this time. "Hurry up and open it already, I'm dying to see what they got you!"

Starting to suspect that she might be the butt of some sort of joke that she wasn't fully aware of yet, Rhen tore off the wrapping paper on her present with a little less gusto this time, finding underneath it another nondescript cardboard box.

Pulling off its lid revealed three things. A long-handled pink plastic bath brush with a round head and soft white bristles, a short-handled wooden bath brush with a flat oval head, and another note.

Plucking up the handwritten piece of paper and blushing a delicate shade of hot pink, she read aloud.

"We weren't sure whether or not Dana liked to spank you over her lap or bending over more, so we decided to get something for each just in case. Make sure you tell us which one you like the best when we see each other again. Have fun, you naughty girl. XOXO. Courtney and Abby."

"Awww, that's so thoughtful of them," cooed Dana, holding out her hands expectantly so that she could get a closer look at the bath brushes her girlfriend was currently glowering at.

Passing them over with a mortified huff, Rhen nodded.

"If you say so."

SLAP-SLAP!

SLAP-SLAP!

"Oooh, you are definitely going to *hate* these," teased her aunt after she'd finished giving each brush a couple of quick test swats against the front of her right thigh. "They're both *very* stingy."

"Lucky me…" deadpanned Rhen, her sarcasm falling somewhat flat as she swallowed nervously and licked her lips.

"Indeed," snickered Dana, before pointing at the final package on the floor with the long-handled bath brush. "One more to go, cutie pie."

Having caught on by now to her partner's and everyone else's game, Rhen snatched up the last package with a harrumph and found its label with a haughty sniff.

"Okay, this one's from Maureen," she declared quickly, before tearing off the wrapping paper and revealing an intricately decorated wooden spoon.

"Huh…" she mused, taken somewhat aback by not finding any humiliating notes or scary looking paddles waiting for her. "This is… kind of cute, actually."

Tossing the torn packaging aside, she hefted the spoon thoughtfully, rotating it slowly in her hands. It was made of a heavy wood that had been stained a rich, dark color not that far off from her ebony hairbrush. Its surface was silky smooth to the touch and bore a faint sheen to it, and painted in swirling, white letters on opposite sides of its rounded head were the phrases "This Side for Scooping" and "This Side for Spanking".

Yeah, as if that weren't readily apparent already, she thought to herself with a snort. *Very funny, Maureen.*

"Oh my, yes! This is *definitely* a keeper," agreed Dana when she took up the spoon, turning it over appreciatively in her hands. "That woman has excellent taste."

"I guess so," grumbled Rhen, trying to sound petulant, but not quite managing to pull it off as she locked eyes with her auntie and smirked. "Although, I still think a gift card would have worked just as well."

"Yes, I'm sure," replied Dana dryly, her lips twitching up toward something devious as she turned to regard the small pile of implements beside her on the couch. "Hmmm... it's funny. Now that I'm looking at all of these wonderful bottom swatters, that reminds me..."

Looking up again, she leveled a disapproving frown at Rhen, fixing her in place with one of her more intimidating hard stares.

"I couldn't help but notice that you neglected to make your bed this morning, little girl."

Swallowing hard, Rhen did her best to ignore the butterflies that had just been whipped into a frenzy inside her stomach.

"I uh... I did?" she asked, feigning a sort of sheepish innocence as her smirk bent into a worried grimace under the weight of her partner's glare.

"That's right," confirmed the older woman with a twinkle of mirth dancing in her dark eyes, setting her wooden spoon down next to the other implements beside her and standing up.

Planting one hand on her hip, she kept her face nice and stern as she wagged an admonishing forefinger at the younger girl kneeling in front of her.

"And just because it's Christmas, that doesn't mean you get to ignore the rules in this house."

"I mean..." stalled a now very flustered Rhen, fidgeting with the hem of her pajama top and casting her eyes about for something to distract her aunt from where she knew their conversation was headed.

Where's a spontaneous group of carolers when you need

one? she whined to herself, drawing her lips into a frustrated pout. *Oh who am I kidding? She'd probably invite them in for cookies and cocoa while they watched her spank me. Humph.*

As she pouted, Dana continued to just stare her down. Waiting patiently for her to succumb to the whirlpool of anxiety and excitement that she knew must be threatening to swallow her adorable twenty-year-old turned teenager up at any moment.

"Okay, *fine*," Rhen harrumphed less than a minute later, putting all of her considerable stores of sass into the single word as she crossed her arms in front of her and whipped her head to the side to glare sourly at the pile of shredded wrapping paper next to her. "I guess that's fair."

It's not like I didn't have a bunch of chances to make it earlier or anything...

"Rules are rules, I'm afraid, cutie pie," replied Dana with a sympathetic shrug and a decidedly unsympathetic smirk.

"Yeah, whatever," grumbled Rhen, deciding that if she was already in trouble, then she might as well act the part.

All her pouting seemed to do though was earn her an affectionate ruffle of her hair as her partner breezed past her.

Moving off toward the entryway hall seemingly without a care in the world, Dana paused long enough to hook a thumb over her shoulder as she looked back and winked.

"I want you to pick out one of those new tushy tanners you just unwrapped, and then meet me upstairs so that we can have a nice, long chat about how you've forgotten to make your bed for... I think it's the fifth time now this semester?"

She tapped a thoughtful forefinger against the side of her cheek as she ran through her mental index of the times she'd spanked her niece in the last few months.

"Yes, it's definitely the fifth," she decided with a delighted grin. "Oh, you are *so* in for it now, you naughty girl."

"Yes ma'am," sighed Rhen with a wan smile that managed to remain partially hidden by the loose curtain of her dark hair.

"Don't keep me waiting, now," purred Dana, disappearing around the corner with a low chuckle.

Once she was alone in the front room, Rhen spent a few satisfying moments balling up a couple loose bits of wrapping paper and throwing them at the pile of other trash beside her, more so out of a desire to be doing anything other than what she'd been told to than anything else as she struggled to master her embarrassment and excitement.

"Humph!"

Truth be told, she was barely even upset with this sudden turn of events.

Despite the swarms of butterflies whirling around furiously inside her stomach, she couldn't have been happier. She'd known that she was probably going to get busted for leaving her bed unmade, and had even decided to tempt fate by leaving the door to her bedroom wide open when she went downstairs after waking her auntie up.

Running the risk of getting caught was half the fun of being a brat, she'd discovered, while actually getting caught was the other half.

Now the time had come to pay, and that was that.

"Ugh…"

That knowledge didn't make it any easier for her to run willingly toward her own doom however.

"Oh well."

Pushing herself back up to her feet on a pair of wobbly knees, Rhen spent a few more moments shaking out some of the more stubborn tree needles still clinging to her hair, before turning to regard the array of spanking implements on the couch in front of her with a sly grin.

Hoo boy... Now this is one heck of a hard choice. Yeesh.

Staring at them, she couldn't help but feel a surge of fondness and gratitude well up within her, filling her from head to toe with warmth and making her beam. She was so lucky to have so many people in her life that cared about her and were looking out for her. And although their preferred method of keeping her on the straight and narrow was highly embarrassing and more than a little painful, she understood that it all came from a place of love, and that was something she wouldn't have changed for anything in the world.

Even if that sense of love left her bare bottom hot and throbbing while she sobbed across their knee.

"It's the thought that counts, right?" she snickered, rubbing her soon to be well-roasted rump through the seat of her pajama bottoms. "And I think it's pretty safe to say by now that I rather enjoy this way of doing things."

She felt her lips curl up into a wry grin then.

"Then again, that doesn't mean I can't hedge my bets just a little bit..."

Grimacing at the pile of bottom blistering items on display before her, she suddenly found herself torn between trying to figure out which of them would hurt the least per individual swat, and which of them would be the easiest to take over a prolonged period of time. However, she quickly abandoned that line of thinking with a grim snort, as it occurred to her that it was rather a moot point anyway.

Dana wasn't going to be going easy on her no matter what she picked out, and she wouldn't be stopping until long after she'd been reduced to a blubbering mess with a pair of cheeks so hot that she could fry an egg on them.

"Heh."

That thought managed to send a giddy little thrill crackling through her entire body, pushing the butterflies in her stomach into overdrive and making her shiver as her thighs pressed themselves together of their own accord.

Oh god, it's going to be such a long day...

Squirming in place and chewing on her lower lip, Rhen had to clamp down hard on a sudden fit of nervous giggling before it could completely overtake her. Luckily though, it was right about then that she heard Dana calling for her from her bedroom, making her jump as she let out a little squeak of surprise.

"Eep!"

"Rhen, I'm waiting. Jingle that butt of yours up here right now, young lady! You *don't* want me to have to come looking for you..."

Realizing that she'd dawdled for just about as long as she could safely do so without running the risk of further punishment, Rhen shrugged to herself and then gathered up all of her new implements.

After all, if she was going to behave like a naughty girl, then she might as well be *thoroughly* punished like one as well.

Cradling her collection fondly against her chest and grinning from ear to ear, she spun on her heal and skipped out of the room, calling out in a breathy sing-song as she went.

"I'm coming, Aunt Dana!"

Life was good.

Epilogue

— *A FEW WEEKS LATER* —

"Have fun at school, cutie pie. I'll see you this evening," Dana Johnson called out after the retreating form of her favorite not-niece before she could get too far.

"Bye Aunt Dana, love you," replied Rhen, turning back and waving with a radiant smile.

"Love you too, hon."

Flashing the younger girl a sly grin, she then added loud enough for all of the other college students milling past her on their way toward campus to hear.

"Now you make sure you pay close attention to your professors today, young lady. I don't want you slacking off just because it's orientation day. You hear me?"

"Yes ma'am," sighed the now junior with a good-natured roll of her eyes, one hand skulking back to smooth down the folds of her skirt over her still warmly throbbing rear end.

She'd already found out the hard way after breakfast that her partner had every intention of making sure she started out the new semester on the right foot, and *apparently* waiting until the very last minute to pick out a suitably cute outfit to make a good impression on her professors counted as procrastinating.

Thankfully though, after stripping her down to her birthday suit and turning her over her knee for a mostly mild hand spanking, her auntie had helped her finish getting dressed. And although she now sported a fresh pull-up beneath her Hello

Kitty leggings, Rhen had to admit that the sassy "Girl Power!" glitter t-shirt that she'd picked out for her did bring her entire ensemble together rather nicely and did an excellent job of making her look like an eager young student.

With a heavy emphasis on being bratty for good measure.

Which was just fine with Rhen, truth be told.

After all, she had a reputation to maintain.

"Good girl," cooed Dana with a knowing smirk. "Oh, and don't forget that we're meeting Courtney and Abby for her birthday dinner tonight, so no dilly-dallying on your way home today, either. You got that?"

"Yes ma'am," chirped Rhen again, unable to resist rolling her eyes one more time.

She'd already been told all of this on their way over, it wasn't like she was going to forget any of it between driving to school and getting out of the car.

Well, probably.

Either way, the warmth pulsating beneath her skirt was enough to remind her to not push her luck just then. Especially not when there were so many low, stone benches within easy walking distance all around them.

Looking down at her watch to distract herself before that particular line of thought could get too far, Rhen blanched.

"Oh crap, I'm going to be late!" she squeaked as her heart leapt into her throat. "Bye Aunt Dana, see you later."

After giving one final hurried wave, Rhen Mathews, the twenty-year-old college junior who spent most of her time in the public eye living as little Rhenny Mathews, the bratty thirteen-year-old niece of Dana Johnson, spun on her heel and sped off toward her first class of the new semester like a raven-haired bat out of hell.

She knew that she'd probably get her bottom busted before

bedtime for being late to class. Heck, her aunt might even let Abby do the honors after dinner that night and just call it a "birthday spanking" or something. But in the end she didn't mind.

She was safe, she was loved, her life had rules and order, she was doing better in school than she ever had, and above all else...

She was happy.

THE END

More Books by Clarine Klein
(Available on Amazon)

Cat and Mouse

Cassidy Coleman is a sassy but introverted college sopho-more out on her own for the first time in her young adult life. At the start of fall semester, she moves into an apartment with a randomly assigned roommate, Lauren Delaney. Lauren is a an outgoing and athletic economics major one year ahead of Cassidy in school, and is just looking for a place to live that doesn't also double up as a party house on the weekends.

Unfortunately, things start off more than a little awkward between the two of them at first, with Cassidy too tongue-tied by the captivating older girl to carry on more than a two sentence conversation before needing to flee to her bedroom. Eventually though, the two manage to bond over a mutual love of video games from their childhood, and overnight an instant and lifelong friendship is forged. From there friendship then blossoms into love when after pushing her roommate into a freezing pool on a chilly winter night, Cassidy suddenly finds herself being hauled across Lauren's ample lap for a bare bottom blistering they've both been dreaming of for weeks.

And it's only the beginning!

The Misty Bog

Clarine Klein
Leila Hann

The Misty Bog

Sally Vinebrook is a young mage seeking adventure.

Fresh from her novice training as a sister of the Celestine Order, she travels the world in search of magical secrets and mystical creatures to further her education in the arcane arts. Following up on a rumor from a town along her journey, she comes across The Misty Bog, home to an ancient and powerful water nymph named Modan.

After begging for a chance to stay with her for a time to study, and a very thorough spanking for being so disrespectful to her swamp upon arrival (and not at all just because she has a cute butt), she is shown a brand new world of magic unlike anything she's ever known!

Though by the end of her stay, she just might not be able to sit down ever again.

The SPANKING of
Sally Marie

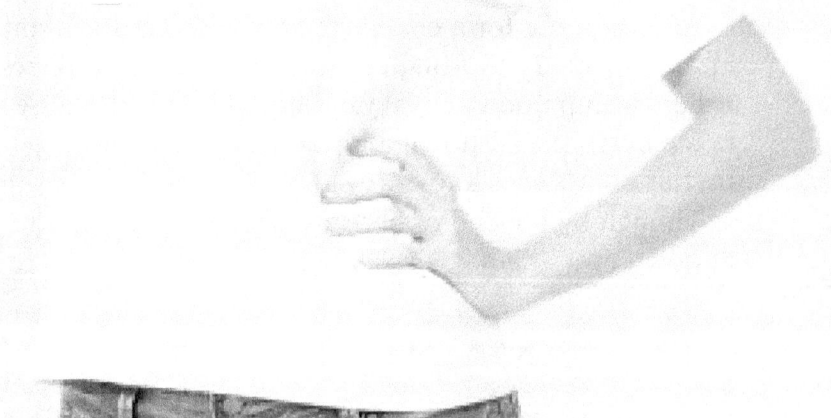

CLARINE KLEIN

The Spanking of Sally Marie

Sally finds herself in trouble once too often, and as grounding and other forms of punishment have had little effect on Sally's bratty behavior, her parents decide to spank their teenage daughter instead. It all begins when Sally stays up half the night playing around on her computer. Her dad is not pleased, and upends her for a bare bottom spanking. It is the first of many such spankings delivered by either Mom or Dad, and things get mega embarrassing for Sally when she's spanked in the Ladies Room in the mall, and in a side room at the local church during the Sunday service. Sally soon finds out the difference between 'attitude adjuster' spankings and the real thing, and her humiliation increases when her girlfriends find out she's still getting spanked - they even seize an opportunity to spank her themselves!

Thank you for reading!

www.ingramcontent.com/pod-product-compliance
Lightning Source LLC
Chambersburg PA
CBHW071727110726
47908CB00006B/1526